License or no license,
this one was hers.

With one mighty kick the door swung inward on its hinges, the lock breaking and splintering the wooden frame. Inside was dark—like that was going to stop her. She wasn't some weak human Venator anymore. Her eyes adjusted quickly to the lack of light.

She walked into the center of the apparently deserted room, knowing he waited for her behind the door. But she was more than a match for him.

The door slammed shut. She flexed her hand around the katana before turning to confront him.

He grinned insanely. The drying human blood was caked on his mouth, making him look like a clown—the kind that sends children screaming in terror to hide under their beds.

Antoinette slipped the sword from its sheath. "So, Pennywise . . . here we are."

By Tracey O'Hara

Dark Brethren Novels
NIGHT'S COLD KISS
DEATH'S SWEET EMBRACE

Death's Sweet Embrace

A DARK BRETHREN NOVEL

TRACEY O'HARA

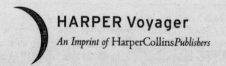

HARPER Voyager

An Imprint of HarperCollinsPublishers

This is a work of fiction. Names, characters, places, and incidents are products of the author's imagination or are used fictitiously and are not to
be construed as real. Any resemblance to actual events, locales, organizations,
or persons, living or dead, is entirely coincidental.

HARPER Voyager
An Imprint of HarperCollins*Publishers*
10 East 53rd Street
New York, New York 10022-5299

Copyright © 2011 by Tracey O'Hara
Cover art by Larry Rostant
ISBN 978-0-06-178314-2
www.harpervoyagerbooks.com

First Harper Voyager paperback printing: February 2011

Harper Voyager and ⟩ is a trademark of HCP LLC.

Printed in the U.S.A.

10 9 8 7 6 5 4 3 2 1

For David,

who is the ink in my pen

acknowledgments

I would like to thank my editor, the fabulous Diana Gill, for her consideration and ability to get the best out of me, and my agent, Jenn Schober, for her patience and understanding. To all the readers and booksellers who have not only read my first book but wrote and told me how much they enjoyed it—words can't express my gratitude.

· I would also like to thank my family and friends for being there when I needed you—especially my parents, Betty and Tim, and my dad, Bob. My wonderful grownup boys, Corey and Seamus, thanks for looking after your mum when the deadlines loom. And Corey's mates Adam and Phil, for their enthusiastic reaction to my books and telling me so. To Cathy—what more can I say that I haven't said before—'cept luv ya. Also, to my work mates for listening to my babble, and to my boss for understanding.

But most of all I want to thank my husband, David, without whom I could never have done this. You make me want to reach for the stars so I can hand them all to you.

1

Angel Heart

The excited babble of female voices floated down the hall toward Gideon. He turned and faced the wall, then pulled a mop from the cleaning cart and began running it over the already shiny floor, pretending to clean.

What are they doing here?

The academy didn't open for classes until this evening. The institution was still officially closed for the holidays.

As two girls neared, he tugged the brim of his cap down over his forehead, keeping his head low as he continued to mop. They walked by without even a glance in his direction, too lost in their own self-important chatter. Maintenance men were invisible, especially janitors, which suited him just fine.

The girls soon disappeared around the corner, talking and giggling, totally oblivious to his presence.

"WELL DONE, MY CHILD." Ealund's translucent form floated across the floor, his ethereal beauty reflecting on the shiny black tiles.

With a quick glance to make sure the girls were gone, Gideon dumped the mop in the cart and pushed it toward his original destination. The incorporeal apparition glowed, his pellucid form surrounded by a silver-blue aura—and Gideon's heart ached just looking upon such unearthly beauty. Ealund only showed himself to Gideon.

He was the image of angelic magnificence with waist-length gold hair floating around his head, pale flowing robes, and terrifyingly exquisite azure eyes—all that was missing were wings. And yet, Ealund's presence of absolute and pure evil almost brought Gideon to his knees.

Apart from the girls, the hallways were deserted. He kept his head down and peered at the security camera in a corner just above a classroom door. They'd been set up everywhere around campus after the first murder several weeks ago, but he had the schematics and knew how to get around most of them.

"HURRY, MY CHILD," Ealund intoned. *"TIME GROWS SHORT."*

Gideon wheeled the cart to a stop and checked the corridor before pulling out the maintenance master key to unlock the heavy wooden door. With one last check, he entered and pulled the cart inside, silently closing and locking the door behind him. Anticipation bubbled up from the pit of his stomach; he wanted to feel the warm blood spilling over his fingers.

"SLOW DOWN," Ealund's rich voice echoed out of the surrounding air—the resonance deep and dark, sending a clammy chill across Gideon's skin. *"FOCUS, MY CHILD. FOCUS YOUR MIND AND LET ME GUIDE YOU."*

Gideon nodded and slipped off his shoes, taking deep calming breaths as he placed them in the cart alongside his backpack. He wiggled his toes in the thin rubber-soled slippers he'd worn like socks in his shoes.

"HE'S HERE." Ealund sniffed the air. *"AHH, THE SWEET SMELL OF DELICIOUS YOUTH."*

The musky, almost feral scent of a prime young male overpowered the stuffy odor of books and knowledge. Gideon stashed the cleaning cart behind the row of book-shelves nearest the door and moved quietly through the maze, guided by the sound of off-tune whistling.

The rhythmic squeaks of a book cart's wheels stopped in a row ahead. Gideon flattened his back against the end of a bookcase and then carefully peered around the corner. The boy was tall, much taller than the others. His handcart was nearly empty. It wouldn't be long now.

Gideon pulled back and leaned against the solid oak end of the shelving, his heart thundering in his chest—partly in fear of being caught and partly in excited anticipation. The hunt was almost as good as the catch. Almost.

Gideon's mouth went dry and his cock hardened as it always did at this point. The hunt began. He closed his eyes for a moment and concentrated on slowing his breathing. The darkness settled the speed of his beating heart.

Again, the cyclic metallic squeaks of the book cart ruptured the deathly silence in the low-lit library. Gideon chanced another quick look.

"HE DOESN'T EVEN SENSE YOU." Ealund sneered, his ghostly form floating out into the aisle between the bookcases. *"THE RACES OF TODAY ARE SO WEAK."* It wasn't the first time Ealund had said this.

The sound of wheels continued to get further away. Gideon hunched low and ran down a parallel aisle. The creaking ceased again as the boy stopped and picked up a book from the cart. He opened the cover and thumbed through a few pages, whistling the catchy little tune he'd begun earlier, then placed the tome on an upper shelf and moved on.

"Shit, missed one," the youth cursed and Gideon heard footsteps turning toward where he was hiding.

He would be seen. Gideon panicked, not knowing which way to go.

A loud bang shattered the still semi-silence. With nerves splintered into a thousand pieces, he crouched ready for flight, heart thundering so loud in his ears, he was sure the boy would hear it.

"What the . . . ?" The boy continued to mutter as he retreated back up the aisle.

"MOVE!" Ealund screamed in his head.

As always, Gideon did as Ealund said. In a crouched run, he returned to the opposite side of the row and flattened himself against the shelf end.

What was that? Gideon thought.

"A BOOK," Ealund replied. *"I HELPED IT OFF THE SHELF."*

His answer didn't exactly comfort Gideon. If Ealund could make books fall, what else could he do? An ember of fear flared deep down, but Gideon quickly dashed it.

The whistling youth returned to the row Gideon had just left and placed the fallen book back on the shelf before moving to the next row over. Gideon was safe for the moment. He slowly expelled the breath he'd been holding. *That was close, and foolish.* He unclipped the small leather case attached to his belt and wrapped his already latex-covered fingers around the T-shaped handle of the custom-made push dagger. It fit comfortably between his middle and forefinger, the tiny detachable blade sticking out at a ninety-degree angle. The squeaky cart was moving back to his end of the far aisle and Gideon ducked behind the books again. Then the repetitive sound moved further away into the study area and stopped, followed by the light scrape of a chair.

Finally, the moment he'd been waiting for. The boy was done shelving books. Gideon had observed this pattern for the past few days and knew that once the day librarian arrived, the boy would go home. His time frame was short, but long enough to do what he had to. His excitement rose.

The boy's head came up, sniffing the air, and he glanced around. Gideon ducked lower behind the stacks. After what seemed like a heart-pounding eternity, the boy shrugged and bent his head over a book.

Gideon waited just a little longer. Careful not to touch the blade, he flexed and relaxed his fingers around the push-knife handle. When the boy seemed engrossed in his task, Gideon made his move.

He raced from behind the bookshelf on the balls of his feet, his footsteps light and silent. As if sensing something, the boy's head began to rise but Gideon hit him from behind before he could turn, then slapped a hand over the boy's mouth before slamming the push knife into the lower part of his neck, right between the C6 and C7 vertebrae. The weapon slid home and the blade detached, just as designed. He placed the remaining knife handle back in his pocket.

"PERFECT!" Ealund crowed.

It *was* perfect.

The boy tried to rise and stiffened—the silver blade, still lodged in his neck, had severed the spinal column. Gideon let him go and reached for the hunting knife tucked inside his janitorial coveralls. The boy folded, falling off the chair and landing on the floor with a heavy thud. His height was not much of an advantage now that he couldn't stand.

Gideon sliced away a large part of the boy's shirt and stuffed it in the victim's mouth. Whether from shock or disbelief, the boy hadn't called out. Yet. Once Gideon went to work, he would soon find his voice again.

"DON'T RUSH IT," Ealund crooned as he floated toward the boy's head. *"YOU HAVE PLENTY OF TIME."*

But not forever. The day librarian would be here soon and Gideon needed to be long gone, yet he still had enough time to have a little fun first.

The boy crawled a few feet on his stomach, his arms having just enough strength to haul his paralyzed body a little. Gideon stalked after him and flipped him over onto his back. With his foot holding the boy's right upper arm, he yanked at the forearm and felt the satisfying snap of the bones beneath. The gag muffled the boy's screams as Gideon repeated the break on the left arm.

The realization he was about to die dawned on the boy's face, his features twisting in alarm. Gideon reveled in it.

Ealund's chillingly beautiful ghostly features glowed a little more brightly as he fed on the boy's terror. Gideon squatted over the victim and cut away the remains of the shirt before carving *the marks* into the boy's heaving chest, then tilted his head to watch the scarring. The silver blocker in his neck not only stopped the boy from moving or transforming, it had slowed down the healing process. The scent of fresh blood tickled Gideon's nostrils and stoked the fiery lust in his groin. The arms had almost healed, so he rebroke them to new muffled screams from the boy.

The ghostly figure floated closer, his crystal blue eyes shining. *"MORE,"* he whispered into Gideon's ear.

A shiver of lust danced up his spine. It wasn't sexual—just

the thirst for blood and pain. His skin flushed with heat as he held the knifepoint above the victim's sternum.

"DO IT NOW."

Gideon complied. The skin parted with ease under the blade he'd honed to a razor's edge and he cut away at the flesh, the tip scraping against the bone beneath. Before the wound had a chance to heal, he dropped the knife, gripped the rib cage in his hands and heaved them apart. As they cracked and parted, hot blood hit Gideon in the face and slashed crimson across book spines on a nearby shelf. The blood was almost as good as his prize, which lay nestled inside the victim's chest, beating double time in terror.

"TAKE IT," Ealund urged. *"IT'S YOURS."*

Gideon wrapped his fingers around the organ, feeling the life-force through the pulsing beat. Then he lifted it from the safety of the chest, pulling it free of connecting valves and blood vessels. He watched life bleed from the boy's horrified eyes as he stared at his heart in Gideon's hands.

"CONSUME THE SOURCE OF HIS DESIRE. FEEL THAT POWER." Ealund's deranged voice sounded frantic with impatience. *"DO IT NOW!"*

The heart twitched its final beats as Gideon brought it to his lips. The flesh was silky and metallic, and sweetly marinated in desires of youth. The delicious hot juices ran down Gideon's chin as he devoured the fresh, young heart.

"YES, YES," Ealund crowed, holding out his arms in triumph, floating higher off the floor and seeming to grow more *there*—almost more solid.

Gideon finished. He stared down at the lump of bloody meat on the floor, no longer a boy, no longer a victim. Now he was nothing. All that he was, Gideon had consumed. He felt little for the male when *it* was alive, and even less now that it was dead.

"YOU DID WELL, MY CHILD," Ealund intoned. *"BUT I NEED MORE. AND SOON."* With those last words, the vision of Ealund dissipated, leaving Gideon alone.

But he was never really alone.

He grabbed the backpack from the cleaning cart and retrieved a large ziplock plastic bag from inside. With quick, well-practiced movements, he peeled off the blood-soaked coveralls, wrapped the hunting knife in it, and placed it in the plastic bag along with his feet coverings and cap.

He took from his pack another plastic bag with a dampened towel inside and wiped the remainder of the blood off his face and hands, then threw the rag in with the soiled clothing and sealed it shut.

He took the last plastic from his backpack, which contained a clean set of coveralls, socks, and cap and slipped them on. He walked around the library, wiping here and there, removing all traces of his presence until no evidence of him remained on any surface. With one last look around, he picked up his pack and placed it in the pushcart, then wheeled through the library door before locking up. He had five minutes before the day librarian was due. Wasn't he in for a surprise today?

Gideon tugged his cap forward to hide his face and moved off down the hall, slow and casual—whistling, as had the boy, the same tuneless melody.

2

A BAD DAY

Kitt's boot heels tapped lightly on the faux marble floor of the NYAPS campus main hall. Academy students were gathered in several groups, calling out and waving to one another, laughing and talking. It had been a while since she was a student, but she still remembered what it was like, and this time she'd be in front of the class. Kitt's stomach rolled with nerves, and nausea made her skin prickle. The discomfort quickly passed, only to be replaced by the growl of hunger.

She glanced at her watch. Maybe she could grab a quick bite from the cafeteria before going to her new office to prepare for class. There were several Animalians in the scattered groups, but none had the distinctive black and silver-white hair of a snow leopard felion.

Kitt could hear a bit of a buzz, people whispering in hushed tones and looking around in a guarded manner. But it was probably just a lot of first-day jitters. Like hers.

One last, quick scan of the faces didn't reveal the twins, though Oberon had told her they'd spent the holidays with the Pride on the reservation near the Adirondack Mountains. Maybe it was for the best she couldn't find them; she wasn't sure she was ready to meet them yet.

The twins.

Her daughters. The children she couldn't see because of the fallout with her people.

Except they weren't children anymore. They were young women.

Anyway what would she say to them? What would they say to her?

As Kitt passed the trophy case, a number of people were pointing at a shiny new trophy on display front and center and she stopped to take a closer look. It belonged to the latest all-state Shadow-combat champion, Mark Ambrosia. Even she, who was usually too busy to keep up on current events, had heard of the young human sweeping the amateur Shadow-combat circuit by storm.

The trophy case was impressive. Lots of photos, medals, and trophies on display. Not surprising, the New York Academy had the well-earned reputation as one of the most prestigious institutions of its kind. Both the physical and academic achievements showed the merits of the programs offered here—and why she was thrilled to be the new lecturer of parahuman forensic pathology. As Kitt reached the elevators, she glanced down.

Oh no.

She transferred the heavy winter coat to her other arm and twisted to look at the thick globs of mud splattering the leg of her new trousers.

Just great.

As she punched the elevator button, she shifted the bag on her shoulder and the strap gave way, spilling the contents of her handbag over the floor. A few of the onlooking students snickered and her face heated. Embarrassment *plus*. She hoped none of these kids were taking her class later tonight.

"Having a bad day?" a male voice boomed from above and the looming shadow dropped.

It was great to see Oberon DuPrie's friendly features smiling down at her. And she couldn't help returning a smile as he helped her pick up the scattered belongings.

"You okay?" he asked, passing her a hairbrush.

"A bit nervous," she admitted. "It's my first time at the front of a classroom."

He dumped the last of her things into the handbag sitting on the ground and swept her up in his huge arms. "Damn, it's good to see you here, Kitt."

"Oberon, put me down," she squeaked with embarrassment, slapping at his massive arms of iron.

He set her back on her feet, his black knee-length leather coat creaking with the effort. "Now, is that any way to talk to the friend who helped you get this job?"

She sighed and looked up as his seven-foot frame loomed over her. "Sorry for taking my bad mood out on you. You know I love you like a brother, especially since . . ." She trailed off, not wanting to bring up Dylan's murder. She was so sick of death. "Anyway, that does *not* stop you from being a pain in my ass."

He leaned in, kissed her cheek, and beamed at her, though she caught the flash of sadness in his eyes. Dylan's death had been just as hard on him. They'd been best friends since childhood.

"Thanks for your help," she said.

"About that," he said, his face growing serious. "I know your first class doesn't start for quite a few hours. I could use your help with something first." He scrubbed a massive hand across his goateed chin.

A bad sign.

Premonition tightened the skin on her face. "What's happened?"

"Come to my office and I'll show you." The elevator doors opened at that moment and he ducked his large dreadlocked head to enter the now seemingly small car.

After spilling her early evening coffee all over her pajamas, getting mud all over her nice, new slacks, and embarrassing herself with the handbag incident, how much worse could the night get?

She was torn. She didn't feel nearly as prepared for giving her first lesson as she should, which is why she'd come in early in the first place. But it *was* Oberon asking and she did owe him.

Kitt sighed. "All right, but only a couple hours."

"Sure," he said and swiped an ID card across a panel, then

hit one of the red buttons on the bottom row under the Staff Only sign.

The elevator descended. Most of NYAPS was underground. It helped to accommodate the more nocturnal of the student body. The buildings had been a secret Aeternus stronghold before the CHaPR Treaty, but now it was used as a center for knowledge for both humans and parahumans.

"Are you going to tell me what's wrong?" she said as they descended.

"I'm amazed you didn't hear about it on the news," he said, not looking at her. "Or at least run into it on the way in."

"Actually I did see quite a crowd when I arrived, so I used the side entrance to avoid them."

He looked down at her. "There's been a murder here on campus."

"Oh no, you don't, Oberon," Kitt said, shaking her head. "I'm not the chief medical examiner anymore."

"I really need your help. It will only take a couple of hours. I wouldn't ask if it wasn't really important." He grabbed her by the shoulders and bent his large head closer. "Please."

Damn him. How could she resist now? He'd used the *P* word. Something he didn't do very often.

The elevator came to a stop and opened onto a lounge with worn stuffed chairs, low tables, and a pot of imitation gruel dressed as coffee warming on the counter. Totally functional, but not exactly welcoming. A few security-guard types sat around talking, drinking coffee or reading the paper.

"Hey, Captain," the guard behind the security desk said.

"Tom," Oberon replied and placed his right palm against the hand-shaped panel on the wall. There was a snick, a beep, and then the red-lit panel turned green.

"Facimorphic test," he said and indicated she step forward. "Anyone who comes into this office must do it."

Kitt had undergone the test many times before; it was standard security in most government institutions. As always, she jumped when the needle pricked her palm.

The guard nodded to them as Oberon opened the door marked Chief of Security. Inside was fairly typical and innocuous—not exactly Oberon's style. He moved behind his desk and grinned as he gripped the edge. Something buzzed and a portion of the wall slid aside, revealing a circular stairwell.

"Come on," he said. "This way."

They descended into an open-plan modern office surrounded by glassed offices and meeting rooms. The place was all leather, chrome, and glass; quite a stark contrast to the lounge upstairs.

"Welcome to the Bunker," Oberon said, shrugging off his coat as he entered and hung it on a coatrack.

The carpet muffled his heavy shit-kicker boots. He looked like a bouncer at a biker strip club with his Iron Maiden heavy metal T-shirt, black jeans, and thick black stainless-steel-studded belt with a large Harley-Davidson buckle. The tribal swirls and points of his scarification were clearly visible on his bare arms.

"Captain, your hot chocolate." The friendly face of Antonio Geraldi beamed at Kitt as he handed Oberon a tall takeout cup. "With extra marshmallows—just the way you like it."

It looked tiny in Oberon's massive ham fist. "Thanks."

The yellow parahuman-friendly lights glowed off Tones's shaven head as he came over and gave Kitt a hug. She hadn't seen him since he'd worked with Oberon and Dylan at the Violent Crimes Unit.

"How are you, Tones?" Kitt said. "And is that a cinnamon latte I smell?"

Tones grinned. "I knew you were coming in today and picked up your favorite."

"Oh my God, I can't believe you remembered. I see you're as thoughtful as always," she said, surprised.

"Yeah, yeah, I know," Tones said and tucked in his chin, dropping his voice. "Someday you'll make some lucky female a good wife, Tones."

His impression of Oberon was so spot on she almost snorted her latte all over his Converse All Stars.

Oberon leaned his bulk against the nearby table. "Not if I strangle you first."

The Aeternus male, Tones, was dressed in his usual attire: a pair of designer jeans and a mustard yellow T-shirt bearing the message KITTENS ARE PEOPLE TOO. For as long as she'd known him, he'd worn shirts with slogans espousing the ideas of a card-carrying member of Parahumans Against Animal Abuse. She was so glad he was working here, too. It certainly made starting the new job a little less daunting knowing friends were around.

A woman with Nordic blond hair stepped forward. Though she looked familiar, Kitt just couldn't place where they'd met before. She wore a dark gray Prada suit over a white T-shirt with a pair of extra-dark sunglasses perched atop her head, which left her deep emerald green eyes visible. On any other woman the outfit may have looked a little pretentious, but on her it just looked . . . lethally professional.

"Kitt, this is Antoinette Petrescu," Oberon said.

The hand Kitt extended stilled, then shook, and she could feel her smile sliding away before she could catch herself. She greeted the newcomer with a rather weak, "Hello."

This was the woman responsible for her brother's death, albeit indirectly. Still, the shock of meeting Antoinette face-to-face for the first time since Dylan's murder was not something she had yet prepared herself for. She took a deep breath and, before she dropped it, placed her coffee cup on a nearby table. This was just enough time to pull herself back together.

"Oberon didn't tell you, did he?" the female Aeternus said.

"No, he didn't." Kitt shot Oberon a narrowed glare. "I'm sorry—it's just the shock. I wasn't expecting to meet . . ."

"I understand," Antoinette said with an awkward little smile.

Oberon's eyes rose to look over Kitt's shoulder and his brow creased into a deep frown.

Kitt sensed *him* long before she saw him. Her whole world bottomed out, taking all the air in the room with it. Her heart leapt into her throat and began beating double time, filling her ears with its racing boom-tha-boomp rhythm. She'd last seen him just over eighteen years ago. She closed her eyes, still not daring to look at him.

"Raven." It came out in a hushed expelling of breath, as if even her voice was afraid to give him form.

As she turned, she opened her eyes. And there he was—just as she remembered—dangerous in every sense of the word. Her pulse quickened, just like it had in the old days.

He leaned against the edge of a desk, his crossed arms stretching the sleeves of a black T-shirt over his flexed biceps and a scar that sliced through his right eyebrow and continued under his eye only enhancing his lethal charm. He hadn't changed a bit—at least not physically. The same devastating sense of danger that had drawn her to him all those years ago was still there.

"Hello, Kitten," he said, his dark-rimmed pale blue irises ripping through eighteen years of carefully constructed barriers to lay bare her soul again.

She swallowed, trying to dislodge the lump that formed in her chest and stopped her breath. She spun on Oberon—right now, she could *not* claim him as her friend. No—a friend would've told her that her ex-lover had returned.

Oberon self-consciously rubbed his chin and jaw and avoided meeting Kitt's eyes. "You were supposed to stay out of sight," he said to Raven.

This night was deteriorating faster than a snowman in the sun. "You could've said something," she whispered.

"I asked him not to," Raven said. "Not until you were settled in here. But when I heard your voice, I just couldn't stay away, Kitten."

"You have no right to call me that anymore." It sounded a lot calmer than she felt. "What are you doing here?"

"I gave him a job," Oberon said.

"You did *what*?" she said, incredulous.

The ursian just shrugged. She had the sudden need to be as far from Oberon and her ex-lover as possible. "What did you need me to do?"

"I'd like you to go with Antoinette to the medical examiner's office and find out what's going on. You know what to look for—I need to know if this body is the same as the last one."

"Shit, Oberon, I resigned from there a couple of weeks

ago. They're not going to just let me walk in and look at a body." Kitt could sense Raven's eyes on her. Her skin heated.

"I'm trying to find out whether Tez is on tonight or not, but she's not taking my calls." Oberon's frown deepened. "If anyone asks, say you're there to pick up some stuff you left behind." Her late brother's best friend took a huge swig from his cup.

"Why don't we just wait for the report to be released?" Antoinette asked.

Dylan had said she was quick, and Kitt could see why he'd admired her.

"Firstly, Kitt performed the autopsy on the first victim and knows the case, and secondly"—Oberon's fists clenched— "that fucking little prick, Neil Roberts, has frozen me out, and if the head of the Violent Crimes Unit is interested, then there's something big going down and I want to know what it is."

Kitt was well versed on what Oberon thought of his ex-boss. She'd heard it so many times she could almost recite it word for word from memory.

Suddenly the room spun, her legs trembled, and she actually felt the blood drain from her face, leaving a pricking sensation in its wake. She felt nauseous and her temples pounded. She'd tried to keep Raven from her thoughts, especially since he'd brought the twins back to mind, but now here he was, standing right in front of her in living color and all she could think of was getting out of there.

"Are you okay?" Antoinette asked, reaching out for her.

Kitt felt disoriented and roughly shook off the female's suffocating touch, pushing away the overly attentive hands. She needed air—

A large dog raced forward, growling and snapping. Kitt dropped to a crouch, her inner cat coming out to protect her. Before she could stop herself, she hissed at the animal and the change prickled along her limbs as white and silver fur sprung through the pores of her skin.

As the animal leapt, a black blur solidified, pushing her out of the way of the snapping jaws and took the full brunt of the attack. The malamute's snarling maw clamped down on Raven's forearm and the dog shook its head from side to side, worrying the flesh. Kitt heard teeth scrape on bone a split second before the dog's sharp canine incisors opened an artery in Raven's wrist and fresh hot blood splashed her face.

3

dead man running

"Cerberus, *NO!*" Antoinette yelled and rushed forward.

"Raven—" Kitt's inner cat was just as unsettled as her human side, but she was aware enough to know not to attack the dog. She reversed the change and returned to full human form.

The animal let go the moment Antoinette grabbed the him.

"It's all right, boy," she said in a soft, calming tone as she rubbed and ruffled the dog's thick pelt to comfort him. "I'm sorry, he's not usually this jumpy."

The smell of fresh blood overpowered everything else and the doctor in Kitt took over, squashing all feelings of insecurity, fear, and doubt. Raven's right arm was a jagged and raw wound, blood spurting with every beat of his heart. It would heal as long as he didn't bleed out first.

"Get me a towel or a clean cloth," she ordered to no one in particular.

"It's not as bad as it looks," Raven said as she pressed torn skin and muscle together.

"Liar," she mumbled as his blood welled between her fingers.

He chuckled, and then hissed as she applied more pressure. "He was only reacting to your distress, you know."

"I know." Kitt glanced at the dog as she took a kitchen towel from Tones.

The animal's head hung low with ears forward and big sad blue eyes looking between them and Antoinette. He'd only been protecting his mistress.

She just had to slow the blood loss long enough to let the wound heal over and seal. While she stood there pressing the makeshift bandage over the shredded flesh, she kept her head down and on her task. If she looked up into those eyes—Raven's eyes—she'd be undone.

"I was sorry to hear about Dylan," he said in a whisper.

She nodded, still not daring to look at him.

"Has your father let you return home?" he asked just as softly so no one else could hear, though she could feel their eyes on her. "Have you seen them yet?"

His free hand wiped the blood from her cheek with another towel and she finally raised her face to him, then shook her head again.

"They look so much like you." His eyes locked on her and he placed the cloth over her shoulder before tucking a stray lock of hair behind her ear. "Same coloring, same features"—the pad of his thumb brushed her lower lip—"same mouth."

Her lip tingled. She could almost smell the pine needles and the loamy scent of the forest floor where they used to make love many years ago. *When had his face gotten so dangerously close?*

"Stop that," she hissed and pulled back. To distract herself, she lifted the edge of the cloth on his arm.

The flow had stopped and she unwrapped the kitchen towel, carefully twisting his arm one way then the other, wiping away the blood. The wound knitted nicely. Finally, she let his arm drop and stepped away, throwing the ruined cloth in a trash can.

"You should be fine now," she said with her back to him.

"I told you it was worse than it looked," he said.

"I'm sorry Kitt," Oberon said. "I shouldn't have asked you down here. It was a bad idea. Tones and Antoinette can go."

Kitt shook her head. "No, I'll go." At least at the M.E.'s

office she knew what she was doing, and for the moment she felt that a sense of the familiar would be good.

"Thank you," Oberon said and nodded at the Aeternus female.

Antoinette stood. "Cerberus, stay with Tones."

The still-shaken animal padded over to lie at the computer tech's feet and dropped his head onto his front paws, his soulful eyes still begging an apology. Kitt almost felt sorry for the big malamute mutt.

Kitt chanced a glance at Raven. His hangdog expression matched Antoinette's animal companion. Appropriate, really. She opened her mouth to say she would talk to him later but closed it again.

Not yet.

She needed a little more time. Maybe a trip to the parahuman morgue might give her more time to think about what she wanted to say to him.

As she followed Antoinette to the door, Kitt stopped near Oberon and looked up. "I'll talk with you later," she said in a calm, controlled voice, once again reining in those rampant emotions.

Oberon had the good grace to at least look sheepish, rather difficult for a seven-foot ursian.

Antoinette glanced at the felian and could tell in the illumination of the green dash lights that Kitt's mood was heavy.

After a few more minutes of silence, Antoinette turned to Kitt. "Are you okay?"

Kitt closed her eyes and sighed. "This is just not the day I'd imagined when I got up this evening."

"I guess the last thing you expected tonight was to get stuck with the woman responsible for your brother's death," she said.

Kitt turned to look at Antoinette, her expression horrified. "I'm so sorry for the way I greeted you. Please, I don't blame you for Dylan's death, it's just you remind me that he's gone, not *why* he's gone. If I'd known we were going to meet, I'd just have been more prepared."

"Oberon's an insensitive son-of-a-bitch sometimes." Antoinette glanced at her, caught the wounded look on Kitt's face, and knew she'd said something wrong. "No disrespect meant. Hell, he's the first person I'd choose to have my back in a fight."

The felian relaxed and smiled. Kitt's resemblance to her brother was uncanny, but the smile made it more so.

"Dylan was a good agent and pretty decent male too," Antoinette said. "I liked him a lot."

Kitt's smile deepened. "He admired you too."

"Really?" Antoinette glanced from the road to Kitt and back again. "He didn't give much away."

"He told me you were one of the sharpest humans he'd ever met, but maybe a little pigheaded and quick-tempered for your own good."

"Pigheaded, hey?" Antoinette smiled, remembering how professional he'd been that night just a few short months ago. "Well, I guess he pretty much had *me* pegged."

After a couple of minutes of silence, Antoinette bit her lip and turned to Kitt again. "Look, I have a brother and can only imagine what you must be going through. I saw Dylan . . . after . . . you know . . . and just wanted to tell you it would've been quick, he wouldn't have suffered. Dante was only interested in prolonging my pain and your brother just happened to be in the way."

"Oberon told me." Kitt looked down at her hands. "But thanks for saying so."

Antoinette glanced at her again. "What's the deal with you and Oberon?"

Kitt's features softened. "He's like a brother, really. We've known each other since we were kids. His Family lived near ours and sometimes did jobs for my father; they treated him differently because he was too small, so he used to hang out with Dylan and me. When we were exiled from the Pride, Oberon came with us and joined the Department with Dylan while I attended medical school."

"Wow, '*small*'?" Antoinette gripped the wheel. "I'd hate to see the rest of his Family."

Kitt laughed. "He's still a head shorter than his father and brother and is considered the runt of the Family. Ursians tend to be larger, and the DuPrie Family is made up mostly of grizzlies, plus his father is polar bear."

Antoinette couldn't help smiling; Kitt had that kind of laugh. It made her look very young and carefree.

"Thank you for taking my mind off what happened back there," Kitt said.

"I'm sorry Cerberus attacked," Antoinette said, feeling more than a little embarrassed.

"It wasn't his fault, with all that confusion and raw emotion flying around, I'm not surprised." Kitt turned to her. "Anyway, can you pull into that convenience store? I need to pick up something."

Antoinette got the impression Kitt didn't want to speak about what went on between her and Raven yet, so she nodded and pulled the car over to the curb. The felian dashed into the store and emerged a few moments later with a large bag of candy.

"That's some sweet craving you have there," Antoinette said as Kitt climbed back into the car.

"It's not for me." She buckled her seat belt and smiled. "You'll see."

Fifteen minutes later Antoinette pulled the cherry red Camaro into the alley behind the building belonging to the Department of Parahuman Security, which housed the Department's Office of the Chief Parahuman Medical Examiner. Kitt had hoped to use the fire exit at the back as a way to enter unnoticed, since she no longer had access to the underground staff parking lot, but smokers, who often propped the door open while they got their nicotine fix, were nowhere to be seen. Tonight, her luck was holding fast—and it was all bad. They'd have to go in the front.

Before entering the building, she felt the weight of the chocolate candy in her jacket pocket and stopped. "Just follow my lead, okay? And pray Stanislavski is not on tonight."

"Who's Stanislavski?"

Kitt sighed. "Just the most uptight, officious, anal M.E. you'll have the displeasure to come across. Trust me—if he's on tonight, we're screwed."

Antoinette nodded. The first hurdle greeted them as they entered the impressive building of faux marble and glass. Like most Department offices, it was open twenty-four hours and a few people buzzed around the foyer. The unsmiling security guard manning one of the two metal detectors between them and the elevators waved them forward. She wasn't used to entering the building this way, and had totally forgotten about them.

Christ, I hope Antoinette doesn't have a gun.

Kitt went first and passed through without a problem. She turned and held her breath as Antoinette did the same.

Nothing. No telltale beep stopped them and they made their way to the elevators with little difficulty. Kitt's back prickled as she waited for him to wake up and challenge them. When the elevator doors closed, Kitt started breathing again.

The guard Kitt had hoped for sat behind the security desk in the basement suite of OCPME and looked up as they walked in, his face almost splitting in half when he saw her. "Hey, Doc! I didn't expect to see you back so soon."

At least something was finally going her way. She took the bag of peanut butter M&Ms from her pocket.

"Looking good, Murray." She dropped the candy on the counter and gave him her biggest, sweetest smile as she ran her eyes over his obscenely bulging biceps. The buttons down the front of his rayon uniform strained to contain his heavily worked pectoral muscles. "How's my favorite security guard? You look like you've filled out a bit more since last I saw you."

The huge human grinned with delight. "I have a competition at the end of the month so I've been doing extra workouts." Murray's eyes dropped to the packet of his biggest all-time weakness.

"I'm sorry I brought these now; I knew they were your favorite." She scooped up the bag of candy. "But you won't want them now."

His bottom lip stuck out like a small child who'd just had his candy taken away. "Since you brought them for me special," he said, eyes fixed on the bright-colored packaging in her hand, "I'll just lift a few more weights."

"Okay, if you're sure," she said and handed him the bag. "By the way, who's on duty tonight?" she asked as nonchalantly as she could manage while her heart hammered away in her chest.

"Dr. O'Connor," he replied, his eyes flicking from the candy on the counter to her and back again.

Thank God.

"I just need to pick up a few things I left in the kitchen and I thought I might say hello while I'm here?" she said, trying to keep the relief from her voice.

The wannabe Mr. Universe reluctantly dragged his eyes away from the confectionary and swallowed—the collar of his uniform straining around his bull neck. "You know I can't let visitors back there, Dr. Jordan. And since you don't work here anymore . . ."

"Come on, Murray, it's only been a couple of weeks since I left." She pushed the M&Ms a little closer. "Can't you make an exception? Just this once? I'll vouch for my friend here; she is another lecturer at the academy."

"Really? I'll have to see some ID," he said to Antoinette.

Kitt swallowed. *Shit.* She should have thought of that.

"Sure," Antoinette said and reached into her pocket. "Will my NYAPS faculty ID do?"

Murray looked at it and nodded. "All right, Doc." He snatched up the phone with the other. "Only for you."

Balancing the handset between his ear and shoulder, he dialed, then mumbled a few brief words, and after a moment hung up. "Dr. O'Connor will meet you in the blue room. Actually, she's expecting you."

"Thanks, big guy," Kitt said.

As she reached the corridor, she turned in time to catch the guard tearing open the candy packet. "Oh . . . and Murray? . . ."

The guard looked up, guilty pleasure written all over his face.

"You never saw us here tonight, okay?"

He frowned and nodded as he stuffed a handful of candy-coated peanutty goodness in his mouth.

Kitt led the way to the blue room, so called for more than

its color; it was also the area people waited in before identifying their loved ones lying on a cold, hard slab in a room beyond, and where they returned to shed their tears after viewings.

"I thought we were in for it when he asked to see your ID," Kitt said. "Lucky you had that card. Is it counterfeit?"

"No, I really *am* a lecturer at NYAPS." Antoinette held out the card.

Kitt glanced at the credentials and read, " 'The Martial Arts Training Department'—so, you are a member of the faculty."

"We all have legitimate jobs. Well, most of us. Tones takes care of the Academy computer systems, Bianca Sin is the head of thaumaturgy, Cody Shields is in admin, and Oberon's head of security. Raven is the only one flying under the radar—mainly because of the . . ."

"Price on his head," Kitt finished for her.

Antoinette looked away.

"He should never have come back," Kitt said. "My father has increased it to one point five million dollars. Every cutthroat and assassin will be looking for him."

"That's why Oberon gave him a place to stay," Antoinette said and smiled. "But from what I've heard, Raven can take care of himself."

The diminutive form of the female medical examiner appeared in the doorway at that moment, looking slightly harassed and more than a little pissed off. However, her features softened as she crossed the floor toward them.

She tossed her glossy black hair over her shoulder and shoved her hands into the pockets of her white medical coat. "Well, I see ya just couldn't keep away from the fecken place?"

4
stone-cold dead

Tez O'Connor looked so innocent, like butter wouldn't melt in her mouth, until she opened it. Then the Irish-accented expletives flowed freely.

"Seems not," Kitt said with a smile. "And you look like you've had better days too."

The M.E.'s shoulders hunched and the frown deepened. "I've fecken reporters ringing every other minute looking for details, and that fecken gobshite, Agent Roberts from VCU, has been threatening my job if anything leaks to the papers"—she screwed up her face—"but that's not your problem. What can I do for you?"

"Actually, I was hoping you'd let us take a look at the body from the NYAPS campus— This is Antoinette Petrescu; she works with Oberon."

At the mention of the ursian's name, a smile split the M.E.'s face. "How's my tall, dark, and shagable?"

"As cantankerous as ever," Kitt replied.

"Hmmm, just the way I like him—all growly," Tez said with a cheeky wink. "Though I'm still not taking his calls for fecken standing me up last week."

Oberon and Tez had a tumultuous on-again, off-again relationship.

"Well? . . ." The medical examiner tilted her head. "You coming or just pissing about?"

"Thanks, Tez," Kitt said.

"Just thank your lucky stars that fecken eejit Stanislavski called in sick tonight or you'd be havin' to deal with him instead of me," Tez said as she led them down the hall.

The stringent scent of antiseptic cleaning products could never completely cover the underlying corruption of death and decomposition that permeated the autopsy suite. Two of the three stainless steel autopsy tables were occupied. The body on the far table was a dark-skinned female with the graying pallor of the not-so-recently deceased. Their body of interest lay on the center steel bench.

Antoinette moved closer to the dead boy. "I know this kid."

The chest gapped open and the hideous mask of fresh death marred the youthful face. Kitt knew that, having once been the most prolific Venator in the trade, the newly turned Aeternus Antoinette had probably seen much worse, though right now it was hard for Kitt to try to imagine what "much worse" could be.

The main reason she had left the medical examiner's office was because she'd started *glimpsing* her late husband's or brother's stone-cold features on the faces of those she performed autopsies on. All the death was finally getting to her after ten years in the OCPME.

But Antoinette was right—there was something familiar about the boy.

And Oberon was right to wonder if there was any similarity to the other murder she'd worked on a couple of months ago. From where she stood, it practically looked like a carbon copy. Though, before she decided one way or another, she'd have to see more.

The Aeternus leaned in close. "I *have* seen him somewhere before." She glanced from the body to Kitt. "I just can't remember where."

"Would you believe he's the son of the fecken ursian ambassador from Russia?" Tez said.

"Holy shit," Antoinette said.

Suddenly it came to Kitt why she recognized him. He'd appeared in the papers a few weeks back with his father at the announcement of a new library wing for the Academy. The ambassador had ceremonially broken the ground on the construction because he was donating a large sum to the library fund.

"That's why the VCU are trying to keep it all under wraps for now." Tez stepped closer to the autopsy table. "I've finished the prelim exam and taken samples. Kitt, it's almost identical to the boy you autopsied from the last murder at the campus. This time we have an ursian male, nineteen years of age and post awakened. As you already know, the first victim was a felian from a prominent Chicago Pride and around the same age."

Antoinette placed her hands on her hips. "So, we may have a racially motivated killer."

"That's for you to find out. I just do the autopsies," Tez said. Heaving the body onto its side, she pointed to the wide fleshy gash in the lower back of the neck. "He was disabled by severing the spinal column between the C6 and C7 vertebrae with a short, wide blade. It was a precise and accurate strike, rendering the victim immediately paralyzed without killing him. The blade was about an inch and a half long and a half-inch wide."

"Some sort of small pocketknife maybe?" Antoinette asked. "Or something with a detachable blade?"

"As you can see by the cauterization around the wound, the blade was silver." Tez turned and picked up a plastic evidence bag from the instrument cart near the table. A small silver blade covered in blood was sealed inside. "This was taken from the neck wound, and matches the first victim."

"So the killer wanted to keep the boy immobilized but alive until he'd finished," Antoinette said. *"Cold."*

Tez turned the body onto its back, resting the head on the special block. "The muscle and tissue were cut here with a knife. You can see the remnant of the same mark as the other victim; it was first carved into the flesh over his heart before the chest was ripped apart—and I mean fecken *ripped*. Whoever did this used their hands to tear the rib cage open. There are only a few peripheral blade marks on the bone. But the worst thing is this. See where the flesh has started to heal around the edges of both the mark and the torn flesh? . . ."

"So he was still alive," Antoinette said, her jaw dropping open and horror creeping into her eyes.

The boy looked so young. Kitt turned off her inner empathy and switched into medical mode. "He would not only have seen his heart removed but would've felt every excruciating second of it because of the precise placement of the blade."

Antoinette shivered. "We'll have to find out if there were any reports of screaming."

"I found traces of fibers on the tongue and inside the nasal cavity that match the shirt found on the scene. The killer used the victim's own clothing to gag him just like the first case," Tez said. "He would've been completely and utterly, bloody helpless to call for help. Poor fecken gobshite."

"So definitely looks like our guy," Antoinette said. "Or girl, I guess. I can't be sexist now, can I? But I think with the amount of strength it would take to rip open a rib cage, we're probably dealing with a parahuman killer."

"What about the blood work?" Kitt asked.

"Sent it away for testing with an order to rush it, but won't see any results for days; pathology is backed up. Situation bloody normal." Tez rolled her eyes.

"They have a lab at the NYAPS campus . . . you don't happen to have a spare set of those samples do you?" Kitt asked.

"Feck me, of course I do. I took extra just in case. I know Oberon—he's going to want this info ASAP." Tez picked up an insulated lunch bag covered with cartoon characters and handed it to her. "I can't give you the blade, but there's a thumb drive in there with the crime scene photos and reports on any other evidence. Just do me a favor—if you do find anything interesting, give me the heads-up." The phone on the wall rang. Tez spat a string of obscenities as she crossed to pick it up. "What?" she shouted into the mouthpiece.

"Shite!" Her face drained. "Try bloody stalling 'em for a few more fecken minutes."

She placed the receiver back in the cradle. "Agent fecken Roberts has just turned up with a couple of his goons, demanding to see the body. If he catches you here with those samples, there'll be hell to pay for us all."

"You got a back way out?" Antoinette asked.

"Yes," Kitt said. "And it leads into the alley where we're parked." She gave Tez a quick nod. "Thanks, and I'll be in touch as soon as I have anything."

The dark-haired human smiled. "Cool. And tell that bear of a man he owes me fecken big-time. And I intend to collect."

Male voices came down the hall.

"Quick, hide in there." Antoinette pointed to the room across the hall.

"No, " Kitt whispered. "This way."

They quickly made it around the corner before anyone was in sight and Kitt led the way to the fire-escape stairwell at the back of the building.

"Won't it set off the alarm?" Antoinette asked when they reached the fire door.

Kitt shook her head. "The smokers disabled it a while ago so they could sneak out for a quick cigarette."

She pointed to a small wedge of wood stopping the door from closing properly. "Looks like someone's out for a nicotine fix right now."

"I'll just check if the coast is clear." Antoinette carefully pushed the door and popped her head out briefly, then signaled for Kitt to follow.

A light snow flurry dusted her eyelids with soft falling flakes. Antoinette stopped dead. She dropped into a crouch and touched the ground with her fingertips, then brought them to her nose.

"What is it?" Kitt asked.

"Fresh blood." Antoinette stood and held a finger to her lips for silence.

She raised her nose to scent the air—her fangs glinting in the light on the wall.

All Kitt could smell with her frozen nose was the stench

of rotting trash and the falling snow. But there was an aura of impending disaster she couldn't quite shake. A noise that could have been a whimper came from the shadows further down the alley. And then a growl—no, more like a purr of animalistic pleasure. Maybe Antoinette should go alone; she was more equipped to deal with this.

"Necrodreniac," Antoinette mouthed as she slipped off her suit jacket and popped the trunk.

"Help," a weak female voice called out.

That tore it. Someone needed help—medical assistance. Antoinette couldn't fight the dreniac *and* treat a human bleeding to death. "I'm coming too," Kitt said.

Antoinette placed the samples from Tez to one side in the trunk and then lifted the floor in the center to pull a long-sheathed Japanese sword from its custom foam housing. "Stay here," she growled as she fixed the sword strap over her shoulder and across her chest so the weapon was in easy reach.

"Not happening," Kitt said.

The ex-Venator closed the trunk carefully, her eyes glittering with an almost fevered pitch. "All right, but just keep out of my way."

She followed Antoinette back down the alley, the scent of fresh, hot blood now apparent even to her slightly enhanced pretransformed parahuman senses. Human form was the only way she could treat the injured.

A whimper came from the darkness, weaker than before. Antoinette raised her finger to her lips again. Kitt shifted her eyes to cat form for better vision, triggering the snow leopard fur to sprout along her limbs under her clothing, but she halted the process enough to keep her enhanced senses while retaining human shape.

The alleyway opened to a small area where a matted-haired male in filthy rags fed on a sagging human man. A few feet away, a skinny female dreniac in a miniskirt with stringy, sandy hair and holes in her fishnet stockings suckled at the wrist of a human woman who sat propped against a Dumpster. The dreniac female had her back turned so she didn't see them approaching. But the woman did. Her eyes

grew round and hopeful, and her mouth worked soundlessly
with three simple words, "Please help me."

The two human victims were obviously the nicotine addicts from the nearby Department offices. They had unfortunately encountered some addicts of a different kind. But
no one expected an attack this close to a parahuman government facility. These dreniacs were unusually bold.

"Hey, ugly and skanky," Antoinette yelled. "This isn't a
takeout restaurant."

The gruesome couple turned as one, the remnants of their
meal coating their mouths and dribbling down their chins.
The glassy-eyed male blinked slowly, obviously deep in the
throes of a death-high, which meant his victim was beyond
help. But the female screeched her frustration, extremely
pissed at being interrupted.

Kitt crept closer to the guy on the ground. She recognized
him as one of the lab techs from the fifth floor. They used to
say hi in the elevators sometimes. She needed to make sure
he was dead or if there was any chance she could save him.

One look and she knew it was a lost cause. Blood congealed around the gaping neck wounds and the glassy eyes
were already clouding in death. His throat was a tattered
mess, ripped and shredded for faster feeding. Even if they'd
arrived the minute he got his wounds, she'd never have been
able to save him.

She turned her attention to the other human. The throat
was still intact and Kitt could maybe save her.

Maybe.

They'd have to get that dreniac away from her if they were
to have any chance.

The former Venator stepped up, distracting the dreniac
female who turned, baring her fangs at Antoinette and
hissed.

Antoinette just laughed. "Come on—really—is that supposed to scare me?" She tilted her head a little to the side.
"You've been watching too many late-night undead movies
and, Honey, we ain't *undead*. And you sure as shit ain't
scary."

The couple seemed a little taken aback by her reaction.

The male crouched low and glowered at her with eyes ablaze. Antoinette, the ultimate warrior, unsheathed her sword and answered with a homicidal grin of her own.

A shiver of fear rattled through Kitt. She didn't know who she was more afraid of at that moment—the bloodthirsty dreniacs or the fucking scary Aeternus who really seemed to be enjoying herself way too much.

While they were distracted, Kitt moved closer to the wounded human female, desperate to staunch the blood loss from her wrist. Almost without warning, the male dreniac launched himself, catching Kitt unawares and unprepared. She didn't even have a weapon to defend herself and no way to stop him.

He moved fast, lightning fast. But Antoinette was faster. The Aeternus leapt high and flipped midair, bringing down her blade in the same moment. One second the male dreniac was racing at Kitt, the next Antoinette had landed in a crouch with one hand braced in front of her on the ground, the other holding the long gleaming sword behind her back—and the blade now sheened with dark blood.

The male's head landed with a meaty thud and rolled a few feet while the decapitated body continued to run a few more steps before toppling sideways. Antoinette glanced over her shoulder at Kitt with a disturbing, almost insanely joyous expression. A spray of dreniac blood covered the lower half of her face, adding even more menace to her features.

The female dreniac screamed in anger and frustration, sending a chill down Kitt's spine. Like her partner, the skanky addict flew at Antoinette with long talon-like nails.

The Aeternus waited, not moving a muscle until the last possible second. Then she thrust up and out so the insane dreniac ran straight onto the blade. The sword entered through the foul creature's open screaming mouth and exited out the back of the head. Antoinette wrenched the blade out and the female dreniac folded like a perverted version of a blow-up sex doll with a puncture.

Kitt was more than a little shaken, by both the violence and Antoinette's obvious enjoyment of the kill. The former Venator's sinister, bloody appearance didn't help matters much. The almost black dreniac blood covered the front of her white T-shirt. But the thing that really chilled Kitt's bones was the on-the-edge-of-insanity glint burning in Antoinette's eyes.

The snowfall grew steadily heavier, and even though the alley was sheltered on three sides by buildings, visibility was getting more difficult.

"Take care of the human," Antoinette growled as she wiped the blade on the fallen female's filthy shirt.

Kitt moved to the surviving human female's side and pulled the winter scarf from around her neck to wrap her torn, bleeding wrist. The poor woman trembled with shock; her eyes darted around, terrified. The falling snow was more a godsend, helping to slow the blood loss as Kitt tied off the makeshift bandage. She heard Antoinette approaching from behind.

"This should stop the bleeding," she said as she turned, "but we'll need to get her to a hospital for a transfusion as—"

It wasn't Antoinette. Another male dreniac loomed over her and licked lips already smeared with drying human blood as he eyed the fresh crimson droplets on the fresh snowfall.

"Hey!" Antoinette yelled from where she squatted beside her dead dreniac female.

He turned his attention toward the sound, then at the blood-soaked cloth around the woman's wrist. Kitt could see his desire to run warring with the opposing instinct to feed and kill. She positioned herself before the human. He'd have to go through her first.

But fear eventually won out. He leapt over the Dumpster to the fire escape above and jumped from floor to floor as he sped to the top of the building. Antoinette raced to Kitt's side and watched as he disappeared over the top.

"After him," Kitt yelled at her. "Don't let him get away in that state of bloodlust."

The Aeternus shook her head. "I can't leave you here alone."

"He's going to kill again if you don't catch him. Don't worry about me. I'll call Oberon for backup. Now go!"

Antoinette stepped toward the fire escape and turned. "What if there are more?"

"Do you think there are?"

Antoinette sniffed the air. "No."

"Then go. Stop him from killing anyone else."

And without another word, Antoinette followed the dreniac up the side of the building.

5

into the lion's den

Antoinette breached the top and looked back down at the felian. Kitt seemed to have everything under control down there, and she was right—in his current state of bloodlust, the dreniac was likely to kill the next human he came across if she didn't get to him first.

Up on the rooftops the snowstorm whipped around her body, but she no longer felt the icy touch. Excitement pulsed low in her stomach. Her first hunt. Well, the first since she'd been embraced months ago. And oh, how she'd missed the thrill of the chase.

In the old days when she was still human, there would've been no way she'd take on two dreniacs at once; and to have gone on a hunt without a pistol loaded with silver nitrate would've been sheer suicide. But now . . .

Things are different.

Now she could rely on her favorite sword, her skill, and her new Aeternus abilities—the ones she'd fought so hard against at first. And for the first time, she was about to find out what she could really do with this new Aeternus body.

The male was gone, but his foul stench was as good as a neon sign pointing, *Bad Guy This Way.*

However, she could quickly lose him in the thickening snowfall if she didn't move fast. Antoinette crossed the rooftop in half a heartbeat and followed the dreniac stench to the edge of the building and across the twelve-foot gap to the roof of the next. She took a few steps back and ran, her leg muscles bunching to launch her into the air. With ease, she made the distance and then some. Landing on her feet, and without breaking her stride, she was on his trail again.

Fuck! That was fun.

He'd turned left and had gone over the side into another alley. Antoinette simply stepped off the multistory building and dropped to the filthy ground below, absorbing the impact by bending her knees. Then she took off at a run. Something else she could never have done as a human.

He tried to lose her several times by doubling back or moving across more rooftops, but she always managed to stay on his trail. She hadn't spent ten years as a Venator without learning more about the devious tricks of the death-high addicts.

After a few more minutes of scaling buildings and dropping into alleys, she spotted him ducking into a back entrance. The roach-ridden fleabag hotel stank with the sour scent of human sweat, stale sex, and incense. It all worked to confuse her senses and mask the trail of her prey.

A fat balding man sat behind the front counter reading a newspaper, sweat circles and God knows what else staining the once-white wife-beater tank top.

"Where did he go?" she asked.

The fat man ignored her.

"Did you hear me?" She dropped her voice. "Or are you just plain stupid?"

A laughing Aeternus male entered the hotel's front door on the arm of a human fang-whore. He glanced up, did a quick double take as he noticed Antoinette, and suddenly seemed to remember he had an urgent appointment elsewhere. It wasn't illegal to feed from a willing human, but it was to supply blood for spiking. And the fang-whore was definitely a spiker.

"Why don't you piss off, cop. You're scaring away my customers," the desk clerk grumbled under his breath, turning the page of his supermarket tabloid. "Come back when you have a warrant."

Antoinette punched through the latest celebrity sensationalist headline and grabbed the insolent shit around the throat. "Who the *fuck* said I was a cop?"

The fat man's eyes practically bulged out of his head.

"I am after a maggoty dreniac who came in here not two minutes ago. Now, are you going to tell me where he went or am I going to have to rip your fucking head off and use the blood to draw him out instead?" Antoinette hissed through clenched teeth.

His eyes grew wide and dropped to her extended fangs. His breath stank and his suffocating body odor made her want to puke, if she'd actually still been able to puke, but she brought her face closer to his vileness anyway.

"Then again, I could do with a bite myself." She sniffed up the side of his face. "And all this fear you're exuding is making you smell rather"—she sniffed him again and fought her gag reflex—"yummy." She may not be able to vomit, but she could still dry heave.

She deliberately touched one fang with the tip of her tongue. His already panicky eyes grew even wider.

Antoinette smiled. "I'm not really into helping myself, but for you I could make an exception."

"That's illegal," he said.

The smell of hot, fresh urine stung her nose and she dropped her gaze to the growing damp patch on the front of his cargo pants.

"So is harboring dreniacs," she said.

His eyes darted to a staircase half hidden by fake plants, giving her the answer she needed. Just in case, she reached over to yank the phone out of the socket.

"Hey . . . th-tha-that's—" he stammered.

She pushed him back. The stool groaned under his bulk. She raced down the stairs and stopped dead at the bottom. Without the conflicting odors above, the place fairly reeked with the dreniac scent, both stale and new, plus a hint of fresh human blood. Her prey had definitely come this way.

The dreniac trail led into the left of two basement suites.

Antoinette nearly choked on the rancid odor of the death-sweat; even when human, she would've had little trouble scenting out this dreniac lair. They'd been here for some time, by the smell of it.

There could be no capture or imprisonment for these insane caricatures of the Aeternus. The Venator Guild had tried in the beginning after the CHaPR Treaty was established, but the dreniac's descent into insanity only accelerated. Without their death-high fix, they tended to prey on each other, or mutilate themselves. With no cure for Necrodrenia, the best and kindest course of action was to put them down. Immediately.

Only a licensed Venator or an agent working for the Department of Parahuman Security were supposed to hunt dreniacs, and she was officially neither. The guild had revoked her ticket when she stood before the tribunal and accused them of corruption. *But, fuck it.* He'd killed and would kill again.

She was right here, right now, and so was he. License or no license, this bastard was hers.

With one mighty kick, the door swung inward on its hinges, the lock breaking and splintering the wooden frame. Inside was dark—like *that* was going to stop her. She wasn't some weak human Venator anymore. Her eyes adjusted quickly to the lack of light.

She walked into the center of the apparently deserted room, knowing he waited for her behind the door. But she was more than a match for him.

The door slammed shut. She flexed her hand around the katana before turning to confront him.

He grinned insanely. The drying human blood was caked on his mouth, making him look like a clown—the kind that sends children screaming in terror to hide under their beds.

Antoinette slipped the sword from its sheath. "So, Pennywise . . . here we are."

Kitt kept the pressure on the wound. It wasn't as bad as it first looked, though it would depend on how much they'd drained from her. The woman's cheeks still maintained a hint of color; her lips were blue from cold rather than blood loss.

Kitt lay the unconscious human down and shrugged off her own jacket to keep the patient warm. With some old boxes from the trash, she elevated the woman's feet. After she checked the scarf-wrapped injury, Kitt fumbled a cell phone from her trouser pocket with one hand while she kept the pressure on her wrist with the other.

On the second key press, something smashed into her wrist and sent the phone flying. She spun, ready to defend her patient, covering the human's body with her own.

Nothing. *No one.*

The heavy snowfall reduced her visibility to a few feet, but the hair on the back of her neck prickled. They were not alone. The woman groaned as she started to gain consciousness. Suddenly her eyelids flung open.

"Shh," Kitt said as she moved the human's unhurt hand to the scarf-wrapped wrist. "You have to press hard on this."

The frightened woman's eyes darted back and forth, sheer terrified panic rising in their depths. Her teeth were chattering from cold fear, and trembling set in from shock. Kitt really needed to get her warm, preferably out of this weather. But no one would hear her, not with this snowstorm.

"Hey, you're all right, you hear me?" Kitt said, pushing down her own fear and clicking her fingers in front of the woman's face. "Here, look. Look. At. Me. It's going to be okay, I'm a doctor. Do you understand?"

The human's eyes settled and focused, her teeth clacking vigorously as she gave Kitt a shaky nod.

"Good." Kitt let out a sigh. "Now, keep up the pressure. Okay?"

The human nodded again.

"I need to call for the paramedics." *And some help.*

Kitt tried to keep her voice calm and her face neutral. She didn't want to spook her patient. The dark alley felt much more dangerous than it had a few minutes ago, and she wished she hadn't sent Antoinette away.

The woman's mouth opened and shut rapidly, her eyes growing impossibly round as the snowflakes melted on her cheeks. "Please," she croaked "please don't leave me."

"Don't talk. I won't be far." Kitt climbed to her feet and crossed to where her phone had landed.

Nothing moved. But the gnawing cold grip of fear didn't lessen in the pit of her stomach. Her hands shook as she bent to pick up the cell and something slammed her against the wall. The force pushed the air from her lungs and showered her with ice and bits of broken masonry. Dazed, she pulled herself into a sitting position and was roughly helped to her feet before being thrown through the air to smash upside down against the opposite wall.

It took a few seconds for the flashy stars to stop and her vision to return to normal. When her head stopped spinning, she found the alley empty again and the falling snow had quickly obliterated any footprints.

Kitt was a doctor, not a fighter, and wasn't prepared for this. Her terror froze her where she lay. Then with thought of her patient, helpless and unprotected, everything shifted. For the second time tonight, the long dormant wildness inside her awoke—the nature of her family, the very nature she'd fought so hard to suppress since she'd moved away from the reservation to live among the humans. She gave in to it because she had a human life to protect.

The woman lay a few feet away, her terrified panting breaths so fast Kitt was afraid she would hyperventilate. A lazy female chuckle crept out of the darkness, from everywhere and nowhere at the same time. Even with her eyes shifted into snow leopard mode, she couldn't see where it came from.

"What do you want?" Kitt screamed into the emptiness.

Her voice startled the human woman; she stilled, and then started panting again even faster. Kitt crawled, watching all around as she felt blindly for her cell phone. Just as her fingers brushed against the hard plastic, someone landed behind and slammed her forward, to lie facedown in the snow.

Black leather-clad legs in five-inch heels kicked the phone out of reach, then circled while Kitt struggled to gain her feet. Another mighty kick, this one to Kitt's abdomen, stopped her from rising and sent her onto her side nursing what she suspected were broken ribs. She curled into a fetal position, trying to suck air into her lungs, and saw the attacker for the first time as her ribs cracked back into place and healed. Broken bones weren't an issue for a Bestiabeo, the true name of her race.

The female who kneeled beside Kitt's human patient was straight out of a 1980s heavy metal video, complete with leopard-print halter top, tight leather pants, heavy makeup, and a teased blue-black perm. Kitt wondered if she'd hit her head harder than she thought until the female turned to her.

"You shouldn't have interrupted my pets' playtime," said the time-warp metal queen as she rubbed the back of her fingers across the human's cheek.

But there was nothing tender about the rock-chick's gesture. And another thing Kitt instantly knew was that the female was Aeternus and not a dreniac like the others. There was no dreniac scent or any sign of death-high addiction, but there was something seriously wrong behind those dark eyes. Lunacy or perversity, she couldn't be sure which.

As Kitt dived for her phone, the Aeternus hauled the human up and wrapped her long crimson-painted fingers around the frightened woman's chin. "Uh-uh-ah . . . smash it against the wall or I'll snap her neck."

The terrified victim's eyes pleaded with Kitt to obey. She had no choice and rammed the cell phone against the bricks with all her weight and frustration. It shattered into dozens of pieces of black and gray plastic and green circuit board.

"There's a good little pussy cat," the rocker chick crooned as she caressed the human's cheek again and smiled widely. "But you're much too trusting."

With a quick flick of her wrist, the crunching snap of the human's breaking neck reverberated off the walls of the surround buildings. Kitt stood stunned—unable to believe or comprehend what had just happened. As the woman's lifeless body crumpled into a heap, shocking anger ripped through Kitt's gut, triggering the onset of transformation.

She tore at her clothes, trying to remove them before the

change ripped them to shreds, but the change was happening too hard and too fast because of her rage.

Within less than a few seconds, a new all-time record for Kitt, her full felian senses were primed and ready for attack. Bloodlust rose as she pinned back her ears and hissed. She crouched and leapt, but the Aeternus swatted her aside like a bug.

She hit the wall with her paws and pushed off to land back on her feet, then crouched again, tail flicking. The metal queen crouched too. Using all of her parahuman strength, Kitt launched herself again and managed to swipe the Aeternus's face with her front paw and scrape across her gut with hind claws.

The metal queen's expression grew murderous. The wounds started to close immediately, but blood still ran down her cheek, dripping on a shredded leopard-print top already soaked crimson from the claw marks on her chest.

"You've ruined my favorite outfit, bitch," the insane Aeternus screamed.

Kitt crouched low and stalked forward on her belly, gathering the strength in her legs. Then she sprang, this time aiming for the female's throat. The force of the impact threw them both to the ground. The Aeternus flipped and gained the upper hand by straddling Kitt and pushing back her head. Kitt struggled to free herself, but the Aeternus had a grip of iron and soon her throat was stretched beyond comfort.

She desperately tried to twist out from underneath, striking out at her with her claws, scrabbling to gain footing on the concrete pavement, but the Aeternus's grip tightened. Kitt's neck felt like it was going to tear open. Panic and darkness crept up her spine with the certainty she was going to die.

When the dreniac's grin grew wider and much more confident, Antoinette had the feeling that being there might not be such a good idea. This lair was his territory—an entirely unknown factor to her—and where he held the advantage.

She caught movement out of the corner of her eye and a female melted out of the closet, grinning like a fool on smack. A soft scrape signaled someone else as another female climbed out from behind a sofa.

Three of them.

Bed springs creaked off to the left and a couple appeared in the doorway of the next room.

Shit . . . five. Not great odds.

The female at the bedroom door wore only a man-sized heavy metal T-shirt, and leaned against the male in a pair of jeans, his lean, wiry torso covered in tattoos.

She shouldn't have been so cocky . . . *But dreniacs don't live in communes. Ever.*

And yet here they were. She'd heard of two or three teaming up for a short time, but they often fell out quickly, usually with fatal outcomes for at least for one of them. Dreniacs didn't know how to play nice with others. From the stench in the room, this lot had been living here for weeks.

Carefully, she backed away a couple of steps so she could keep all five within her periphery—and hoped to hell there weren't more of them. She raised the sword before her and tried to figure which one or ones would attack first.

"Where's Joaquin?" the female who had come from behind the couch asked.

Antoinette guessed Joaquin was the headless male back in the alley.

"This bitch wasted him and Tiggy, then came after me," Pennywise said, confirming her suspicions.

"No!" The despondent female turned her haunted, hate-filled gaze on Antoinette.

Bingo!

Within the time it took to tense for the attack, the dreniac female flew at her with a hollow wail. Antoinette braced back on her left foot, and just before the enraged female reached her, she sliced low and brought the blade back up a little higher. The razor edge found little resistance as the katana's blade sliced cleanly through the dreniac's body. The female fell to the floor with three ugly wet splats. The head rolled a little, rocked back and forth, and stopped, facing away from her; the legs kicked and twitched a little at Antoinette's feet, and the torso oozed dark dreniac blood onto the carpet.

The others stood staring at the pieces, stunned into silence. All except the guy with the tattoos—he just tilted his head and looked at her with amusement.

Antoinette wasn't about to wait for them to regain their senses. Keeping momentum, she continued, striking the female on her right through the throat, then, with a twist, freed the head from the dreniac's shoulders.

The last remaining female turned and ran into the bathroom, locking the door with a snick. It wouldn't keep Antoinette out for long . . . but she did still have two males out here to deal with first.

Pennywise circled around behind her, while the tattooed guy smiled and moved right. There was something familiar about him: his sunken cheeks were covered in a light beard; dark circles ringed his eyes. And even though he had the typical appearance of a dreniac junkie, something about him pricked the back of her mind.

Antoinette tried to keep both males in sight without giving them an opening to strike. Pennywise came for her but broke off at the last minute. A distraction. Giving Tatts-guy enough time to grab a weapon, a sword much like her own—and the way he was twirling that blade, he knew how to use it. The stench rolling off him meant he'd already fed tonight, so he'd be sharp.

"Well, well, well. The great Antoinette Petrescu is one of us now," Tatts-guy said.

"I'm nothing like you," she spat, wondering how he knew her name.

Pennywise stopped and looked at her in openmouthed surprise.

"Not yet, but give it time. Patience was never one of your strong suits," Tatts-guy replied. "Wait until the hunger gets to be all you can think about, when it eats away at you."

"Been there, done that—"

"Bought the T-shirt." He finished Antoinette's quip while twisting his sword around in the air. "You really don't recognize me do you, Antoinette?"

"Sure I do—you're just the same as every other dreniac piece of shit I've ever put down over the years."

"I'm hurt. After all we shared in Reno. Though, I guess it was a few years ago," he said, raising the tip of his sword.

Shit, it couldn't be.

Her eyes dropped to his left shoulder. And there it was, almost lost in the intricate skin art: a tattooed caricature of a grinning skull with vampire teeth, a sword speared through the top so the blade showed through one eye socket, and a rose wrapped around the pummel.

"J.J.?" She breathed his name in disbelief.

He'd been a year above her at the Petrescu training school, even though she was five years younger; and she'd had a bit of a crush on him, more because of his abilities than any real desire for him. But some years later they'd crossed paths again while hunting the same dreniac. He'd been very human—but then again, so had she. "What happened to you? You were one of the best."

He smiled. "That's right, baby. Remember that weekend? I was turned two days after you left me sleeping alone in that hotel room."

After she'd bagged the dreniac and the bounty, she'd given J.J. a consolation prize: a weekend of drinking, partying, and sex. It'd been a brief interlude for a couple of Venators—but whatever they'd shared then wouldn't stop her from taking him out now that he was a filthy, murderous dreniac.

The whole time J.J. had kept her talking, Pennywise inched closer. She saw him out of the corner of her eye just before he lunged from the left, forcing her to sidestep into the bedroom. She didn't have room to swing her weapon and could only kick out, landing her foot in the middle of his chest, sending him crashing back into the wall.

Sentimental feelings didn't stop J.J. from thrusting his sword at her either. She leapt back just before the tip entered her gut and slammed the bedroom door on him hard, trapping his forearm and forcing the blade to drop from his hand. She slid her toe under the fallen weapon and flipped it up, catching it midair with her left hand.

Now she had both weapons. She spun them with a flick of her wrist. *Nice.* Both blades had perfect balance, not surprising since they were made by the same master.

Why had she never thought of using two blades before? Because it hadn't been practical then; she'd needed one hand for her gun. But now, now it felt . . . right.

Pennywise ducked left, picked up a beat-up metal coatrack from just inside the bedroom door, and swiped at her head. Antoinette leapt backward over the furniture and shoved the bed forward with her foot. It crashed into Pennywise's knees, his bones crunching with the impact as he fell on the dirty gray bedcovers. He started to rise almost immediately, his bones popping as they began to heal. She had time to cross her arms behind his head, each sword placed on either side of his neck.

Then before he had a chance to spin around on her, she uncrossed her arms and the blades sliced through bone and sinew with ease. The body fell forward as the head dropped to the bed and rolled, landing with a dull thud on the floor. Dark dreniac blood sprayed across the bedcovers and up the opposite wall. She doubted they'd be getting the deposit back on this room.

Antoinette shoved the bed out of the way and moved into the outer room. The door to the suite was open and the room empty. J.J. had run. But there was still one more thing she had to do.

She kicked in the bathroom door and found the girl crouching in the bathtub, shaking violently and crying.

"Please," the girl said, holding her hands up, tucking her chin into her chest. "Please don't kill me."

Now that the others had been taken care of, Antoinette realized the girl's scent wasn't tainted. And she was terrified, her raised hands shaking and tears coursing down her cheeks, dragging mascara into black smudges. This *didn't* mean J.J. hadn't already embraced her, for if she had taken the eternal kiss, then she was still doomed.

"Did you take his blood?" Antoinette asked.

"What?" The girl's trembling hands dropped a little.

"Did you taste blood when he kissed you?"

"N-n-no." The girl completely lowered her hands and looked at Antoinette. "I don't think so."

She leaned closer to the girl. J.J.'s dreniac scent was all

over her, but Antoinette still couldn't tell if she'd been embraced. The best thing to do was take her in and watch if she went into the transition. Then if need be, she could be taken care of.

"Stay here," she told the girl and went back into the bedroom, closing the door behind her before taking out her phone.

6

A Beastly Rescue

The Aeternus female tightened the grip on Kitt's jaw and panic screamed in her mind as her head was pulled further back. Kitt's limbs trembled as they started to change back to human form, but she fought it. If she transformed, she'd lose much of her felian strength and abilities. *Can't change back.* She closed her eyes and concentrated, trying to quell the panic and stay in cat form.

The strain on her neck reached unbearable agony, cutting off her airway. She reached up with partially transformed, fur-covered human hands to break the iron grip. But the Aeternus shifted her hands to Kitt's evolving human forehead.

Just when she felt her body and mind couldn't take the lack of oxygen, something slammed into them both, breaking the hold. Air rushed back into her lungs as she scrambled further away from her assailant while gulping air into painful, screaming lungs. Furious sounds of fighting added speed to her escape. When she was far enough away, she glanced over her shoulder at the large black mannish shape grappling with the Aeternus.

Her eyes had changed back to human along with the rest of her and didn't have the energy or the mental capacity to switch back to felian form. She could barely feel the falling snow on her naked skin as she watched the battle before her.

The humanoid black form snapped elongated jaws, tearing at the Aeternus female with ferocity. Kitt searched for her clothes and glanced at the fight going on behind her. For a single instant, the shape came out of the snow and into light. Her breath turned to ice in her chest, freezing her vocal cords as well as her ability to process oxygen.

Raven. Her dark warrior.

His head and jaws were lupine, his body human shaped, covered in thick black fur, and he still wore jeans. He'd retained the best of both forms—the strength and speed of the wolf and the dexterity and balance of a human. To have halted the transformation that far advanced took an incredible amount of power and control.

Kitt located her clothes: the shirt had lost several buttons, her new slacks, the ones she'd stressed over getting mud on, were completely shredded, and her underwear was useless. Then she noticed her abandoned thick coat on the ground beside the human woman's body and slipped it on.

Raven's claws sliced and teeth snapped. The female Aeternus gripped the fur on either side of his face and head-butted him right between the eyes. He staggered back, shaking his head as a growl slowly built and erupted from deep within the half-human, half-wolf creature. He launched himself at the female, hitting her with enough force to propel them both to the ground, and managed to twist her under him. Finally, he had the upper hand.

Antoinette dropped to the alley floor not far from the tangled heap of limbs and fangs. It was enough of a distraction for the feral female to shove Raven off and speed off down the alleyway.

Raven skidded to a stop beside Kitt as he reverted to human form. "Are you okay?" he asked, touching her face, turning her arms, running his hands up her calves as he checked for any damage.

"Yes," she croaked.

Her wounds had stopped bleeding; cuts, scrapes, and gravel rash healing quickly.

"Get her back to the Bunker," he said to Antoinette, stripping his jeans as he changed to full wolf form. Then took off after the escaping female.

Antoinette tilted her head and frowned. She squatted beside the human woman's body and placed two fingers on the side of her throat feeling for a pulse. "What happened?"

"She came after you left," Kitt said, slowly gaining control over her trembling. "And just murdered the woman, in cold blood. Snapped her neck without a second thought." Kitt pulled her thick coat tighter.

At least the snowfall was slowing. The male human's body was crusted with snow and ice. She'd failed to save either of them.

Antoinette pulled out her cell phone. "I'm going to call this into base for Oberon to deal with."

"Did you get him?" Kitt asked.

"What?" Antoinette said in the middle of dialing.

"The dreniac . . . Did you get him?"

She answered with the same killer grin, though this time Kitt was glad for it. After witnessing what that cold bitch did to the woman, she was happy that Antoinette was on their side.

Oberon was there to meet her and Antoinette when the door slid open. Kitt must've looked a sight, dressed only in her knee-length tan coat. His face turned to stone and he pulled her against his big body.

"Kitt, I'm so sorry." His voice hitched slightly as he guided her down the spiral stairs.

"It wasn't your fault." She hugged him more for his sake than hers.

"How could you have put her in such danger?" he growled at Antoinette.

Kitt pulled away and looked up at his thunderous features glaring at Antoinette.

"You're right. I shouldn't have left her alone." Antoinette hung her head.

"Don't you dare blame her—I insisted she go," Kitt said, her own anger surfacing. "How was she to know an insane bitch waited in the shadows?"

"She wasn't there to hunt dreniacs and shouldn't have gone into that alley," Oberon said.

Kitt shoved her hands on her hips and planted her feet. "And *what*? Just let those people die?"

"They died anyway," he yelled back.

"I would've saved that woman if not for that crazed eighties reject," Kitt hissed. "And maybe if you and Dylan taught me to fight instead of wrapping me up in cotton wool, I could've taken better care of myself."

Oberon's mouth dropped open. Surprise and hurt replacing the anger.

"I'm sorry, I shouldn't have said that," Kitt said softly and put her hand on his arm.

I let them protect me. It was as much her fault as her brother's and Oberon's.

Antoinette cleared her throat and flicked her gaze to Kitt's chest. She realized a small group of stunned people gathered to watch the show, and if her coat crept open much more, they'd all get a peep show to go with the verbal boxing match.

"Why don't we go get cleaned up," Antoinette suggested. "I have some spare clothes you can borrow."

Oberon's brows relaxed and his face softened. "I think that's a great idea. And when you're finished, meet me in the conference room for a debriefing."

A shower was exactly what she needed to wash away all the blood, filth, and chill from her body. She followed Antoinette to the unisex locker room.

The Aeternus undressed and turned on the communal shower faucet. Steam swirled in an enticing seduction of heat and Kitt noticed how frozen her toes were. Antoinette stepped into the stream and lifted her head, the hot water sluicing over her face.

"God, that feels good for the soul," she said and looked over her shoulder at Kitt. "Nothing like a hot shower to wash away the stench of dreniacs."

The tan coat was all that stood between Kitt and nudity.

She shed the wrapper and stepped onto the tiled floor of the showers.

Antoinette reached for the soap and worked it into a lather.

The hot water slammed against Kitt's skin like a thousand needles. It soon became a soothing steady stream, both relaxing and remedial as the knots in her shoulders loosened and the last of the chill left her.

Antoinette continued to wash, turning around in the stream of running water. "You were pretty impressive tonight."

Kitt shook her head. "You fought them off, I didn't do anything."

"Are you kidding me?" Antoinette's hands stilled and she glanced at Kitt. "The way you went in after those humans. That took real courage. Never come between a dreniac and its food."

"But Oberon's right, it was all for nothing," Kitt said and let her head fall forward so the shower pounded on the back of her neck.

"You tried, though," Antoinette said, rubbing white foamy suds into her shoulders. "So . . . I take it you and Raven had a thing?"

Kitt fought her instinct to turn away. Antoinette's expression was neither accusatory nor judgmental. It was a simple honest-to-goodness question for the sake of the answer.

"A long, long time ago."

"And this stuff with your family?" Antoinette cupped her hands to the falling water, her mouth open to catch the stream, which she spat out and glanced over at Kitt again.

"What do you know about it?" Kitt asked.

The other female shrugged. "I know your Pride placed a substantial bounty on his head because they believed he killed your husband."

Kitt picked up the soap.

"Even though there was never enough evidence for the authorities to officially charge Raven with the murder," Antoinette went on.

"That doesn't matter to the Pride," Kitt said. "Human rules mean little and Pride law is complex and archaic."

"But you obviously don't believe he killed your husband."

Kitt shook her head.

Antoinette watched her face for a moment. "Does anyone else know Raven is the father of your twins?"

Kitt dropped the soap in shock. For a moment she thought of denying it, but she had the feeling Antoinette would not be easy to convince. "How did you know?"

"I pieced it together. The twins were found, what, three months ago? And shortly after, Raven shows up here and Oberon takes him in, just like that—" Antoinette clicked her fingers with a wet snap under the stream from the shower. "Then there was the way you reacted when you saw him, and the way he protected you in the alley. That cuts much deeper than just a quick sport-fuck."

Kitt nodded. "Of course Oberon knows, so did Dylan, but no one else does."

"That's why you're sure he didn't do it?" Antoinette reached up and ran her hands through her wet hair.

"Not exactly. We found Emmett's body after spending the night together. The shock sent me into labor."

Antoinette didn't seem at all surprised by this news. "How do you know he didn't arrange your husband's murder?"

"Two reasons. First, if he'd wanted someone dead, do you think he's the kind of male to get someone else to do it?"

Antoinette shrugged, and then shook her head slowly. "I guess not."

"And second . . . he had nothing to gain. Emmett and I were husband and wife in name only. We protected each other's secrets." Kitt stepped from the shower and reached for a towel hanging above the wooden bench. "I loved Emmett, just not in that way."

Antoinette turned off the taps. Heavy drops falling into the water pooled on the floor and replaced the constant drum of the shower. She slicked back her wet hair and cocked a dubious eyebrow.

"We were happy, but when it came to sex, I wasn't his type. As I said before, Pride law is rather archaic, including their views on homosexuality. It would've been impossible for either of us to take a lover from within the Pride. So we used to get away to a human town a few hours from the resort. And that's where I met Raven . . ."

She trailed off, remembering the first time she laid eyes on Raven in the bar they used to frequent, but shook herself out of useless reminiscence. "It seemed the perfect solution at the time. The Matokwe Pack and the Jordan Pride had never been what you would call friendly, and Raven didn't even get along with them. All that sneaking around also made it more exciting and . . . the sex really hot." She whispered the last part.

Antoinette grinned and wrapped a towel around her long, athletic body. "Did Emmett know about Raven?"

"Yes. So did Dylan and Oberon. In fact, they all got along extremely well—until I got pregnant that is. Then things got . . . complicated."

"I guess it didn't help that Raven disappeared around the same time as the murder, and especially because after the murder he was seen in the area?" Antoinette asked.

"You really have done your homework," Kitt said.

"I got curious when Oberon brought him in, got Tones to do a check on him . . . so who do you think really murdered your husband?"

"No idea." She sat down on the bench. "Everyone liked Emmett. He was an expert in the old laws. What's troubling is the similarities between the current deaths and Emmett's murder."

"Probably just coincidence," Antoinette said as she crossed the room and opened a locker. "Here, this should at least get you through your lecture tonight."

She passed Kitt a dark blue suit similar to the one she wore earlier. The pants were a little long in the leg and the jacket reached her knuckles but didn't look too bad. As Kitt dressed, the Aeternus also pulled out a pair of Department sweatpants and a tank top.

Before they left the locker room, Kitt placed a hand on Antoinette's arm. "Please, don't let on you know."

Antoinette gave her a small nod and a reassuring smile. "Your secret's safe with me."

*　　*　　*

Oberon met them as they came into the main office. It reminded Kitt of the law enforcement offices she'd seen on TV, complete with modern furniture and high-tech equipment.

Tones sat in front of three computer screens, each one displaying something different, and he got up as they came in as if he'd been waiting for them.

"I'd better go prepare for class," Kitt said, eager to escape sympathetic, concerned glances.

Oberon crossed his arms over the massive expanse of his chest. "Can you stay a bit longer? I need your expert opinion."

Kitt looked at her watch. She didn't have much time to spare.

"It'll take twenty minutes—max," he said. "I promise."

"Okay. I can do that, but no longer."

He nodded his large head. Several dreadlocks hanging down his back fell forward. "Let's go into the conference room."

Kitt followed Oberon, Tones, and Antoinette into the room to the right. Dominating the room was a long, wide glass table surrounded by a dozen high-backed leather swivel chairs. A large flat computer screen hung on the far wall displaying a slow-spinning Department of Parahuman Security logo.

Oberon nodded in the direction of the screen. "While we aren't officially on the Department's books, we do have some connections. I'll be back in a minute; I'm expecting another consultant."

"So, the captain's pulled in the day shift." Tones walked down the table and held out his fist to the surfer-looking guy in jeans, a T-shirt, and an open black silk shirt with a yellow fire-breathing Chinese dragon. "How you doing, dude?"

"Hey, mate." The sun-bleached blond man knocked knuckles with Tones in greeting.

Kitt couldn't quite place the man's accent but it was familiar. She smiled at the ethereally pale Bianca Sin, head of thaumaturgical studies, sitting next to the stranger. She'd worked with her on a couple of cases for the Department. The witch was often called in to consult as a forensic thaumaturgy specialist. She acknowledged Kitt with a tip of her head—one professional to another. Kitt did the same.

The man smiled as she sat across from him, his long sensuous fingers caressing the glass tabletop as he would a lover's thigh. Stroking and touching. Her breath caught in her throat, her nipples tightened, and her heart beat a little faster. *Why am I thinking of him stroking my thigh?*

"This is Cody Shields, our very own pet Australian Incubus." Antoinette leaned forward, elbows on the table beside Kitt. "Hey, Cody . . . how 'bout turning the juice down a bit?"

Australian, of course. She should have known.

"Oh shit, sorry." His accent only added to the surfer-boy charm. "Oberon called us in just as I was preparing to feed. I'm overly sensitive."

She'd never met an Incubus before, and the fact that she now felt a little uncomfortable meant he wasn't trying to manipulate her emotions in any way, consciously or unconsciously. She leaned back in her chair, trying not to look like she was distancing herself. The last thing she needed right now was enhanced sexual desires.

"Where's Raven?" Cody asked.

"Last I saw, he was chasing after a murderous Aeternus metal-head groupie who'd"—Antoinette growled—"attacked Kitt."

"Dark hair, eighties dress, fond of leather?" Tones asked with a frown.

"Yeah, sounds like her," Kitt answered.

Oberon came in at that point, cutting off further conversation. He took a seat at the head of the table.

"So, Captain, what's up?" Cody asked.

Oberon steepled his fingers under his chin. "It seems we have a serial killer in our midst—a sadistic, ritualistic murderer. I've brought in someone who's got a theory."

A frail old man entered the room, his cane tapping on the floor with each step. Antoinette jumped from her seat to envelop him in what looked like a bone-crunching hug. Kitt recognized him as the well-respected academic of the ancient codex and NYAPS's lecturer on modern CHaPR governance.

"Rudolf! What're you doing here?" Antoinette pulled back and smiled at him.

Kitt was amazed at the brilliance of the Aeternus's smile for the old man. It was nothing like the horrific visage back in the alley. *Had it only been a couple of hours ago? . . . Somehow it seemed longer.*

The man was definitely human. And yet, Kitt got the impression he was even older than he looked.

He patted Antoinette's arm in a fatherly manner and moved to a nearby chair. "Patience, my dear. First things first. How's your father?"

Kitt could barely believe the wizened human's voice held such command.

Antoinette's smile widened. "Grigore and Lisbet have gone to London to be with Nici for the birth of his and Tatiana's child. Lisbet is so excited about the baby, she can hardly wait."

"Sounds like your cousin is getting used to life outside of captivity." He patted Antoinette's arm. "I'm so glad she's blossoming. It can be hard for someone like her."

"Yes. But people are finally realizing that though she may look like a little girl, she *is* a lot older. They've started treating her more like an equal, though she still enjoys playing the innocent-little-girl card when it suits her."

Rudolf nodded sagely. "Well, being a century old and trapped in the body of a six-year-old must have its problems but—now I must talk to you all about something important."

His movements were deliberate and slow as he crossed the room and sank into the empty chair on Oberon's right.

Kitt tilted her head and watched him move. *That cane is more a prop than a necessity.*

His head whipped around toward her. His narrowed eyes were cloudy with age, yet still pierced with a sharpness she'd seen in few others.

Could he read minds?

Just as quickly, his eyes switched to the Incubus, making her wonder if she'd just imaged it all.

"We can't wait for Raven, so I'll brief him later," Oberon said. "Kitt, you go first."

7

the rise of darkness

As the ancient little man took his seat, Oberon leaned back in his chair, raising his arms and placing his hands behind his head as he looked around the table. Kitt eyed him as she rose to her feet; he could feel the sting in her gaze. She'd forgive him for Raven when she was over the shock of it all—realize that he could not have turned his back on Raven, a wolf with his talent. They would need all the skills they could get in the coming days if what Rudolf had told him earlier was true.

Kitt cleared her throat. "The latest victim was a young ursian male, killed in the same manner as the felian male found in the campus hunting run just over two months ago."

The wide screen filled with an image of the two victims side by side. Oberon had had Tones dig out crime scene photos from the last murder and load the images onto a thumb drive Antoinette had brought in with images of the latest victim.

Kitt glanced at the screen—surprise flashing across her face. Her eyes shifted to Tones, then she covered up being caught unawares with a professional mask. "As you can see, the wounds are identical . . ." She walked closer to the screen and pointed. "The victims were immobilized by a silver blade lodged in the base of the neck."

Underneath the main images was a row of small, thumb-nail pictures. She touched four of them and they enlarged to replace the two large images of the victims. Now two of the four images showed the neck wounds, and the two others displayed the blade with a ruler, which illustrated its inch-and-a-half length.

As Kitt went on explaining the similarities between the murders, Oberon zoned out. He'd seen enough to know this was the same killer and not just some copycat. What disturbed him now was how they would receive Rudolf's theory.

He watched the faces around the table. Each person had been handpicked for their skills, each agreeing to work for him. All except for Kitt. He'd intended to pull her into the team when things had settled down a bit. But now, with the murder and what Rudolf had told him earlier in the after-noon, his timetable was brought forward somewhat.

Kitt had stopped talking and he realized everyone now faced him.

His gaze locked with the old man's steely eyes. "Why don't you tell them what you know?"

The old man nodded and rose to take a position in front of the screen. "At the turn of the last century, an ancient tomb was discovered dating back to before the existence of most of our known sedentary civilizations. It was one of the most significant finds ever discovered, and in that tomb was a book unlike any ever seen."

"Why haven't we heard of this before?" Antoinette asked.

"The contents of the book were sealed by order of the Council of Aeternus Elders," the old man said.

"Why?" Antoinette asked.

The old man nailed the Aeternus female with an unblink-ing stare. "I see you've still to learn the virtue of patience."

Slightly rebuked, Antoinette sat a little straighter under the scrutiny of her former teacher. Even Oberon found him-self leaning forward, eager to listen again to the theory of this ancient human. Rudolf placed both hands on the cane in front of him, looked around the room, and continued.

"As I was about to say"—he shot Antoinette a marked

look—"it was a tomb of an ancient Aeternus king. The book is written in an ancient parahuman language, and describes a power so strong, so powerful, the very knowledge of it puts the world as we know it in mortal danger."

Like a master of theatrics, Rudolf took a moment to let the information sink in. Oberon had to admire the old man—he sure knew how to string his audience along. They all sat transfixed, hanging on his every word.

"Several decades ago, the book disappeared from the secured vault of the CHaPR headquarters. No one knew how—what or who took it—but many theories were bandied about and no evidence found. The mystery was solved when the book turned up in what remained of a former NYAPS board member's home."

Antoinette's head shot up, her eyes growing large as she shook her head. *"No."*

The old man's eyes softened at her distress. "That's right, Antoinette. Lucian Moretti—the man who searched for a way to genetically annihilate the parahuman races."

Oberon pushed down the familiar feelings of helplessness he felt whenever his former captor was brought to mind.

"But you have the book back now," Bianca said. "What does it have to do with this serial killer?"

The old man dragged his hand across the smart screen until the first two images showed again.

"Sorry, can you make these areas larger?" Rudolf asked Tones as he indicated the marks carved into the boys' chests with his finger.

Tones tapped the keyboard to zoom in. The image resolution wasn't the best but clear enough for the group to see.

Rudolf reached into his pocket. Oberon knew what he was after and held his breath as the old man unfolded a piece of paper and held it up.

"It's the same symbol," Bianca said.

"What is it?" Kitt asked, sitting forward in her seat.

Rudolf stopped, leaning on his cane and stood straighter. "This is the mark of the Dark Brethren—an ancient and powerful enemy of your parahuman ancestors."

* * *

Kitt's head hurt.

"What the hell is the Dark Brethren?" Antoinette asked.

The old man frowned, this time with sorrow. "That is what the name in the old language roughly translates to, and they were the masters of the ancient tribes that spawned the parahuman races of today. The Brethren came to earth ten millennia ago to the ravaged immature population who were starting to form intelligent civilizations. They had done the same on many worlds before. But this time their servants rose up with the help of some earthly beings and overthrew the Dark Brethren. Beyond that, we know very little else at this point."

"So again—what does it have to do with our serial killer?" Bianca asked.

Ancient kings, mysterious books, and unspeakable demons—it all seemed too much. Kitt really didn't have time for this. Her first class started soon and she started to wonder if this wasn't some cruel initiation joke Oberon played on her. She looked at his dark face. He definitely didn't seem to be a man having fun, but that could just be for show, to string her along. He'd done it before.

Enough was enough.

She had a class to get to and rose to her feet. "I really have to go."

Oberon looked at his watch, then at her. "Five more minutes? Please!"

Kitt reluctantly sat back down, gritting her teeth.

"To answer your question, young witch," Rudolf said, "this symbol has been turning up at other murder scenes. Do you have those images I asked you to load, Tones?"

"Yes, sir," Tones said.

A picture filled the screen of a large room with exquisite furniture. It looked like the kind of room that belonged in a European castle or manor house. A bloody, headless body of a woman along with the blood that had splashed across the antique furniture and rug marred the setting. The Dark Brethren mark, as the old man called it, was painted on the wall—in blood. The next image came up, similarly European, similarly bloody, and similarly marked. Then another image, and another and another and another—all the same. Kitt felt a little queasy at the sight of so much violence and death.

"These are the crime scene photos taken at the height of The Troubles in France, Germany, and Italy. As you see, the symbol is prevalent at each and every one." Rudolf looked at Antoinette, who appeared quite pale, even for an Aeternus.

The next picture caused a collective intake of breath. Even she recognized the converted concrete sewer junction as the torture chamber of Dante Rubins—Dylan's killer and Antoinette's torturer.

She glanced over at Antoinette. A muscle ticked along the female's tensed jaw; a sickly expression hung on her face. Kitt was willing to bet she hadn't seen the place, not even a photo, since it had all happened—the place where she had suffered unspeakable torture and pain.

"I'm sure you all know this scene from a few months ago." The old man tapped the cane on the floor for emphasis.

Amid the photographs and other crazed scribblings of a lunatic, written in chalk, pen, and what could possibly be dried blood, were several examples of the same mark—drawn by a lunatic who both killed Kitt's brother and tortured Antoinette.

This is insane.

"I've been scanning the news channels and there are plenty of reports coming in," Tones said as he hit a few more keys and the screen filled with a broadcast. "This one in particular; I recorded it earlier."

"The vicious attack on the monkey house late last Friday evening looks to be the work of Satanists. Several of the animals were skinned and ritualistically laid out in a large satanic symbol, painted with the animals' blood," a WTFN news anchor reported as he sat behind a news desk.

His schooled expression showed just the right amount of concern and seriousness as he read on. *"Experts are unable to say if that attack has any relevance to the latest ritualistic murder, discovered earlier today on the NYAPS campus, but we have our reporter, Trudi Crompton, on the scene. Come in, Trudi."*

"Thanks Larry." The young female reporter, dressed in heavy cold-weather gear, hooked the windblown hair out of her eyes with one gloved hand and held the WTFN microphone with the other. *"Behind me is the New York campus for the Academy of Parahuman Studies. The scene of not one, but two, grisly murders, thanks to the body found in the library earlier this morning—in a scene that could only be described as a slaughterhouse. Now the question on everybody's lips is, are our children safe?"*

The melodramatic fresh-faced newswoman didn't look much older than most of the students attending the Academy. She turned slightly to her left. *"To help me with that answer is the head of New York's Violent Crimes Unit."*

The camera panned back to reveal a smug, smiling man standing next to her, and Kitt recognized him instantly.

"Fucking little ass-wipe," Oberon spat at the screen.

Kitt glanced at the ursian with sympathy. Roberts had manipulated and connived behind the scenes to get Oberon kicked out of VCU.

"Agent Roberts, are there any similarities between this body and the murder victim found in the campus hunting run just over a month ago?" The woman shoved the mike toward him.

Agent Roberts smiled widely and leaned in. *"There seems to be several similarities, Trudi, and we're just waiting on confirmation from the autopsy report."* He looked directly into the camera as he spoke, and not at the attractive young reporter.

"The bastard wouldn't know if his ass was on fire," Oberon rumbled.

From the few times Kitt had met Roberts, he'd come across as smooth, almost smarmy. But his cunning political savviness didn't make him any more competent as the head of VCU—a job that should have gone to Oberon.

The reporter asked a few more questions and Agent Roberts artfully answered without giving any real information or committing to anything concrete. Kitt watched the thunderstorm roll across Oberon's face as he sat glued to the news report on the large monitor.

Trudi nodded a small frown meant to give the air of attention, but the tilt of her shoulders gave away her frustration at not getting the answers she was after. *"One last question— how do you intend to protect the students of NYAPS from further attacks?"*

"Well, Trudi," Roberts said and smiled into the camera, *"if campus security"*—the agent's nose screwed up with distaste—*"keeps out of our way and lets us do our job—"*

Anything else he'd said was drowned out in the tirade of profanity streaming from Oberon's mouth.

Then ursian threw a coffee mug. With a bang, the glass wall shattered into a million tinkling pieces onto the floor. Maybe glass walls were not the best idea with Oberon around.

Agent Roberts knew which buttons to push with Oberon. The ursian leaned back in his chair and fell into a sullen silence. And she knew he was sulking more because he'd let that weasel get under his skin. Again.

Kitt turned her attention back to the screen as the camera zoomed in on the reporter's perfect features. *"Thank you, Agent Roberts. This is Trudi Crompton coming to you from NYAPS campus for WTFN News."*

Oberon picked up the remote and turned the screen off. "So people—it looks like we have a serial killer stalking our campus. What do you think, Rudolf?"

Rudolf looked at each of them. "I think the Dark Brethren are stirring."

8

AN Apple for teacher

As Kitt's hand rested on the door handle, she took in a deep cleansing breath. Her first night at school had not been as she'd imagined it—and now it was time to give her lecture, which she felt less than prepared for. But there was no putting it off. She just had to suck it up and get it over with.

She inhaled back another deep breath and held it before opening the lecture hall door. The buzzing chatter dropped off as she made her way to the slightly raised platform, front and center.

"My name is Dr. Kathryn Jordan and I will be lecturer for this class in Parahuman Anatomy." She placed her notes in the middle of the desk and looked up.

Dozens of students sat in the stadium seating, apparently with varying degrees of interest. As she glanced around, she swallowed the uncomfortable lump forming in her throat. In a morgue she didn't have an audience—and this one was a little more daunting than she'd expected.

She swept her gaze over her students. "We will have one practical—"

Perfect. Just perfect. This really was her night of all nights.

Two pairs of intense blue eyes bored into her. One girl sitting forward in her chair, smiling and ready. The other slumped with a scowl, tapping the tip of her pencil against the cover of a notebook. They had their father's eyes, but apart from that it was almost like looking in a double mirror.

My daughters. My flesh.

She glanced down at her notes to compose herself again and continued. " . . . session per week. Over the next semester we will be covering the anatomical composition of all human and parahuman beings. Today I'm going to start with the skeletal composition Homo sapiens." She turned and pulled down an anatomical chart of the human body.

Kitt closed the door to the small office and leaned back against it, closing her eyes for a moment. All things considered, it hadn't gone too badly, though her hands shook and her heart thumped heavily at the base of her throat.

A titanium flask sat in the middle of her desk with a note. *Good for settling nerves. A.*

Bless Antoinette. Kitt smiled as she opened it and sniffed. The sweetly pungent fumes brought tears to her eyes even before she took a large, burning swig. *Brandy.* More tears and burning.

She shook her head and blew out a liquor-fumed sigh. Although the medicinal value was highly dubious, it did make her feel warmer and slowed the beat of her heart. Though the effects of the alcohol wouldn't last long, at least it was enough to calm her shakes.

She landed heavily in the chair behind the desk and took another mouthful. A knock rattled her office door; she quickly replaced the top and slipped the flask into the draw. The last thing she needed was to be found drinking on the job after her first class.

"Come in," she croaked and cleared her throat.

Two blurred figures filed in from behind the frosted glass panel in the door and her heart leapt into her throat, again.

She came to her feet as they stopped on the other side of the desk. "Ah, hi. I'm Kitt," she said, stumbling over her words. "But of course you know that."

Her nervous laugh had a slightly hysterical edge to it.

"Um," she cleared her throat and rubbed shaking hands together. "I can't believe you're here."

"Hello, *Mother*." This one of the twins practically sneered, earning an elbow in the ribs from her sister.

"Uh . . ." Kitt said, the shakes doubling. She indicated two chairs on the other side of the desk. "Please, take a seat, and call me Kitt, if you prefer."

Their silver blond-and-black hair was cropped short, displaying the snow leopard pattern. They moved in unison as they sat, like choreographed dancers.

"I've been so looking forward to this moment." *And dreading it*. Kitt sat back down. What would she say to them?

The happier twin leaned forward. "We're glad to finally meet you too—aren't we, Seph?" Her face lit up with a stunning smile. Another legacy of their father.

Seph . . . Persephone. And Calliope. Their accents were very similar to the Incubus, Cody; and considering they'd spent the last eighteen years in the Australian tropics of Far North Queensland, it wasn't surprising.

"You don't know what it means to meet you girls," Kitt said, determined not to let the emotion overwhelm her at the risk of isolating them further. She shuffled around papers to cover her trembling hands. "So, you were with the Pride? Did you see your grandmother?"

Calliope's face fell and nodded. "She misses you and is still grieving for her son. She didn't want to let us come back here. But you know what it's like, women of the Pride don't get much of a say in anything."

"Yeah, right," Persephone said, her face screwing up in disgust.

"Don't worry about Seph," Calliope said and gave her sister another scathing scowl. "She's in a foul mood because Tyrone won't let her become a tracker."

"I don't see why both of us have to be healers; surely they only need one of us." Persephone folded her arms and scowled.

Kitt remembered what it was like not being able to do what she wanted when she was their age. "I'm sure he thinks he's doing what's best for you."

"Like he did for Nathan? . . . No, thanks," Persephone said.

"Seph," Calliope hissed.

"She's right, Calliope. My brother's attitude is the result of my father's protection," Kitt said.

The twin screwed up her nose. "Please call me Cal. Calliope makes me feel like I'm in trouble."

She felt the same way about being called Kathryn. "Okay, Cal." Kitt smiled. "Nathan has been seen as unlucky since his littermate died at birth. The Elders wanted him abandoned in the forest, lest his bad luck infect the Pride. Only Tyrone fought their edict; and it was only his position as the Pride Alpha that saved Nathan. I guess, in a way, Tyrone both loves and hates Nathan, which can put a burden on a person."

"Yeah, well, I think their superstitious beliefs are ridiculous." Seph's lips curled into a sneer. "Anyway, Nathan doesn't need much protection anymore. He's just an uptight asshole whose life is ruled by Pride law."

Hmmm. Nathan had always been an officious little shit, even when they were kids.

"You don't believe in their ways either, do you?" Cal tilted her head.

Kitt noticed again how much their eyes resembled Raven's. While hers were amber, the twins' were blue. Thankfully, Emmett's white tiger heritage wouldn't raise any questions in the Pride, even if they had the same dark ring around the irises as Raven's. The girls waited for her answer, looking at her expectantly—Cal with interest and Seph with a frown.

"No. But I wouldn't admit that to the Pride council, if I were in your shoes." Kitt folded her shaking hands together. "Speaking of the council, how have they handled your return?"

"Okay, I guess," Cal answered—she seemed to be the talker of the two. "Some are a little more suspicious than others."

"That Leon guy is one seriously creepy dude." Seph's shoulders shook in an exaggerated shiver.

Kitt leaned forward and dropped her voice. "Watch him—he's a very dangerous male. Don't ever get caught alone with him."

Seph shrugged and fiddled with a penholder at the edge of Kitt's desk. "We can take care of ourselves."

"And at least the council stopped grilling us about Mum and Dad . . . ah . . . I mean . . . our foster parents," Cal said.

Kitt could see the raw grief in her daughters' eyes. The only parents they'd known were recently killed in a horrific car accident. The Hennesseys, the people she'd arranged to care for her babies all those years ago.

"What about Raven?" Kitt asked. "Do they know he helped raise you?"

"No, but they know he's returned," Cal said. "Tyrone raised the price on his head when he received reports of Raven being spotted in a bar in Lake Placid."

The bar we used to meet in. "So I'd heard. He should've stayed away," Kitt said.

Cal looked down at her hands while Seph's expression darkened. They obviously didn't like hearing their father criticized.

"I meant for his own safety," Kitt added.

"Raven can take care of himself," Seph grumbled.

"He's always been there for us, teaching us about being Bestiabeo," Cal said. "We knew he was our real father, but he never tried to take that way from our dad. I loved him for that. After we went through our Awakening and came out as felians, Raven stepped up our training. Just in case anything like this happened."

Seph looked away, hiding her feelings with a frown. She missed him—that much was obvious. Her heart went out to the girl.

Her daughter.

It was still so strange to think these two grown young women were the babies she gave birth to several years and a lifetime ago. Kitt knew what it was like to be pushed into something you didn't want to do. It was only after she was exiled from the Pride that she'd been able to follow her dreams to study medicine.

"So, Seph," Kitt said, stacking and restacking her notes. "What would you rather be doing other than sitting in my anatomy class?"

The sullen twin met her eyes for the first time and smiled. "Shadow-combat."

"She was the captain of the Cairn's Marauders, and she made the team here yesterday," Cal explained. "Her first match is in a couple of days."

"Really?" Kitt was impressed. "I'm surprised Nathan would let you compete."

"It was a compromise; my price for training as a healer." The girl straightened and sat forward. "You should come to the match." Then she caught herself and slouched back in her chair, growing sullen again. "If you want to, that is."

Cal nodded enthusiastically. "That'd be great."

Kitt had never seen a Shadow-combat match before; the craze had taken off in the last few years, but she'd been too busy with her work. "I'll see what I can do."

"Well, we'd better get going or Nathan will wonder what's happened to us," Cal said and stood, stretching to offer her hand over the desk. "I think they're still a little suspicious of us."

Kitt took the warm, dry grip with a nice firm shake. There was no jolt of recognition or flood of overwhelming maternal feelings, but it did feel nice.

Seph just stood and gave a minute incline of her head before she left the room.

Cal followed, but stopped at the door and turned to look at Kitt. "I'm glad we've finally met. Raven spoke about you all the time." And then she was gone.

After the girls left, Kitt slumped back in her chair and took another swig from the flask. It was obvious Cal was the more outgoing of the two, and Seph reminded her of Raven, with the same reserve. The road was going to be a little tougher with her. It hadn't exactly gone as she'd dreamed it would, but then again it could've been worse. After all, they had come to her.

Kitt entered the Bunker and Antoinette looked up from behind several piles of reports, her frown of concentration smoothing into a welcome smile.

"How did it go?" she asked.

"Okay, I think. Thanks for this." Kitt flopped into the chair opposite and passed over the flask. "And I met the twins."

"How did that go?" Antoinette sat back ready to listen.

Kitt sighed and shrugged. "I guess I've been imagining our reunion for over eighteen years, but never really expecting it." She picked up a report sitting on top of the pile to change the subject. "What's all this?"

"Murders going back over the last couple of months. I'm trying to work out the dreniac hunting grounds by tying the murders to possible dreniac feeds." Antoinette held up the buff-colored folder. "This one, for example, is a storeowner stabbed several times during a robbery. Investigators assumed he just bled out into a drain near his body. Yet the stab wounds were made in the shoulder, wrist, and groin. No fang marks to attract attention, but the knife wounds correspond with key feeding areas on a body. This lot is far too smart."

"So you think it could be the work of a dreniac gang?"

"Sure of it. There are several others they'd most likely be responsible for, but we could never pin it on them. I'm just trying to find a pattern so we can work out where they might strike next. I'm dividing them into categories—definites, possibles, missing persons, improbables." Antoinette placed her hand on the largest of the piles. "This is the possibles. I *have* managed to find one thing, though." Antoinette passed her one of the files. "Recognize her?"

Kitt opened it up to find a missing person's report complete with a smiling photo of a Boston college student. The kind of picture you find on the family home mantel or in the school yearbook. Her ash blond hair was pulled neatly back, highlighting her clear, healthy complexion and bright eyes. Vastly different from the strung-out dreniac in torn stockings with ratty hair that had been feeding on the wrist of a human in a dirty back alley.

Antoinette rested her elbows on the desk and linked her fingers. "She was reported missing over three months ago. The Boston police are informing her parents as we speak."

Kitt looked at the stacks of files, especially the possibles pile. "There has to be over fifty here. Wouldn't someone have noticed dreniacs were active in the area and called in the Guild?"

"Ah—but as I've said, they're smart and hide their tracks well, something not usually associated with dreniacs. They don't fit the usual profile. In these files there are robberies, holdups and kidnappings. Some victims have just bled out and look like simple murders or even suicides. Dreniacs usually drain their victims; but to get the high, all they have to do is take the blood while the heart beats the last beat. They can forgo the rest if they're not real hungry."

"So you're saying they masked their killings—dreniacs don't do that." Kitt picked up a report of a young girl's beheaded body found on the side of the road, thought to be a hit-and-run accident.

"No, but then again, they don't live and hunt in packs either. When I found them in that fleabag hotel, it looked like they'd been there for weeks, maybe longer."

Tones came out of the communications room and beamed. He raced over, his excitement almost palpable.

"I'm glad I found you two together." He turned around a print of a black-and-white arrest photo. "Is this the Aeternus you saw in the alley?"

Antoinette took the page and glanced at it. "Could be, but Kitt got a better look." She passed her the picture. "What do you think?"

The woman in the photograph had streaked and running mascara, hollow eyes, and messy hair, but Kitt recognized the sneer immediately.

"That's her," she said, glancing from one to the other.

"I knew it." He took the photo back, pleased with himself. "As soon as you described her, I knew it was Marvella."

"Marvella?" Antoinette leaned back in her seat.

If he had a tail, Tones would be wagging it like there was no tomorrow. "Marvella Marie Molyneux, from an old New Orleans Aeternus family. She had some success in the eighties as a rock star by the name of Marie Vella. When groupies and hangers-on started disappearing, they discovered she'd been feeding them to a bunch of dreniacs she had locked in the tour bus. Apparently, she got off on the killing and then had sex with dreniacs while they were still in the throes of their death-high. She was arrested and put into a maximum security parahuman prison, but escaped about a year ago. Some suspect she was helped."

"So she's not a dreniac, but a twisted Aeternus like Dante Rubins," Antoinette said.

Tones's smile slipped at the mention of the monster's name and glanced at Kitt before nodding slowly. A now-familiar hollow sensation settled in the pit of Kitt's stomach with the mention of Dylan's killer, though the feeling wasn't as heavy as it used to be. *Maybe I've finally started to move on?* Time would tell.

"Looks like she's returned to her old ways." Antoinette changed back to the subject at hand. "But seems she's now gotten smarter about it."

Kitt placed the file on the Boston girl back on the tiny definites pile. "Do you think this has anything to do with the serial killer?"

"I'll do more checking," Tones said. "But I don't see how."

Antoinette nodded. "They're too different. Though, maybe this Dark Brethren stuff Rudolf was talking about has something to do with it."

Tones's lip curled into a snarl. "I don't think it's really feasible to jump to that conclusion just yet. We need more proof than the existence of a supposedly ancient book and the interpretations of an old human."

"You don't believe him?" The timbre of Antoinette's voice rose a little in disbelief. "Why are you so dead set against it?"

Tones sighed and ran his hand back and forth over his bald scalp. "My family is one of the oldest of Aeternus blood-lines, which means we have responsibility as protectors of the lore. You can't change the beliefs of a lifetime overnight. To think our ancestors were mere servants—no, more like slaves . . . it's a really hard thing to swallow."

Kitt's reservations were more basic than fearing the loss of some perceived superiority. It just contradicted every-thing she knew to be true.

"What's going on?" Oberon interrupted their little confer-ence.

"Tones has identified the Aeternus from the alley," Kitt said, trying to cover their misgivings.

Oberon took the picture from Tones. "Good work. Now see if you can find any connections between the two cases."

"Already on it," Antoinette said, lifting a pile of reports.

"Excellent, but let's call it a day," Oberon said.

"Has Raven come back yet?" Kitt asked.

Oberon shook his head. "But he's a big boy and can take care of himself." He looked at Antoinette and Tones. "You two had better get home before dawn."

"Good idea." Antoinette linked her fingers and stretched her arms above her head. "What'd'ya say, boy? Ready to go home?"

The large pale-eyed malamute came to his feet, his tongue lolling and curled tail wagging.

"I'll walk out with you," Kitt said, glad the night was finally over.

She couldn't believe how much had happened in the last hours. Suddenly her weariness weighted her down.

Oberon put his hand on Kitt's arm as she rose from her chair, his face softening. "You okay?"

"Nothing a nice hot bath and a good night's sleep won't fix," she said.

Since Dylan died, Oberon had kept an eye out for her; and most times she was grateful, but tonight she needed space. After looking at her closely, he nodded and leaned in to plant a kiss on her cheek. "Go home, get some rest."

The underground car park was deserted. Night classes had long finished and day classes were still a couple of hours away. It was that in-between time, when hardly anyone was about.

"Heavy first day," Antoinette said, their footfalls echoing in the manmade concrete cavern. "What're you thinking?"

"You could say that," Kitt said. "By the way, one of the twins is competing in a Shadow-combat match. I know we've just met and all, but would you come with me?"

"Sure." Antoinette stopped by her car and pulled the keys from her pocket. "But wouldn't you prefer that Oberon go?"

"It'd be nice to go with someone who isn't watching me

every second"—she pulled her coat tighter around herself—"making sure I'm okay."

Antoinette nodded with understanding. "I've never been to an actual match before—could be interesting."

An invisible weight lifted from Kitt's shoulders. She hadn't realized until that moment how difficult the idea of going alone had been.

"Why don't we—"

A hooded figure appeared from behind a pillar and clamped a black-gloved hand over Antoinette's mouth, cutting off whatever she was about to say. A low snarling bark came from Cerberus and his hackles rose.

"I've been waiting for you," the would-be mugger's voice rasped.

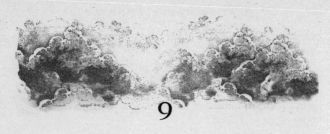

9

LOVER COME HOME

Kitt didn't know what to do. She froze in terror. The dog barked, snarled, and snapped, saliva droplets pattering the cement floor. Antoinette's eyes went wide, then narrowed. She twisted and grabbed her assailant by the shirt and slammed him back into the pillar.

"About time, you bastard," she growled as she pulled him into a full-mouthed kiss. "Any longer and I was going to start playing with my food."

She stood back grinning, her hand dropping to clutch her attacker's.

The man leaned into the light and pushed back the hood. "How you doing, Kitt?"

Christian Laroque. Kitt knew him from her job in the Department's morgue, though it had been a few months since she'd last seen him.

Cerberus's tail beat double time and Christian bent to ruffle his fur. "Gave you a scare too, old man."

The dog answered with an excited yip, but it took a few more seconds before Kitt could slow her hammering heart.

"Now look what you've done," Antoinette punched him in the arm. "You've scared her half to death."

"I'm sorry, Kitt." Christian's handsome features softened into genuine regret. "I didn't mean to frighten you."

"I thought I was about to have the perfect end to a perfect night," she said, giving the Intel agent a tight smile.

"That bad, huh?" Christian asked and looked at Antoinette, his eyes filling with concern.

"It was eventful but nothing we couldn't handle." She leaned in to kiss him again and grinned. "But right now I just want to get you home and jump your bones for several hours on end."

Kitt's face warmed and she looked away, partly with embarrassment and partly with envy.

"Sounds good to me," Christian said when they broke apart. "Because I leave for New Orleans this evening. This is just another flying visit I'm afraid. We've got a new lead."

"Shit, Christian, that bites," Antoinette spat. "Are we ever going to spend more than a few short hours at a time together?"

"I'm sorry, baby." He cupped Antoinette's cheek and planted a kiss on the tip of her nose. "Soon, I promise. Now let's get home—I have some bones that need jumping."

Antoinette looked over her shoulder as she walked away with Christian's arm around her waist. She got the impression Kitt could do with some company but couldn't pass up the chance to spend some time alone with her lover. As they approached the black stretch limousine, the driver stepped out and opened the back door. Cerberus jumped into the passenger seat through the open window. He loved riding up front—and it would give her more time alone with Christian.

She placed a hand on Christian's shoulder and leaned in to plant a quick kiss on his lips before climbing in.

"You seem a little preoccupied," Christian said as he settled in beside her.

She leaned back against the seat, searching every inch of his face. *God, it is so good to see him.* "I'm just a little worried about Kitt. She went through a lot tonight and now she's going home to an empty apartment."

"Why don't you give Oberon a call, let him know what you think," Christian said, reaching for the bottle sitting in the custom-built warmer.

She smiled and took out her cell. "I knew there was a reason I love you."

Oberon answered on the second ring.

"It's Antoinette. I'm a bit worried Kitt may need some company after all she's been through tonight. Maybe you could check in on her and make sure she's okay."

"I'll do it later on my way home," the ursian replied, concern apparent in his voice. It seemed strange to her, Oberon showing so much concern for someone. Kitt must mean a lot to him.

"And I may be in a little late tomorrow night." She smiled at her lover as he poured a splash of crimson into a brandy balloon. The scent of warm blood stirred her hunger.

"I guess that means Christian's in town," Oberon said with a chuckle. "Then I'll see you when I see you."

She slid the phone shut and leaned forward to take the offered glass. Christian filled one for himself and clinked it against hers.

Antoinette drank deeply. The flavors played across her pallet with delicious delicacy. She closed her eyes to savor the aroma and the taste.

"Fresh, young," she said as she lay back against the seat and smiled. "And female."

Christian beamed. "You're learning to tell the difference."

She grinned. "Thanks to Kavindish."

Christian's friend and butler could teach her that at least. The rules of polite Aeternus society were not something her rigorous Venator training had prepared her for; and much to her and Kavindish's dismay, she was failing dismally at Aeternus etiquette. Instead of sipping, she drained the last few drops and held her glass out to Christian. Though her hunger for sustenance was abated, she wasn't yet satisfied.

"Now what shall we do?" Christian asked, taking the glass and leaning in close.

She laid her legs across his lap. "I can think of a thing or two."

"Shall I tell Anton to take the long way home?" he suggested.

"You've been away for a while," she said with a wink. "I don't think it will take that long."

Christian leaned forward and pressed the button to raise the privacy screen. "Anton, we're not to be disturbed."

"Yes, sir." Antoinette could hear the smile in the driver's voice.

"Well then." Christian reached beneath her tank top and tweaked her nipple.

"Well then," she repeated and pushed him down before straddling him. "What have you got for me?" She unzipped his fly and freed his straining hardness. "Oh yes, that'll do nicely."

She ripped off his hoodie and the T-shirt underneath.

God, it'd been so long.

With fresh young blood coursing through her veins, she was past ready and impatient to have him inside. She quickly divested herself of her sweatpants and pulled his jeans off his hips.

"Hey, how about a bit of foreplay?" Christian said with a devious smile.

"Just shut up and fuck me." She placed one hand on his chest and used the other to guide him to her entrance. "Foreplay later."

He groaned as she slid him inside, and he gripped her by the hips. "I love it when you talk dirty."

The tip of his cock hit the entrance to her womb and filled her, and her turn to groan. He lay down along the seat and she leaned back to raise the tank top over her head. He lifted his head, watching her face, then her lips, and then her breasts. Teasing him, she cupped a breast in each hand and rocked back and forth in a steady building rhythm. His head fell back and he growled with pleasure. This power over him was such a trip.

Antoinette felt her orgasm building quickly. She'd been hyper horny for days now, and it wasn't going to take much to tip her over the edge. He slipped his thumb between them, rubbing her in just the right spot, with just the right pressure. She was close. So close. But she needed something else. Her gums tingled, her fangs slid to nestle in a groove beside her top front teeth. She stretched her jaw to make way for them and looked down into his face.

"Come on, baby. Do it." His voice was husky with the same need and his fangs glinted in the limo's interior lighting.

She leaned forward, her sensitive nipples brushing his flesh as she pressed her breasts against his chest. She kept on rocking her hips as she opened her mouth. The hot scent of the fresh blood he'd consumed drove her wild and she sank her fangs into the side of his throat. Her orgasm crashed down on her, rocketing through her body as his blood filled her mouth and slid down her throat.

As the last of the aftershocks subsided, Christian sat up, still buried deep within her, and brought her mouth to his. They shared the taste of his blood as he pressed his hands against the small of her naked back, then flipped her over, pushing even deeper inside her. She locked eyes with him, his face only inches above hers, and bit her lip, piercing it with one of her fangs. He licked away the blood that formed and leaned back to watch her as he thrust in and out, his speed increasing. She loved the expression on his face, one almost of reverence, and she could tell how close he was just by the glazed look in his eyes. Then with a long, low moan, he thrust deeper and shuddered to a stop.

Collapsing on top of her, he rested his head between her breasts and absently brushed the peaks of her still-erect nipples as he lay there. Antoinette stroked his hair, enjoying his weight on her. She missed this quiet time—when lovemaking was over—but not the physical connection between them.

Clothes were strewn around the large interior of the stretch limousine, and she chuckled.

"What's so funny?" Christian sat up and pulled on his jeans.

"I told you it wouldn't take that long."

"Just wait till I get you home, then I'll show you how long I can take." He threw her tank top at her. "You'll be begging me to stop."

"Oh, promises, promises."

As he pulled on his T-shirt, she noticed he wasn't wearing a suit. "I thought you were back here for a meeting?"

"I am," he said absently.

She sat forward and fingered his shirt. "Then why aren't you wearing a suit? You always wear a suit."

"Actually, I wasn't here to meet with my superiors. I was here to see Rudolf." He captured her hand and brought her knuckles to his lips. "He was after information on the labs. We discovered another one last month and have a lead on two more."

"So, Lucian wasn't in it alone."

"I've no doubt that Lucian was behind a lot of this, but I think he was just the tip of the iceberg. Too bad he died before we had a chance to question him." He turned her hand palm up and nipped at the skin on her wrist before continuing up her arm.

"Maybe, but I'm glad he's dead." Antoinette's fingers curled as delicious fire burned beneath her skin. "What else did Rudolf tell you?"

"Nothing," Christian looked up, his brow forming a V. "Why?"

"Oh, nothing," she said, smiling quickly. "He gave us a bit of a pep talk."

She hated lying to him, but Oberon had been adamant. The information must stay secret until they knew what they were dealing with. Christian's brow smoothed out. She could tell by his tight smile he didn't quite believe her, but he wasn't going to press the issue either. After all, working for intelligence, she was sure there were lots of things he couldn't tell her.

"So how do you like the new penthouse?" he said, deftly changing the subject.

Christian sold his brownstone and bought a grand penthouse apartment a few weeks ago. The old place just felt too much like Viktor. His malamute, Cerberus, missed his former master terribly and was always down. Even Antoinette could feel the memories of their friend haunting the rooms, and suspected Christian felt the same way though never admitted it.

He chucked the balled-up hoodie to the seat opposite. "I'm looking forward to spending some more time there soon."

"When?" she asked.

"Soon, baby." He cupped her cheek and kissed the spot between her eyebrows. "I promise."

Yeah, right. I'll believe that when it happens. She sighed. There wasn't much point thinking about it when they only had a few hours together. Better to just make the most of it now.

10

The Ghost of Darkness Past

The dark apartment felt cold and empty. Kitt's handbag hit the floor before the door even clicked shut, and her coat quickly followed. She stepped out of her borrowed shoes on her way to fall face-first onto the sofa. Bath, food, and bed—all too hard. She needed to shut her eyes. *Just for a minute . . .*

Kitt opened her eyes, blinking in the gloomy morning light. She lifted her head from the patch of drool on the cushion and disgustedly swiped the back of her hand across her mouth.

Lovely.

She suddenly realized she was still on the sofa and still dressed in the clothes Antoinette had loaned her. The clock on the wall read three past eight, which meant she'd slept for over two hours instead of just a few minutes.

Someone's in the apartment. She instantly froze at the thought.

Nothing indicated the feeling was a reality, but she *knew* it was true. There was something not right; something she couldn't quite put her finger on. She wasn't alone.

Kitt rolled off the sofa into a crouch on the floor and came up onto the balls of her bare feet with her hands resting on the coffee table. Nothing moved in the shadows and nothing made a sound. Time ticked by on the wall clock. Mere seconds seemed to stretch into a lifetime. Her heart thundered against her chest wall, and the roar of blood pounding in her ears almost deafened her.

She waited a moment longer before creeping into the kitchen, keeping low. She slid out the biggest stainless steel carving knife from the woodblock beside the stove. The weight felt comforting in her trembling hand as she crept from the kitchen. Maybe leaving the medical examiner's office wasn't such a good idea after all—before today, she'd never been attacked by any insane females or had intruders breaking into her apartment.

But what if it was more than just an intruder? *What if it's that psycho Aeternus bitch come to get me?*

The drawn blinds gave the apartment a ghostly atmosphere of shadows and filtered half-light. She contemplated transforming completely, but switched her eyes instead and made a mental note to put in a request for a gun. *Make that two. Big ones.*

Everything seemed quiet—well, as quiet as it gets in a city waking for a day's work, with tooting car horns and the occasional wailing siren. She flexed her fingers to loosen the white-knuckled grip on the knife handle.

The corridor to Dylan's room seemed both endlessly long and dangerously short as she reached into her pocket for her cell.

Damn. No cell anyway; she'd smashed it against the wall in the alley. *Double damn.* Not even her pockets.

No landline either. Since Dylan's death she didn't see the point in keeping it up. Nothing she could do about it now.

Kitt crept along the wall until she reached the bathroom door, which was slightly ajar. A soft scrape came from inside. Shifting her grip on the knife, she kicked open the door to find a man sitting on the edge of her bathtub. Relief washed over her fear, stopping her heart for a split second before being closely followed by anger.

Raven cleaned dried blood off his chest and torso.

"What the hell are you doing here?" she demanded.

His eyes dropped to the knife she held as he continued to clean his own wounds. "Are you going to use that?"

Kitt looked down at the forgotten blade in her hand and placed it on the nearby counter. The cuts looked deep and he was pale with blood loss. To distract herself from looking at his nakedness, she opened the cabinet beneath the double sink and pulled out some medical supplies. The alcohol stung her nostrils as she filled a kidney dish; then, with a pair of forceps, she dipped a clean swab in the clear fluid and turned to him. He hissed sharply as she touched the alcohol-soaked gauze to the jagged cut running across his shoulder.

It wasn't that bad, but with the number of wounds he'd sustained tonight, Raven's parahuman healing abilities had taken a bit of a battering. Risk of infection, while still minimal, was higher in times of decreased immunity. He trembled under her touch. She couldn't tell if it was shock or something else. She distracted herself by hitting the foot pedal on the trash can to dump the used swab, then reached for a fresh one.

"Now, are you going to tell me what you're doing here?" she asked as she worked.

"I'm not really up to making it back across town and I knew you were close," he said.

She stopped and looked at him. "So you broke into my apartment . . . haven't you ever heard of knocking?"

"I wasn't sure if you'd be asleep, and you looked so exhausted crashed out on the lounge that I didn't have the heart to wake you." He moved a little closer, his naked thighs flanking her legs. "Besides, your father is having you watched."

She froze, the forceps shaking in her hand. "I didn't know that," she said and grabbed another fresh swab.

"Hmm. Oberon does."

Kitt gritted her teeth. She was going to have words with that bear. "Are these wounds all from that Aeternus?"

He shook his head and looked up at her with those familiar deep blue eyes. "I ran into a couple of bounty hunters, courtesy of your dear old dad. That's why I came here; it's the last place they'd expect to look."

So, he sought sanctuary—not her.

Damp locks fell forward as he hung his head, his arms

snaking around her waist. "Besides, I *really* wanted to see you again."

Blood rushed to her head, his touch setting a different heavy beat to her heart. If she didn't get away now, she'd never get out of here.

Stepping beyond his reach, she turned to tip the alcohol down the sink. "Why don't you take a shower and I'll make you something to eat. You need some meat to heal properly."

On her way out, she grabbed a couple of fresh towels from the closet beside the bathroom door and sat them on the counter.

"Thanks, Kitten."

There he goes, using that name again. She turned to rebuke him, but he looked so beat up and miserable she just nodded and shut the door.

Kitt hadn't been in Dylan's room since he died. Not once. She took a deep breath and opened the door, feeling like an intruder. Raven needed fresh clothes and hers sure as hell weren't going to fit him. She grabbed the first things she came across and hurried from the room, dumping the clothes on the back of the sofa before going into the kitchen and opening the refrigerator. There wasn't much in there; some eggs and a few rashers of bacon, but she had a couple of steaks in the freezer and some bread too.

She chucked the steaks into the microwave to defrost and put on a pot of coffee, then threw some bacon in a frying pan. Raven would need the protein to replenish his strength. The microwave pinged and she added the still slightly frozen meat to the frying pan.

"Something smells good."

She turned to find him standing in the kitchen doorway, drying his long dark hair and wearing nothing but a towel around his waist. Her mouth went dry at the sight. It'd been a while since she'd had any man in her apartment. Actually, it'd been a long while since she'd had a man, full stop. She tried to ignore the way his muscles rippled across his shoulders as he rubbed his hair, and the way his abs flexed and relaxed when he moved.

The yin- and yang-style double dragon tattoo on his chest

drew her gaze, which then led her to look lower, at his well-defined abdominal muscles disappearing beneath the towel hanging low on his hips.

It was several seconds before she realized he'd stopped, and just stood, watching her with a knowing smile. She dropped her gaze, her cheeks burning.

"There's some of Dylan's clothes on the sofa that should fit you," she said and turned back to the steaks.

The meat was ready, seared and warmed through to rare perfection. She placed them on plates with the bacon, eggs, and toast.

Raven came into the kitchen buttoning the black fitted shirt. "Is there anything I can help with?"

God, even dressed he looks so damn good. "You can take out the coffee and orange juice."

She placed the food on the dining room table as he took his seat and filled the juice glasses. Her appetite deserted her as she sat opposite and glanced across the table at him. Freshly washed hair hung down his back and his fresh male scent spiked her appetite for something other than food, something she hadn't had in a very long while, and something the felian in her craved. She managed to suppress her inner cat for so long, but Raven just brought back too many memories of wild abandon under nature's canopy.

Kitt pushed the eggs around on her plate and sipped at the juice while Raven fell on his food like a man who hadn't eaten for weeks. Fatigue descended on her again, but the thought of bed raised other images. Images she shouldn't be picturing. Dangerous images. Her animal lust threatened to overwhelm her, so she picked up her plate and carried it into the kitchen.

She stood at the sink, scraping the barely touched meal into the trash, when Raven came in. The room suddenly felt smaller than it did a moment before. She could feel his eyes burning a spot between her shoulder blades but didn't dare turn. It would be her undoing. His breath touched her skin as he came nearer and reached around to put his empty plate on the sink.

"Here, let me." His fingers closed over hers and he took the plate from her hands.

Her fatigue fled. She turned around to look at him. *Big mistake*. His wide soft mouth was close, very close. She snagged her lower lip with her teeth and pressed herself back against the counter.

He closed his eyes and inhaled deeply. "You smell so good."

"So do you," she admitted, her voice barely above a whisper. "Too good." Her inner snow leopard growled.

He placed his hands on the counter, either side of her body, still not touching her. As he leaned in, she leaned away, keeping her eyes locked on his full sensual mouth. Memories of what those lips could do to her sent a flush across her skin.

His chin brushed the tip of his nose as he planted a kiss between her eyebrows, then he tilted his head to her neck and breathed in deep. When he raised his head again, his eyes were closed, as though he was savoring her scent. Then his lips burned the indentation at the base of her throat. Her head fell back, granting him greater access, and she clutched his shoulders for support.

Raven pressed one hand on her lower back and the other between her shoulder blades. His hands traveled down to her hips and slid up her sides, dragging over her top. She allowed him to unzip her slacks and untuck her shirt. He pinned her with his hips, and his fingertips trailed down her inner arms, tracing the ridges of her ribs through the thin shirt material. She buried her hands in his hair and crushed his lips to hers. She wanted to breathe him in, to quench her hunger and her felian lust.

His hands slid inside the trousers to grip her ass; he pulled her against the erection still bridled by his black denim jeans. She groaned and leaned back against the counter, wrapping one leg around him.

He lifted her onto the counter, grabbed her hips, and again pulled her hard against him. His right hand slid under her shirt and up the furrow between her breasts to wrap around her throat; the tips of his fingers caressed her earlobe and her jawline, sending shivers straight to her groin.

She ran her palms over his chest and pressed her pelvis against his. The groan that crawled up her throat and escaped through her mouth sounded like someone else's.

She needed more of his warm, naked flesh next to hers and reached for the front of his shirt, trembling fingers fumbled to free each button.

The hard muscles of his abs rippled under her palms before she pushed the shirt off his shoulders and let it slip to the ground. Her hands moved to the top button of his jeans; with no control over her hands, they half unzipped his fly. Raven's chest stilled, eyes slowly closing as his face tilted toward the ceiling, his long dark hair cascading down his back. His bronzed skin glowed in the morning sunlight streaming through the small kitchen window.

He looked back at her through hooded eyes, blue eyes, the same eyes she'd seen last night in her children.

Our children.

"No," she said, pushing him away.

Confusion and hurt replaced the desire in his expression. "Why?"

"I can't do this again," she said. "We can't—"

He dropped his head.

Her newfound resolve and strength crumbled. She stepped toward him. "Raven—"

The front door rattled with a loud banging.

Who could it be at this hour? She tucked in her shirt and zipped up her slacks as she crossed to answer it, signaling him to stay in the kitchen. She opened the door, half expecting one of her neighbors and found Oberon on the threshold.

"Hey," he said, stepping into the apartment without invitation and holding out a bottle of slightly cloudy pale violet liquid. Atropa wine.

His head tilted to the side, still his dreadlocks brushed the top of the doorframe. "Are you sure you're feeling okay? You're looking a little flushed."

"I . . . I . . ." Her mind worked quickly, trying to think up an excuse.

"Hello, Oberon," her ex-lover said from the kitchen doorway, his shirt neatly buttoned.

The ursian's fingers curled, forming massive fists; his lips peeled into a snarl. "I thought we'd agreed you'd stay away from here."

11

A clash of Titans

Oberon took a step forward, looming over her as he moved toward the canian. She pushed back against his chest with her free hand, ready to smash the bottle of potent belladonna moonshine on Oberon's thick skull if she had to.

"It was an emergency," Raven said in a calm tone, as if he wasn't about to have his head ripped off his shoulders.

"Oberon, please," she begged, trying to calm him before the rage took over.

The ursian strained forward again and said, "Tyrone probably has men watching this apartment right now!"

Raven propped himself against the kitchen doorframe with his shoulder. "The Tiger Twins are in an SUV across the road; another watches from the apartment in the building opposite, tenth floor."

Oberon gently swept her aside and stormed toward the canian, but she inserted herself between them.

"You done?" Raven asked.

"Yeah, I'm done." Oberon unslung the backpack he carried over one shoulder. "Here's the stuff you asked for. I really wish you'd pick somewhere else though."

"You knew?" Kitt said. *Unbelievable.*

"I left him a voice message to meet me here," Raven said, taking the bag. "But, dude—*timing.*"

Oberon frowned and looked at Kitt. No matter how hard she tried to stop it, the blush heated her cheeks.

"Did I interrupt something?" he asked.

"No—" Kitt spat.

"—Yes," Raven said at the same time.

"Okaayyy," Oberon said and turned toward the door. "Well, I can see you have things to sort out—I'll be leaving."

"Wait," she said a little too quickly. If he left now, she'd be alone with Raven again, and that was far too dangerous. "You brought some moonshine—stay for some. I'll get glasses."

Oberon's gaze flicked from Kitt to Raven and back to her. *Can he sense my desperation?* She refused to look at her ex-lover.

"What'd'ya say, Raven? Join me in a drink?" Oberon said.

"Why not." Raven moved to the sofa. "It's been a long time since I last had a taste of belladonna."

Kitt grabbed three shot glasses and joined them in the living room. The two males sat side by side on the sofa: Oberon taking up one and a half cushions, Raven sitting back, with one arm causally extended along the back of the lounge and his left ankle resting on his right knee.

She kneeled on the opposite side of the coffee table, sitting back on her feet as she pulled the cork stopper. The liquor was made from the berries of the deadly nightshade plant that Oberon's family brewed up in the backwoods. Called Atropa wine, the spirit was extremely intoxicating at this illegal strength to the Bestiabeo, but fatally toxic to humans.

Déjà vu hit as she poured the first shot, throwing her off. They'd done this before. A little of the cloudy liquor splashed onto the glass tabletop, and she willed her hand to steady as she continued to pour.

Oberon took the glass she offered. "This reminds me of another time," he said as if reading her mind.

"With a couple of differences," Raven said and held up his glass. "To absent friends—Emmett and Dylan."

"Emmett and Dylan," Kitt and Oberon chorused, then downed the bittersweet liquor.

"Whoa, that's got quite a kick," Raven said, smiling and placing the tiny glass back on the table.

"Just like old times, hey?" Oberon grinned.

"After I taught you some manners." And Raven's lopsided smile deepened.

"Yeah . . ." Oberon put his glass beside Raven's and indicated a refill. "Hell, you really kicked the shit out of us both."

"What?" she asked. "When?"

"When we first met," Oberon replied.

"But I introduced you," she said, confused. "We had a very pleasant evening."

"That wasn't exactly our first meeting," Oberon admitted.

"Emmett, Oberon, and your brother decided to run me off when they found out we were seeing each," Raven said. "What was it Dylan said? 'We don't want no Matokwe scum touching our women—especially not my sister.'"

Oberon laughed and nodded. "But I think it was 'Matokwe piece of shit.'"

The two males picked up their second shots, clinked them together with a laugh, and drank. Kitt downed hers in one swallow. The tingling buzz started in her extremities: her fingers, toes, and even her lips. She'd been surprised at how smoothly that meeting between her new lover and her friend, husband, and brother had gone. Now she knew why.

Separately, Dylan and Oberon had been dangerous, to say the least, but together they were lethal. And Emmett was no pushover either. So to have beaten all three must have been some accomplishment. Oberon's temper was legendary. However, one thing that trumped it was respect.

"So what happened?" she asked.

"Raven went through me, Dylan, and Emmett like butter—before we even had a chance to get our shit together." Oberon stared down into his glass.

"Well, serves you right," she said, setting the bottle down.

"Dylan was impressed. He said if you could do that to the three of us, then you'd have no problem protecting Kitt." Oberon looked up a little sadder. "He respected you, man."

In a way, she could understand. It'd been the same sense

of controlled danger that'd attracted her to Raven in the first place. She filled the glasses again and they all lifted them, this time in silence to absent friends.

The corner of Oberon's lips quirked. "So, do Tyrone's men know you're here?"

"Of course not." Raven sniffed. "They're idiots."

"He's upped the price on your head again." Oberon held out his glass for another refill. "One point seven mil now."

Kitt froze midpour and stared at Raven. It was obvious this wasn't news to him.

Oberon swallowed the rest of his drink. "From what I hear, Tyrone thinks these latest murders are by Emmett's killer."

So did Kitt. Even though Emmett's death was more frenzied and brutal, the similarities were too great.

"And since they started around the time of your return and happened to be centered around the institution his granddaughters are attending . . ." Oberon left it hanging for a moment before continuing. "He's garnishing support from many other frightened Bestiabeo families. Especially one very prominent and grieving Russian ursian ambassador."

Raven shrugged and tensed a little more around the shoulders, but not enough for Oberon to notice. Kitt knew him all too well though.

"Have another drink," she said, holding out the bottle.

"Better not or I'll never get home," Oberon said.

"Then stay here," she said. "You've slept on the sofa bed before."

Raven frowned slightly, and Kitt knew he read her just as well as she could him. With an air of resignation, he leaned forward and pushed his glass forward. "Come on, old bear. Or are you afraid I'll drink you under the table?"

"Why the hell not?" he said and placed his shot glass beside Raven's, signaling a refill. "Let's go."

Kitt's head was already spinning but poured herself another, just the same. *As Oberon said . . . why the hell not?*

"Raven can have Dylan's room," she said.

"Now, hang on a minute . . ." Raven began. "Oberon can have the room and I'll take the sofa."

"Actually, I'm happy . . ." Oberon lifted his glass to her and as he drank, he winked— "Me and the sofa; we've spent many a night together; we're old friends."

Maybe he isn't as unobservant as he appears.

Kitt struggled to her feet, her head whirling and her legs feeling like they belonged to someone else. "I'll get some bedding."

Kitt woke in her darkened room, her head pounding and mouth dry. She climbed from her disheveled bed still dressed in one of Dylan's T-shirts. She must have made it to bed somehow, though the last thing she could remember was trying to get up off the floor without falling over. That Atropa wine sure kicked like a mule, especially if you weren't used to drinking.

She stumbled out into the living room. Oberon lay sprawled diagonally and facedown on the sofa bed, his feet hanging over the edge. Wearing only a pair of fitted red cotton boxer shorts, his tribal scars were clearly visible over his back and upper arms. The sun was still up. Just.

Kitt locked the bathroom door and showered quickly. Time for an early evening meal before going into work, though the thought of food churned her stomach. Some fresh meat would do her a world of good. Like most of the Bestiabeo races, she remained mainly nocturnal. In this day and age, it was more habitual instead of a necessity, though. Hundreds of years of conditioning were a hard thing to break.

She schlepped into the kitchen and checked her freezer. Nothing. She'd cooked the last of her steaks this morning— hers now lay wasted in the bin. Luckily there was a twenty-four-hour Bestiabeo friendly store just down the street. Kitt dressed quickly before going out for provisions.

When she returned, Oberon was up, dressed in his black leather pants. His huge platinum metal belt buckle was hanging loose and undone along with the top button and half the zipper. He took a mouthful from a large mug of black coffee and reached for one of the fresh-made rare roast beef rolls Kitt placed on the kitchen counter.

"You're a genius," he said and kissed her cheek before stuffing half the roll into his mouth.

Raven wandered into the kitchen looking like she felt. The top button in his jeans was also undone and shirt unbuttoned. He leaned back against the counter and rubbed his hand to his face.

"You look a bit rough there, dog," Oberon said.

"I feel like a herd of elephants tap-danced on my skull," Raven croaked as she handed him a mug. The walk to the store got her blood pumping, and she didn't feel quite as bad as she first did.

"Why do you look so chipper?" he asked Oberon.

"Mother's milk." Oberon grinned around a mouthful of roast beef and bread. "Raised on the stuff. Have something to eat—it'll make you feel better."

Raven grabbed a roll and sniffed before taking a tentative bite.

Oberon took another. "Now, how're we going get you out of here without getting you killed?"

Kitt's heart stopped. She hadn't even considered that.

"Same way I came in," Raven said. "I'll take care of it myself. But I could do with a lift—meet you two blocks away in fifteen minutes."

"Yeah, well after those bounty hunters found you last night . . ." Oberon picked up the backpack he'd brought with him and tossed it at Raven. You'd better dress up. And you'd better stick close to the Bunker from now on."

Kitt pulled into the campus lot and parked beside Oberon's Harley; Raven climbed off the back. Wearing sunglasses and a beat-up old cowboy hat, his hair tucked inside, even she had trouble recognizing him. No one spoke on the elevator ride down. Raven's mood seemed as dark as the long black leather coat he wore.

Antoinette and Tones were sharing a joke as they came down the staircase. Their heads both turned at once, the laughter dying as they stood.

"Geeze, you guys look like shit," the computer tech said.

"Fuck-you-very-much too, Tones," Raven growled.

Tones stepped back and out of his way as Raven brushed past.

"God, he's in a bad mood. I only meant—"

Kitt put her hand on his arm. "It's nothing to do with you."

"What's happened?" Antoinette asked.

Oberon sighed. "He was attacked by bounty hunters last night. With every influential Animalian family in town out for his blood, we'll soon have all the contract killers on the East Coast hunting him down. He's done well to stay under the radar so far, but that can't last forever." As Oberon headed into his office, he added. "At least we have a chance of protecting him here."

The magnitude of what he said hit and Kitt's legs trembled. She realized he and Raven had been playing down the danger in front of her. That, on top of the drinking session, had her reaching for the nearest chair. She landed heavily on the seat before her legs gave out altogether, then hung her head between her legs.

"Are you okay?" Antoinette asked. "You don't look too hot."

"Just a little hung over on some illegal-strength belladonna moonshine."

Antoinette cocked an eyebrow and crossed her arms as she straightened. "Hmmm, does Oberon know?"

Kitt grabbed her pounding head with both hands. "Who do you think brought it?"

Antoinette chuckled. "Now, why doesn't that surprise me?"

Kitt just remembered . . . "Speaking of lack of sleep, how was your day?"

Antoinette beamed and stretched. "Not much sleep for me, but I feel *fine*." Then the cat-got-cream smile slid from her face. "He's already left and I don't know when I'll see him next."

"So Christian is away a lot these days?"

"Yes. Intel has him searching for lab complexes similar to Lucian Moretti's."

"Have they found any more?" Kitt asked.

Antoinette nodded. "Three. And they all seem to be linked to Lucian's network some way."

It was the first time Kitt had seen a trace of fear mar her pretty Aeternus features. From what Oberon told her, the torture and trauma she'd gone through was enough to emotionally scar even the most balanced person.

"There will be more labs found," Rudolf said from the bottom step of the entrance and walked over to them. "If the humans wipe out the parahumans, who will protect them if the Dark Brethren get loose? I think these people are doing the Dark Brethren's work, and I fear that this is only the beginning. My research says they feed on negative emotions and death."

The girls looked at each other as the old man walked into Oberon's office.

"Hmm, that's some fucked-up theory," Antoinette murmured and shook her head. "But if it's true, then God help us all." She straightened and turned to Kitt. "You want to walk me to class and tell me what went down today?"

"Why not," Kitt said. "It might help to clear my head."

12
Gladiators

The arena was packed. The crowd noise buzzed through the air like ten thousand whiny insects.

"Tones said he'd meet us here," Antoinette said, looking around.

Kitt pointed at a frantically waving figure. "There he is."

They made their way down to the front, where Tones was waiting for them. Kitt had never seen anything like the Shadow-combat arena before. The rows of seating were high, surrounding a sunken area in the middle where a sort of playing field resembling a gladiatorial coliseum was arranged like the rooms of an old abandoned house. Large screens hung suspended above the arena, showing in rotation images of players with their match statistics.

Persephone's serious features appeared in high-definition glory. It was a little surreal, thought Kitt, almost like seeing herself up there. Antoinette elbowed her gently in the ribs, gave her a thumbs-up, and Kitt couldn't help smiling, suddenly and unexpectantly overwhelmed by what could only be maternal pride.

Then the crowd erupted as the image of the new NYAPS all-state champion filled the screen. The boy's lopsided grin had the girls screaming even louder.

Antoinette leaned in close. "That kid used to go to my

uncle's school and got the shit kicked out of him not long ago. Always was a cocky little shit."

The guy next to Kitt tilted open a panel in the arm of his seat and plugged in an earpiece. When he found her staring, he smiled awkwardly and looked away quickly. The small screen could be tilted for better viewing and she could hear the tinny buzzing coming from the man's earpiece.

Another roar filled the arena.

Kitt laughed. It felt so good. The crowd was cheering, clapping, and screaming—happy spectators waiting for the games to start. The atmosphere was contagious, but she couldn't help thinking of gladiatorial combat in an ancient Roman arena—where the masses would gather and bay for blood; the players ready to give it to them. This was definitely a modern-day equivalent, and the danger was just as real. People got hurt in these matches; sometimes fatally, though not often. Still, a lead weight settled in the pit of her stomach at the thought.

Then out of the corner of her eye, she caught a glimpse of someone she hadn't seen in a very long time; he hadn't seen her and yet his good-time smile slid a little. He began looking around the crowd, eyes searching.

At first, his gaze washed over and passed her by. Then it flicked back, after less than a heartbeat, the recognition instant. His mouth disappeared into the thin line of disapproval she remembered so well. The one he'd given her more times than she could count. Just as quickly, he looked away.

Cal sat beside him, smiling and clapping with the rest of the audience, totally unaware of Kitt's presence.

Antoinette leaned in again. "That has to be your other daughter."

Kitt nodded, not trusting her voice.

"Who's the guy with her?"

"Nathan," Kitt hissed. "My big brother."

As if sensing they were talking about him, he glanced their way again and stiffened in his seat.

"If looks were silver, you, me and every parahuman within five yards would be dead."

"Nathan and I have"—Kitt searched for the right word to explain their complicated relationship—"issues."

At that moment, the crowd roared as a team of four entered the arena from one end, dressed in black with stripes of red and gold running down their left sides. Then different voices swelled as the opposing team in dark purple and silver entered from the other end.

"Welcome to tonight's feature event. The visiting Pittsburgh Reapers versus the home-team favorites—the New York Demons."

The crowd cheered for their team and jeered for the opposition.

"Tonight for the Demons, we have the captain: a human, and the all-state champion—Mark Ambrosia."

The crowd went wild. Even those rooting for the opposition seemed to be cheering. The boy acknowledged the crowd with an almost humble wave and turned back to his team. Antoinette chuckled beside her.

"What's so funny?"

Antoinette smiled and said, "He seems to have learned a bit of humility since I last saw him."

The loudspeaker crackled into life again once the crowd had settled a little. *"Joining him is the current runner-up in the women's division and a Facimorph, Diane Curran."*

The girl dressed in Abeolite, in the team colors, with her dark hair hanging loose, stepped forward for her turn to acknowledge the crowd.

"And in her farewell performance is the former Demons' captain, amateur women's singles champion and Thaumaturgist, Sandie Hudson." The crowd drowned out the announcer's voice. This time wolf whistles and suggestive remarks had the boys making more noise than the girls.

The witch stepped forward and threw kisses to the crowd above. Her beautiful silver-gray hair was secured on top of her head with what appeared to be pair of chopsticks. Her Lycra Demons' bodysuit molded firmly to her shapely figure and a thick albino python was draped over her shoulders, its tail curling around her upper right arm. Her familiar.

When the noise died down, the announcer continued.

"And the Demons team rounds out with a rookie in her inaugural first-grade match—the felian Persephone Jordan."

The Demons supporters erupted into a crescendo of clapping and cheering, drowning out the jeers of the Reapers' supporters. Kitt clapped her palms so hard it hurt, getting just as caught up in the excitement like everyone else. Tones stuck his fingers in his mouth and whistled shrilly. Antoinette yelled encouragements. The girl gave a nervous smile and stepped back with her team.

"For the Reapers we have the former all-state champion and ursian Davis Jones as team captain."

He was huge; not surprising for an ursian. He wore only Abeolite pants so his ursian Family scars marking his torso and arms would be visible. He also sported several black tribal-design tattoos.

The roar from the audience was deafening.

Tones leaned forward. "Ambrosia took the championship from Jones a few weeks ago and this game has been touted as a bit of a grudge match."

Kitt sat straighter in her seat. This sounded interesting.

The loudspeaker crackled. *"Joining him is his sister, Stacy Jones."*

The ursian female, not quite as big as her brother, was solidly built yet retained her femininity. She also had ursian clan scars and tattoos.

"The third member for the Reapers' team is veteran Shadow-combat player John St. Johns who has just been drafted into the National Shadow-combat League team the L.A. Fireballs. Tonight will be his last match as an amateur before turning pro this spring."

At this stage the announcer could probably read out his shopping list and the crowd would cheer.

"And the final participant in tonight's match is a U.K. exchange student and druidess playing her first game stateside, Penelope Peabody. The match will commence in thirty seconds."

The druidess was dressed differently than all the rest. In accordance with her religion, she wore a traditional long ankle-length robe in the team's colors, purple with silver stripes on the sleeves. It was open down the front, revealing that she wore very little underneath. Her long black hair flowed over her shoulders and past her waist; it was streaked with purple, red, and white. The druidic people were an earthy, naturally sensual people.

A counter appeared on all the screens, starting at 00.00.20. When it reached 00.00.00, the observation area darkened and a hush fell over the audience. From now on the participants wouldn't be able to see or hear the spectators.

She could sense someone watching her in the dim light and caught Nathan glaring at her. He didn't look away. Instead, he lifted his chin a little higher and kept scowling at her. This time it was she who turned away first, trying to concentrate on the match or at least give that impression. She was *not* going to give him the satisfaction of knowing how much his presence bothered her.

"If your brother frowns any harder, I think he's going to blow a blood vessel," Antoinette whispered in her ear.

The short laugh burst out before she could stop it, and she glanced again at Nathan. His brow only deepened. He couldn't have heard them, but he seemed to know he was the butt of their joke.

"Shh," she whispered back at Antoinette.

"What's the joke?" Tones had that dense grin of someone who's laughing with you but is clueless as to why.

"Never mind, just watch the game," Antoinette said, patting his hand and winking at Kitt.

With the tension broken, Kitt relaxed back into her seat and watched the Demons enter one of the rooms on half of the large split-screen; the other team's close-up occupied the second half of the display. Mark held up his hand for them to stop, pointed ahead, and nodded to the witch Hudson. She lifted her hands and blew a golden stream of energy into the room. Two live rats hiding inside the room lit up like Christmas trees.

"What an opening move by the Demons. They are off and running with the first points of the game," the caller announced.

The scoreboard ticked over, giving 10 points to the Demons.

"What just happened?" Kitt asked.

Tones leaned across Antoinette and whispered, "The Thaumaturgist used a spell that identified life-forms in the room. If she had discovered one of the other team's members, it would have been fifty points; and if nothing living was in the room, then they would have lost points. The rule of three applies to all magic, meaning they can only use each individual spell in their registered repertoire three times a match. They have to be careful when and what they use it on."

"Wow, you really do know this game," Antoinette said, impressed.

Tones pulled back his shoulders and beamed. "See how they have no weapons? They have to find them; it's part of the game."

The Reapers' team members entered another room and began searching through boxes, old furniture, and litter scattered around the room. The female ursian, Stacy, forced open an old bureau draw and slammed it shut, then turned the painting on the wall. She pulled an orange card from where it was taped on the back and grinned.

"The Reapers are now off and running with the discovery of a twenty-point spell card."

She handed it to the druidess, Peabody, who took it and shook her head.

"The more powerful or stronger the spell, the more points it's worth. They get the points, but I don't think the druidess can use it," Tones whispered. "Still, they've stopped the opposition from gaining a valuable spell and a possible advantage."

The Demons came to a locked door. The shape-shifter Curran shrank into a perfect replica of the witch Hudson's familiar, the snake, and slithered through a crack in the door. Then Hudson shoved her teammate's Abeolite suit through the crack—and a few minutes later, Curran opened the door from the inside and came out holding a red-handled fire ax, which she passed to the team captain. The scoreboard clicked over another 80 points for the Demons' team.

"Well played," the commentator roared. *"Entering a locked room and finding the first weapon."*

"They opened the door without breaking it down or busting the lock," said Tones, "which gained them thirty points, and the fire ax can be used as a weapon, which gives them another fifty points. If she'd found a gun, it would have been one hundred; a silver-bladed sword, one hundred and fifty; and a gun loaded with silver nitrate, two hundred points. Though it isn't really silver nitrate; they try to avoid accidents."

The arena afforded a wider view of the game, but it wasn't always possible to see what was happening. The large screens were there for the close-up action. However, this got more complicated as both teams split into pairs. Seph and the ax-wielding human captain formed a pair.

With the commentary and Tones's explanations, Kitt was really getting into the game. Cal sat forward on the edge of her seat, totally engrossed in the game like the rest of the audience. But not so with Nathan—every now and then she could feel the weight of his stare, those cold tawny eyes a shade or two darker than her own.

Seph and Ambrosia made their way along a corridor. The attention to detail they paid to setting the scene was impressive. Yellowing stained paper hung off the walls in torn strips, some of the wooden floorboards were missing, and antique lights flickered, adding to the eerie atmosphere.

Seph said something and the team captain nodded. Kitt wished she could hear what was going on. Wait, she could. She opened the panel in the arm of her chair and selected Seph's image on the small screen then inserted the earpiece.

They were silent now. A frown of concentration creased Seph's brow. The overhead screen flicked to show the Reapers' captain, Jones, and his teammate St. Johns waiting in the opposite room. They were setting up an ambush. St. Johns had a lethal-looking crossbow. A collective gasp from the crowd echoed her own.

Antoinette grabbed her hand. "Don't worry, it's been tipped."

But accidents happen. With the amount of force it took to launch a bolt, it would be *very* easy for it all to go wrong with that particular weapon.

Seph stopped suddenly and pulled up her captain, Ambrosia. She leaned in and whispered so quietly, Kitt couldn't make out a word. The tension was building and she moved forward in her seat.

Did Seph sense something? Does she know they're there?

Seph and Ambrosia flattened themselves against the wall and carefully moved along it. Kitt's heart thundered in her chest. Seph pointed at a spot on the wall and Ambrosia positioned the ax, then snow leopard fur rippled up Seph's right arm. When he gave the nod they struck together. The ax bit into the wall beside the ursian Jones's head, then Seph punched her partially changed arm right through and wrapped her fingers around St. Johns's neck. She yanked her arm back, slamming the human's head into the torn plaster and wood.

He crumpled to the floor, clutching his face and screaming.

Seph ran into the room and tried to pull his hands away. "I'm sorry. I'm sorry," she cried. "Please let me look."

The nearest camera zoomed in on the injured man. A large splinter of wood had lodged in his left cheek, close to his eye.

Seph reached to pull the splinter out.

"NO!" Kitt yelled. Tones and Antoinette turned to look at her, confused. "If she pulls the splinter there's a danger of rupturing the eye, and he could lose it," she explained.

"Shit," Tones said.

Seph's hand wavered over the sliver, then she tilted her head in the direction of the audience, almost as if she'd heard her . . . or someone else.

"How did Seph know where Jones and St. Johns were?" Antoinette asked.

"She probably heard her opponents' heartbeats," Tones offered.

Kitt shook her head. "Not unless she transformed her ears, but we would've seen that." *Come to think of it, why hadn't she?*

"A hit that precise took more than a guess," Antoinette added.

"But how did she know?" Kitt wondered out loud. A yellow light started flashing above the room and everyone froze.

"What's going on?" Kitt asked.

"The match is suspended until they get the injured off the field," Tones said.

"John St. Johns will be withdrawing from the match due to injury," the commentator announced.

Paramedics entered carrying a stretcher. The Reapers' captain, Jones, held his teammate's hand in his massive fist and talked to him. He stood back and let the paramedic load the wounded man onto a stretcher—worry clearly etched his features. Ambrosia clapped a comforting hand on Jones's shoulder, which the ursian acknowledged with a quick nod. Then it was game on as usual.

Outnumbered, the Reaper took off to rejoin his team and Mark Ambrosia gave the opposing team captain time to rejoin his other teammates before continuing, earning him a roar from the crowd.

After a half hour, the tension was palpable for those who watched. The scoreboard showed 395 points to the Demons, and 375 for the Reapers. The Reapers' druidess Peabody and ursian Stacy had taken the Demons' shape-shifter Curran out of the game. And now the two teams had just a room between them. No one in the crowd dared to even breathe. Not even a whisper was audible.

Antoinette gripped the arm of the chair until it creaked. Tones sat forward resting his chin on the back of his hands and fell silent. Kitt could almost taste the adrenaline released from the pores of the excited spectators. The entire audience held a collective breath as the two teams stepped into the same room to face each other for the first time.

The Demons' witch flung a stun spell she had picked up along the way. The spell exploded in a splash of color against the chest of the Reapers' captain, sending him backward onto the floor. He twitched like an electric current was jolting his body.

"Ohh," the commentator announced. *"The Reapers have lost their captain to a paralyzing spell. A mighty painful one*

by the looks. The Demons lose twenty points for the spell, making them dead even with the Reapers. This is a close game, folks."

"What?" Antoinette said. "Why did they lose points?"

"Some spells cards found have a points cost if used, especially if they cause pain," Tones said. "And that one caused a lot of pain."

"Shit, that bites," Antoinette said.

Tones looked at her. "I think it might be worth the sacrifice, look."

The female ursian Jones flew into a rage, her body rippling with the effects of the transformation, anger at her brother's cruel disablement speeding her change.

The witch Hudson's python hissed at the furious female black bear as she reared up on her back legs. The witch's hand shot out, conjuring another spell. The druidess dug her hand into a pouch under her robe and threw something on the ground. It sprouted into thick green tentaclelike vines.

Most thaumaturgy came from life and nature—familial witches through animals, and the druidic through plants. Seph was midway through her transformation when the vine tendril whipped around her arms and waist, lifting her off the ground.

Then Hudson conjured a phantom bear to combat the real one, and the two animals met in a clash of teeth and claws. Mark Ambrosia took the animated vine tentacles with the fire ax and a sword he'd found along the way. Delicate purple-red petals unfolded along the tendrils, bursting into beautiful blooms. The flowers immediately began to shoot thorny darts.

One of the tentacles wrapped around Seph's throat and began choking the life out of her. Kitt looked away and caught a glimpse of Cal looking pale and panicky at her sister's plight. No, it was more than that, she clutched at her throat, like she was being choked too.

Ambrosia pulled out a thorn lodged in the side of his neck and stumbled forward. He shook his head, his movements slow. The thorns were venomous. He brought the sword down and severed the tendril wrapped around Seph's throat and then fell forward onto the floor. The vine withered, freeing Seph, who immediately leapt for the druidess, hitting her chest and knocking her back against the wall. Her snow leopard jaws clamped down on the forearm of the mostly naked magic wielder, though not enough to draw blood. With her attention broken, the plant withered and died just as the phantom bear knocked out the ursian.

"THE DEMONS WIN THE MATCH," yelled the commentator. *"What a masterful piece of teamwork displayed by both teams here today. I cannot remember a more exciting match."*

Cheers and screams erupted from the crowd and then the commentator's words were entirely lost to the voices of the audience—the arena silencer must have turned off. And the Demons could be seen waving to the crowd, then they turned to help the opposing team members. The two team captains, both looking a little worse for wear, clasped hands and pulled each other into a manly, backslapping hug. Both teams' members shook hands.

Tones was on his feet clapping wildly, cheering and screaming at the top of his lungs, *"FANTASTIC. WELL PLAYED!"*

Antoinette looked at Kitt and directed a tilt of her chin over Kitt's shoulder. She turned to find Nathan standing in the aisle a few feet away, with Cal and four burly bodyguards.

Kitt's throat closed; she stood on wobbly legs. Antoinette discreetly tapped Kitt's inner arm to show that she was nearby if needed. Nathan's pale eyes burned under his scowl. "What are you doing here, Kathryn?"

13

Brotherly Hate

"Nice to see you too, Nathan," Kitt said, trying to smile, but feared it came off more as a grimace.

Her brother's frown deepened. "You were never interested in contact sports."

"How would you know what I'm into, Nathan? It's been years since we last saw each other."

"Hi." Tones put out his hand. "Antonio Geraldi. I used to work with your brother."

Nathan glanced down at the outstretched arm, and ignored Tones's offer.

She could've just kissed Tones for trying to diffuse the situation a little, and patted his shoulder as he backed off. "Not that I need to explain myself to you, but I came to see my daughter."

Out of the corner of her eye, Kitt glimpsed Raven standing near the arena exit in the same dark clothes he was wearing earlier. His wide-brimmed hat was pulled down low in front, but she knew he was watching. When Nathan turned to look at Cal, Raven took a step forward and she gave him a slight shake of her head. She could handle this.

"So, what did you think of your sister's first game?" Antoinette asked Cal, trying to distract the twin from the tension between her uncle and mother.

"Seph did really well, I think"—her eyes darting nervously between Nathan and Kitt, then Antoinette—"and what do you think?"

"I thought she played brilliantly," Tones interjected. "The way she dispatched St. Johns was awesome. She must be very strong to have such control over her transition at such an early age."

"Yes, yes she is." Cal dropped her eyes to the ground. "But she's going to beat herself up for injuring him."

"Tell her not to," Antoinette said. "These things happen in a match like this."

The girl nodded. "True, but knowing Seph as I do . . ." Then she looked at Kitt and smiled.

"Cal, please wait for me outside," Nathan said.

"But . . ."

"I said wait outside," he growled.

"Okay." Cal turned to Kitt. "Thanks for coming. I know Seph will really appreciate it."

"I'll walk you out," Tones said.

"That won't be necessary," Nathan hissed.

"Maybe not, but I'm headed that way myself," Tones said in a hardened voice. This was a side of him Kitt rarely saw. Nathan always had a knack for bringing out the worst in people.

Her brother signaled a couple of the bodyguards to follow them, leaving two to remain on watch with him.

Kitt waited until Tones and her daughter were far enough away before confronting her brother. "That was rude and uncalled for."

"I'm not here to make nice with you or your friends." He clasped his hands in front. "But I *do* have a message for you—"

"What, stay away from the twins?" she cut in quickly, not wanting to play his nasty little mind games. "That'll be a little hard since they're in my class. And we're going to cross paths while at the Academy. You're on the board and the girls are attending— Can't we at least be civil to each other?"

Nathan stepped closer and dropped his voice. "I trust you will respect the edict of the council and keep contact with Pride members to an absolute minimum." He glanced toward the exit as Tones and Cal disappeared. "I tried to have them transferred when I learned you would be taking some of their tutorials, but there are no openings at the academies we deem suitable. They're in your class and that's as far as it goes. All other contact with them is forbidden without my express permission." By the look on his face, she knew that would never happen. "Do you understand?"

"Nathan, they're my daughters."

"They belong to the Pride and you don't." He couldn't have said it with more sting if he'd tried. He turned on his heel and headed in the direction of the exit without another word or a backward glance.

"Is he always so charming?" Antoinette asked when he was gone.

"This is one of his better days." Kitt watched him disappear with his men in tow.

"I promised Tones a drink," Antoinette said. "Why don't you join us?"

"Thanks for the offer, but I think I need to go see Raven. He was here, at the game." She had to try to make him see sense; for the moment he was in danger and had to stay hidden.

"Okay, then," the Aeternus said. "Maybe next time."

Antoinette pulled up next to a dilapidated warehouse on the docks by the river. She'd left Tones at the bar in the care of a lovely young vegan donor and went off to take care of some important semi-personal business.

She climbed out of the car and scanned the area for her contact, an ex-con by the name of Tripper McKee.

The nearby building stank of rot and decay, and the stench from the river wafted in on the wind. Her brother Nici and Tripper had been pretty tight a few years back, before Tripper had been sent to prison on a five-year stint for reckless endangerment causing death.

She leaned through the open window to grab her cell phone to call him. A low whistle of appreciation came from a nearby warehouse and she looked over her shoulder to see him standing in the doorway. When she approached, she could smell the strong odor of a freshly smoked joint clinging to his clothes.

He flicked his long light brown hair and grinned. "Still a great car."

"How's it hanging, Tripper?"

"Not bad, fang-hottie." His smile widened as his eyes traveled down her body and then back up to her face. "Come on in. I think I've got something for you."

He crossed to the faded green van parked inside and hit the button. Motörhead blared out from the speakers sitting on the ground next to the van. An old large dog lifted his head from a fluffy blue rug and gave her a lazy, halfhearted woof.

"Yeah, yeah, Dog. A bit late to tell me we have visitors." Tripper ruffled the old dog's head as he went past. Antoinette followed him onto a large square of the moth-eaten Persian carpet. A faded fat, stuffed leather chair sat to one side under a giant open pink-and-green beach umbrella.

Dog sniffed her shoes and her trousers and gave a little growl at the scent of Cerberus. She squatted down and scratched behind his big ears. He lifted and dropped his tail three times, as close as he could get to actually wagging it these days.

"Hello, old boy," she said.

"I think he's going deaf, maybe blind too." Tripper looked at the old animal and his expression filled with fond sadness. He looked away. "Stupid dog."

"Can I get you anything—a smoke, a drink, a vein?" He turned his head to the side to offer his neck.

She narrowed her eyes and crossed her arms.

"Okay, just trying to be hospitable," he said with a wink and pulled a joint from his pocket.

The pungent smoke filled the air and he placed his hand on the back of the leather chair.

"I ran into J.J." She turned to gauge his reaction.

Tripper exhaled sharply and screwed up his nose. "What is that son of a bitch up to these days?"

"Hunting down innocent people and sucking them dry."

Tripper's eyebrows raised, the only sign of his surprise. "You'd better step into my office."

He crawled into the back of the van and sat down on one of the two office chairs inside, she took the other. A corkboard attached to the wall above the computer station had newspaper clippings and notes pinned to it with little colored tacks—however, Antoinette's gaze was drawn to the snapshot of three young men laughing with their arms around one another. She'd taken that photo of Tripper, his brother Cleb and her brother Nici. She remembered the day well; it'd been just before Tripper's world fell apart.

He saw her looking at the picture and turned back to the computer screen. "I keep it as a reminder never to take anything for granted."

Antoinette looked at her brother's laughing boyish face. At least she could still talk to him, even if he was miles away in London. Tripper didn't have that luxury. Cleb was dead. Killed in a hunt gone wrong, and Tripper charged with negligence for his death.

"Do you ever wonder what if?" he asked, still not looking at her.

"I try not to," she said. "It only ends up making things worse." She knew that from experience.

"Well, I do. Like what if we'd kept our mouths shut about that damned blood farm; what if I'd trusted my instincts and not taken that job?"

She placed her hand on his shoulder. "You weren't to blame."

"No, the Guild was . . ." He looked at her. "And one day they'll pay."

"We have to get enough evidence first," she said.

He grinned, and there was no humor in it. "I'm working on it."

"Yes, we both are."

"So, J.J.'s gone bloodsucker, then?" He suddenly looked up in horror. "Sorry, no offense meant."

"None taken." How times had changed—not so long ago she'd had the same prejudices. "He's with some bent Aeternus called Marvella."

Tripper tapped the keys at the first console. "Would you mind grabbing me a soda?"

She scooted back a couple of feet to grab a soda from the small fridge under the microwave. He had a pretty good setup here really, several computers networked together down one side and a drop-down bunk on along the other.

"Where are you getting the power to run all this?" she asked.

He took a large puff on his joint and pointed at the cable running from the back of the van to the power pole outside.

"Shhh, it's a secret," he said in that half-talk, half-sucking way potheads use as a way to keep as much of the aromatic smoke in their lungs for as long as possible.

He blew out a stream of bluish white smoke. "I'll have a week, two tops before they become suspicious of the power drain and I have to move on so they don't catch me." He pulled a yellow folder from beside his computer. "Here, a present."

There were several emails from a Guild insider with whom Tripper had made contact. It turned out there were a number of people with the same suspicions and stories of secret goings-on. He was beginning to build quite a little network of contacts.

"There is nothing substantial here we can use," she said. The emails showed large amounts of money being siphoned off to a secret account and little else.

"No, but it shows my contact has access to some highly classified files. We don't have anything yet, but soon."

He was right. This did show a potential good source of intelligence.

"Okay, fine—keep digging."

"Is this her?" He brought up several photographs on the screen.

Shit, the picture.

She pulled out a piece of folded paper from her pocket and opened it. The Aeternus Marvella with long, teased dark hair matched the ones on the screen.

"Yep, that's her," she said. "We encountered her a couple of nights ago, but she's gone to ground with J.J."

He took another puff on the joint. "Okay—I'll put out a bulletin."

"Excellent," she said. "Let me know as soon as you hear anything, night or day."

When Kitt got downstairs, she found Oberon in his office reading through reams of research Tones had produced. As she leaned against the doorframe watching him, he looked up.

"Game over already?" he asked. "Did we win?"

"Yes and yes. Where's Raven?"

"Down in the rec room, I think. Why?"

"He was at the game," she said. "And so was Nathan. You shouldn't let him just wander around."

"I can't really stop him." Oberon laid the papers on the table. "He's not a prisoner."

"I know," she said. "It'd be better if he'd just return to where he came from."

"Better for him?" Oberon asked. "Or better for you?"

"I really don't know." She sighed and pushed herself away from the door. "I'd better go find Raven."

She found him half sitting, half lounging on the sofa with his feet up on the coffee table. He'd removed the jacket but kept the hat on. He was flicking through the channels on the big screen TV and glanced over as she came into the room, dragging his feet to the ground as he sat up.

"Great game," he said, flicking off the TV.

"Yes, it was. Too bad my brother had to ruin it."

"Wanna tell me about it?" he asked.

"Not really." She leaned against the doorframe, almost afraid to take that final step.

Unshed tears burned behind her eyes and made her temples throb. He patted the cushion beside him and held out his hand. She knew the moment she sat down, those tears would come. It had been building for days really. New job, meeting the girls, him; Nathan was the last straw.

And she was right. The moment her ass hit the cushion the dam of tears didn't just break, it shattered apart with an explosive force. The sobs tore through her body, the unfairness of it all ripping her insides with grief and anger. Once the tears started, she couldn't get them to stop.

Raven wrapped his arms around her and pulled her against his chest. He held her against his warmth, his strong hand soft against her hair. He'd done this long ago, and she felt as safe as she had back then. Curled against him, Kitt clutched his shirt and soaked his chest as she poured out all her hurt.

14

prime time

Gideon hid in the shadows, watching long after the fans had left. The team hadn't come out yet. He dropped his chin to his chest, his eyes feeling heavy. If he waited too much longer, he would run out of time.

"WAKE UP," Ealund shouted in his ear, jolting him.

Gideon looked at his watch. Dawn would be in a few hours. Where were they?

Laughter burst out of the opening back-door entrance to the stadium. The three people emerged, jostling each other, high on their victory. They looked so young, so healthy, so alive.

A car door opened not far from Gideon and he shrank back further into the shadow of the nearby building. A girl climbed out wearing tiny denim shorts, a tank top, and cowboy boots. She sat on the car hood and tucked a piece of honey blond hair behind her ear. Her large silver hoop earrings glinted under the streetlight.

"Hey, baby," she called and waved. The boy's head shot up and he grinned as he waved back.

He leaned in and gave each of the women he was with a kiss on the cheek, lingering a little longer to whisper something in both of their ears. Then he jogged over to the girl on the car and buried his hands in her hair while kissing her deeply.

"FOCUS," Ealund hissed. *"STAY ON TARGET."*

Ealund was right. Desires of the flesh were just a distraction. They were so close, he could almost reach out and touch them.

Ealund floated toward the couple. *"CAN YOU TASTE THAT POWER?"*

"Hey, baby," the boy whispered when he came up for air. "Wanna fool around?"

"Sure, what do ya fancy?" She wrapped her legs around his waist. "A quickie in the back of the car. I gotta be home by dawn."

"I got a surprise for you," he said. "Come with me."

He took her hand and pulled her off the hood.

"Where?" she said, laughing.

"You'll see." He pulled her toward the back door to the NYAPS arena.

"Hey, we could get in trouble."

"I paid the tech guy to leave early and turn off the CCTV to give us little privacy." He grinned as he tugged her closer into an embrace, his hands kneading her ass as he nibbled at her neck. "I want to do you in the ring."

"Eww, gross."

"No," he said, "in the arena." Then he gave her rear end a sharp slap. "On second thought, the other could be kinda kinky."

"Don't even think about it, mister." She stepped away from him and ran his hands down the front of her scantily clad body. "Not if you ever wanna tap these again." She cupped her breasts and squeezed.

The boy growled and stepped toward her. She squealed in delight and ran; he was hot on her heels, obviously letting her stay ahead. He caught her around the waist just as she reached the door and yanked it open. He lifted her up and she wrapped her legs around his hips and her arms around his neck. They continued to kiss as he carried her through the door.

"THIS IS GOING TO BE QUITE A SHOW." Ealund chuckled and cupped the bulge at the front of his robe. *"AND ISN'T THAT A LUCKY BREAK. THE CAMERA'S ALREADY TAKEN CARE OF."*

Yes, it is. Gideon's own cock hung flaccid in his pants. There was only one thing that would get it hard.

"What will I do about the girl?" he asked Ealund.

"OF COURSE."

"But she is an innocent."

Ealund's form darkened with what Gideon had come to know as anger. *"YOU DISAPPOINT ME."*

Gideon picked up his bag and crossed to the door after he checked that no one was near. With one last look around, he slipped inside after the lovers.

15
Blood

Kitt woke in the dark. The narrow bed wasn't hers. The smells in the room weren't hers. Feeling the wall beside the bed, she found a switch, hoping it was for the light.

Bingo.

The soft glow revealed a spartan room with a single cot, a chair, and very little else. It must be one of the unused guest rooms. Her shoes were off, but apart from that, she was still fully dressed. Raven or Oberon must have put her here after she'd cried herself to sleep. She stretched and yawned, feeling better rested than she had in quite a while.

There was a tentative knock at the door.

"Come in," she answered, sitting up on the bed.

Antoinette entered. "How are you feeling?"

"Really good, actually."

"Just as well, because you're going to get very busy tonight," the Aeternus said, passing her a large mug of steaming coffee. "I thought you could do with this."

Kitt took a sip and it warmed her right down to her toes. "Thanks."

"And you probably should take a look at this." Antoinette handed her the paper she had tucked under her arm.

THIRD STUDENT FOUND AT THE ACADEMY OF DEATH, screamed the headline.

Kitt glanced up at Antoinette's worried face and read on out loud.

" 'In the early hours of this morning another student was brutally mutilated on NYAPS campus grounds. The current reigning all-state champion, NYAPS student Mark Ambrosia . . .' "

Kitt stopped reading. "The boy from last night? He's *dead*?" she asked in disbelief.

The Aeternus nodded.

If Antoinette was here, then she must have slept through the entire day. "What time is it?"

"About nine thirty," Antoinette said. "The paper just came in, but Oberon called us all before sunset to get here as soon as possible."

Kitt got up and slipped on her shoes. "So what's happening?"

"Tez has just sent over some pictures; Oberon wants you to take a look."

"She sent them? What about VCU?" Kitt asked as she pulled on her shoes.

"The CHaPR chairman has pulled rank and given Oberon special dispensation as the former head of personal security and current chief of security at the Academy. They want him brought in on this operation."

The office was abuzz with everyone answering phones, yelling, or bustling about. Oberon had even brought in Cody and Bianca from the day shift. The ursian was standing and writing on a white board covered with pictures of the victims taped to it. He turned and smiled at her as she came up behind him. No—more than smiled. Oberon beamed.

"Antoinette's told you the news? You're now an official member of the team and we have lots of work to do."

"Hang on a sec, don't I get a say?" *How dare he assume*.

Oberon stopped and turned to her, frowning. "What?"

"I agreed to help you out once, not join the team. I came here to teach."

It was obvious he hadn't even contemplated her saying no. "Kitt, please, I need you."

"I will help you out for now, but as far as joining the team is concerned, I will have to think about it." *And if the last couple of days were anything to go by, then it's not bloody likely.*

Oberon nodded. "Okay; for now, then. Tones is updating the data since this victim is human and not Animalian. We need you to analyze the photos; Tez is waiting at the medical examiner's office for you to assist on the postmortem."

"I don't want to step on Tez's toes, or put OCPME off-side." Kitt stood before the case board looking over Ober-on's scrawled notes. "You know, Oberon, we have more high-tech equipment you can use for this."

"I like the old-fashioned method." He turned and smiled at her. "We've been asked to consult on this case because of the special circumstances; Tez is more than happy to work with you again."

"Okay, when do I have to be there?" she asked.

"That's why I sent Antoinette to wake you," he said with some measure of excitement. "We're meeting VCU at the medical examiner's office." He was like a kid who'd won the playground turf war.

"Oberon, a boy is dead," she said. "Can you be a bit less happy about this?"

The smile slid from his face.

Kitt took the coffee to her desk and sat down, shaking off the last of her lassitude. Oberon's phone rang. He glanced at it and his smile returned. He let it ring a few more times before finally answering. "Neil—always such a pleasure. Yes, we're leaving immediately."

Oberon slid the phone shut. "Okay, Kitt, let's go. You too, Cody."

The Incubus looked up in surprise. "Really?"

"Roberts has a way of getting under my skin—if I start to get too upset, zap me with your happy juice."

Oberon had waited several years for some payback, and now the day had finally come. Neil Roberts was his bitch. But Kitt was right—a boy had died and that soured his taste of revenge.

The agents stood around looking uncomfortable and the head of VCU scowled.

"I'm not happy about this DuPrie," Agent Roberts growled. *Situation normal. No preliminaries, no niceties, just straight for the throat.*

Oberon gave his former team leader the best fuck-me grin he could summon. "Do I look like I give a shit?"

Tez rolled her eyes. "Dr. Jordan, shall we get started?"

"Fine with me," Kitt said. "But should we leave the children alone. Someone might get hurt."

Oberon could feel his temper rising; Neil Roberts tended to have that effect on him. Cody came to stand on one side of Oberon, then Kitt on the other.

Oberon looked over at Tez and noticed how plump and delicious her lips looked with bright red do-me lipstick. A tingling warmth spread from the center of his chest and he melted into it.

Agent Roberts also seemed to be wearing the same goofy grin, his eyes distant and unseeing. Even the other VCU had relaxed their stiff stance. Oberon glanced at Cody. The Incubus's eyes glowed soft violet. He'd diffused the growing tension and Oberon duly noticed. He gave Cody an inconspicuous thumbs-up.

Agent Roberts shook himself. "Okay, we'll leave, but I want a copy of the report on my desk ASAP."

"In triplicate," Tez said and smiled sweetly.

The head of VCU signaled to his men and they withdrew. As he passed by Tez, he stopped. "Document everything, and I mean everything."

Obviously, thought Oberon, the agent didn't know of his relationship with Tez or he would've insisted on another doctor. Still, he wasn't about to let that little detail get in the way.

Kitt snapped on the latex gloves and carefully unzipped the body bag. The boy's face bore little resemblance to the one she saw at the games—that something-special, that vibrancy he had last night, was gone.

"He must have been a good-looking kid," Tez said under her breath.

Kitt remembered the reactions from girls last night. "Yeah, he was."

She unzipped the body bag completely and they dragged it from the gurney onto the stainless steel table before rolling the corpse onto his side. The sliver of metal remained embedded in the back of his neck.

"Tez, can you pass me—" She didn't have to finish as Tez placed a set of forceps in her outstretched hand.

"Just like old times." Tez grinned at her.

Yeah, it was, only this time it should be Tez taking the lead. "You know, I can observe if you want to do this."

The M.E. shook her head. "I'm happy having you as the expert consultant. Between the two of us, we hopefully won't miss much."

Kitt extracted the metal and held it up to the light. Definitely silver, and definitely the same dimensions as the others. But more important, the placement is precise and consistent with the others. Even if the method of disablement had been leaked to the public, the exact placement, with such exacting precision, would have been damn near impossible to do without a lot of practice.

"He's human—why use silver?" Tez asked in a flat, far-off voice.

"I suspect it was more about the ritual," Kitt answered and looked at the younger M.E. "You doing okay?"

"Yeah," Tez said, her spark returning. "But it just doesn't fecken add up—why use a ritual perfect for Animalians on a human?"

"Maybe it was a case of mistaken identity," Kitt said without much certainty.

"Maybe." Tez didn't sound convinced either.

Kitt turned the body onto its back. "Let's look at the chest wound for any differences."

The ribs were torn apart in the same brutal manner, and the heart had been ripped from the gaping hole in the chest just like the rest. There seemed to be more marking on this body than the previous deaths, more superficial cuts on the chest.

"Take a look at this," Tez said. "I think we have another symbol."

These marks were too uniform to be random wounds. And the one thing that made this death different was giving them another possible clue: an Animalian would have had time to heal these kind of injuries, humans couldn't.

"I'm pretty convinced it's the same killer," Kitt said. "The MO is the same, but his victim typology has shifted."

"I agree," Tez said. "Let's finish the autopsy."

Kitt peeled off the latex gloves and dumped them in the special trash can. Then she crossed to the phone on the wall and dialed.

He answered on the second ring. "Oberon!"

"We're done," she said and looked down at the mark, the one simple pattern that confirmed all their fears. "And it's definitely our killer. But we've found something new."

The team gathered around the conference table. Bianca, Cody, Raven, and Rudolf sat to the left; Antoinette, Tones, and Kitt on the right, with Oberon at the head. They all stared at the photograph on the screen, all silently contemplating the symbols carved into the victim's flesh, comparing them against the one in Rudolf's book. They matched. One, the mark of the Dark Brethren, and the other couldn't be deciphered.

"It could be a coincidence," Tones said. "I mean, up until a couple of days ago, we'd never even heard of these Dark Brethren."

Rudolf sighed. "I wish I could agree. But these events are coming together. I'd say the Dark Brethren are building their strength for a push to free themselves from the imprisonment placed on them by our ancestors. I have done some more research, which has been difficult because most old texts have removed any reference to the Dark Brethren. Apparently, they prey on the immoral or malevolent among us. They twist and manipulate the individual until they control them and make them a disciple of the Brethren. Once a disciple, every negative emotion such as greed, lust and envy is exacerbated. Our problem is how to identify these disciples and stop them from freeing the Dark Brethren from their imprisonment."

"Then how would we stop them?" Oberon asked.

"I don't know yet," Rudolf said. "But my research seemed

to also indicate the need for some kind of blood sacrifice. I think this second mark may be the personal identifier of the Brethren controlling their disciple."

"So we need to stop the sacrifices to stop the Dark Brethren?" Kitt mused aloud.

They all looked at her, as if she'd said something stupidly insane. All except for Rudolf, who tilted his head as a slow smile creased his aging, withered face.

"Well, maybe not *stop* them, but at least slow them down," he said and turned to Antoinette. "We need to identify any other murders similar to this—murders that may be Dark Brethren influenced; murders that bear the same Dark Brethren mark."

"You mean like blood sacrifices to ancient powers of old," Bianca said.

"That's exactly what I mean," Rudolf said. "The more violent and bloodier the death, then the stronger the Brethren grow."

Tones raised his head from where he'd been resting it in his hands. "But how're we supposed to find them all?"

Antoinette stood straight up and looked around at them. "Maybe we need to recruit some more operatives."

Raven had been silent throughout the entire discussion, frowning and in deep thought, but now his face suddenly changed. He looked over at Oberon and exchanged one of those annoyingly male, tiny reverse nods that other males instantly understand. Being around Dylan and Oberon all these years, Kitt had learned to interpret some of them. This one said, *"Dude, we need to talk"*—and with exactly the same replying head movement, Oberon said, *"Later."*

The ursian then moved on. "Tones, run an analysis on all the violent crimes in the area and see if there are any others bearing these marks. Then cross-reference with other ritualistic murder cases in the state, looking for any evidence with the same patterns from this area, then widen the search to the rest of the country."

Tones braced his arms on the table. "Do you think it's possible Marvella's latest dreniac recruitment drive is linked to this Dark Brethren thing?"

"Good point," Oberon said. "Let's split our efforts. Antoinette can you continue to handle the dreniac case?"

The Aeternus female gave him the same terrifying, deadly grin that Kitt did in the alley. She suppressed a shudder; the look still creeped her out.

"Excellent! Now, Bianca, can you hit the Academy's database and student records to see what you can find out in the way of exceptional students, so we identify any potential new recruits? And, Cody, I want you to help Kitt. I'll keep everyone off your backs. Share nothing of what we've discussed here, especially not with anyone in the VCU."

They all rose with purpose and filed out of the room.

Kitt tapped Cody on the arm. "Can you take me to the latest crime scenes?"

"Sure." He slid his hands into the pockets of his khaki cargo shorts, his sun-bleached hair flopping into his eyes. "But why?"

"I just want to get a feel for the kill zones."

"Good idea." Oberon followed them out of the conference room. "Take Raven with you."

"What?" she said. "I don't think that's a good idea after last night. Shouldn't he just lay low?"

"He'll be more useful out there than sitting around here on his ass." His eyes flicked past her. "Take him with you."

She turned and found her ex-lover standing in the doorway. "How long have you been there?"

"Long enough," Raven said and crossed his arms. "And you don't need to worry about me."

"Hey—she's only trying to protect your ass," Oberon interjected and frowned heavily at Raven. "Rightly or wrongly you're a hunted man, so don't get too blasé about the danger you're in or the danger you put her in."

"Come with me," Cody said, steering Raven toward the back rooms. "No one will recognize you once I'm done."

"There's a janitor's uniform back there," chimed in Oberon. "The guards sometimes use it in the outer office—no one pays much attention to a janitor . . ." For a moment, Oberon's mouth hung open, his eyes glazing, and his internal cogs spinning double time. "*Tones*. I need you in my office— ASAP."

Tones gave him a distracted wave from his computer terminal. "Just a minute, Captain."

"*NOW!*" the ursian yelled.

As Tones scurried to comply, Oberon dropped his voice to her. "You can't keep him locked up down here, even for his own good. He's just not the kind you can keep penned in."

Another reason she'd been attracted to Raven—no commitments, no long-term aspirations: the perfect material for an extramarital bit on the side. Oberon was right about one thing, though. Raven was not a man who took well to restriction.

After several minutes, Cody led a hunched, portly blond janitor back into the room. If Kitt hadn't known who it was, she would never have recognized him. Cody did good.

"Let's go get this over with," she said.

Classes had already started, so there were only a few students in the halls. The library was still closed, and yellow crime-scene tape barred access. Cody unlocked the door and they all ducked beneath the tape.

The smell of old blood and violence was ripe in the enclosed area.

"Why aren't there cameras in here?" Antoinette asked.

"There were." Cody shrugged. "Apparently they malfunctioned a couple days before the murder."

Raven straightened, immediately becoming the hunter. His eyes went lupine as he sniffed at the air. "The victim was in here awhile with the killer, not knowing he was being stalked."

He moved between the rows of books, occasionally stopping to breathe in deeply. "The killer is definitely male and in an extremely excited state. There's trace pheromones just under the latex smell on everything he touched. Like here, where he stood leaning against the shelf. And here, where he moved these books aside."

"Could you trace him through this scent?" Kitt asked.

Raven's features froze in concentration. "Yes, I think so."

They moved to where the body had been discovered. The carpet would need to be replaced; a large blood-stained area surrounded a spot in the vague shape of the body. Blood spatters covered nearby shelves and book spines, a table, and the back of a chair lying on its side. Kitt stared at some smudged footprints but couldn't discern any shoe pattern.

"With this much blood, he must've been covered," Raven said. "Which would've made him very visible."

Cody squatted to look at the dried blood. "Unless he changed. There *was* a janitor on the monitors outside the library, but we couldn't be sure he came from or into the library—however, we do know the usual janitor was off sick that night. We have no idea who that was on the surveillance cameras."

"Of course it was," Kitt said. "He'd have to plan this to know the best time to strike and how to avoid detection."

Cody pulled out a small notebook from the pocket of his cotton shirt and started jotting notes. "I'll get Tones to check out the CCTV again to see what he can find. The crime scene cleaners will be here shortly to get the library reopened as soon as possible; Oberon has stalled them for as long as he can." He closed up the book and looked at them both. "Do you want to take a look at the fresh scene now? The arena scenery is due to be rebuilt tomorrow."

"Sure." Raven looked at Kitt and frowned. "Unless *she's* had enough."

"Of course we'll take a look," Kitt said nonchalantly, trying not to let his little barb sting.

Why is he so pissed with me?

Raven shifted to his wolf senses as they entered the arena. This place was worse than the library. From the looks of the kill room, there was a definite struggle, with broken over-turned furniture and lots of blood. But in the end, the human had lost, unlike he had earlier that night.

The strong scent of the same pheromones he'd found in the library lingered on the walls and the floor. He followed the smell and it led him to a room across the corridor. Behind an old cupboard was where the killer hid; there, a condensed patch of scent had collected. He had waited here, maybe watching his prey. Raven also caught the fresh, strong scent of lust and sex by that wall, and it was mixed with the lingering odor of a woman's perfume.

"In here," he called out to the others.

Kitt's amber eyes were wide and her face flushed with excitement as she joined him. *God, I love that look on her. It's the same look she had last night, before Oberon's interruption.*

But this time it wasn't for him; the hunt sent color to her cheeks.

"What happened in here?" she asked.

Was it the scent of lust that stoked his desire, or the scent of her? He felt himself responding to Kitt's nearness with a familiar stirring—his hunger for her growing stronger.

Cody's eyes glowed and narrowed. Raven's lust had stimulated the Incubus's hunger as well.

"Raven, what happened here?" Kitt repeated when he didn't respond.

"Uh." He snapped himself out of it, for the time controlling his wayward desires. "The victim had a female in here . . . on that old desk over by the wall, to be precise. And the killer watched them from here, his bloodlust rising."

He concentrated on the perfume and followed it. "The girl left not long after sex, but the boy stayed and moved into the room opposite."

Raven closed his eyes, scenting the air, reading what had happened. "The boy must have sensed the killer as he came in after him. He turned and fought back. A scuffle ensued. But eventually the killer overpowered and disabled the human."

"Can you tell if the killer was human or not?" Cody asked, writing notes on a small pad.

"Usually, yes," he said and frowned. "There's something different about this scent, though, like several meshing into one, nothing identifiable." He'd never come across anything like it before in all his years as a tracker.

"The killer wasn't wearing shoes but wasn't barefoot either. Look. Another smudged bloody footprint here has nothing definable," Kitt said.

"The scene has been fully documented and photographed; let's get this info to Tones," Cody announced.

This killer enjoyed his work and he wouldn't stop. Raven hoped everyone had strong stomachs, because he had the feeling the body count was about to rise.

16

Lovers Lost

"Where's everyone?" Kitt asked Tones as they walked into the nearly deserted Bunker.

"Huh?" He looked up from the computer screen and glanced around, amazed. "Um, I don't know. I've been working."

"I got some more data for you," Cody said, sitting on the chair next to him. They soon had their bent heads together, going over the notes in Cody's notebook.

Kitt rubbed the tension knots in the back of her neck. The last few days had been more than eventful. All the talk of bloody violence freeing an imprisoned race that sounded like demons from hell had taken its toll.

She was tired, sore, and hungry, and didn't feel like returning to her cold apartment alone. As if reading her mind, Raven came up behind her and started working on the knots with sure, strong yet gentle hands. She dropped her head forward and moaned—his fingers knew exactly where she needed them to go.

Raven leaned forward, his lips close to her ear. "Why don't you let me cook you something to eat? Oberon's stocked the kitchen."

She could really do with some protein to help build her strength, and her growling stomach answered for her.

He chuckled low and seductive against her hair. "I take it that's a yes?"

The other two seemed caught up in the computer screen.

Raven left her in the kitchen and disappeared to change. She walked around opening cupboards and looking in drawers. She was constantly amazed by this place. It had everything that was needed. When Raven returned, he wore combat pants and a tank top, all in black, and was barefoot. She loved him barefoot.

"I wonder how Oberon got this place set up so well," she said. "It must've taken some time to get it all fitted out."

"It used to belong to a black-ops team disbanded years back."

"How do you know?" she asked.

"Heard rumors in the service." He pulled some meat from the refrigerator and ripped at the plastic covering.

"You told me Seph wanted to go into the service as a tracker. She seemed fairly capable last night— Did you train both her and Cal?"

He looked at her then. "I wanted them to be able to protect themselves should anything happen."

"I want to show Oberon what they can do." If he was going to recruit students to the cause, maybe Seph could be one of them. What she'd seen of the girl's talent last night would be a shame to waste, especially on something she didn't want to do. Kitt placed her hand on his forearm and stepped closer. "Trust me."

He turned the meat over in the pan. His muscles flexed under her fingers.

A sudden need clenched her stomach. The past few days of serial killers, dreniacs, and demons made everything else seem insignificant for the moment. An Animalian could not exist on protein alone—there was something else she needed to feed, and she'd been ignoring her physical appetites for far too long.

Watching him work, she realized how much she needed him to make love to her like he used to. She needed the contact, the touch of him, to soothe the beastly desire, if only to relive the carefree days of their love affair for a few short hours.

She stepped closer and ran her fingers up his bare arm, over bunched, corded muscle, over smooth, supple skin. But it wasn't enough to touch him with the tips of her fingers; she needed to feel him with her entire palm. His hand stilled above the meat, the fork he used to turn the steaks trembling.

She reached down, turned off the stove, and stood on tiptoes to kiss lips that tasted of green forests and wild mushrooms. He dropped the fork into the pan and gathered her against him—deepening the kiss to consume her very soul, it would seem.

"Take me to your room," she whispered.

He pulled back, his gaze searching her eyes.

"I'm not promising anything more than just *now*."

He swung her into his arms. "I'll take it." He kissed her again. "For *now*."

She wrapped her arms around his neck, clinging to him as he carried her to his room.

He kicked the door open and she looked inside. It was identical to the one she'd woken in this morning, with a single bed, chair, dresser, and very little else. Spartan and martial.

He dropped her feet to the floor and took her face in his hands. "Do you know how long I've waited for this?"

She answered. "Far too long."

He smiled and nodded. His eyes searched hers, drinking in her face. His fingertips brushed her earlobes and caressed her jaw.

"I feel like I'm dreaming and any moment I'll wake and find you gone." His hot breath brushed her lips, leaving her wanting more.

"I'm here," she whispered back.

He touched his lips in turn to each of her eyelids, kissed her forehead, her cheeks, the tip of her nose, and finally her mouth.

No man knew her as Raven did—no man got to see the part of her she kept only for him. She'd had other lovers, but she kept them at a distance. And for the first time in years, she relaxed.

Kitt dropped her hands to his waist, pushing her thumbs through the side belt loops of his jeans. He moved to her throat, and she tilted her head back, giving him greater access as he trailed burning, feverish kisses along her collarbone. His skin smelled so good, so familiar—the earthy wildness of woods mixed with the warmth of a still summer night. Her breath caught as he nipped the skin where her shoulder met her neck—and she couldn't have stopped the moan if she'd wanted to.

He chuckled against her skin. "I remember how much that used to drive you crazy."

She let go of his jeans and dug her fingers into his shirt. He continued to snag her skin gently with his teeth. Their familiarity drove her to a new level of confidence. Memories of Raven making love to her on a carpet of fall leaves or under the waterfall where they used to swim flashed through her mind.

She pushed him down onto the chair and unzipped his fly. Freeing his erection from the confines of the jeans, she ran it through her hands, his skin silky smooth under her fingers, and brushed the tip of one finger across the swollen head.

She stood, slipped off her panties and straddled him, then stopped to look at him, savoring the moment.

They locked eyes, the tip kissing her opening. She wanted to watch his face as he entered her, wanted to breathe in the air that left his lips. She pushed down, and he filled her perfectly.

Oh God.

His eyes softened as they fell to her mouth. He pulled her face to his and snagged her lower lip, sucking it between his teeth, nibbling it. She rose up and down slowly, and he let loose her lip for a brief second as he gasped. She rocked back and forth. The pressure was building fast. It was going to be over quickly. She could feel him rising to meet her and she could tell he was close by the change in his rhythm. Then he stopped kissing her, and held her face inches away from his.

"I want to watch your face as you come," he whispered.

His voice sent her over the edge. The orgasm started hard in her groin and spread to her limbs, making every nerve in her body tingle. He pulled her close again so their foreheads touched, breathing out hard followed by a short intake of air and then out again—once, twice, and then a long low moan and he shuddered with his release as the tremors of her orgasm rippled to a stop.

She wrapped her arms around his neck and burrowed into his shoulder. Both were panting hard and unable to speak for some time.

Finally he stood up with her in his arms and looked at her. "Round two," he said, carrying her to the thin military-issue cot.

She was not about to argue.

Kitt had known Raven a long time, but there was still so much she didn't *really* know about him. When they were together before, it'd been about sex and secrecy. They didn't talk much about themselves, their hopes or dreams or the future.

Kitt traced the black tribal tattoo on his left pectoral muscle. He'd had it as long as she knew him.

"Does this have meaning?" she asked.

The dragons—one in black, the other in negative—lay head-to-tail in a yin and yang style.

He raised his head, watching her fingers. "It's just something from my past."

"And this?" She traced the scar across his eye that could only have been made with silver.

"Yep, that too."

Kitt could see he wasn't about to tell her anything more.

"You've never told me about your past." She came up onto her elbow beside him. "Why not?"

He reached up and traced the edge of her face with his fingertips. "Because until I met you I was damaged and had no past worth remembering. You saved me. And our children gave me a reason to be."

"To be what?"

"Alive." He kissed her cheek.

He avoided her questions, kept her out. And she remembered how he'd done the same, even back then. Suddenly she remembered there were bad times as well as good—bad times that left her alone. She'd lost her husband, her children, *and* her lover.

"I'd better go and see what they've found out," she said.

"Stay," he whispered and pulled her down to meet his lips.

She melted against him again, her free will dissipating. She could think of nothing but his lips on hers, his hands running down her body, his hardness growing against her stomach.

"Has anyone seen Kitt?" she heard Tones asking outside the door.

"No, why?" That was Cody.

"I think I've found something," Tones said.

"Maybe Raven's seen her," Cody said as a knock sounded at the door.

"Shh!" She put her finger to her lips and broke away to gather her clothing before making a run for the bathroom.

Raven was pulling on his pants as she closed the door behind her.

She slipped into her panties and clipped her bra into place, then buttoned her shirt and tucked it hastily into the skirt before doing up the zipper. She looked at herself in the mirror, at her flushed cheeks and glowing skin. She padded her face with cold water.

Kitt opened the bathroom door to find Raven sitting on the edge of the bed.

"Raven," she said, searching for something to say, "I . . . ah . . ."

She didn't want to give him the wrong idea about what had just happened between them.

"Don't say it." He stood up, jeans still unbuttoned, his torso bare and no shoes. "It was just a thanks-for-the-memories fuck, wasn't it?"

She couldn't look at him and dropped her eyes. "What we had was great twenty years ago, and what we just did was fantastic, but it doesn't change anything. The girls need one of us there. I must get accepted back into the Pride to protect them. For that to happen, we can't be together."

"Why not?" he said, anger flashing in his midnight eyes. "I turned my back on my Pack years ago when I chose our daughters. Your family abandoned you, kicked you out, dropped you like yesterday's garbage." Instant regret crossed his face. He stepped forward and reached for her. "I'm sorry, I didn't mean that."

"Yes, you did." She backed away from him. "I miss my family and my home, and I want to go back."

His eyes flashed with pain as she yanked open the bathroom door and slammed it behind.

What had started out as something amazing had ended by leaving a foul taste in her mouth, and she was the shit who had caused it.

Raven was nowhere to be seen when she finished fixing herself and left his room. She made her way back down to the office.

Antoinette pushed out the slow, controlled Tai Chi movement. Raven came into the workout room without seeing her and struck at the punching bag several times before tearing it from the ceiling, and kicking it across the room.

"I think it's dead," she said as he was walked over to stand above the torn equipment, fists clenched.

He turned on her, eyes blazing and teeth bared. His eyes closed for a second and his hunched shoulders loosened as he stood straighter. She knew that expression, had it herself many times when the hunger came upon her, but he seemed to have little trouble reining in the beast.

"Sorry. I didn't mean to destroy the bag. I just had to hit something. Hard." His face and shoulders relaxed further.

"Do you want to spar with me? I could use the practice."

"I don't think so." He turned toward the door and started walking.

"Afraid of getting beat by a girl?" She placed her hands on her hips.

He stopped but didn't turn around.

"Come on, I'm a trained Venator and Aeternus female. I doubt you could really hurt me."

Raven threw her a look over his shoulder, an amused glint in his eye. "Okay, little girl. But don't say I didn't warn you." He pulled his long dark hair back and tied it with an elastic band he wore on his wrist.

Antoinette took a moment to admire the view. As he

claimed the mat, he rolled his head and his shoulders and shook out his arms. He fell into a stance, feet apart and knees bent. She didn't let him get too comfortable and flew at him, intent on driving her knee into his solar plexus. By the time she reached where he stood, she hit thin air. The next thing she knew, she was staring up at the ceiling as he swept her feet from under her.

She knew he was good, but he was still in human form, with hardly any of his enhanced abilities. How could he possibly match her Aeternus speed? Okay—she'd underestimated him that time.

Not again.

They fell back into their stance facing each other off. This time she'd wait for him. But he didn't move. After nearly a minute she could take it no more and attacked. He blocked her punch with practiced ease, and then twisted her arm behind her. The only thing that hurt was her pride.

The tinkling chime of her cell broke the tension and he let her go so she could answer it.

It was Tones. "We have reports of a male and female matching the dreniac and Marvella. They are down by the homeless camp."

"On my way," she said.

"So I guess the sparring session is over," Raven said. "Just as well. I think you were just about to beat the shit out of me."

Not a freaking chance in hell. "You better believe it, buddy," she said, grinning, yet she got the distinct impression he was toying with her. "Though, I want a rematch."

"Okay," he said with a smile. "Next time."

"Yeah . . . next time."

Cody looked up sharply as Kitt entered the room. His eyes sparked and narrowed, his nostrils flared, and he licked his lips.

To avoid his intense examination, she bent to look at the computer screen. "Find anything?"

"I think we have." Tones looked from the image of a body already stitched up post-autopsy and smiled. "This is the second body, from the library. I have blown it up as much as the image resolution will allow, and you can just make out the marks."

She peered closer and frowned. "I don't see anything."

"Here, let me help," Tones said, clicking a few buttons.

Red slashes matching the marks found on the third body overlaid the photo.

Oh my God.

"Turn the lines off," she said waving her hand at the screen. Tony complied.

The result was unmistakable. She could even see it clearly now without the enhancement. Above the mark of the Dark Brethren was the second symbol carved into his chest before he died—but because of his Bestiabeo abilities, it healed beyond visibility. Well, almost.

"What about the first body?" she asked.

"That one's trickier," Cody said. "He must have survived longer. Show her Tones."

A few keystrokes later and another image appeared, and he made the red lines appear again.

This time there were not many strokes that could possibly correspond.

"You think it's possible that was once the same symbol?" she asked Cody.

Tones placed the symbol over the marks and they seemed to fit. "I'd say in all likelihood it is but can't be conclusive."

The outer door slid open behind, but they were all too intent on the screen to look around.

"I agree," said Cody. "Maybe it's there because we want to see it, maybe it's real. Who knows?"

"Who knows what?" Oberon asked.

Cody straightened. "We think other bodies also had the symbol carved into their chest."

"Send them to me in an email. I'll be in my office," Oberon said and walked away.

Tones jotted down something on a notepad and Kitt noticed a small double yin-yang dragon symbol in the corner.

She took the pad from Tones and looked at it closer. "Where did you get this from?"

Tones glanced up at her half preoccupied. "I found it with some old stationery back in the storage room. Why?"

"Nothing," she said and followed Oberon into his office.

"Do you know what this is?" she asked.

He looked up as she closed the door. "I can see you've finally put two and two together."

"Raven's tattoo?"

He nodded and leaned back in his seat, with hands behind his head; the chair groaned under the pressure.

"Are you going to tell me what it means?" she asked.

"The Draconus Nocti was a team of Department-trained assassins and covert-ops agents set up during World War I to be dropped behind enemy lines. They were active through all the wars including the cold war until they disbanded around twenty years ago. This was a real bunker, and used to be their headquarters."

"Trained assassins," she said, falling into the chair opposite. "And they broke up before we met. No wonder he said he was damaged." She looked at the ursian, suddenly afraid. "Apparently he's trained the twins to defend themselves. I thought that meant a little kung fu or something. What if he's been teaching them to kill?"

"If he trained them that well, then who better to start training those new recruits?" Oberon said. "Why do you think I want him involved? His skills as a covert operative are invaluable. You don't survive that long on luck alone."

She could see his mind ticking over. "If we catch the real killer, my father would have to remove the bounty. He'd be in the clear."

"Only if we can prove the killer is the same one who murdered Emmett," Oberon added. "Though, now knowing his past, and from what I've seen of Emmett's case file, it was rather messy for a man of his talents."

She sighed and slid in her seat, the worry over what Raven had taught the girls gnawing away.

"Well," he said, "if you really want to know, ask him. But I'd still like to put the girls through their paces and see what they can do. I'll get Antoinette to set it up."

Cody burst through the door. "There's been another body found. This time at a Web design place that hired NYAPS students."

17

murder most Bloody

Raven stretched in the night air. He was going stir crazy and had to get out for a run, especially after what had just happened with Kitt. The attempt by the Aeternus to take him on had only exacerbated his need to get out of there.

He hadn't had time to put on any Abeolite, just wanted a run. He stood in the park slipping out of his jeans, then hung them on a tree branch and willed the change. His body spread, contracted, and popped into place. It was never like those old horror movies: his muscles didn't tear apart, there was no pain, and it didn't take nearly as long as they made it look. But the movies were all about effect, not truth.

His wolf form was as much a part of him as his human one. Raven threw back his head and let the wolf cry of freedom float into the night air before loping off into the woods. Once off the campus grounds, he decided to do a bit of exploring in the nearby urban areas. As he came to one street, a white cat rose up and hissed. It was time to get back at another feline by having a little fun with this one. It ran off down an alley and he gave chase.

He did not intend to catch or actually hurt the cat, but a nip or two on the tail every now and then kept the small animal on its toes. The feline seemed to know it was just a game and never got too far ahead.

As the cat tracked out onto another street, Raven came to a dead stop and lifted his head, scenting the air. The dark corruption of fresh blood filled his nostrils. The cat jumped up on a brick wall, its tail flicking back and forth; it began cleaning its front paw and pretending not to watch him.

Raven loped to the nearby Dumpster where the scent grew stronger. It wasn't enough to be a full body, only part of it—and the person who'd dropped it there had gotten into a vehicle and driven away, but not long ago. He didn't want to disturb the forensics just in case, so he left whatever it was undisturbed. He could call it in to the police and let them handle it. But first, he needed to follow this trail to the source in case someone was in need of help.

Raven tracked the scent across the street and down another alley. As well as the blood, he could distinguish traces of terror, and adrenaline. It grew stronger the further he went. He continued tracking the scent to a back door that stood open, and he scurried inside to investigate. The blood was strong and not long spilled, but it was dead blood. Whomever it belonged to was no longer living.

Wait. Two kinds.

He padded into a room filled with computers, following a new scent. An eerie bluish light flooded the room from glowing LCD screens. The body of a young girl lay slumped against the table in front of a computer, her head on her outstretched arm; her eyes stared off to nowhere and an ugly yawning gash split her lovely throat. Blood had pooled on the table and the keyboard was sitting in the middle of the tacky puddle. Arterial spray had sliced across the computer screen, slightly cooking on the hardware's heat.

It looked like she'd been sitting at the computer working when the killer snuck up behind and slit her throat. Raven returned to human form to examine the body as much as he could without touching her. The chest was intact, she had no other wounds he could see, and her blood wasn't the blood he'd started following. Hers was sweeter, more innocent. *She never knew what hit her.* There was movement in the next room, familiar footsteps stomping as they moved around.

"In here," he called and stood up.

Oberon appeared in the doorway within seconds.

"What are you doing here, Fido?" The ursian crossed his arms and looked at the slumped figure.

"I was about to ask you the same thing."

The canian was standing next to what looked like another body, and was completely naked. Oberon's gaze fell to the yin-and-yang dragon tattoo on his chest—the mark of a Draconus Nocti operative.

"Can I see the body, please?" Kitt said as she tried to squeeze past Oberon. She came up dead when she noticed Raven.

"You've found the other body?" Raven asked, tilting his head.

"Yes—in the other room," Oberon said, not surprised. "But how did you know?"

"This is not the campus killer; this is something else," Raven said. "I tracked it from a couple of blocks over. You might find in the alley what it was she threw away; it's in the Dumpster."

"*She?*"

"I detected estrogen in the nervous sweat." Raven moved out of the way so Kitt could examine the body. "She's either human or pre-awakened, though I tend to think the former."

Kitt pulled the girl's head from the sticky pool of blood covering the table. The gaping wound in the neck yawned wider as the head tilted back.

"So, you don't think it's the same killer?" Oberon asked, knowing Kitt had just told him a spreader was used to open the rib cage.

"I'm positive it's not," Raven said, peering closer. "There're no traces of the pheromones found at the other kill sites, only the terrified sweat of someone who's killed, but not for pleasure."

Raven glanced around at the banks of computers. "What is this place?"

"It's kind of a Web sex sweatshop dressed up as a software company," Oberon said. "The owner, Carin Engels, employed several students from the campus on a part-time basis." He looked at the naked canian, up and down again.

"One second," Kitt said and disappeared, then came back a few minutes later with his knee-length leather coat and a pair of pants. "Tones had these in his car."

"We discovered you were gone after the call came in," Oberon said.

He glanced up at them as he finished zipping his fly. "Call?"

"Yes, someone phoned in an anonymous tip." Oberon frowned. "A woman, in fact."

"That's never happened before," Raven said. "Could be our killer."

"Hmmm, interesting theory, but I think I'll wait for the proof first. You'd better come see the other body, or should I say bodies? . . . I think you'll be interested in one." Oberon crossed his arms.

"Right," Raven said, frowning. "Let's take a look, then."

"Are you okay here, Kitt?"

She nodded to Oberon and waved them off, already focused on her task.

Raven pulled on the coat Kitt had given him as Oberon led the way to the next office. Raven's face screwed up when he saw the body of a bird on the floor, its neck broken and black feathers scattered everywhere. It could've been a crow or a raven, Oberon couldn't tell, but the look on the canian's face was worth it.

"Very funny." Raven sneered, then bent to have a look at the body.

Oberon stepped closer for another look. Her dark brown hair lay in a pool of congealing blood. Kitt came in just as Tez entered, carrying her M.E. case. The two women greeted each other and began an animated discussion.

Tez looked good. *Real good.* Oberon couldn't remember exactly how long since they'd been together, but it'd been a while. Maybe too long. She was still pissed at him for standing her up the last time he'd had to follow a lead.

Bianca came into the room next, her pale face hardening when she saw the body on the floor.

She glanced up at Oberon, then back to the body.

"Did you know her?" he asked.

"Only by reputation," Bianca replied. "It was rumored she dabbled in a little gray thaumaturgy to make her business more successful."

"Gray thaumaturgy?" Raven asked, standing up.

Bianca's gaze traveled up and down Raven and then flicked to Oberon, raising a questioning eyebrow.

He gave her a slight nod.

"Gray thaumaturgy uses the practitioner's own blood. While it's not exactly black magic, it isn't exactly white either. There are no human sacrifices or the use of unborn fetuses, but it can involve some animal parts and other unsavory practices. Not exactly illegal, but a very fine line."

Oberon's eyes never left Tez; he watched as she followed Antoinette into the other room.

"So is it him?" Bianca asked.

"No!" Raven said at the exact time Oberon muttered, "Possibly!" They looked at each other.

Kitt showed Tez the body next to the computer. The M.E.'s raven hair spilled over her shoulder as she leaned in for a closer look.

"She was killed quickly," Tez said. "And there are no symbols that I can see either."

Kitt agreed and said, "I think her throat was cut before she even knew what hit her."

Tez straightened and stood from her crouched position beside the body. "Poor fecken kid."

"I'll show you the other victim if we can get that lot in there to move out of the way." Kitt led the medical examiner back to where the others were still gathered.

Tez stopped and looked at the twisted little feather body beside the dead witch. "Why kill the bird?"

"So the witch couldn't use her magic," Bianca said with more than a touch of something akin to sadness or regret. "She'd be powerless until she bonded with another familiar."

The ethereally pale Thaumaturgist stood away from

the body and absently fiddled with the red-and-black egg-shaped pendent hanging around her neck.

"Right . . ." Oberon said, breaking the melancholy mood. "Time to see if the victim has the wound in the back of her neck."

Tez and Kitt crouched on either side of the body and turned the dead witch. The skin was still slightly warm.

There was the wound, but it seemed a little too messy. Kitt looked up at the others waiting intently for the verdict and shrugged. "Hard to say until an autopsy."

"Shit," Oberon spat. "All right, we'll let the forensic boys in to do the rest of their job. You okay with that, Tez?"

The medical examiner stood up and placed her hands on her hips. "Feck, yes."

They were such an odd couple in some ways, and yet so perfect in others, Kitt thought. The top of Tez's head barely reached the center of Oberon's chest—and yet she had an outsized personality that would take none of his crap.

"We'll take over from here, DuPrie." The VCU agent-in-charge sauntered into the room in a dark gray suit and mirrored shades.

What the hell was with the sunglasses at night? Roberts is human.

Raven glanced at the agent and quickly pulled back into the shadows. Roberts was so intent on the dead body, he hadn't seemed to notice him.

Oberon crossed his arms, the leather of his jacket creaking. "I was wondering when the smell of carrion would draw you out, Roberts."

He ignored Oberon and signaled his men with a wave of his hand. They filed in carrying equipment and cases for forensic analysis. "I can't stop your people being involved in the autopsy, but we still have jurisdiction over the crime site."

Oberon's expression darkened like the sky before a winter storm. Kitt could almost hear the rumble of thunder.

"Okay, Dr. O'Connor"—the agent swept his suit jacket aside and placed his hand on his hip, then whipped off his mirrored sunglasses—"is this our guy or not?"

The man had obviously been watching too many TV cop shows. Kitt looked at Tez; the corner of the M.E.'s lips curled as she stifled her own smile.

Tez went all serious-faced as she turned to the agent. "It's too early to tell, but there are similar markers."

"Hmm." The agent turned his back on them. "I want everyone not VCU out of here."

None of Oberon's people moved.

"DuPrie, don't make me call in the heavies." Agent Roberts put the arm of his sunglasses to his lips.

Oberon gave a nod and Kitt followed Bianca through the door and out of the building, the ursian right behind. Kitt could hear the heavy clomping of his boots on the floorboards. Bright lights zeroed in and camera flashes went off as the group left the building. Kitt shielded her eyes with her hand.

The reporter Trudi Crompton stood before them, microphone in hand. "Can you please confirm the latest body is a woman?"

Oberon held up his hands. "Sorry, you will have to direct all your inquiries to the head of VCU, Agent Roberts." Then he pushed past her and the rest of the reporters to join his people waiting by the ambulance. EMTs were racing inside the building with stretchers to collect the bodies.

"This is turning into a circus," Oberon said as he approached.

"I saw VCU," Cody said. "How did it go?"

"We had a good look at the scene before they arrived and got some good insights." Oberon glanced around the gathering crowd. "What about out here—did you sense anyone who might have been involved?"

"The tension in the air is what you'd expect," Cody said. "But I'd rather talk about it when we get back to the Bunker. By the way, Raven stopped by and had me grab some surgical gloves and a plastic bag off one of the EMTs. He said to tell you he would pick that little something up on the way home."

"Good point," Oberon said. "Let's wait for the bodies to come out so we can see about the autopsies."

Kitt watched the faces in the crowd. Most were confused and shocked. But they were also terrified. The killer had struck again—this time, outside all expectations. Everyone was waiting in silence to see what was going to happen with the bodies.

A buzz went up in the media as Agent Roberts exited the building. He put on his sunglasses as the reporters started snapping pictures.

"Now I know why he needs those glasses," Kitt said.

"Gobshite," Oberon said, borrowing one of Tez's favorite words.

"Is this the work of the same killer?" the tenacious Ms. Crompton asked.

A stream of questions followed. The throng of journalists and cameramen was so focused on Roberts that Tez was able to slip past and join the team.

Agent Roberts was in his glory. "At this point I think I can safely say we are looking at the same killer."

Oberon spat on the ground and glared at the well-dressed agent as he preened before the cameras.

Another string of questions swelled as the press crowded closer to the agent.

"What?" Kitt said and turned to Tez.

She shook her head. "Don't look at me. All I said was the markers possibly indicated the same killer, but there were some discrepancies and we would need an autopsy to confirm it. If he ends up looking like an idiot, not my problem."

"Oh, Tez, you're evil," Oberon said. "And I love it."

"No," the agent continued, "I don't know why he's started killing outside the campus or why the murders are escalating—however, this business did employ many students from NYAPS. We will have an official statement for you once our medical examiner has performed her examination."

As he finished, the EMTs wheeled out the two stretchers, each bearing a black zipped body bag. Again, the press went into a frenzy of flashing cameras.

As Tez grabbed Kitt's hand, she said, "I'll ride with the bodies. See you at the morgue?"

"Sure," Kitt said. "I'll catch a lift with Oberon."

* * *

Raven waited in the Bunker for them to return. Only Kitt didn't come back with them.

"So do you have a death wish?" Oberon asked.

"Not really." Raven kept it cool. "Where's Kitt?"

"I dropped her at the morgue." Oberon's face thundered. Raven could see he was struggling to keep his temper in check, and thought of giving him his little present. Raven got up and retrieved a plastic baggie from the small-drinks refrigerator kept in the office and placed it on the desk in front of the big male.

"I retrieved this from the Dumpster."

Oberon picked it up by the top and looked at the bloody clump of human heart inside. "We've never found the heart before."

"Like I keep saying, it's not the same guy," Raven replied.

"He could be right," Cody said. "The emotions I sensed from the crowd were mixed. There were the usual anger, fear, and terror, but also hate and a sense of relief. I interviewed a few of her employees in the crowd. Seems like she wasn't that well liked. In fact, from what I could gather, she used to bully her employees and would often single out one to pick on until he or she either quit or was too stressed to perform and was fired. Then she would move on to the next."

"Hmm, doesn't follow our normal victim pattern in any way." Oberon frowned and scratched his goatee. "Let's see what Kitt comes up with in the autopsy."

"Check this out," Tones said and hit a button on the remote that turned on the large LCD screen.

Trudi Crompton was reporting from outside the medical examiner's office, and again Agent Roberts was her interviewee.

"What are your theories on this case?" Trudi asked.

The agent turned to the camera.

"Did he just do a head flick?" Tones asked. "I can't believe he just did a head flick."

Raven couldn't stop himself from chuckling along with the rest but leaned forward to listen to what the head of VCU had to say.

"Well, Trudi, I don't want to preempt the medical examiner's findings, but I suspect what we have here is the work of a satanic cult, possibly dark witchcraft." And then his lips parted and stretched into a for-TV smile showing off his perfectly straight, white teeth. *"My men are cracking down on any and all such groups as we speak."*

The footage cut away to a team of black-uniformed men crashing through the door of a thaumaturgical sorority, grabbing screaming and terrified young witches out of their beds or away from their studies.

Oberon spun, his dreadlocks whipping through the air as he slammed his fist into the wall. The sound of cracking bones filled the room and a crater was left in the plaster as he pulled back a misshapen fist. The ursian shook out his hand, flexing it as the metatarsals popped back into place and healed.

Raven sympathized. He'd used pain in the past to control rage, though he'd try to direct it on things that could take it, like punching bags.

"What a drop-kick," Cody said.

"A what?" Tones asked.

"It's an Australian term for idiot, moron, or ass-wipe," Raven said, keeping his eyes on the screen.

"Yeah—what a drop-kick," Tones said and grinned as he and Cody knocked knuckles.

More images filled the screen—this time the raid of a Goth club, confused screams, and outraged objections were heard from the patrons being bundled into waiting VCU paddy wagons.

"You got that right," Oberon said with a groan. His hand was almost fully mended; just because Animalians healed quicker, it didn't lessen the pain.

The screen filled with the faces of Trudi and Agent Roberts again.

"That reporter chick is fairly creaming her pants over this killer," Cody said. "She sees it as a career maker."

"We hope to soon have some hard evidence, to put a stop to these gruesome killings once and for all." Agent Roberts smiled widely into the cameras again.

"You'd think he'd try being a little less cheerful considering the subject matter," Tones said.

"Whatya expect—he's a wanker, pure and simple," Cody
said and the two of them knocked knuckles again.

Oberon barked with laughter.

Raven came to his feet. "If you have a moment, Oberon,
can I talk to you in your office?"

The ursian sobered and stood up, slapping Raven on the
shoulder. "Sure, come this way."

Raven closed the door to Tones's and Cody's laughter and
turned to Oberon, not really sure where to start.

"What's on your mind?" Oberon leaned back in his chair.

Raven stood with his hands behind his back, looking up
and straight ahead. "I want to resurrect the Draconus Nocti."

The ursian's eyebrows rose and he leaned forward. "Well,
you certainly don't beat around the bush, do you?"

"I don't think we have time for that"—Raven dropped his
eyes to meet Oberon's—"do you?"

"No, I guess we don't." The ursian looked hard at him
for a moment, then lowered his gaze to his hands clasped
in front of him. "Do you know how to get in touch with the
others?"

"A couple." They were a hard, ruthless bunch and Raven
would only bring back a select few. "But I don't want to go
back to old ways either. We need new blood."

This time only one of Oberon's eyebrows went up. "Like
the twins?"

18

DRACONUS NOCTI

Antoinette took her seat in the conference room across the table from Raven. Kitt came in with Oberon a few minutes later and pulled up just inside the door for the briefest of seconds, then she moved into the room.

The first of the autopsy photos appeared on the screen in gruesome color. "On past victims we found that the wound was started with a knife and ripped the rest of the way." Kitt ran a finger along the image. "These edges are too precise to be anything but a blade."

She dragged a picture in from the side to replace the current shot. Just as well. Antoinette wasn't squeamish. The open chest cavity was a mess.

"Here and here are marks on the bone to indicate a rib spreader was used to open the chest—a major inconsistency. We also found a couple of long blond hairs caught in one of the grooves. Then there was the method of disablement—the one thing we have kept out of the press. This victim appeared to be disabled in the same way, but on closer inspection . . ."

She pulled the next image in from the side with her finger. The screen filled with a close-up of the back of the victim's neck.

Kitt reached out and pointed to the gash. "This wound is a lot less precise than the others. While placement is almost correct, it occurred postmortem and the dimensions of the blade are inconsistent; however, the main thing that screams copycat is the absence of the Dark Brethren or any other symbols."

"So if not our killer, it's someone who knows almost all of the gruesome details," Antoinette said, leaning forward. "Could we have a leak?"

"Maybe," Oberon mused. "Raven thinks the assailant was female."

Cody, looking like a model out of a surfer catalogue, stood up with a small notepad in his hands. "I might have some insight into that."

Antoinette settled back in her chair.

"From what I've gathered so far, Carin Engels was an office psychopath. She would bully and pick on her employees, play favorites, then play them off against each other.

"Why?" Tones was asking what everyone seemed to be thinking.

"Psychopaths are all about power. They get their kicks by psychologically destroying others. I've done some digging and there was someone Ms. Engels currently targeted. This girl, the latest in a long line of victims, was at the scene, but she managed to evade me every time. And she was a blonde."

"Excellent. Why don't you and Bianca go have a chat with this girl," Oberon said.

"Right on it," Cody said, putting his little notebook into his pocket.

"The rest of you keep working on your assigned task."

The ursian glanced at Antoinette and Kitt. "Can I speak to the two of you in my office before you go?" His eyes flicked to Raven, who gave him a discreet nod.

Oberon held the door and closed it after them before moving to his side of the desk. "I've been thinking about the twins and what we discussed earlier," he said to Kitt. "And I think you're right."

"Good, so you'll evaluate them?" Kitt asked.

He nodded. "I'm going to get Antoinette to put them through their paces."

Antoinette felt totally lost. "What the hell are you two talking about?"

"Have you ever heard of the Draconus Nocti?" Oberon asked.

"They're just a myth, a conspiracy," Antoinette said, but the look on their faces told a different story. "Aren't they?"

"Not exactly." Oberon stood up and pulled a folder from the filing cabinet, then threw it on the desk in front of her. "They were elite covert soldiers for CHaPR—totally off-the-books black-ops."

On the front of the folder was a yin-and-yang double-dragon symbol. Antoinette had seen it somewhere before, but couldn't exactly pinpoint when and where. Inside listed the operations performed by the team, which were not only impressive but downright scary. The list of dead agents was even scarier.

"So who do you want me to evaluate?" Antoinette asked, still not sure where this was leading.

"My daughters," Kitt said.

"But according to this file, the group was disbanded nearly twenty years ago. What's it got to do with them?" Antoinette asked, confused.

Oberon sat back to take a folder from his draw, glancing at Kitt before handing it over to Antoinette. "This is a file on the Draconus Nocti's top operative."

Antoinette opened the file on an agent, code name Black Wolf, and Kitt craned over her shoulder. The stats on this agent were impressive: 1,493 successful missions and an indeterminate number of enemy kills all happening over a sixty-year period that included several wars. And his skills were also remarkable: sharpshooter, assassin, and tracker just to name a few. Then she turned to the photo of a man in an army uniform.

"Oh my God." Kitt exhaled the words.

His hair was short but there was no mistaking those eyes. *Raven.* The Black Wolf.

That's where she'd seen the symbol before—Raven's tattoo. She knew he'd been holding back. And no wonder—he was lethal on legs, and probably off legs as well.

Antoinette looked up at Kitt. "Okay. When and where?"

Kitt walked to her car in the predawn darkness. It'd been a long night and she just wanted to get home, have a long soak in the tub, and fall into bed. She hit the unlock button on her keys, the taillights flashed. As she reached out for the handle, she got a sudden impulse to open her door, jump in, slam it shut and get the hell out of there. Her skin tingled, her scalp crawled, and she had the distinct impression of being watched.

The parking lot was almost empty—a couple of cars, a pickup truck, and a big black SUV. Nothing moved even when she flicked her eyes to felian vision. She was out of touch with many of her Bestiabeo instincts and was probably just being paranoid. But every nerve in her body jangled like an alarm bell going off.

Kitt climbed in behind the wheel and tried to jab the key into the ignition, but missed. Her hands were shaking so badly, she dropped the keys on the floor. Taking a deep breath, she closed her eyes and slowly released the air from her lungs. This serial killer on the loose had her imagining dangers that probably weren't there. She snagged the keys off the floor with her fingertips and jammed the ignition key in. It wasn't going to start, she just knew it . . . The engine roared into life on the first turn and she sighed, her head falling with relief onto the back of her hands clutching the steering wheel. After another moment, to pull herself together, she reversed the vehicle and drove out of the parking lot.

The early morning bluish gray sky was stained with splashes of pink and orange as she drove toward her apartment building. Kitt glanced up automatically at the rearview mirror, then looked to the road ahead but immediately flicked back to the reflection of a big black SUV with no lights following at a distance.

Was it the same one from the parking lot? She couldn't tell, but wasn't about to take any chances.

At the next intersection, she turned right instead of her

usual left. The SUV turned right too. A couple of streets down and she took a quick left without indicating. Luckily, the roads were nearly deserted.

The SUV turned as well, but still kept its distance. She was pretty sure it was following her now. *Right. Time to lose them.* She hadn't been the sister of an agent without learning a thing or two about driving, if nothing else.

After another right, she floored the accelerator then took the next quick left and a right again before reversing into a one-way lane. Less than a minute later, the black SUV sailed past without noticing her. She immediately backtracked the way she'd come and headed toward home, checking the mirror for any sign of her pursuer.

She parked in her spot near the apartment building and hefted her bag onto her shoulder. A few feet from her building's door, the black SUV pulled alongside and a hulking great lump of a man in dark glasses and a dark suit jumped out and blocked her way.

She recognized him immediately by the close-cropped orange-and-black tiger-striped hair and the Celtic tribal tattoo on his right cheek—one of the Tiger Twins, she couldn't remember which, Jericho or Joshua. They were the only set of rare identical twins in the Pride, until Kitt gave birth.

"Your father wishes to speak with you, Miss Kathryn," he said, his eyes completely hidden behind the dark shades.

"It's Dr. Jordan, and hasn't he ever heard of a telephone?" Trust Tyrone to *summon* her presence like this.

"Sorry, ma'am," he said. "But you'll have to take that up with the Alpha, I'm afraid. Please. Get in the vehicle."

The SUV was the same one that followed her earlier. "Couldn't you just have approached me back at the Academy instead of scaring me half to death?"

The dark glasses made it difficult to gauge his mood, especially with his stony facial expression. "We were only ordered to keep watch over you at that point."

"Keep watch? Why would you need to keep watch?"

"That is also something you must take up with the Alpha"—he waved to the back door he held open—"Now, please, ma'am. Come with us."

She didn't have a choice. If she refused to get in the car, then they would just make sure she got in. She did as was told and after closing the door, he came around the vehicle to get in beside her.

The driver looked in the rearview mirror and gave her a quick-greeting nod before driving off. The identical tattoo to his twin was mirrored on his left cheek. The two brothers sat in silence the entire trip through the city, until they pulled up outside The Plaza. Her father liked the atmosphere of the historic hotel, especially if he wanted to impress. Only she wasn't the one he'd be trying to impress. She was just a blip, an annoyance he had to deal with.

The hotel door attendant opened the SUV door and held out his hand to help her from the vehicle. She climbed the red-carpeted steps and entered the beautiful marble lobby with the Tiger Twins close behind. Last time she was here was to attend the murder of a couple of fang-whores.

The elevator seemed very small as she moved to the back with the Tiger Twins standing in front.

"Wait for the next one," one of the brothers growled as a well-dressed elderly couple tried to enter.

"We can wait a few more minutes." The elderly man pulled his wife back a few steps.

"But, Henry . . ." She started to puff up self-righteously.

"Zip it, Mavis. What's a few more minutes?"

Wise man, Henry. He could obviously tell trouble when he saw it.

Kitt's stomach flipped as the doors closed. It'd been several years since she'd seen her father, and then he'd been angry and disappointed. Not because she'd defied him, but because Dylan had taken her side, forcing him to exile them both. As the Pride Alpha, he could not afford to look weak, and Dylan had been the son he started grooming to take over from him until the exile.

Alpha males had to step down after fifty years to stop the Pride from stagnating under the same leader. Her father's term was almost up; Nathan was out of the question to follow him, given his unfortunate birth. The Pride would never follow an unlucky leader.

The elevator came to a stop and opened. Her heartbeat picked up. Now it was more the excited terror of seeing the male who had sent her away in shame. *Would he still be angry?* She'd soon find out. One of her escorts knocked on the door.

"Come in." She could hear her father's growl through the closed door, and all of a sudden she realized how much she'd missed him.

The door opened from the inside. Several other dark-suited men sat or stood around the opulent suite. All her father's men.

Tyrone Jordan's midnight black hair kissed the collar of his expensive Italian suit as he stood with his hands behind his back, looking out over Central Park. He didn't turn to greet her. Nathan sat on the sofa in pale gray Armani, his legs crossed and sipping tea.

"Hello, Tyrone."

His broad shoulders stiffened slightly, as if he steeled himself to look at her. He turned, his eyes softening for a brief second before hardening and looking away again. She'd forgotten how much Dylan resembled him, and the knot in her chest tightened. Had her father missed her?

At least a little?

"Thank you for coming," he said with a formality he usually reserved for strangers or outsiders.

In a way, she was both.

"It's not like I had a choice," she said, using anger to mask the knife twisting in her heart at his refusal to even look at her.

"I asked you here, Kathryn"—he always used her proper name—"because we have heard about the murders at the campus and have several students attending this year. Do we need to fear for the Pride children's safety?"

Is this all he has to say to me after eighteen years?

She sighed. "We don't know. There are people looking into the deaths, but at this point there are no answers."

"I hear that my s—" He stopped, pain flashed briefly and he blinked it away. "That your brother's former partner is looking into it. Is this correct?"

He was about to say *his son*—he was grieving for Dylan, after all. But the knowledge only made her angrier. He could've acknowledged him if it wasn't for his stupid sense of duty.

"His name is Oberon. Remember? Once you treated him like a son." When Oberon chose to leave along with Kitt and Dylan, he'd left behind his welcome in Pridelands.

Her father's stony silence was the only answer she was going to get.

"Okay, so he's involved," she said.

"She's not telling you everything." Nathan looked over the top of his teacup at her.

Why did her brother hate her so much? "He's head of security at the campus and asked me to consult on a couple of autopsies."

"I want you to find out everything that's going on." Her father walked around behind her.

"I'm not part of his team," she said.

"You have access. If you want back in, prove your loyalty." Tyrone came around to the front, again standing close.

"Okay, but there's a price." She looked at him. "I want some time with my daughters."

"Out of the question," Nathan spat, rising to his feet.

Tyrone leaned in, searching her eyes—looking not only at her but into her. "Done."

"But, sir—" Nathan started to object.

"I said, *done*." Tyrone's voice held such command. "You can have an hour at Nathan's house."

Her brother closed his mouth, and his eyes burned with pure hatred.

"I want two hours, and alone," she said. "No bodyguards and on neutral ground."

For a moment she thought her father would refuse, but then he nodded slowly. He moved away and locked eyes with his son. Something she couldn't read passed between them.

"What can you tell us about the four murders so far?" Tyrone said, his gaze still holding her brother.

"There have been three by the serial killer," she corrected.

His head snapped around, eyebrows raised as he hit her with the full force of his gaze. "How so?"

"The latest killing was a copycat." She felt Nathan's scowl boring into her. It didn't matter what she did or said—while Nathan had any sway, she was never going to be able to convince her father to let her back into the Pride.

"Good," Tyrone said, satisfied, and continued to stare at her as he moved in so close they almost touched. He leaned in over her shoulder, his mouth ending up by her ear. "But you jerk me around on this and you're done."

He knew.

Somehow he knew that the latest killing was a copycat. It was a test. One she'd passed.

"Your mother wishes to see you," he said softly.

Kitt turned her head to him. "How is she?"

"She grieves for the children she's lost." His grief was raw; the naked hurt clouded his blue eyes.

He blamed her. "Father, I—"

The shutters closed; his face grew stony and unreachable as his gaze flicked to the men behind her.

"If you want to see her, you must go with Jericho and Joshua now." He turned and started to walk away. "It's a once-only deal."

The Tiger Twins stepped forward, one taking her gently by the elbow.

I'm going home.

They guided her to the elevator.

I'm going home.

There was only silence in the ride down to the lobby.

I'm going home.

One of the twins nudged her. The elevator doors opened and she stepped forward. She was halfway across the lobby when she was shoved face-first against a marble pillar, smashing open her lip.

"What the *fuck* are you playing at—" Her brother's voice hissed hotly against her cheek.

19

Family Ties

Then his weight was gone. When Kitt turned, Oberon was holding Nathan by the throat. The ursian's eyes flashed with rage, and Nathan's flashed with fear.

Kitt put her hand on Oberon's arm. "Let him go; he's not worth it." She looked at Nathan, then back to Oberon. "You'll have the Jordan pride down on you if you kill him, and I don't want to lose you too."

Oberon pushed her brother backward as the Tiger Twins closed in from either side. Nathan fell onto an armchair that toppled over with the force, and he landed on his back. The tigers held Oberon back by his arms. Nathan climbed to his feet. He dusted off his suit and looked at her with a humorless grin.

With a jerk of his head, he signaled the men to let the ursian go. "It doesn't matter what you do, your daughters belong to us." His grin grew wider. "Belong to *me*. And they *will* learn to respect the pride laws, one way or another."

"If you lay one hand on either of them," she hissed and took a step toward him, "I'll kill you myself."

Oberon dropped a hand on her shoulder to stop her from getting too close. "That goes double for me."

This was one time Kitt didn't mind him being overprotective. Nathan shrugged his shoulders, then spun on his heels and walked away.

"Let's go," Oberon said, taking her elbow and guiding her toward the exit. She could've just kissed him at that moment.

"How did you know I was here?"

He kept walking, not even slowing to look at her. "I had intel your father was in town and my informant here called me as soon as he saw them bring you in."

"You knew he was here and didn't tell me?"

"Yes," he said as he dragged her out the door.

She stopped and yanked her arm out of his hands. "Why?"

"Your family walks a fine line between legal and illegal activities, same as mine"—he placed one hand on the handlebar of his large black Harley-Davidson—"and I like to know where they are when they're in *my* town."

He was right. She knew about the money laundering and that her family dealt with shady characters all the time, and there must be other stuff. Of course Oberon was interested.

The twin brothers stood a short ways off, waiting patiently. With everything that had just happened she'd almost forgot. There was no sign of Nathan.

"Stop," she said. "They're taking me home to see my mother."

"Are you sure?" Oberon asked, watching the felians with suspicion.

"Yes," she said. "I know these men, and while they might step in to save Nathan, they are my father's men. And even with all his dubious activities, you know Tyrone is a man of his word."

The door attendant started to look a little edgy. A seven-foot dreadlocked ursian in black leather on a Harley-Davidson and two almost-as-large tiger felians in expensive suits and wraparound sunglasses were probably enough to make The Plaza's clientele more than a little nervous.

Oberon looked past her. "Maybe I should come with you."

"No, I need to do this on my own. I'll be fine."

Oberon looked about to argue, but then shut his mouth and climbed onto the motorcycle. "All right. Call me when you're coming back and I'll pick you up." He turned to the two males. "Look after her."

The helicopter swept in over the frozen Jordan Lake with the midday sun bravely trying to break through gray winter sky. The land surrounding the renamed body of water had been the Jordan Pridelands ever since the Adirondack reserve was turned into the biggest Bestiabeo reservation in North America, just over a hundred years ago. The resort occupied one end of the lake while the village sat on the opposite side, isolated from the resort visitors. She'd been living in the city since her banishment, and now the desire to run free among the trees of the mountain wilderness filled her with a yearning she'd thought long dead.

The weak shadow of the helicopter grew larger on the pure white snow. The throbbing rotors kicked up a swirling snow flurry, obscuring the elegant red cedar buildings of the resort lodge. The cloud quickly dissipated once they landed to reveal a lone male figure, heavily dressed against the weather, standing beside a company jeep. Behind him rose the exquisite Jordan Pride Lodge, an exclusive resort for the rich and dangerous. But this was not home—this was just the family business.

As the whirling rotors slowed down, her welcome committee of one approached and opened the helicopter door. She began to climb out of the chopper and froze when she looked up at a familiar face, her smile of thanks sliding away.

Leon.

The last person she expected or wanted to see. His smile deepened; he knew that his presence was getting to her. She steeled herself and ignored the hand he offered to help her out. He would not ruin this for her. Not today.

"Hello, bros," he said to the Tiger Twins.

They took turns in greeting their brother by clasping right hands between them as they hugged with thumping backslaps.

Leon led them to the jeep and opened the door for her. "The Primara doesn't know you're coming. Your father didn't want to get her hopes up in case things didn't go right."

"How is she?" Kitt asked, the concern over her mother momentarily overshadowing her hatred for Leon.

"Honestly?" He looked down at her. "She's a shell of what she used to be since your brother's death."

Exactly what she'd been afraid of. A chill skittered across her skin and it was more than just the icy wind blowing down from the mountain through the snow-laden trees. She climbed into the backseat and pulled her coat tighter. Leon walked to the front of the van and slapped something into one of the twins' hands, then leaned in through the door and reached into the back to fish out a thick blanket. "This will keep you warm until we get you to the village."

As he smoothed the blanket over her legs, he locked eyes with hers. His smile twisted as his hand lingered a little too long on her thigh; and no matter how much her skin crawled or his nearness made her want to throw up, she would *not* give him the satisfaction of reacting.

He let out a chuckle and climbed in next to her. Jericho and Joshua got in the front. Joshua, the one with the tattoo on the left side, as she'd finally remembered on the trip up, turned the key in the ignition and Jericho reached down to crank up the heating.

The village was only a few miles from the resort, but the ride seemed to last forever. It'd been nearly twenty years since she'd last seen her mother and now every second that passed seemed too long. She endured Leon's hungry stare, trying hard not to flinch.

"You are looking well," Leon said as the jeep hit a bump in the road.

Joshua's intelligent amber eyes locked with Kitt's in the rearview mirror. He seemed troubled under his heavy brow and broke off to exchange a silent communication with his twin. Jericho tensed and turned around in his seat, watching them. The twins could not be more unlike their older half-brother. While Joshua and Jericho had inherited their tiger mother's genes, Leon had taken to their shared father's lion side.

The Jordan Pride took the three brothers in quite young—the only survivors of a tragic forest fire that wiped out the neighboring Pantella Pride. She had spent many nights crying herself to sleep, wishing the fire had consumed the man sitting next to her too. But as the village came into view, she forgot about him and leaned forward, bracing her hands on the back of the seat in front.

The village was almost invisible among the trees. Perfect for the kind of isolation from the rest of the world the Pride craved. The scent hit strongly, reminding her of her roots. There were a few people on the narrow streets. They all lifted their hands in greeting as they passed, and while Kitt recognized most of them, there were a few new faces.

When they finally reached her mother's house, she suddenly felt dizzy and sick. The house was just the same. Even before leaving Pridelands, she'd moved out to live with Emmett, yet this would always be her childhood home. With shaky hands, she reached for the handle, but Joshua beat her to it and opened the door from the outside.

Her legs were numb as she walked down the drive toward the front door.

"She'll be in the clinic at this time of the day," Leon said.

Of course she would. Her mother was the village Primara, or midwife in the ancient sense of the word. The people of the Pride came to her for everything from advice for treating poison oak to attending childbirth. While the Alpha kept the Pride in line, the Primara was the soul and spiritual center of the community.

The clinic was attached to the side of the house. There was no sign, no opening hours displayed, no announcement that the clapboard extension was anything other than a garage or just another add-on to the house.

There didn't need to be.

Everyone in town knew where they had to go. Everyone knew it didn't matter what time of the day or night it was, the clinic would always be open. Everyone came here at one time or another. She missed that.

The clinic door opened and a heavily pregnant woman stepped out as Kitt's mother was stroking the back of the female's hand. "Everything is progressing fine. Your babies will soon be here, in a few weeks."

Mem. A lump formed in Kitt's throat. Though Serena mostly looked the same as she always had, she also looked a little thinner and less vibrant. She turned to greet them as Kitt and the others got closer.

Her face broke into a smile. "Leon, your children grow strong and healthy. I was just telling your wife—"

Their eyes met.

Serena lifted shaky fingers to her lips, her eyes brimming with unshed tears.

"Hello, Mem." Kitt used the Pride version of Mom and stepped closer.

Her mother reached out and took Kitt's face in her hands—"Oh my God. I can't believe you're really here"—then pulled her into a fierce embrace.

Kitt hugged Serena back, breathing deep the scent of her mother, reminding her of pine forest and fresh-baked cookies. What she didn't enjoy was the feel of Serena's backbone under her fingers or the stick-thin arms her mother had wrapped around her.

"Let me look at you," Serena said, pulling back. "How long are you here for?"

"Until nightfall tomorrow," Leon answered for her.

"Such a short time." Her mother's face fell. "We best not waste it, then. Come into the house."

The pregnant woman hung back awkwardly. Serena seemed to notice that she was still there. "Kitt, you remember Rainbow."

Remember? Hell . . . Besides Dylan and Oberon, Rainbow had been her closest childhood friend. Dark rings circled her pretty hazel eyes. The pregnancy must be taking its toll.

Leon came up beside Rainbow and draped a protective arm across her shoulders. "My wife."

For a moment, Kitt could've sworn she saw the woman flinch under his touch. Maybe she'd just imagined it.

"Hello, Kitt," Rainbow said. "It's been a long time."

"It's good to see you again, Rainbow. It looks like you're due soon." Kitt turned to Leon. "Congratulations to you both."

Tears filled Rainbow's eyes as she looked down and rubbed her large tummy. Leon hugged her closer. This time

Kitt didn't mistake the flash of fear on her old friend's face. Not all was happy in the house of Leon and Rainbow.

"Come on, I'll give you a ride home and you can tell me about the checkup," Leon said. It wasn't a request either.

"If you need anything, call me." Serena took her hand and squeezed it. "Night or day. Okay?"

The female nodded her head. She turned to her husband and kissed him quickly. There was no lingering, no tenderness. A simple duty-peck.

"Nice to see you again, Kitt," Rainbow said as she passed.

On impulse, Kitt reached out and grabbed Rainbow's hand as she passed. She couldn't think of anything to say, but words weren't needed. The woman squeezed her hand and nodded. The silent communication of the abused. This could easily have been her life if she hadn't rebelled.

Leon put his arm around his wife again and walked her to the Jeep. Just before she climbed into the passenger seat, Rainbow glanced back at Kitt with one last haunted look. Both of the twins shuffled awkwardly, pretending they didn't see it.

"Come in the house," Serena said. "I'll make some coffee."

Kitt watched Rainbow, framed in the car window; she lifted her hand in a sad little wave and Kitt reciprocated. Then she turned and followed her mother to the porch as the Jeep pulled away.

"Go on into the sitting room," Serena said. "I'll put on the coffee."

"Thanks, Primara, but we're fine out here," Jericho said, shaking the snow and mud off his shoes.

"Nonsense. You boys are hardly dressed for the outdoors." There was no arguing with the woman using that tone of voice. "Go inside where the fire is warm."

"Yes, ma'am," the twins chorused.

"I'll help you with the coffee," Kitt said.

It would give them a few moments together, alone. She followed her mother into the kitchen—the same kitchen it was when she was a child, the same little pink rosebuds painted on the drawers and cupboards, the same old red cedar table with matching chairs, the same old hardwood floors, and the same old woodburning stove.

Nothing has changed. Especially not Leon.

"What's happening with Rainbow?" Kitt asked. "She looked exhausted."

Her mother stopped taking cups from the cupboard beside the sink and turned to her. "She's having a difficult time with the pregnancy."

By the look on her mother's face, Kitt knew there was more to it. "I bet this isn't her first pregnancy either; there've been others but she's lost them."

Her mother didn't need to answer, the way she turned away. Avoiding the question said enough.

"Everything's the same," Kitt said. "I can see the Pride still allows men to beat their wives."

"It's not the Pride's way to interfere with a mated couple," Serena said, the sadness in her voice breaking Kitt's heart.

This was supposed to be a joyous occasion, the first time she was spending time with her mother in nearly two decades. "I'm sorry, Mem—I didn't come here to fight with you."

Serena's face broke into a brilliantly sad smile and she cupped Kitt's cheek with her warm hand. "I've missed you, especially since your brother . . ."

Kitt pulled her mother close. Her mother's thin frame shook with great choking sobs. Soon Kitt's own grief resurfaced and she was crying along with her mother. After a few minutes, Serena pulled back, picked up the apron hanging over the back of a nearby chair, and dried Kitt's tears.

"I'll just go wash up," Serena said.

Kitt moved to the sink and washed away more tears, then dried her face on a kitchen towel. She'd cried for her brother's death and because she was now alone. But this was the first time she was actually crying to say goodbye. For the first time since losing him, her world didn't feel as empty.

"I'm sorry," Serena said when she got back. "That's the first time I've really been able to cry—*really* cry."

"I was just thinking the same thing," Kitt admitted.

Her mother reached out and ran her fingers down Kitt's cheek. "Your daughters look a lot like you. I thought it would be like having you home again. But it wasn't."

"They seem like pretty good kids."

"They've never known the Pride's upbringing, so they don't behave as expected. It's part of the reason your father sent them to the Academy, to get Nathan to teach them away from here. They're headstrong and independent like their mother." Serena smiled, lighting up the whole room.

"I've missed that smile," Kitt said, hugging her mother again.

"I really think that's why your father sent you here," Serena said. "He said the same thing a few weeks ago."

"I think you're right." If there was one thing Kitt had always been certain of, it was how much her father loved her mother.

"Well, let's get this into those tiger boys." Serena placed some homemade cookies on the tray with the coffee.

A child of around seven or eight appeared at the back door looking flushed and terrified, her hands covered in blood. "Rainbow fell—she's bleeding. *Please come!*"

20

TO ERR IS INHUMAN

Serena hugged the shaking girl, Rainbow's little sister. Kitt was crammed in beside her while Joshua drove her mother's old jalopy and Jericho sat with his fingers digging into the dash, his usual stony expression now pure granite. According to the girl, she'd stopped by to visit her sister and found her in a pool of blood at the bottom of the stairs. Rainbow had sent her for the Primara.

Joshua brought the car to a skidding stop by the front porch. Kitt was out of the door before the engine even died, Jericho hot on her heels. They found Rainbow propped against the bottom stairs sitting in the blood, her face scrunched in agony as she clutched her stomach, and Leon nowhere to be found.

"Okay. Rainbow, I am going take a look at you," Kitt said, coming to her side. "Are you having any contractions?"

The female nodded through gritted teeth and her stomach tightened under Kitt's palm.

Serena kneeled on the other side and took Rainbow's hand. "What happened, sweetheart?"

The woman's eyes filled with tears as she looked from Serena to Kitt. "I slipped on the stairs."

Amniotic fluid was mixed with the blood around Rainbow. A few feet away there were several smudge marks, too big to be the little girl's.

"Rainbow, Rainbow," the child screamed as she flew past them to hug her sister. "I brought them as soon as I could. I'm sorry it took so long." Tears streaked her rosy cheeks.

Rainbow stroked the child's hair as her face contorted in pain. "No, my darling. You did good, you ran like the wind."

"Jericho, take Elsie outside," Serena said.

The burly twin gently pried the sobbing child off her sister and carried her out the door.

"How many weeks is she?" Kitt asked her mother as she palpated Rainbow's stomach.

"Thirty-seven weeks," she answered. "I have some magnesium sulfate back at the clinic we could use to slow the contractions."

Kitt shook her head. "It's too late for that. But we do need to get her back there."

"My babies," Rainbow cried.

"Sh-sh-shhh . . . lie still," Serena soothed. "It's going to be all right."

"We have to get her to the car," Kitt said.

Joshua lumbered forward and carefully lifted Rainbow off the floor with such tenderness. Kitt raced ahead to get the doors and Serena climbed into the backseat to support Rainbow's head in her lap. Joshua got in behind the wheel and Kitt jumped into the passenger side and turned to face the back.

Jericho remained on the porch, cradling the child on the swing seat as they drove away. Both the twins displayed a kindness Kitt never thought possible of Leon's siblings, and her new respect for them increased another level.

Rainbow was bleeding heavily. Her skirt was saturated and so was the old rug her mother had placed on the seat under her. Serena looked up, worry clouding her eyes, and Kitt reached over to squeeze her mother's hand.

"We're nearly there, Rainbow," her mother said. "Just relax and you will soon be holding your sweet babies. I promise."

One way or another. Kitt just hoped they could save both them and their mother.

Even though it was only a few minutes' drive, the journey

seemed to take forever. When they eventually reached the clinic, Joshua drove right up to the door, jumped out immediately, and gently lifted Rainbow out of the car to carry her into the clinic.

Serena's hand on Kitt's arm stopped her from following. "Is it what I think?"

Kitt nodded. "I'm afraid so. The continual bleeding indicates a severe placental abruption. If we don't hurry, we could lose them all."

"Do you think we'll need to operate?"

It'd been years since Kitt had operated on a living person and she hoped she didn't have to today.

Kitt sighed. "Hard to say until we examine her fully. Can you check her dilation?"

"Yes," Serena said, looking around. "We should send for Leon."

"No," Kitt hissed, a little too forcefully. "He's the cause of this, you must know that."

"It's not the Pride way to interfere—"

"FUCK that!" Kitt took her mother by the upper arms. "He may just have killed three members of the Jordan Pride. How do you think the council would view that?"

Serena straightened—the uncertainty disappearing from her face. "I'll speak to your father as soon as I can, but right now we need to save Rainbow and those babies."

Kitt followed her mother into the clinic, and while Serena performed the internal exam, she went through the clinic inventory in case she needed to perform an emergency C-section. A lot of the equipment was old and outdated, but adequate for their purposes. Just. In general, most of the Pride was fairly healthy, but the children were practically human until their eighteenth year, and some Latents still lived among them. She would have to make sure the Pride updated the equipment when . . .

If . . . she corrected. *If she came back.*

She pushed away her self-pity. Three lives depended on her and her mother and she had to be completely focused on the task ahead.

"Nine centimeters," Serena said, peeling off a pair of surgical gloves. "And her contractions are coming very close together. Joshua, go into the house and bring back as many pillows as you can find. We need to make her more comfortable."

The twin moved quickly. Most women in the village gave birth in their own homes and in their own beds. This examination table wasn't the most comfortable, but it was sufficient. Kitt wheeled the ultrasound machine close.

Serena cut open the girl's ruined dress while Kitt turned on the machine and spread the gel over Rainbow's stomach. She rolled the handheld scanning device over the pregnant female's abdomen. The black-and-white image on the screen showed the babies, top to tail. It also showed where the placenta of the breech baby had come away from the wall.

"You've had much more experience at this than I. What do you think?" Kitt said to her mother.

"It's not a full abruption, so hopefully there will be enough oxygen getting through for the birth."

"Do you want me to perform a C-section?"

"Not yet," Serena said. "This labor is happening fast."

"Okay, but I'll stand by in case there're any complications." Kitt moved the machine out of the way.

Joshua came back with several pillows, which they propped around the patient. The female's eyes filled with tears of terror and uncertainty. Her mother really was the expert when it came to birthing babies.

"You're doing really well, Rainbow," Serena said.

The female clutched Kitt's offered hand fiercely. "Can't you stop it? They're not supposed to come yet."

"No, sweetie," Serena said. "Your water has broken and you're almost fully dilated. These babies are coming today."

Rainbow shook her head. "No, I'm not ready. You must stop it." Her voice rose to near hysteria.

Joshua took the hand of his brother's wife and began to hum a very old lullaby, one Kitt hadn't heard for many years. It seemed to do the trick. Rainbow calmed a little, then she lay back and closed her eyes until the next contraction ripped through her.

When Joshua looked up, his eyes were damp. Kitt put a comforting hand on his shoulder and patted it gently as he continued to hum the beautiful, haunting melody and stroked the pregnant female's brow.

Rainbow let out a heavy pain-filled groan. Kitt worried the babies were in distress.

"She's crowning," Serena yelled with excitement.

Kitt moved behind her mother. The matted mass of red-gold hair showed from between Rainbow's thighs. With one more push, the head was free and the infant's body slid out on the next contraction.

"It's your boy, Rainbow." Serena beamed as his wail filled the room. She wrapped him up in a fresh warm towel Kitt handed her and laid him on his mother's stomach while she clamped off and cut the umbilical cord.

"Here, let me clean him up a little," Kitt said. "Okay?"

Rainbow clutched her baby close and glanced at Serena.

"She's a doctor and will take good care of him," her mother said. "I promise."

Wiping off the blood-streaked white vernix caseosa coating gave her a chance to check the infant for any injuries. At this stage, she didn't want to distress the new mother any more than she needed to. Rainbow's *fall* could have caused all kinds of damage—broken bones, fractured skull, or even internal bleeding. Kitt had to make certain he was okay.

He was perfect—a little undersized given he was slightly premature, but his color was good and he breathed well without assistance. She wrapped him back up in a tight little bundle and passed him to Joshua while Rainbow prepared to give birth to his littermate—the breech with the placental abruption.

Rainbow let out another low guttural cry—her hands balling the bedding as she pulled herself forward to push.

Serena looked up at the pale and exhausted expectant mother. "We have to take this one a little more slowly."

Breech babies weren't unusual in Bestiabeo births; her mother had delivered them dozens of times. The placental abruption caused Kitt the most concern. If the baby had been starved of blood and oxygen, it could cause major complications.

Serena worked the baby's rump out of the birth canal until the legs were free, though it took quite a few more minutes to carefully ease out the arms and shoulders. As the minutes ticked by, Kitt stood by helplessly as her mother worked.

The baby had to come out, and soon.

Then Serena lifted the body and eased out the head. The baby lay still in her arms. She glanced up, clearly worried. Kitt wrapped the small body in a towel while her mother separated the cord.

Kitt placed the tiny bundle on the special heated table and unwrapped it to find the lifeless pale gray little girl. She picked up the suction bulb and cleared the airways, but still the little girl didn't cry.

"What's happening to my baby?" Rainbow asked. "Where is she?"

Kitt ignored her and placed the stethoscope on the tiny chest. The baby lay still, deathly still, but her heartbeat fluttered weakly. She reached for the mask, placed it over the tiny infant's mouth and nose, and squeezed the bulb. Bruises covered the poor little mite's body, and while some were from the trauma of birth, Kitt suspected others were compliments of Leon.

She would not let Leon destroy this tiny girl, her mother, or her sibling. Death of a littermate was considered extremely unlucky, and these children were already unfortunate enough to have Leon as their father.

The tiny arms and legs lay lifeless, but Kitt kept pumping the resuscitation bag, not giving up. She closed her eyes in silent prayer and gave the bag one last squeeze before she'd finally admit defeat.

She looked down one last time, just as an arm twitched. Then a foot. Then arms and legs clenched and drew up as the tiny girl let loose an almighty wail, turning her blue-gray complexion purplish red.

"That's it little girl, complain hard and loud," Kitt said as she wrapped her into a warm towel.

* * *

Kitt came forward in the old stuffed chair as her mother opened the door. One of the babies snuffled in sleep, but didn't wake. Neither did Rainbow, who lay curled up in the bed beside her tiny bundles. Serena padded over and checked on the sleeping family before tiptoeing to where Kitt sat.

"The babies are both looking pink and healthy, and are breathing well," Serena whispered. "Why don't you go get some sleep and I'll take over."

She exchanged places with her mother and quietly left the room. The vision on the bed of the mother and her babies brought a lump to her throat. She never got a chance to have that with her own children. She'd known she would have to give them up, so when she gave birth, she couldn't bear to look at them. If she had, there was no way she could have let them go.

Looking back was never good. She now saw opportunities she couldn't back then. Opportunities that would've let her keep her daughters close. Hindsight is such a wonderful thing.

The Tiger Twins came to their feet when she stepped into the living room, their expressions worried and expectant.

"They're all fine," she said. "Rainbow and the babies are healthy and sleeping."

The two large males relaxed. They seemed really concerned about their sister-in-law. *Or maybe it's guilt for allowing this to happen.*

"Have they found Leon yet?" she asked.

Joshua shook his head. "He was seen up at the lodge earlier on, but disappeared a few hours ago."

"Well, it's been a hell of a day and I'm beat. You boys should get some rest too," she said and left them to sit in front of the fire.

The twins had their own homes in the village, but with Leon on the loose, they decided to stay in her mother's tiny parlor.

Kitt warmed milk on the old stove and made several mugs of hot chocolate. She took some to Joshua and Jericho, then a cup to her mother before taking her own to her old room.

It hadn't changed it at all—girly things still lined the shelves above her pink bed.

Looking outside, the thin cloud cover cleared to reveal a full moon shining brightly down onto the wilderness below. The houses of the village were purpose-built for felians and had easy access to the ramps that led down to the tree line.

The sudden urge to run through the snow among the trees suddenly overcame her. She found an old Abeolite suit in her closet and undressed before she changed her mind.

The cold crisp air caressed her skin with icy fingers, covering her with goose bumps and contracting her nipples to painful little nubs. The familiar prickling sensation started along her arm and moved to her stomach. The thick fur chased the chill on her skin as it spread down her limbs and across her back. She dropped to all fours as her backbone began extending, pushing out into a tail, and her arms thinned to become powerful front legs. Within seconds, she'd fully transformed and sprang down the ramp to hit the snow.

It was fresh and clean and crisp under her paws. The air sang with life, and above her billions of tiny pinpricks shone from the heavens. She'd forgotten how beautiful this place was.

Oh, how she'd missed it.

Like a kid again, Kitt leapt and ran, jumped from rock to rock, bounded over fallen tree trunks, and rolled in the snow. She enjoyed every minute of her snow leopard form—every minute of freedom. She lay down on a rock and licked the fur along her front paws, cleaning off the snow. A hare darted away to her right. The predator in her stirred for a second and she crouched, but she wasn't hungry for fresh flesh or in the mood to chase, not even for fun.

The snow-covered branches hung heavy in the moonlight; the wind blew through the trees, carrying the scent of the wilderness. It stirred her blood.

This was where she grew up.

This was where she belonged.

This was her home.

Kitt sighed contentedly, lay her head down on her paws,

and closed her eyes. Music and laughter drifted on the breeze. She lifted her head and listened.

Since I'm here, I may as well take a look.

Kitt padded around the lake. The closer she got, the brighter became the lights from the lodge. This was the other side of the Pride life, the sordid side. Far removed from the simple village on the other side of the lake.

The Jordan Pride Lodge supplied them with the money to be able to live a simple life in the wilderness. It took care of every male, female, and child. The Pride referred to it as the Family Business. While it actively improved the lives of all Jordans, other more illegal activities allowed them power.

Pride activities allowed them to expand their land further, buying up other surrounding Bestiabeo holdings. It was why they warred with the neighboring Matokwe Pack: they both vied for the same land and the same business.

Kitt changed back to human and entered the lodge. The large central fireplace added to the warm glow of the wood-paneled lobby with cathedral ceilings. Several people occupied the lounge bar. All the women were young, attractive, and expensively dressed; men's wear ranged from expensive suits to designer ski wear.

The lodge was gilt and glitz. A false promised land. It offered a retreat to some of the most powerful and dangerous people in the country. The patrons, both human and parahuman, were men of power and men of wealth, not to mention men of questionable business practices.

Here they could relax far from the prying eyes of the country's law enforcement agencies to conduct business in private on the pretext of skiing or hunting. More under-the-table deals were done here than in boardrooms. Some of the most powerful underworld figures in the country, if not the world, had permanent bookings here and brought their mistresses along for a little pampering in the Pride's health spa.

"Miss Kathryn," a voice called from the office behind the concierge desk. "It's so good to see you after all these years."

She looked at the old man, taking another moment to recognize him. "Cuthbert, you're still here."

Her father's hotel manager smiled as he walked toward her. He was the only human Tyrone entirely trusted; the only outsider he'd allowed to marry into the Pride. When she'd last seen him, he'd been a man in his prime; now he was on the far side of middle-age.

"They told me you were home, though we didn't expect you to visit us here." He looked around nervously.

"What's wrong, do you have orders to keep me out?" she asked.

"No," he said quickly and patted her hand. "No, not at all. It's just Leon was here earlier, drinking heavily and cursing your name. Belladonna wine. Then others came looking for him."

"It's okay. I just wanted to see the place again before I left tomorrow." She patted the old man on the shoulder. "Say hello to your wife for me."

"I'm sorry your stay couldn't be longer. I'm sure she would've liked to see you." Cuthbert's smile grew wider, trying to cover his relief. "How about going out the back. It's faster to get back to the village."

Kitt followed him through the office and down a service passage. They moved through what seemed miles of tunnel and came out where she knew they would. The ski shed. Hanging on the wall were several heavy anoraks and insulated ski pants. Cuthbert handed over a pair of each, which she slipped on over her Abeolite. He also grabbed a set of keys from the small cupboard hanging on the wall and tossed them to her. The number on the key tag matched the snowmobile she stood beside.

"I'll send one of the boys to fetch it from your mother's tomorrow," Cuthbert said.

Sleep and a nice warm bed called her name. The trip had been both emotionally and physically exhausting. The snowmobile would get her back to her mother's much faster than on foot, even four of them.

"Thank you," she said to the old man.

Kitt climbed into the saddle and fired up the machine as Cuthbert pushed open the shed door. She gunned the engine and waved goodbye as she shot out into the night.

Traveling through the snow and forest on the snowmobile was almost as good as running in felian form. She kept the throbbing machine on the well-worn track between the lodge and the village, its lights shining in the darkness, showing her the way.

A bright flash exploded behind her eyes. She found herself flying through the air.

She tumbled.

And landed hard on her back.

The air expelled from her lungs in an almighty *wump*, and she gasped to refill them.

The sound of the snowmobile continued away from her until it sputtered and died. Kitt struggled to breathe and tried to rise. The world spun, her head pounded, and her vision swam.

"Well, now," Leon's voice slurred from somewhere nearby. "Talk about the right place at the right time. I knew that old fool would send you this way."

He'd been watching the lodge. Kitt opened her eyes and reached up to the pain in her forehead. Her hand came away wet and sticky. She struggled to sit and Leon forced her back with his foot on her chest. He stood over her, a large naked branch in his hand.

Her head still swam, though the pain abated and a spark of fear replaced her confusion. He'd used a tree branch to knock her from the speeding snowmobile.

Leon fell down to his knees, straddling her. "You come back here. Mock me in front of my wife. Make me look a fool."

"I didn't do anything," she said, fear pitching her voice slightly higher.

He heard it. His smile deepened and his lips peeled back from his teeth.

"No matter," he said. "It's not a total loss." His gaze dropped to her chest and he shifted his weight, forcing her legs further apart.

Pain shot up from her hip and she almost blacked out. The fall had dislocated her hip. She screamed as his movement popped it back into place. This only seemed to encourage him, spur him on, and he ground his erection against her groin.

No!

He would not do this to her again. She curled her fingers and forced the heel of her palm up and into his nose. He rocked back enough for her to struggle out from under him, then she turned and kicked him on the side of the face. Her head still spun and she stumbled, falling to her knees.

He snarled loudly. The sound drove her to her feet and she ran blindly forward, struggling to get out of the heavy anorak and pants so that she could transform. She looked over her shoulder as she ran.

Leon shredded the clothes on his body, claws turning into large powerful paws. The full red-gold mane spread over his shoulders and down the center of his back. He dropped onto all four paws and tossed back his head in a full-throated and deafening lion's roar.

Kitt was no longer in danger of being raped. If Leon caught her now, he would kill her. She finally managed to shed her jacket and kept up her stumbling run to put as much distance between them as she could. She struggled out of the pants and fell backward.

His flat yellow eyes burned as he dropped his head and charged forward on powerful legs, his mane rippling with the speed.

21

Return from Oz

I'm going to die.

As the thought ripped through her head, two blurs whirred past her straight into the path of the charging lion. Leon skidded to a stop, growling with frustration as he met the wall of tigers. Jericho and Joshua had come after her.

Leon padded back and forth, his throaty rumble occasionally becoming a snarl. The snow and chill seeped; her teeth chattered loudly. Leon finally stopped pacing and transformed back to human. His chest rose and fell, the visible fog of his breath panting into the cold night air.

"This has nothing to do with you," he growled at his transforming brothers.

"She's under our protection," Jericho said and crossed his arms over the black-and-orange tiger-patterned Abeolite suit.

Joshua fetched Kitt's discarded anorak and wrapped it around her shoulders. She smiled her thanks, and not just for the jacket.

The snowmobile had crashed nose first into a snowbank, so she wouldn't be riding that home.

Jericho led Leon in the other direction, talking in low tones.

"Can you make it back to the lodge?" Joshua asked.

Kitt shivered. "I think so."

"Good. We'll pick up a truck there and take you back to the village," he said and watched as his brothers walked away. "Don't worry about Leon. Jericho is going to stay and watch over him until the Alpha works out what to do."

Well, at least she didn't have to worry about him getting to Rainbow.

The helicopter rotor blades whirred into life behind Kitt as she held tightly to her mother's hand.

"It wasn't enough time." Serena swiped away a tear that spilled onto her cheek. "I wish you could have stayed for longer."

"So do I," Kitt said, holding back her own threatening tears. "Maybe Tyrone will allow me to return soon."

Serena just nodded, more tears sliding down her rosy cheeks. Kitt's heart contracted at the sight of her mother's red-rimmed eyes.

"Take care of Rainbow and those precious babies," Kitt yelled above the sound of the rotor blades as they picked up more speed.

Serena nodded, fresh sobs wracking her shoulders as she buried her face in her gloved hands. The snow swirled around them from the down draft of the chopper blades, and Jericho tapped her on the arm.

"I have to go," Kitt cried and her mother seized her into a frantic hug, as if she couldn't bear to let her go. She returned Serena's embrace with just as much fervor. The thought of letting her go now was almost too much.

"We have to leave now, there's a storm headed this way," Jericho spoke into Kitt's ear.

She released her mother and nodded, wiping away the tears that she could no longer hold back. They turned icy in the bitter wind kicked up by the swirling rotors.

Her mother clutched her hand in desperation one last time before finally letting go. Kitt ran to the helicopter and turned to wave just before she climbed into the cockpit behind the pilot.

Serena blew her a kiss with both hands as the machine lifted off the ground, and Kitt returned it. Then she sat back and let the tears fall as she watched her mother's lone figure grow smaller the higher they climbed.

Jericho handed her a handkerchief, his sad eyes reflecting her sorrow.

"Where's Joshua?" she asked behind a sniffle as she wiped her cheeks dry.

"He stayed behind to *mind* Leon until his fate is decided by the Alpha and the council," the twin said, his eyes taking on a rare animosity. "This time he's gone too far."

Ya think?

But Kitt kept the retort to herself. She remembered how Jericho and Joshua had always been loyal to their brother, the last of their Pride. While the Tiger Twins were large and proficient bodyguards, they also didn't suffer the same aggressive tendencies as Leon. To hear him talk with such bitterness about Leon was something she never even contemplated.

Oberon pulled the Harley up outside her building. Kitt climbed off and slapped him on the back, then walked inside, straight past the doorman without her usual friendly greeting. She just didn't have the energy.

He followed her into the elevator and pressed her floor. "Are you sure you're okay?"

"Yeah, just tired." She glanced at him and placed her hand on his arm. "Thanks again for picking me up."

The elevator stopped after two floors and the door opened. An elderly woman stood frozen and slack-jawed on the other side. Her hand flew to her mouth as she took a step back and stared at Oberon.

"Evening, ma'am," Oberon said and stepped aside.

She gave a nervous little smile and gingerly stepped in, throwing anxious glances at the seven-foot male in leather. Any other time, Kitt would have found it amusing.

After a couple more floors, the old woman stepped out in a hurry, throwing worried glances over her shoulder as she raced down the hall.

"Have a nice day, ma'am," Oberon said cheerily and gave the old woman a friendly wave.

The poor thing almost dropped dead from fright as she looked at him with alarm and hurried away even faster, clutching her bag close to her chest. Oberon chuckled as the door closed.

"What?" he said with an innocent shrug of his shoulders when he caught her scowl. "I was just being friendly."

"I have to live here you know," she said.

The elevator finally reached her floor and they stepped out into the hall. Kitt just wanted to curl up and go to sleep. As soon as she entered and closed the apartment door, she threw her bag on the counter and turned to Oberon.

"Thanks for seeing me home."

He walked in and pulled back the curtain to look down onto the street. "I just wanted to make sure you were safe. What happened up there?"

"I'm very tired," she said. "Can we discuss this later?"

"Sure." He nodded and turned to the window. "Here come your babysitters."

The large SUV pulled up across the street. She could make out the tiger-striped hair on the driver and smiled.

"What does he expect you to do?" Oberon finally asked.

She knew he meant her father. "He wants me to spy for him—tell them everything I know about the campus murders. In return I get to see my mother and I also get two hours alone with the twins." She looked up at his face, bracing herself for the tirade she was sure would follow.

"Good." Oberon simply nodded as if he'd been expecting her answer. "That will give us time to evaluate them."

Suddenly the past thirty-six hours hit all at once. Everything Leon had done—or should she say, had almost done . . . Her legs collapsed and she found herself sitting on the floor, looking up at Oberon.

He was by her side in a flash. "Are you okay?"

"I had a bit of a run-in with Leon," she said as he helped her stand and move to the sofa. "He's so much stronger and I felt so helpless. Please promise me you won't tell Raven. He'll want to kill him."

"He'll have to stand in line—that evil bastard deserves everything he gets." Oberon's obsidian eyes grew even darker.

"He should've been taken care of years ago for what he did to you."

She sighed and lay against the back of the sofa. "Everyone knew I had a crush on him. I was young. No one would've believed it was rape."

"So the only punishment he gets for nearly killing his wife and children, and assaulting you, is a demotion and a slap on the wrist." Oberon's hands curled into white-knuckled fists. "What's to stop him from hurting them again?"

Joshua had relayed the verdict to the helicopter before they landed in New York.

"If he does, I will kill him myself," she said, meaning every word of it.

Antoinette waited in the gymnasium for Kitt's twins. Tonight she would see what they were made of. A few people were limbering up on the mats. She'd picked some of her top students to help evaluate Raven's training.

The twins came through the door looking a little confused.

And right on time.

"Umm . . . hi, there. We were supposed to meet our mother here." Antoinette recognized Cal from the Shadow-combat match.

Seph crossed her arms with attitude. "Yeah, we're looking for Kathryn Jordan."

Interesting. Not ready yet to call her Mom.

Antoinette held out her hand. "Thanks for coming. Seph, isn't it? Cal and I already met at your game the other night, which I thought an extraordinary match."

"Thank you," Seph said, her expression improving. "And I'm impressed you can tell us apart. Most can't."

"Actually, you're very different. Cal has light in her eyes that's hard to miss and, Seph, you have the carriage of a warrior."

Both girls puffed up under her observations.

"Your mother will be here soon," Antoinette said. "I work with her and Oberon. We just want to see what you've got—what training you've had."

Seph straightened. "So this is just between us; you're not telling our uncle or grandfather about it?"

"Hell, no," Antoinette said. "This is definitely between us. We just want to see how well your father taught you."

Cal glanced at her sister, then turned back to Antoinette with a cautious tilt of her head. "What do you know about our father?"

Antoinette smiled and crossed her arms under her breasts. "I work with Raven too."

The twins locked eyes again and something passed between them. They turned as one and nodded in unison.

"Are we to fight you, then?" Cal asked.

Antoinette shook her head. "I'm here to observe and referee. I'll evaluate your technical abilities and your reaction. Besides, I'm still learning to control my Aeternus capabilities and don't want to hurt you."

Both girls laughed. There was no arrogance or cockiness in it; they just truly believed she couldn't hurt them.

"First we are going to try hand-to-hand combat, one on one. Do you want to change?"

They nodded, looking at each other with excitement. It was infectious—a tingle fluttered in Antoinette's stomach. And it made things easier that they were willing to do this.

"There's Abeolite in there," she said, showing them to the change rooms.

As the girls disappeared, Antoinette approached her people. She'd handpicked her best, all proficient in various forms of martial arts.

"Mike, Jasper," she said pointing to her two black belts. "You're first up. Start off slow, but don't be afraid to push them."

The students bowed from the hips.

The twins returned dressed in black and red Abeolite and approached the middle of the mat. They stood with feet apart and hands behind their backs. Antoinette's four students lined up opposite, in the same stance. There was also an Aeternus that Oberon had arranged to participate in the evaluation; he was leaning against the wall. She hoped they didn't need to use him because something about him didn't feel right.

Antoinette walked down the two lines. "Today we'll go through a number of bouts to see what these newcomers are capable of. I want each of you to give your best at all times. The first round will be hand-to-hand, unarmed combat—one on one. The second round will be weapons capabilities, using staffs and Animalian abilities. The final round will be all in, anything goes, but I will reserve judgment on final combatants after the first two rounds." She looked from one side to the other. The twins stared straight ahead, like soldiers. The students watched her.

Hmm, this could get interesting.

"Okay, first-round combatants." Antoinette moved to the side. "Please take the mat."

Cal and Seph stepped forward and maintained their previous posture as they watched their opponents limbering up before them. Antoinette put the whistle to her lips and blew.

It happened so fast, Antoinette almost missed it. One second the two highly proficient black belt students began their attack, and the next they were both on their backs, stunned and staring at the ceiling. The twins had barely seemed to move.

So much for taking it slow.

Antoinette blew the whistle again to stop the bout. The twins moved in unison, this time holding out their right hands and helped their opponents to their feet.

She wanted to see if they could do it a second time now that Mike and Jasper were ready for them.

"Shall we go again?" she asked.

The two students bowed at the hips and took up a more aggressive stance opposite the two girls. She blew the whistle again. While not quite as fast this time, the result was the same. Antoinette's students attacked, the twins countered in perfect unison, and the boys ended up on their backs staring at the ceiling.

Oberon stepped out of the office behind the mirror-lined wall and stood beside the door, signaling Antoinette over.

"Everyone stand down," she said and crossed to meet him.

"Did you see that?" she whispered. "They laid out two of my best like they were yellow belts."

"I know," he said in a low voice. "I think we're wasting time here—go straight to the final round."

"Okay." She glanced over her shoulder. The two who'd just had their asses kicked, twice, didn't seem worse for wear as they endured the ribbing from their classmates. "I'll use your guy and one of my other students."

He pierced her with her obsidian eyes. "Use them all."

"I watched Seph in the Shadow-combat match. She was good, though nothing extraordinary."

"I have a theory," he said, half distracted, then he focused again. "Trust me. I want you to push them. Hard."

"What about Kitt?"

"Leave her to me," he said and returned to the office.

Antoinette rejoined the rest. "Okay. Change of plans. We're going to go straight to the final bout."

"Excellent." Seph smiled, her eyes lighting up. "Bring it on."

Antoinette hid a smile. She was really starting to like this girl.

"We're going all in," Antoinette said. "It's anything goes, to a point. You can use weapons, bare hands, and abilities. But if you hear the whistle, you stop immediately. Is that understood?"

"Hai, Sensei," her students chorused and the Aeternus pushed himself off the wall to join them.

"Right, choose your weapons if you want them."

The two boys who'd been shown the ceiling, twice, moved to pick up weapons. One took a staff and twirled it around his body with precision, and the other chose a katana, her personal favorite. The two others, both canian from different Packs, remained unarmed and so did the Aeternus.

She signaled over the squad of five she was about to send against the twins. "I want you to really push these two. We need to see what they are capable of."

"Are you sure?" said the Aeternus male.

Antoinette didn't even know his name, and she was now certain she didn't want to. "Within reason. I don't want anyone getting hurt."

"Right," he said as the corner of his lip twitched.

I don't like him at all. Where did Oberon find this guy?

She considered dismissing him altogether, but that would mean she'd have to step in to see how they went against an Aeternus. No matter what Antoinette had seen the girls do, she was still genuinely afraid of harming them.

"Okay, let's go free-form." She blew the whistle and hung back.

Jasper attacked first, swinging the staff at Cal's head, who ducked as Seph grabbed her hand and somersaulted over her back, striking him in the chest with a sidekick that sent him across the room. *Such strength, while in full human form.*

They moved to defensive mode, back to back. The other boy, the one with the katana, seemed to lose his nerve and dropped the tip of the sword to the ground. One of the canians transformed into a large gray wolf and circled the twins.

She caught a movement out of the corner of her eye as the Aeternus male swept in from the side, sucker punching Seph on the side of the head, dropping her.

"Hey," Antoinette yelled.

The girl rose to her hands and knees on the mat, shaking her head. Cal had dropped beside her, and seemed a little dazed, like she'd been struck as well. But then murderous eyes narrowed on the male. Her change started midleap and by the time she landed on the Aeternus's chest, she was in full snow leopard form. Cal's powerful jaws clamped down on the fallen male's forearm and dark Aeternus blood sprayed everywhere, coating his white gi and her silver-gray fur. The other combatants hung back, stunned. Antoinette signaled the students to leave as she raced forward to separate the snow leopard from the bleeding male just as Kitt burst through the door with Oberon close behind.

The Aeternus staggered up, holding back the snarling snow leopard by the scruff of the neck, and slammed her head against the wall before Antoinette could stop him.

Seph struggled to her feet, fury radiating from her like a white-hot heat. Oberon stalked forward, lip peeled back in a growl. He grabbed the Aeternus by the throat and they smashed through the mirrored wall into the office behind.

Antoinette bent over the girl, who'd transformed back to human and opened her eyes.

"Are you okay?" Antoinette asked, helping Cal to her feet.

"Just a little shaky," she replied, and as she glanced past Antoinette, her face fell. "Oh no, Seph. You didn't."

Antoinette turned around to find Kitt wide eyed and pale; shaking fingers touched her lips as she stared at a silver-gray wolf.

What the fuck? "I thought you were both snow leopards."

"We are," Cal said. "And we are both wolves." Cal changed to match her sister before padding over to lick the side of Seph's face.

Kitt blinked slowly and rallied a little. "How?"

The girls transformed back and Seph placed her hand on Cal's shoulder. "I'm sorry, I was confused and didn't mean to . . ."

Cal wrapped her arms around her sister and kissed Seph's forehead as she glanced at her mother. "It's okay, it's all okay." Seph may be the warrior of the two, but Cal was the strength.

Oberon came to Kitt's side and slung an arm around her. He seemed just as shaken by this turn of events as the felian.

Then he smiled at the twins. "It'll all be okay; in fact it's perfect."

Raven flicked to the next channel, the next, and the next. Being stuck down here was starting to drive him insane. He was certain the room was bigger yesterday. Someone had come in and removed several feet sometime during the last twenty-four hours. He stood up and began to pace up and down the room. Maybe a workout would work off some of this frustration.

He stood in front of the chin-up bar and peeled his shirt off, then jumped to grip the bar. Bending his knees and crossing his ankles, muscles strained as he pulled his body up to tap his chin on the bar. He slowly dropped for maximum muscle control. Up he pulled and down he dropped, getting into a slow steady rhythm, exhaling on each lift, inhaling on each drop. He didn't bother counting. He'd just keep going until he'd had enough, until his arms could take no more.

He couldn't bear to watch the twins' evaluation; as much as he wanted to be there, his presence would distract them from their task. They had to do this on their own.

He sensed her, even through the adrenaline haze, and glanced at the clock on the wall as he dropped to the floor. *Half an hour.*

It was over already?

As he saw Kitt, he let go of the bar and bent to pick up a towel from the bench. A certain look didn't leave her eyes as she swallowed hard. He watched her throat work, then the way she licked her lips.

Raven dried the sweat on his face. "From your face, I can see it didn't go well."

His gaze traveled down her body, his insides turning to molten lava. Even after all these years, she was the only one to turn him on with a simple glance. But there was something wrong. Nervousness, more than was usual, haunted her eyes.

He moved closer, stopping mere inches away. "What's the matter, Kitten?"

She leaned forward with that far-off look in her eyes and he doubted she even realized she was doing it. When he reached to pull her into his arms, she blinked.

The spell was broken. Her eyes returned to their usual color. She shook her head, more like shaking off a stupor than indicating no.

"Why didn't you tell me?" she said, the accusation hanging in the air between them.

"Tell you what?" He ran the towel over his chest and under his arms.

Her eyes followed the movement. "About the twins; about what they can do."

What was wrong? "I taught them how to defend themselves. They're good. I know."

She snagged her bottom lip with her teeth and tilted her head, frowning. "You don't know, do you?"

"Know what? Look—something I taught them obviously has you distressed."

She shook her head again, her frown deepening. "It's not what you taught them, it's what they can do."

"I have no idea what you are talking about?" he said, turning out his hands. "What *have* they done?"

She glanced over his shoulder, that far-off look returning.

"Kitt, what is it. Tell me what's wrong?" Worry gnawed at the pit of his stomach. She was really starting to scare him. He reached out and took hold of her upper arms.

She dropped her eyes to his chest and then raised her chin, focusing on him again. "Get dressed and meet us in the conference room. There's something you've got to see."

Kitt made her way back to the conference room. Was it possible he really didn't know about them?

"Are you okay?" Oberon asked from just outside the room. Through the glass she could see the twins sitting with blankets wrapped around their shoulders, clutching each others hands.

"I'm fine," she said, taking a bottle of water from the small fridge and unscrewing the top. "It's just the shock."

Antoinette placed her hand on Kitt's shoulder. "They're scared and confused . . . Could someone tell me what's going on?"

She took a large swallow of water to soothe her dry mouth as Raven came into the room, his hair still damp from a really quick shower.

Raven glanced around the room and his face transformed into pure delight—then quickly fell at the girls' disconsolate postures. "What's wrong?"

Oberon frowned. "It's probably best to see for yourself."

Raven looked at Kitt closely. She couldn't meet his eyes, in case he saw the fear in them.

"Let's go in," Oberon said.

"RAVEN!" the girls yelled in unison and ran to him, almost knocking him off balance with the force of their contact. He wrapped an arm around each of them and stroked the back of their heads, the concern on his face increasing.

"Hey, hey," he said. "It's all right."

Kitt stood in the background. He had a connection with

them she would never have. He'd helped raise them, tended their scraped knees, chased away nightmares in the middle of the night, and tucked them into bed at night. She was just the woman that gave them birth.

"Show him," Oberon said.

"Will someone please tell me what the fuck is going on?" Impatience strained his tone.

"Just watch," Oberon answered.

The girls stepped back and threw the blankets off their shoulders; they were still wearing the Abeolite suits underneath. Fur spread across their skin as they dropped to their hands and knees. The change came quickly and smoothly: one turned into a snow leopard, the other a wolf. Raven stumbled back, his hand out searching until he found a chair, then he fell heavily into a nearby seat.

"They were both felian, at the Awakening. No—" He shook his head. "This isn't right."

"Show him the rest," Kitt said.

They turned their heads as one and gave a little nod. Soon the snow leopard thinned out and legs grew longer, while the other's legs shrank and rounded.

Where once stood the cat, there was now a wolf—and vice versa.

Raven's mouth opened and shut soundlessly, his eyes wide as he tried to grasp the enormity of it. "This is impossible."

His surprise was real. He couldn't possibly fake his reaction. He really had no idea. The girls changed to human form and picked up the blankets again.

The room was silent. The twins hung their heads as if they'd done something wrong. Kitt didn't know what to say to make them feel better.

"Both of you?" Oberon said. "You both can do this?"

The twins nodded their heads in unison.

"We mustn't let anyone else find out they're Dúbabeo," Kitt said. "Especially the Jordan Pride."

"What are we?" Cal asked, fear causing a tremble in her voice.

"I'm sorry, Dúba-*what?*" Antoinette asked. "Isn't it good they can take both forms?"

Kitt laughed. Even in her own ears, it sounded half hysterical.

"They are a myth, a legend," Oberon said from where he leaned against the wall. "They're not supposed to exist."

"So they do, isn't that good?" Antoinette sat on the edge of the table and crossed her arms.

Oberon came away from the wall. "Good? It's fucking miraculous. These girls defy the odds on every count. Identical twins are rare; for a mating of two different Bestiabeo lines to result in a pregnancy is so low, it's near enough to impossible. And while Dúbabeos have been recorded in the far recesses of our history as a myth, they were seen as something to be honored and feared. Something that only existed to serve the Bestiabeo people."

Oberon walked around to the twins. "To put all that on the head of these girls would be monumental—they'd never be free again."

22

Angel in Disguise

Gideon waited outside the Academy. He leaned against a tree, watching a piece of trash driven by the wind cross the parking lot. The door opened. A male skipped down the steps. Gideon pushed away from the tree trunk.

"NO, HE'S NOT THE ONE," Ealund said.

Gideon relaxed again and crossed his arms.

And then he saw *her*.

His heart pounded heavily against his chest. Years ago, he'd escaped a prison and seen the most beautiful thing ever created. *Her.* And then he'd been locked away again.

"WHO IS SHE?" Ealund asked.

"My angel," Gideon replied. "My own personal angel."

Now here she was again, even more beautiful than before. Twice as beautiful—no, three times. And she was headed his way. He panicked and looked around. She mustn't see him. The time was not right. He hid behind the tree and circled the trunk as he watched her pass.

Her perfume wafted on the air. He closed his eyes and inhaled. Oh. My. God.

She's mine.

"PATIENCE," Ealund whispered in his head. *"NOT YET."*

He was right. Not yet. He wasn't ready.

"HE COMES." Ealund looked at the male descending the stairs. *"YOUR NEXT SACRIFICE."*

"No," Gideon said. "Not him. He's not even a student."

"HE IS MY CHOICE," Ealund said. *"MAKE IT SO."*

23

Taste of Blood

The twins were silent on the drive home. Kitt glanced in the rearview mirror. They just sat on the backseat, heads together, holding hands—fear etched on their young faces. She wished she could do something to alleviate their worry.

Kitt pulled up in front of the Pride's city residence. A huge concrete wall surrounded the grounds, and the house sat about six hundred feet from the front gate. More than anything, she didn't want to return them to her brother—but Oberon was right when he said if they didn't go back, it would just make her brother and father suspicious. She and Raven had no choice.

Kitt climbed out of the car and stood in front of them, feeling a little nervous herself.

"Just be careful and everything will be okay"—again wishing she could wipe away their discomforts, their scared and confused expressions—"and there's nothing wrong with what you are," she said in a low voice so no one could overhear. "You are very special."

They both smiled the same resigned smile, and she got the impression they were now trying to make *her* feel better.

"What if they want to know what we did?" Cal asked.

"Ah, that reminds me." Kitt opened the trunk and took out retail shopping bags from some of the trendiest stores, which contained items that Bianca had picked up. "Just say we went shopping and had a bite to eat."

A private security guard in a cheap black suit and tie stepped out of a small booth near the thick perimeter wall. The way he held his left arm was a dead giveaway: he carried a gun beneath his jacket.

"Here comes Uncle Nathan," Cal said, nodding to the large late-model car that came along the street and pulled into the drive beside them as she took the bags from Kitt.

The guard in the booth hit a button and the immense iron gates slowly rattled open.

The tinted black window of the car lowered with an electronic whir and Nathan's disapproving features appeared. "You girls, head up to the house—I want to talk to your . . . to Kathryn."

Her stomach sank. The last thing she needed right now was any more of his bullshit.

"Don't worry." Kitt hoped the twins understood what she was referring to. "Just go on in."

The girls looked uncertain. Cal glanced at her uncle and then grabbed her sister's hand and started up the drive.

Kitt gave them a little wave goodbye as they turned before walking through the gate, then they continued up to the house.

"Well?" Nathan said after they'd gone.

"Well, what?" Irritated, her foot started tapping as if she was in felian form, her tail would be flicking like mad.

His brow creased in his I'm-disappointed-in-you expression. "What did you find out about the campus killer?"

"You're joking, right? Besides, if I knew anything more, as I mentioned the other day"—she approached and placed her hands against the window, leaned in a little—"I'd report it to Tyrone, not *you*."

His lips thinned and tightened, the surrounding skin turned white, and a muscle ticked with the tension in his jaw. He waved off the security thug in sunglasses who started toward the car.

"I see you've taken to hiring humans," she said.

"You know the appeal a newly Awakened female has on felian males. The girls have no training on how to tone down their attraction. The other males were getting too distracted; humans aren't as susceptible."

Maybe, but she'd seen how the guard looked at the girls as they passed; the way his head tilted to the side watching their asses as they climbed the drive to the house.

"Is everything okay here, sir?" the armed human asked.

"Yes." Nathan tapped his driver's shoulder. "She's just leaving."

His window rose, dismissing her. The car moved forward and up the driveway to the house. The bodyguard stood inside the closing gate, watching her from behind his dark shades. If she transformed, she could rip out his throat before he had a chance to pull the gun.

Where had that thought come from?

Nathan wasn't a total fool. He would've hired humans who'd been training to deal with Animalians. In fact, the Family *business* offered just such a service to train bodyguards for their wealthy, questionable clients.

He stood there long after the gates closed, staring her down as she got back into her car. *Time to go home.* As she drove back to her empty apartment, she was tempted to go to the Bunker but knew it was just an excuse to see Raven, no matter how she tried to justify it.

The delicious smell of food cooking greeted her as she opened the door to her apartment. Maybe Oberon had decided to stay in the spare bedroom after all, knowing she would need some company.

She dropped her bag on the table and went into the kitchen.

It wasn't Oberon.

Raven stood shaking spices into something bubbling on the stove. He looked up and smiled. "Pasta will be ready in five; there's a bottle of red breathing on the table— Why don't you pour a glass?"

"Oberon's going to kill you when he finds out you're gone again," she said, actually relieved he was here.

"He'll have to catch me first," Raven said and dropped the smile. "I think we have to talk."

Her cell phone rang. She scrabbled through her bag trying

to find it. It rang out by the time she finally fished it out so she looked at the missed caller ID. Oberon's number flashed. She hit redial.

"I think you're busted," she yelled into the kitchen.

"If that shit is there, I'm going to rip him a new one," Oberon growled when he answered.

"Yes, he's here," she said. "Cooking me dinner."

"Does he understand the danger he puts you both in?" Oberon growled again. "Do you want me to come get him?"

"No, I think we have a few things to discuss."

"Tell him, next time he wants to go out, at least let me know first. And call me if you need anything. I can be there in twenty minutes."

"I will and I'll see you later," she said and hung up the phone.

The wine sat on the table just where he said. She poured two large goblets and carried them into the kitchen as he spooned rich red sauce over a bowl of spaghetti.

As he picked up the bowl of pasta she held the glass to his lips. He took a sip and then gave her cheek a quick kiss before carrying the food to the table.

"I learned this recipe from a little Italian woman on a cane farm where I was working near Cairns."

"What was it like?" she said.

He scooped out a serving of pasta and put it on her plate, then sat down and passed her the salad before serving himself. "Dig in while it's hot."

The rich aroma made her mouth water and her stomach growl.

He picked up his fork. "The Hennesseys were great parents and never stopped me from seeing the girls. They spent every other weekend with me as their uncle. Come on, eat—it's getting cold." He shoveled a large forkful of pasta into his mouth and grinned.

She got the impression he was avoiding the subject but let it drop.

The smell was divine and her stomach gurgled, reminding her how hungry she was. She lifted her own forkful for a taste. The flavors burst in her mouth . . .

She swallowed and wiped away the excess sauce with her napkin. "Oh my God—that's so good."

"Oh no," he said jumping up. "Almost forgot the bread."

He raced into the kitchen and came back with warm crusty rolls from the oven. The males of her people didn't cook, so this was luxury. The fresh doughy scent filled the apartment as he pulled apart the bread and slapped on a large dab of butter. Her mouth watered as he leaned across the table and held it to her lips. The buttery bread melted on her tongue, helped by his heated gaze.

They talked very little while she dug into the pasta and ate the bread. It was good, filling food. After a while she sat back, stuffed. As she wiped her mouth with the napkin, and reached for her glass of wine, Kitt noticed Raven watching her.

"What?"

"That is the first time I've seen you relaxed."

"I've had a lot to be tense about lately." She took a sip from the glass. Even the wine was perfect.

"And I haven't helped."

"Maybe." She sighed, putting her glass back on the table. "But there is just so much to take in. With my father, our daughters, a serial killer stalking the campus, and my brother's hostility—I just want to forget about it all, even if just for a short time."

He stood up, picked up her glass, and held out his other hand. "Here, come sit on the sofa."

For a moment she thought of refusing, but then reached and took his hand. He led her to the sofa, placing her glass within easy reach, and then pulled her back against his chest.

It was nice to be surrounded by his protective warmth—nice to feel safe again in his arms.

"Is that better?" he whispered in her ear.

She closed her eyes and sighed. "Yes, thank you." She twisted and looked up at him. "This Dúbabeo thing with the twins must be worrying you as much as me."

"I wish they hadn't kept it from me. I would've protected them better, kept them hidden. He wrapped both his arms around her. "I'm afraid that the longer they stay with the

Pride, the more it increases the chance that one of them may slip up."

Not if she could help it. She *had* to get back into the Pride. At least that way she'd be there to shield them and help keep their secret.

He caressed her hair and she snuggled deeper into his warmth, not wanting to think. As she closed her eyes, his stroking turned from comforting to something more sensual. This could only lead to one thing . . . but it felt too good to stop him.

He planted kisses on her shoulder, her neck, and cupped her breast, rubbing the pad of his thumb over her peaked nipple. She wanted to give in, she really did. Her stomach flipped and her core grew heavy with need. But giving in would not help her or the twins, would only make it harder to leave him later. And that's exactly what she'd have to do if they couldn't get the twins away.

"Raven." She sighed and leapt off the sofa. "We can't do this."

She wanted him more than anything but moved out of his reach, and turned her back on him.

His fingers trailed down her back. "I need you." His voice cracked. "I've needed you for so very long. That one taste of you has only made me want you more."

She turned and leaned against the wall, his crushed, broken expression melting her heart.

"Please," she said. "Right now I just need space to think."

"Fair enough," he said, dropping his gaze to his hands. "You need time. I get it. But know this—I want you now as I wanted you then. And without the shackles of the Pride, we have a better chance to be together."

After a moment, she heard the front door close and a tear fell down her cheek.

"Not if they kill you first," she whispered. The most dangerous thing for him was her. If he stayed near her, then the Pride would find him. And if not one of them, then one of the hired killers who would collect the bounty they'd set. Either way, he'd be dead.

* * *

The alarm buzzed loudly. Kitt hit the snooze button and rolled over to find an empty pillow beside her. Her body ached, the dull throb of needful pain clenched her lower abdomen—and she wished she hadn't turned Raven down. It was already too late to stop herself from falling for him again; she doubted she'd ever stopped.

He was right about the girls. The longer they spent with the Pride, the more the danger they were in. She had to figure how to get the Pride to take her back, or try to get them out. It would take some time and some careful planning.

Kitt arrived at the campus and climbed out of the car with her coffee in one hand. As she slung her handbag over her shoulder, the familiar black SUV pulled into the lot. The twins sat in the front, watching her. Joshua gave her a small wave and she returned it before heading for the main hall.

No one was in the Bunker operations room. She dumped her things on her desk and made her way down to Raven's room to make sure he got back okay.

She found him hitting the punching bag in the workout room and watched the way his muscles bunched as he struck and perspiration gleamed on his skin.

"Do you always work out this hard?" she asked.

He grabbed the bag with both hands to stop it from moving. "Only when I'm frustrated and there's nothing else to do."

"Well, I have a solution for that. We're going to get you to start training any recruits we find." Oberon said from behind her. "But first we have to figure how we're going to get those girls of yours away from Tyrone and Nathan."

"We were going to talk to you about that," Raven said, pulling off the gloves and dumping them on the weights bench beside him. "It should be easy enough if we grab them here at school, hide them away—I could even take them back to Australia."

"No. We need them here, at least for the time being," Oberon said and turned. "Let's discuss it in my office—I want to show you something."

Kitt and Raven followed the ursian down the hall and took a seat as Oberon sat opposite, behind his desk.

"Where is everyone?" Kitt asked.

"Bianca and Cody are investigating a lead on that copycat killing."

"And the others?" she asked.

"Tones is following something up in the Department archives and Antoinette is chasing her own leads," Oberon said.

"So what did you want to show us?" Raven asked.

"This." Using two fingers, he typed something into the keyboard on his desk and turned the screen around so they could see.

The twins sat in a classroom with two large men in suits sitting behind them.

"What?" Raven asked.

"I had a call from the head of the NYAPS board not long ago, informing me your father has demanded these body-guards escort the girls to all their classes and activities. I have no say in this at all, even as the Academy's head of security."

"Shit, that means they will never be alone," Raven spat. "Can he do that?"

"My father is either scared or suspects something's up," she said, yet was pretty sure the girls wouldn't have told Tryone anything. And maybe that was the problem: if they were silent about what went on, he'd know they were keeping something from him.

"What do we do?" Kitt asked.

"Nothing," Raven said. "We'll bide our time and trust in the twins. They're safe enough where they are at the moment. They know to be extra careful."

"But—" She just wanted to get them away.

"He's right," Oberon said. "If we act too soon, we could just blow our chances altogether. If the Pride withdraws them from the Academy and moves them back to the Pride-lands, they'll be well out of our reach."

She slumped back into her chair, defeated.

Raven reached over and took her hand. "I don't like this any more than you do."

She had to get out of here before the hot tears pricking her eyes made an appearance. "I'd better get ready for my class."

"Kitt?" Raven called after her, but she didn't stop.

It took several deep breaths to stave off the tears and pull herself together. By the time she reached the lecture hall, she'd regained her composure. She sat behind her desk and opened up the lecture notes in front of her, but the words just danced around on the page.

When it was time, Kitt picked up her papers and entered the lecture hall. The murmured discussion died down as she took a seat on the edge of the desk. The twins sat in the second-to-last row with their two human minders behind them. While Cal looked quite unhappy, Seph's face was positively thunderous as she glanced over her shoulder at one of the babysitters.

Kitt placed her notes on the desk beside her and stood up. "Today's class will go into the impact of Necrodrenia on the Aeternus metabolic system."

Kitt finished class and went back down to the Bunker. Antoinette looked up from behind her desk and smiled.

"Oberon said you were in Boston." Kitt sat heavily in a chair.

"One of the perks of having a rich lover with his own private jets," replied Antoinette.

Bianca and Cody also were at their desks and a sense of excitement filled the air. Oberon was talking animatedly on the phone in his office, seeming very pleased about something.

"What's going on?" Kitt asked.

Cody brushed his hair out of his eyes and smiled. "We found Carin Engels's killer. The employee we suspected is a medical student with access to the tools she needed to perform her little heart-ectomy, *and* a first-rate computer hacker. Tones helped track her down."

Tones was almost leaping out of his skin with excitement. "She hacked into the VCU system. That's how she knew details about the case we hadn't released to the papers and why she didn't know about the Dark Brethren symbol, because we hadn't told the VCU about it yet. Oberon's in there talking to CHaPR and the Department, which are not too happy with Neil Roberts's performance right now."

"Especially after the very public witch hunt he held in front of the press," Antoinette added.

Raven was there but remained silent in the background.

Oberon came out of the office looking like a bear who'd just stumbled across a honey factory. "It's official. We're to take over this case completely. CHaPR has just recognized the team and we've been officially added under the Department umbrella. The campus-killer case is now ours."

"What about VCU?" Tones asked.

Oberon's face broke into a shit-eating grin. "Neil Roberts has been reprimanded for security leaks and the team suspended, pending an investigation."

Raven rose from his seat and left the room. Kitt watched him go.

"You look like you could use a drink," Antoinette said.

Kitt smiled at her. "I think I could use a dozen."

"Then I know the perfect place. Come on. And get your boot-scooting boots on. Tones—you too," Antoinette urged. "We're going dancing—anyone else want to come?"

Oberon shook his head. "The mound of paperwork on my desk keeps growing."

"Cody and I have paperwork as well, on this girl we caught," the pale witch said.

Surfer-boy shrugged his shoulders, looking like paperwork was the last thing he wanted to do. "Maybe next time."

"But it's almost dawn," Tones said.

"You got somewhere better to be?" Antoinette placed her hands on her hips. "Come on, I thought you'd jump at the chance to escort two beautiful women for drinks and dancing."

His face beamed. "When you put it like that, how could I refuse?"

"Right!" She threw the keys at him. "You can drive."

24

sweet betrayal

The winter-kissed wind sliced through Gideon with the promise of snow. His face froze, but he hardly noticed. All he wanted, all he waited for, was a glimpse of *her*. Just one glimpse and he could go away happy.

Until next time.

The cold ran down the back of his neck like icy fingers as Ealund appeared at his side.

"YOU WASTE PRECIOUS TIME."

He shivered and hunched his shoulders as he turned the collar of his jacket up around his ears and ignored the tug of fear in his gut.

"SOON. IT MUST BE SOON," Ealund demanded. *"I MUST HAVE THAT SACRIFICE."*

"I'm almost ready," Gideon said distractedly, watching the doors. "The time is almost right."

What if she'd left already? What if she'd gone out another way? What if her car wasn't in this parking garage?

As if he'd summoned her with his mind, she appeared with another female beside her.

Ah . . . my angel—my sweet, sweet angel.

She stopped and pulled on some gloves, and a male followed. He linked his arms around the waists of both women as they walked. She laughed at something he said and looked at the other female laughing too.

Gideon stared at the male. His features burned into his brain. He recognized him instantly, and it made things a little easier.

All three climbed into a black Jeep Cherokee and drove off, leaving Gideon empty and seething. His fingers curled into fists, balled so tight the nails bit into his frozen palms.

His angel. His sweet, sweet angel.

Right now, he wanted to kill something. Wanted to strike out and destroy something to make this pain in his heart go away.

He turned to Ealund's ghostly figure. "Looks like you'll get your wish sooner than later."

"EXCELLENT!" the hollow voice of his master intoned.

25

Dance with the Devil

Antoinette walked in and waved to Buddy behind the bar. She'd been here often since she returned to New York; it was a great way to keep herself occupied while Christian was away. She learned to let go and enjoy herself in this place, and just being here reaffirmed the simple joys of life.

"Hey, Sherry," she called to the waitress busing tables on the other side of the room.

"Well. Hi there, sugar. Take a seat and I'll be right with y'all." Sherry placed beers in front of a couple of tourists—Antoinette could tell by the shiny new boots and creases in their new shirts.

"A Western bar?" Tones's jaw hung open. "I would have pegged you for a Goth girl or something."

"Hell no. I love this place. It may be a big tourist draw, but quite a few parahumans frequent this place too. Mostly Animalians and magic-wielders, but we do get the occasional Aeternus. The owner, Buddy"—she nodded to the guy behind the bar—"is a canian."

"Hey there, Antoinette." Sherry placed her hand on her hip. "What can I git y'all."

"It's okay, Sherry. These are my friends."

"Oh, thank goodness," the blonde whispered, her Southern accent switching to a broad Brooklyn one. "I'm just about to finish my shift so me and Buddy can go home to the kids. Hard to keep up this act when I'm tired."

"Sherry is Buddy's wife," Antoinette explained to the other two.

"How'do," Tones said, looking around all excited.

Antoinette knew he'd like this place. "Sherry, how about the usual for me. A glass of your finest vegan for my humegetarian friend here." She slapped Tones's shoulder. "And a Viktor Special for my felian girl."

"Comin' right up." The waitress smiled and squeezed Antoinette's shoulder before heading off toward the bar.

"You sure they have real vegan blood here?" Tones asked, his eyebrows rising with skepticism. "I'll be able to tell."

"What's a Viktor Special?" Kitt asked.

Antoinette just smiled and remembered when her friend Viktor Dushic had ordered her something fruity with an umbrella in it. It'd become known as a Viktor Special in honor of his memory. He would've been proud.

However, this was not a time for maudlin thoughts; it was a time for fun. She was determined to pass on the lessons Viktor taught her to someone who needed them: Kitt.

"I think I should go," the felian said.

"Hell no. We're just getting started," Antoinette said. "Why do you want to leave so early?"

Kitt glanced around uncertainly. "I can't shake this feeling someone is watching me."

"Then let's give her or him something to look at." Antoinette leaned over and popped open a couple of Kitt's top buttons. "Now take off your jacket and let down your hair."

The felian stood up, slid off her suit jacket, and untucked her white button-down shirt from her black linen pants. She pulled loose the ponytail and fluffed out her hair, then looked at them uncertainly. "Is that better?"

Antoinette gave her the thumbs-up. "Much."

"You look ready to par-tay," Tones agreed.

Sherry arrived with the tray of drinks. She unloaded crimson-filled glasses in front of both Tones and Antoinette, then placed an innocent-looking exotic cocktail, complete with a little paper umbrella and decorated with fruit, in front of Kitt. Antoinette knew from firsthand experience that looks were deceiving—the drink was practically pure alcohol.

Kitt took one sip and her eyes widened with surprise. "WOW! That packs quite a punch, doesn't it?"

"That's a Viktor Special, God bless him, and Buddy added a dash of belladonna just for you," Sherry said, laughed, and put a hand on Antoinette's shoulder. "We're off now, hon. You take care."

She walked back to the bar and passed her tray to Buddy's littermate Jenni. Buddy helped his wife into her coat and the two of them walked arm in arm to the door. Just before they left, Sherry gave a little wave to Antoinette and Buddy inclined his head in her direction.

"They're good people," Antoinette said after they were gone.

"How old are their children?" Kitt asked.

"About five or six, I think—why?" Antoinette looked at her.

"It can be hard on an Animalian to watch his human loved ones grow old and die if he marries a human." Kitt looked down at her hands. "Especially if the children don't awaken to their Bestiabeo heritage either."

"What are the chances they will?" Tones asked.

"Less than fifty percent," Kitt said.

"A little more than that in this case," a deep female voice said from behind.

Antoinette turned to find Buddy's sister with a tray of drinks balanced in one hand. She smiled, placed the tray on the table, then picked up a chair and turned it around, straddling the seat and resting her forearms on the back. "Here's a round on the house," she said.

"Kitt, Tones—this is Jenni," Antoinette said.

The female was Amazonian in physique. She extended a muscular arm to each of them. She had a jagged scar running across her throat.

Antoinette caught a glimpse of a tattoo on the canian's chest, half covered by her tank top. She glanced at Kitt, whose eyes were also glued to the same spot. It was hard to tell from the little that showed, but it looked similar to Raven's.

Antoinette leaned back in her chair. "Are you looking after the bar today?"

Jenni glanced over her shoulder. "Yeah, but we're breaking in a new guy, a coyote from up country. And I'm giving him a solo run to see how he handles it."

"What's your Pack name," Kitt asked with a slight tremble in her voice, her eyes flicking between the canian's face and the tattoo.

"Goodblood." Jenni frowned, becoming a little cagey.

"Buddy and Sherry's kids . . ." Antoinette interjected, hoping to distract them before Kitt said something Oberon might regret, "Why do you say they have more than a fifty percent chance?"

"Uh"—Jenni dragged her wary gaze back to Antoinette—"Sherry's mother was canian."

Kitt leaned forward. "Well, that's not so bad."

"What do you mean?" Tones asked.

"Being a latent Bestiabeo gives her a chance of a longer life span; not as long as a full Bestiabeo, but at least a couple of hundred years."

Jenni relaxed a little. "And she's expecting again. Which is why we're taking on extra staff. Last time nearly killed her and Buddy's real worried."

"I can understand that," Kitt said. "Bestiabeo pregnancies are demanding, especially in a human's body. And the last trimester can be very dangerous."

"Yeah—but she wants those pups so damn much." Jenni shook her head.

Voices started to rise over by the bar, and Jenni glanced over her shoulder again. "Shit! Looks like my cue. That coyote has a bit of a quick temper." She grinned. "Might have to beat that out of him."

Antoinette had no doubt she could. Kitt leaned into Antoinette. "That tattoo—I think she was a Draconus Nocti operative."

Antoinette watched Jenni walk back to the bar. "We should tell Oberon. Maybe Raven knows them."

"I'd say that would be a yes." Tones gave a slight nod to the door. Raven was standing there, looking at Jenni.

The Amazonian glanced over and broke into a grin, which Raven returned. His eyes swept the room—past his table of friends for a split second, then back, stopping on Kitt. He turned away and walked toward Jenni with purpose. Antoinette wondered if they'd been lovers—and from the looks of it, she wasn't the only one: a slight frown creased Kitt's brow, her eyes following his progress toward Sherry's sister-in-law.

Jenni came around the bar to meet him and gripped his right forearm with her right hand, as he did hers. A handshake of warriors. They exchanged soft words—so soft that Antoinette couldn't make them out with all the background noise, even with her enhanced hearing.

As he said something to Jenni, she turned to look in their direction. She nodded and returned to behind the bar as Raven made his way over to them.

"I didn't know you were coming here," he said, his eyes never leaving Kitt's face.

"Antoinette brought us," she replied, raising her chin a little higher. "I didn't know you knew *anyone* here."

"Who? *Jenn?*" Raven glanced back at the bar. "The Goodbloods and I go way back. Before us," he said, looking straight at Kitt.

"The Draconus Nocti?" Antoinette asked.

The canian raised an eyebrow in surprise and gave a simple nod. Tones gave a low, impressed whistle.

"Anyway, I'm here on business," Raven said quickly. "I'll leave you to your drinks." He bent low to whisper into Kitt's ear. Antoinette managed to make out *"I'll explain later."*

"No need," she said in a curt tone and picked up her cocktail. "It's none of my business."

Raven opened his mouth but closed it again—leaving whatever he was going to say unsaid. He turned on his heels and stalked back toward the bar, his hands clasped into fists at his side. Jenni greeted him with a tilt of her close-cropped head and led him behind to the office door at the end of the bar.

Antoinette leaned forward and picked up her glass. "How about we forget all about the Dark Brethren, campus killers, and Draconus Nocti for now and just enjoy ourselves."

"Hear, hear," Tones agreed, picking up his own drink and sniffing it. He took a tentative sip. His face lit up and he took a bigger mouthful. He eyes closed and he made a funny little noise in the back of this throat. He placed the glass back on the table and noticed them watching. Antoinette laughed at the expression on his face.

"Very good vegan," he said, smiling sheepishly. "I really didn't expect it to be genuine."

A band on the small stage started tuning up when they were on their third round of drinks and Kitt was just beginning to feel relaxed. The belladonna in the drink wasn't like the moonshine she drank with Oberon. This was a legal-strength kind—just enough to give her a nice, mellow buzz and enhance the effects of the other alcohol in the drink. At least enough to take her mind off the fact that Raven was alone with another woman only a few feet away.

What are they doing in there?

"Oh yes. The Blast," Antoinette said, watching the band. "They're great to dance to."

"You dance"—Tones's eyebrows rose high in disbelief—"to this?"

"Yeah, why?" Antoinette's voice took on a defensive tone.

Tones shrugged. "I just thought you would be more into alternative music, like pagan rock or something."

"I'm very eclectic with my music tastes, and I was recently introduced to the joys of a good boot-scooting, honky-tonk hoedown."

"Eighties music for me, especially British bands like the Smiths, the Cure, U2, Spandau Ballet, Duran Duran," Tones said and beamed. "But nothing beats a good Carpenters melody."

Kitt smiled. From his devout humegetarian practices, to his animal-activist activities, it didn't surprise her in the least to find out he liked the Carpenters. But eighties' British bands?—that was really different.

"You just continuously surprise me, Tones," Antoinette said, tilting her head. "However, today you are going to dance with a couple of females to the dulcet tones of the Blast."

As if hearing her introduction, the band started a rocking honky-tonk rhythm. Antoinette grabbed Kitt by the hand and pulled her out of her chair.

"No, I don't know how," Kitt said, trying to drag herself back to the table.

"I'll teach you." Antoinette's smile was pure joy.

Tones followed with a big, cheesy grin on his face. He really did worship the ground she walked on. A fact Kitt was sure Antoinette was not totally oblivious too, but she never encouraged him.

They joined a line forming in front of the stage. For the early morning, there were quite a few people here. Parahumans need to let their hair down too. Kitt saw a few students from her class, and was surprised to see Cal joining in the line behind her. All she could do was smile and wave as the lines started to move to the tune.

At first, Kitt mixed up her feet and went left as everyone went right but soon got into the rhythm. Tones was really good. He tucked his thumbs into the top of his jeans and stepped in time to the music with all the flourish of a seasoned professional.

With her head light from the belladonna, the music and other people's enthusiasm, Kitt started to giggle and then laugh. It was silly, heady fun—she hadn't enjoyed herself so much in a very long time. Antoinette grinned. Kitt wouldn't have thought the frightening Aeternus she'd seen in the alley was capable of having such simple fun, but here she was, dancing her ass off.

Kitt was a little sorry when the music finished, until another song started—this time a different repetitive dance sequence, but she soon picked up the steps. She couldn't keep the grin from her own face and suddenly worked out why Antoinette came here.

To do and be something completely different.

And to get away from all the death.

The real world would come crashing down on them soon enough; there was no point dwelling on it now. All she had to do was enjoy herself.

Kitt hugged Antoinette, then Tones. Someone tapped her on the shoulder. Cal stood behind her and Kitt hugged her too.

"What are you doing here?" she said in the girl's ear.

"Having fun, just like you," Cal replied.

Kitt grabbed her by the hand and dragged her off the dance floor to their table.

When they were seated, Kitt asked, "How did you get here?"

She pointed to some girls on the dance floor. "Some friends of mine from the Academy heard about this place and decided to check it out."

"What about your uncle? Does he know you're here?"

The girl shook her head. "Seph and I tricked the bodyguards. Today, I go out while she covers for me, and tomorrow I cover for her while she gets to escape. They're all way too serious—no one has any fun back there. It's the only way we can stay sane."

A shadow fell across the table. Antoinette looked up, half expecting Raven, but a heavyset male with the physique and dress sense of a long-haul trucker placed his hand on the back of Kitt's chair and leaned in. "Hey, pretty lady. How 'bout a dance?"

Kitt looked up at him. His mouth twisted into something that resembled a smile, but his eyes were narrowed and predatory. Even if she had been tempted to dance, she would've said no.

"Hey, thanks for the offer, mate." Cal winked as the corners of her mouth turned up sweetly. "Maybe later. Right now, we're talking."

Another male closed in behind Cal, obviously his friend, from the way they similarly dressed. "Who said it was an offer?"

Kitt shifted in her seat. This was not good. *Not good at all.*

From their tribal scars and snow white hair, Kitt knew

they were ursian, of the polar bear Family—the more aggressive of the Bestiabeo races. And there was one thing she
knew for sure—these guys were *not* going to take no for an
answer. If only Raven was out here. *Damn him.*

She looked around for backup and saw Antoinette coming
off the floor still laughing, but she slowed a few feet away
when she glanced over at them. The Aeternus seemed to
take in the situation with one intense and calculating frown,
then with a slight nod at Kitt, she plastered the smile back on
her face and approached.

"Well, you gals can talk all you want after we have a
dance." The male behind Cal moved in closer to block any
avenue of escape.

"Is there a problem here?" Antoinette asked as she came
around to Kitt's side.

"What's it to you?" asked Kitt's would-be sweetheart.

Antoinette's hand kneaded Kitt's shoulder with a posses-
sive squeeze. "You harassing my girl?"

"Your *girl*?" The guy snorted. "Yeah, *right*."

Antoinette buried her hand in Kitt's hair, and gently
yanked back her head. Then before she had time to prepare,
Antoinette kissed her. Not the usual peck on the cheek a
friend gives a friend, but a full openmouthed, tongue-
tangling, toe-curling, passionate embrace.

When she drew back, the Aeternus gave Kitt a cheeky
wink. Kitt could hardly breathe, partly out of shock and
partly because she was a fraction turned on. She'd never
kissed a woman before, never even thought of it, and never
really wanted to again. But that kiss had been something.

Antoinette turned back to the two slack-jawed ursians—
hand on hip. "She's mine and she's not interested."

"Way hey, hey," said the guy nearest to Cal, his cheeks
flushed. "That was the hottest thing I've ever seen."

The other one didn't look so excited. "All we want is a
little dance with these gals, and maybe then show them what
they's missin' out on."

Antoinette sighed, looked up, then dropped her head with
a shake. The two males closed in even more aggressively
than before. Kitt had a feeling this was about to get ugly and

looked around for the bartender, Raven, or Jenni before it got out of hand.

Antoinette's smile sent a familiar tremble of dread down Kitt's backbone.

"I tried, but fuck it." Antoinette grabbed the nearest male's shirt with both hands. He easily outweighed her by two hundred pounds, but when she smashed her forehead into the bridge of his nose, he stumbled back, his hands flying up to his mangled face.

His friend leaned forward and extended a right hook to Antoinette's jaw, sending her flying into the table behind.

"Hey!" Cal shot to her feet and jabbed a punch into the second male's gut. As he doubled over, she slammed the heel of her right hand against his nose.

The people sitting behind, whose table Antoinette had crashed into, weren't the least bit happy about having their evening interrupted. Not taking anyone's side, they pushed her away with an excessive amount of force. Antoinette spun around, hands up in apology when one of the guys at the table hit her full in the face, rocking her head back but not much else.

The Aeternus female got that lethal look in her eye and Kitt jumped up to stop her from taking the human's head off. For her trouble, she got slammed in the side of the face by another human just as one of the ursians recovered enough to spin Antoinette around for a teeth-rattling blow. Kitt grabbed the human by the arm, twisted it around behind him, and slammed him face-first into his table. Antoinette grinned widely and gave Kitt an approving thumbs-up before kicking the other advancing ursian hard between the legs.

The bear of a man collapsed to his knees with a crashing thud as he clutched his precious, wounded jewels. Cal leaned sideways and smashed the other ursian in the face with her foot, sending him to land on his friend.

Out of nowhere, Tones flew in to land on top of the duo. They didn't take long to recover, and a fist thrust out of the pile of arms, legs, and fat to collect Tones on the chin. He climbed from the floor a few feet away, his shaven head shaking. Cal and Antoinette stood side by side ready, waiting for their opponents to get up as Tones leapt on the table beside them and kicked the first one in the head before launching himself on the back of the second.

The fighting had spread to the dance floor too. Kitt watched as a couple of males crashed onto the stage and into the twin Marshall amps behind the bass player wearing a Blast T-shirt with a semi-faded *Tom* written across the top. The other members in the band kept playing as Tom brought down his bass guitar on the heads of the wrestling fighters and kicked them off the stage. Literally. Then without breaking his stride, he turned around and picked up another instrument from the stand, plugged it in, and continued to play.

"Behind you," Cal warned.

Kitt turned to find the human with a bloody face and a butterfly knife in his hand. Raven appeared behind the knifeman, his face a lethal mask of rage, with bared teeth and dark intense eyes. He snapped the human's wrist with a quick twist, and spun him around to face him.

"DON'T KILL HIM!" she yelled.

Raven looked through her as if he didn't see her, then his features relaxed and he dropped the man. With two striding steps, he was at her side and wrapping her in his arms as Jenni waded in to pluck Tones off the pile of bodies with one hand.

"Take him," the Amazonian growled and shoved him toward Antoinette. "How many times have I told you two?" Jenni picked the ursians up by the scruff of their necks. "No fighting in my place."

"We only wanted a dance with the pretty girls," the first ursian mumbled.

"Yeah," the second said with a bit more force. "Just one innocent dance."

"Hey!—No means *no,"* Jenni said as their fight started to come back and they both began to struggle. She brought their heads together in an almighty crack and the ursians crumpled to the floor, unconscious. It took a lot of force to knock out any Bestiabeo, let alone a couple of hardheaded bears.

The burly female bartender picked up one, slung him over her shoulder like a sack of corn, and carried him out of the bar. A moment later she stalked back into the bar and did the same with the other one.

Then the coyote bartender righted tables and piled together pieces of broken chairs.

Kitt's hands were still shaking. That fight had been as scary as hell, but at the same time, she'd rather enjoyed it in a perverse, adrenaline-pumping way. And maybe, just maybe, she wasn't completely helpless after all.

Raven picked up an overturned chair and sat her down at the table. Miraculously, their table was still upright with her drink intact. She drew a long mouthful of alcohol-laced fruit juice through the straw. As she sat back, a strange aftertaste coated her tongue.

"Maybe we should go . . ." The words sounded slurred in Kitt's ears.

Surely she wasn't that drunk. The cocktail. *The aftertaste*. Her blood ran cold. "Heeeyyyy," she drawled. "Tha's not m'drink."

Kitt's vision swam and her head spun. She clutched the edge of the table and tried to stand, but her legs wanted to go in the opposite direction she did.

"Kitt?" Raven's voice was distorted, sounding both far away and close at the same time. "Are you okay?"

"Shit . . . aconite."

Kitt couldn't tell who said that—her hearing felt just as blurred as her vision. Wolfsbane, *Aconitum vulparia*, was toxic to Bestiabeos. Her heart seemed to be beating inside her eardrums. She swayed, her vision doubled, trebled, and then clouded. The floor rushed up to meet her.

"Can you hear me?" The voice came from far away. Too far away. "Kit . . ."

26

poison dreams

Raven paced the floor of the recreation room. Antoinette
had convinced him not to go to the hospital with Kitt by
having Jenni knock him out. By the time he came around,
he was already back at the Bunker.

"She shouldn't have been there."

"They were only having a drink and some fun." Oberon
sat with his right ankle resting on his left knee and his left
arm resting along the back of the sofa.

He looked far too relaxed for Raven's liking. "And Cal,
what about her?"

"Tones took her straight home—"

Raven stopped, frustrated and afraid. "Who would do
such a thing?"

"We don't know. Antoinette's back at the bar questioning
the patrons and staff," Oberon said, his voice annoyingly calm.

"No, I'm not," Antoinette said from the doorway. "I called
Bianca to go to the hospital."

Oberon came to his feet. "Did anyone find anything?"

"Not really, but Buddy came back in and gave me the surveillance video," she said, holding up a CD. "Jenni's really
beating herself up over this."

Oberon stood and took the CD from Antoinette. "I'll get
Tones to go over it as soon as he gets back."

"I'll go over it now," Raven said and reached for the CD.

"No, you won't." Oberon put a hand on Raven's chest.

He dropped his gaze to it. "You going to move that or am I going to take it off at the elbow?"

"You're too close to this." Oberon didn't move for a second, then leaned in so he spoke only to Raven. "And it won't do her any good. Just take a deep breath."

His eyes rose to the ursian's face—they locked in a silent battle of wills, and then Raven turned to slam his fist through the wall.

Oberon crossed his arms. "Feel better?"

"Hell yes," Raven spat and then shook his head. "I haven't felt this fucking helpless since they took the girls away."

The ursian clasped his shoulder. "I know."

Raven could see that, despite his outward appearance, Oberon really was just as frustrated.

At a noise in the hall, Antoinette disappeared. "Bianca's back," she called. "With Kitt."

Raven raced out the door to find Bianca supporting the woman he loved—pale, shaky, and very vulnerable.

He stomped forward and swept her up in his arms despite her weak protestations. She was light as he carried her to his room and laid her tenderly on the bed.

"You should've stayed in hospital," he said. Some of the pain and frustration he felt made his voice harsher than he intended.

"You don't have to worry," she whispered.

She knew him so well.

Her weak smile made her pale face a tiny bit brighter. "I'm fine. They pumped my stomach and gave me a shot of digitalis to counteract the effects of the *Aconitum*."

He smoothed back her hair. She'd nearly died. If Cal hadn't been there to recognize the poison that could fatally harm an Animalian, he would have lost her. The words caught in his throat, choking him. He knelt beside the bed and laid his head just below her breasts, wrapped his arm across her stomach, holding her as tight as he could without crushing her bones.

The moment her fingers stroked his hair his control broke.

* * *

Oberon stood at the door watching Raven's shoulders shaking as he clung with desperation to a very pale and fragile Kitt. He pulled the door closed to give them privacy.

The canian confused him. Oberon could see how much the two were completely lost without each other. Why couldn't they see it too? Raven's devastation at her condition had to prove something to Kitt. It broke his heart to see the pain they were both in, but they would have to sort that out for themselves. Other things needed his attention right now.

Tones was back and stood in front of the large smart screen.

"What've we got?" Oberon asked as he stopped beside the Aeternus and looked at the frozen bar scene on the screen.

"There are multiple cameras to work from." Tones reached up and touched a symbol to the side of the picture. The screen split into four images, each showing a different angle of the bar. "It is a really good setup, very professional. I've set it up to go frame for frame in sync from each angle."

"When is this?" Antoinette said, coming up behind them.

Tones turned to her. "See, there's you leaving the dance floor. And there's me talking to a couple of hot babes." He turned around grinning. "They liked my dancing."

Oberon crossed his arms, mainly to stop from reaching out and shaking the shit out of Tones. He seemed to sense Oberon's impatience because the grin disappeared and he turned back to the board.

Tones cleared his throat and tapped a symbol to start the video moving again. "Anyway, here's Kitt and her daughter talking to the ursians."

Antoinette leaned in. "Stop a minute and go back a bit."

Tones did as she asked and Oberon tried to see what she caught. "There, stop. Can you bring this up and go frame by frame."

The three other camera angles disappeared and the lower bottom image filled the screen. Tones tapped the side and the video moved forward one frame at a time.

"There," she said. "Did you see it?"

The one behind Cal looked over his partner's shoulder and nodded to someone off camera.

"Can we track it back and find out where these two came from?" Oberon asked.

"Sure thing, Captain." Tones moved his fingers around the screen; pictures flew past as Tones's eyes flicked from image to image. Then he stopped— "*There.* At the bar." The screen paused. "See the guy talking to the ursians?"

He started the images moving again at quarter speed. The new player kept his head down and the brim of a cowboy hat pulled low, but he wore a suit.

The ursians nodded, looked over toward Kitt and Cal, and nodded again. Then the guy with the cowboy hat slipped something into one of their hands.

"Do you think he's paying them?" Antoinette asked.

Tones said, "Let's take a look at what he's doing during the fight."

The images streamed by at top speed, then Tones froze the screen to show the man in the cowboy hat keeping his head down as he leaned back against the bar, propping himself up with his elbows.

Oberon slapped Tones on the shoulder. "Can you zoom in on him?"

Tones tapped the screen several times and with each re-rendering the image deteriorated a little more, but got the close-up enlarged enough to show a gold-coin ring on the ring finger of the man's left hand and a small birthmark near his wrist.

"I'll make a hard copy of that," Tones said as he hit a button on one side and reset the screens again.

Tones may be quirky, but he was a true genius when it came to this stuff. He took the frames forward slowly, using the other camera angles to track the suspect. The male knew cameras were on him because he never lifted his head high enough for a camera to get a full shot of his face.

With head down, the man in the hat snuck a look over his shoulder and slid a hand into his pocket.

On another screen, the fight broke out. The hat guy turned and watched; they couldn't see his face, but Oberon could tell from the male's stance that he was satisfied with the outcome. A drink identical to Kitt's sat on the bar beside him. The coyote barman stood back from the bar, looking around uncertainly—Jenni Goodblood, nowhere to be seen. When the Amazonian female came through a side door carrying a box of liquor a few moments later, it was all over. She quickly surveyed the scene with narrowed eyes and zoned in on the huddled fight in the middle and turned to silently yell through the open door.

Raven appeared in the doorframe a second later.

Oberon glanced at the other screens. Kitt handled herself very well, especially with the humans; she'd watched the others, her face focused, looking for an opening to jump in.

"I didn't think she had it in her," Antoinette said. "But look at the way she watches, tense and on the balls of her feet, ready to pounce if necessary."

Pride welled in his chest. "Kitt's always been a fighter, but usually does it with her brain rather than actual physical fighting."

The brawl stopped as the bartender slammed the two heads together.

"*THERE!*— Did you see it?" Tones yelled.

"What?" Oberon asked.

Tones took the video back several frames. "Watch the lower right-hand corner of the top left screen."

Everyone had their backs turned away from the table Kitt, Tones, and Antoinette occupied, which had miraculously survived upright. The man in the hat slid by smoothly, pulling his hand from his pocket and tipping over Kitt's drink before slipping away and out the door. He left the unrequired cocktail sitting on the bar.

Oberon got Tones to rewind and play it again. The move was so smooth, so effortless. No one noticed him. Everyone in the bar was focused on the action in the center of the room.

Tones zoomed in on Kitt's image as she sat down and reached for the drink. She took a long pull on the straw. The color drained from her face as she turned to speak on the soundless video. She staggered slowly to her feet as she tried to stand up but knocked over her chair and fell forward to brace herself against the table.

Then her knees gave out and she collapsed sideways. On the screen, Cal picked up the cocktail, dipped her pinky finger, and sniffed.

"That's where Cal detected a large quantity of aconite in the drink. She was amazing—she stuck her fingers straight down Kitt's throat, making her vomit up the poison," Antoinette said.

"It saved her life." Bianca came up behind them. "Do you think it has anything to do with the Dark Brethren?"

"No—this seems personal and calculated, different from either the dreniac attacks or the campus killer," Tones replied. "Too cowardly."

He was right. It lacked the bloodiness.

Oberon had his suspicions. "I've a feeling we're going to have one pissed-off wolf on our hands."

Kitt snuggled against the warmth and opened her eyes to find Raven staring at her.

A slow smile stole across his mouth as he reached up and tucked a lock of hair behind her ear. "Do you know how much you scared me today?"

"Probably as much as I scared myself." She leaned forward and kissed the tip of his nose. "But I'm all right now."

"What happened?" he asked, stroking her face.

How was she supposed to think with him touching her like that? She closed her eyes and tried. "I remember the fight breaking out. And afterward I sat down and took a drink, but it tasted different. It's my fault for not checking. I'm sure it was just a mistake."

"Hmm . . ." Raven frowned. "I'm not sure anyone else thinks that."

"What else could it be?" *Why would anyone want to kill me?*

"Let's just see what the others come up with," he said, his expression guarded.

His touch was soothing and she soon found it difficult to

keep her eyes open. The sound of his voice was almost hypnotic and lulling.

Raven leaned over and kissed her. Kitt murmured in her sleep as he snuck out of the room, and closed the door quietly. He could hear hushed voices coming from Oberon's office. They stopped the moment the ursian spotted him through the glass panel wall as he came down the corridor.

"What've you found out?" he asked without any preamble.

Oberon leaned back in his chair and crossed his arms. "Nothing much yet."

Tones seemed to be avoiding him. The Aeternus looked down at his hands, at Oberon, and anywhere else that wasn't in Raven's direction. He knew something. And Raven had a better chance of getting something out of Tones than Oberon, but not while the ursian was around. He'd have to wait for the Aeternus to leave and ask him then.

As if reading his thoughts, Tones stood up. "I think I'll head home now."

Oberon nodded as he picked up some papers and glanced at Raven before waving Tones off. "I've a few more things to do here before I leave. I'll see you tomorrow night."

The Aeternus male left the room with a cursory nod to Raven.

"I'd best get back to Kitt. I don't want to leave her alone too long."

"Before you go, I'd like a word."

"Okay." Raven could still see Tones as he headed toward the Bunker exit.

"I know you and Kitt have history." Oberon stood, towering over Raven. "But you hurt her again and I'll tear you apart."

"If I hurt her again," Raven said, looking up, "I'll let you."

Oberon inclined his head once, a small predatory smile tugging at the corners of his mouth. "Then, that's a promise. And close the door on your way out."

Raven pulled the office door shut and hurried back down the corridor to his room.

Kitt was still sleeping when he crept in. Careful, so as not to wake her, he grabbed his shoes and a shirt and walked into the sparse bathroom. He slipped on his shirt and climbed onto the toilet cistern.

The screws on the vent cover were bogus. He tugged off the metal grate held on by the magnetic clips he'd attached fifty years ago. He could never cop to the fact there was only one way in and out of the complex—if they ever got cut off, they'd be trapped in here. And that scared the shit out of him. So he'd set about making his own back door for emergency use. He tossed in his shoes first and hauled himself up to the metal opening. It was a tight squeeze, but not impossible; and he'd done it many times before in years gone by.

Halfway down, he slid open another metal panel and crawled out into the old airshaft. From there it was an easy climb up to the exit hidden on the Animalian reserve.

Tones would've had a head start. Raven just hoped he hadn't left the parking lot. A large section of the car park was under cover so the Aeternus faculty and staff didn't have to worry about direct sunlight.

Tones's Jeep was still there, but no sign of the Aeternus. As he was walking through the parking lot, a familiar dark scent wafted on the wind.

The killer.

He's here.

Raven loped forward, following the fresh trail. He was close. Very close. He changed his eyes and his face to enhance his canian senses. A few feet from Tones's car, he saw a dark droplet. He squatted and dipped the tip of his first two fingers into the sticky spot, then rubbed it with his thumb pad and sniffed. The dark metallic scent confirmed his worst fears.

Blood.

He sniffed the smear again.

Aeternus blood. *Tones's blood.*

The scent trail led to the small gap between two buildings, and Raven raced across the grass to continue following it. He entered a recess used as a make-out spot, given the privacy of the eight-foot wall at the end.

Grunting sounds greeted him from within the darkness. They could be mistaken for the sounds of just another amorous couple having a semi-public fuck, if it wasn't for the strong scenting of fresh Aeternus blood. In the corner of the alcove, a hunched figure leaned over something on the ground. Raven crept closer. The smell of the blood grew stronger.

The figure wore some sort of camouflage coveralls and a hood or beanie. He turned around and stared directly at Raven. Whether it was male or female, it was difficult to tell. The figure spun. It was definitely a beanie, and ski goggles covered the face. The figure stood, raced for the wall, and started to climb within a blink of an eye. Raven gave chase, but as he passed the body on the ground, he looked down and saw Tones's eyes staring up.

Go after the killer or get Tones to help. He was torn. The predator in him said chase; the man in him said help. He ran and prepared to jump after the fleeing killer. The thought of Kitt entered his head unbidden. If Tones died, she'd never forgive him.

He stopped.

Punched the wall.

And turned back to Tones.

His chest had been ripped open and wasn't healing as it should be. Dark Aeternus blood soaked his clothes and was splashed on nearby walls; his mouth was stuffed with a gag. Raven yanked it out and tossed it aside. He scooped the male up into his arms and Tones's limbs flopped to the side, unmoving.

The only way to go to the hub was through the front door. People turned and gasped as he carried Tones's bloody body across the lobby to the elevators. No one stopped him—no one even tried. They all stood back, stunned.

The elevator doors opened and he pressed the lowest level on the panel with his toe while he juggled to hold Tones steady. Nothing happened. He stared up at the camera in the corner, sending the watcher a silent message, hoping to communicate his meaning. Suddenly the elevator started to descend. The Aeternus was conscious, but paralyzed, and didn't utter a sound the entire trip in the elevator.

When the doors slid open, Oberon was waiting for him. *"What happened?"*

"Your killer. He's struck again." Raven let Oberon help carry Tones. "He's in a pretty bad way."

The ursian nodded. "Let's get him inside quickly."

Navigating the circular stairs was difficult, but they got him downstairs.

Oberon carried the wounded male into the conference room and lay him on the table. "Go wake Kitt."

"I'm already here." She raced forward, but slid to a halt as she saw blood covering Raven. Her eyes widened.

"It's all his," he consoled. "Go. See to Tones."

"I need hot water and fresh towels," Kitt said as she raced to Tones's side. "Fetch me some surgical instruments."

Oberon obeyed without hesitation. This was her world and she was in total control.

27
Beautiful Evil

Gideon threw the coveralls into the incinerator. The drying blood bubbled and blackened as the flames consumed the heavy material.

"HE WAS THE WRONG ONE." Ealund spoke quietly from behind.

A chill crawled up Gideon's spine and terror prickled like a thousand tiny bugs crawling beneath his skin. He didn't want to turn, but had to. Tears spilled from his eyes.

"I *couldn't* wait for the bear, it was getting late."

"AND STILL YOU FAILED ME," Ealund said, waving his hand across his body.

Gideon flew across the room and slammed into the wall. With each death, Ealund had grown stronger. Gideon had considered stopping, but it was too late. After Carin's death, Ealund's fury had been terrifying to behold. She was to serve the Dark Brethren and they'd been cheated out of a recruit. Even though Gideon wasn't responsible, he bore the brunt of Ealund's enraged frustration with a pain so excruciating, he broke into a sweat just remembering it.

"I'm sorry, my lord," Gideon said, climbing to his feet. "I was interrupted."

"YOU COULD'VE DEALT WITH THE DOG." Ealund

sneered. *"INSTEAD YOU RAN AND CHEATED ME OF MY SACRIFICE."*

"He was too powerful for me. I've seen him before; I would've been caught or worse, and you'd have no more tributes."

The vaporous form threw back its head and cold, dark laughter shattered the last of Gideon's nerve. *"DID YOU REALLY THINK YOU WERE THE ONLY ONE?"*

"I . . ." Gideon closed his open mouth. That's exactly what he'd thought. Now he felt cheated. He'd been promised greatness. "Then let others serve you, lord, if I am unworthy."

"AH, BUT IT DOES NOT WORK THAT WAY." Ealund lifted his ghostly hand, pressure coiled inside Gideon's heart and tightened. *"YOUR WORK IS UNFINISHED AND I NEED YOUR SACRIFICES. FEEL MY GROWING POWER."*

Gideon's fingers scrabbled at his chest, trying to release the force squeezing his heart before it exploded. Ealund's smile twisted in macabre delight. The pressure forced all the air from Gideon's lungs; his temples thudded from the lack of oxygen, and his terror.

"NOW"—Ealund opened the fingers of his fist and then clenched them tighter. *"NOW YOU MUST MAKE THE SACRIFICE. WE'VE TALKED OF IT. YOU KNOW WHOM I WANT. BRING THEM TO THE SACRED PLACE."*

"Please, don't make me—"

"YOU WILL DO THIS." Ealund tightened his fist again.

Gideon felt his eyes would burst from their sockets at any moment. He nodded.

"GOOD." Ealund dropped his hand. *"WHEN YOU DO THIS, I WILL FREE YOU FROM YOUR PRISON FOREVER."*

Gideon fell forward on his hands and knees, gasping for breath. He looked up, but Ealund was gone. A giddy wave of nausea swept over him and he rolled over onto his back. He wanted to get back to his cell, where he was safe. He didn't even know if he wanted freedom anymore.

28

agent down

Bianca brought the towels and a kettle while they waited for Oberon to get back. Kitt dipped the cloth in the warm water and wiped it over Tones's torso. Aeternus blood didn't clot like human blood and came off easily.

Oberon returned a few minutes later with a tight roll of clean, white cloth.

She unwrapped the bundle to reveal surgical instruments. "The chest wound is deep and isn't healing as fast as it should, due to the silver blade lodged in the back of his neck. I must remove it carefully or it might kill him." Kitt looked up at Oberon. "I'll roll him onto his side; I need you to hold his head."

Like all the others, the blade was lodged perfectly between the C6 and C7 vertebrae. She had to remove it in one piece. If even a tiny sliver broke off and entered his bloodstream, it could prove fatal.

"Hold his head still," she ordered.

Oberon braced his massive hands on either side of Tones's head as she picked up her instruments and went to work.

She cut the skin and peeled it back, then cut through the tissue. Tones screamed. There was nothing she could give him, nothing to deaden the pain. She just had to try to work as fast as possible.

As the edge of the blade became visible, she picked up the forceps and carefully worked it loose. Once the silver metal was out, the wound closed and began healing completely. Oberon carefully turned him onto his back. The broken rib cage bones reconstructed and the chest wound started knitting.

Tones began to move. Oberon helped him to sit. Though he was still very shaken, he tried to stand, but his legs collapsed underneath him. Oberon caught him before he fell and held him while Kitt lifted his face and looked into his eyes.

"You're in an Aeternus form of shock. You need fresh blood and lots of rest." She turned to Oberon. "Set him up in a room here where I can watch him."

Tones looked around with haunted eyes. It was more than physical injuries that plagued him. While his body healed, it was going to take a while for the psychological scars to disappear. Beside all that, the killer was still out there. Maybe she could get Antoinette to have a word with him.

"I'm fine to—"

Kitt held up a hand to stop him. "I insist. It's going to be a few days to make sure that nothing happened when I removed the blade."

"Do what the bloody doctor tells you," Oberon growled.

She looked up at him. Now the danger was over, he could give in to his angry fear.

"But my cats," Tones frowned. "Who will feed Millie and Casper?"

"I'll go get them. A couple more animals around here aren't going to make much of a difference." Oberon scowled.

Kitt smiled. He really could be thoughtful when he tried.

"But"—he pointed at Tones—"the first cat shit I stand in comes out of your hide."

"They're house-trained, Captain," Tones said with a gratified smile.

The phone rang and Bianca picked it up.

"They'd better be," the ursian grumbled as he started to stalk away, saying, "Where the hell is Cody?"

"He's upstairs calming things down," Bianca quickly replied as she was covering the mouthpiece and holding out the phone. "And Agent Roberts would like a word."

"Tell him to go fuck himself." Oberon crashed out of the room like a receding storm.

"I'm sorry Agent Roberts, Captain DuPrie is unavailable right now. May I take a message or have him return your call at a later time?" The pale witch winced and held the phone away from her ear.

Raven came in showered and changed. The memory of him covered in so much blood made Kitt's heart skip another beat. The thought of losing him . . . it was too much.

Kitt placed a hand on his arm. "Can you help Tones to one of the rooms? He needs blood. I'll prepare some from his stash in the fridge, but I'll have to get Antoinette to organize a donor for a fresh supply."

"I have a card in my jacket," Tones said as Raven moved under his arm to help him to stand. "They're my regular suppliers. Then I can be sure I have proper vegan blood."

"Okay, go lie down and don't worry; we have it under control." Kitt turned to Bianca. "Do you know where Antoinette is?"

"I'll try her cell," the witch said. "Oberon is pretty pissed—he must like Tones a lot."

"Yeah," Kitt said. "They've always been pretty tight."

Kitt stopped at Tones's desk to pick up his cup. Lying on top of some other papers was a close-up print of the back of a male hand wearing a ring, pouring something into a cocktail that looked like the one she'd been drinking at the bar. The ring had her family symbol and a distinctive birthmark marred the skin near his wrist.

She slipped the picture into her jeans pocket and pulled her shirt down over the pants. In the kitchen she pulled out the special warmer Tones kept in the cupboard and filled it up with water. She grabbed one of the bottles from the fridge and put it in the warmer, then snuck another look at the print. It had something to do with her poisoning.

She tucked the print back into her pants and twisted the bottle sitting in the warmer. Microwaving tended to destroy the cells, breaking them down, making it useless to the Aeternus. This way warmed it slowly while still maintaining the structural integrity of the blood cells.

The drink would tide him over for now, but he needed fresh blood from a living source for faster, more complete healing. The Aeternus would remain weak for several days while enzymes rebuilt his body.

The timer on the warmer finally chimed. She lifted the bottle from the warm water and filled his cup. She met Raven coming down the hall.

Kitt placed a hand on his arm. "Thanks for your help."

"What else could I have done?"

"You could have left him and gone after the murderer." The thought terrified her. What if Raven had caught him and gotten hurt himself, or even killed?

She took a mental breath. "What room is he in?"

"The third on the right."

"I'll come find you as soon as I've seen to Tones," she said.

He leaned forward and kissed her softly, his lips barely brushing hers. "I'll be waiting," he said as he drew back.

The dark smolder in his eyes set her blood racing. Again, she realized, it was too late to guard her heart against him— she was going to lose herself in those eyes. But first she had a patient to attend to.

"Come in," Tones answered to her soft knock.

She handed him the warm mug as she sat on the side of the bed. "How are you feeling?"

"Woozy, a little shaken, and"—he dropped his eyes—"a lot scared."

"Do you want to tell me about it?" she asked.

He shook his head. "Not yet. Oberon will want to question me later and I don't think I can tell it twice."

Hmm, Oberon had the tact of a sledgehammer; she might talk to him about that.

"How 'bout we talk about this instead?" Kitt pulled the photograph from her pants and handed it to him.

He took the picture and his eyes widened. "Where did you get this?"

"From your desk."

"Shit," he spat. "He's going to kill me."

"Who is?" she asked.

"Oberon." He sighed. "You weren't supposed to see this. You or Raven."

She stood, no longer able to sit still. The cold stone of dread lodged in the pit of her stomach. "What do you know?"

"Nothing." He tried to bluff her, but she stared him down and he finally threw up his hand. "Okay. Not a lot, though."

"Tell me what you *do* know." She sat back down on the bed.

"All we know is that this guy paid the ursians to approach you and then poured the poison into your drink while everyone was distracted."

She stood again. "I thought it was just a mistake, the heavy hand of an inexperienced barman."

Suddenly there was no air left in the room. The walls seemed to close in on her. Who would want her dead? Who would rather not have to deal with her existence, enough to hire someone to poison her?

Her father.

With her gone, he wouldn't have to face the embarrassment of letting her back into the Pride. And he would have complete control over her daughters. *Did I embarrass him that much?*

Yes. Yes, she did.

She had openly opposed him once, but only once, when she refused to marry Leon. He had banished her then. But she'd followed all the rules to gain reinstatement into the Pride in the proper manner; and later she hadn't opposed her brother's guardianship over her children, even though it almost killed her to know they were with him.

The anger boiled over. "Is there anything else?"

He shook his head. It was too much. Kitt snatched back the print and raced from the room and out of the Bunker. When she reached her car, she began searching the pockets of her jeans for the keys.

Shit. She'd left them behind.

The lights of the now-familiar black SUV flicked on. She ran toward it, yanked the back passenger door. "Take me to my father."

* * *

Jericho pulled up at the front gates of Nathan's house. If Tyrone had moved his base to Nathan's house, it meant he must be worried about security. Maybe it had something to do with the twins' bodyguard detail.

"My father has changed his mind about returning home, I take it."

"The Alpha has decided to remain in the city indefinitely," the driver said.

When the SUV stopped in front of the house, she leapt out without waiting for someone to open the door for her. She found her father in the large formal sitting room.

He had guests.

Corey O'Shea, gangster and known drug lord. His long-haired personal bodyguard and brother, Seamus, stood behind him and Tyrone with hands clasped low in front of his ankle-length black leather coat. Rumor had it that Seamus O'Shea was also his brother's assassin-for-hire. One look at his cold eyes and Kitt could definitely believe that.

"I need to talk to you. Alone," she said to her father.

Tyrone refused to look at her. "I'm busy. You'll have to wait."

"*NO. NOW!*" She dropped the print on the coffee table in front of him.

29

can't pick your family

Raven lay on his bed looking up at the ceiling while he waited for Kitt to return to the room. *Where could she be?* It'd been over an hour.

"Shit." He climbed off the bed and opened the door.

"*What* did she say?" Oberon's raised voice bounced down the corridor from Tones's room.

"I didn't know she'd left the building," Tones said.

She? Raven's heart stilled in his chest, then started with a sluggish *ker-thump.* Were they talking about Kitt?

He hurried down the hall and slid to a halt just inside the door. "What's happened?"

Oberon ran a massive hand over his dreadlocked head. "Kitt went off after she discovered a picture we took from the surveillance video."

"What picture?" Raven growled. *They had information they hadn't told him about?*

Oberon looked at him, his brow knotted mid-forehead. "The one with a hand wearing a Jordan Pride ring."

Her family? Why would they want to kill her?

If Tyrone found out about his and Kitt's past or present relationship, or worse—the twins, they could all be in danger. And now Kitt had stormed into the lion's den.

Raven knew that's where she'd be. "We must go after her."

"I know," Oberon said. "I'm just working out how to approach it."

"Work it out on the way," Raven said. "She's in danger."

That seemed to polarize the ursian. He nodded his large head. "Okay, but you can't come."

"Like hell, I can't," Raven said.

"Are you insane?" Oberon scowled down at him.

"After this it won't matter, because—"

Raven woke in his room to his head pounding and jaw aching, and sat bolt upright.

Kitt.

Oberon must've slugged him good. He leapt off the thin mattress and raced into his bathroom. The cover over the airshaft didn't give way on the first tug. He changed his angle and pulled harder, but it still didn't budge.

"I wouldn't bother if I was you," a feminine voice said from behind.

Bianca Sin was leaning against the doorframe with arms crossed and an amused expression. "He said it's for your own good. It's too dangerous to let you go after Kitt. You'll be dead before you get near her."

He looked closer at the screws. They weren't just glued-on heads, but brand-new shiny screws, firmly fastened.

"FUCK!" he yelled and slammed the grate with both hands.

"That won't help either." The pale witch smiled. "He also said to tell you to review and weigh up the mission risks like you used to do in the old days, and also that you should know, Tyrone would never order his daughter's death.

Raven climbed down from the toilet. "He's right." He clasped his hands together and leaned forward, resting his elbows on his knees. He'd been too angry and frightened for his family's safety to think straight.

"So he found out my secret escape route?" Raven reached up to scratch a tickle on the side of his neck and touched something foreign.

No, he couldn't have. Raven stood and looked in the mirror. A braided leather cord surrounded his neck, clasped with a tiny combination lock.

He did. Oberon had fitted him with a change inhibitor. While he wore the leather-encased silver cord, Raven couldn't take wolf form.

"Fuck! *FUCK!*"

Tyrone picked up the picture and glanced at it before raising his eyes to meet hers. "Corey, can you give me a few moments with my daughter?"

She sucked back her breath and stilled. He'd referred to her as his daughter.

The drug lord raised an eyebrow and stood, rebuttoning his expensive suit jacket. "Of course. Family always comes first." He nodded to his brother and they both left the room.

"I want privacy," Kitt said when Tyrone's bodyguards made no move to leave. "Complete privacy."

Her father turned and waved his men out.

"What's this?" he asked, holding up the picture.

"The other night, someone tried to poison me. And this is what was caught on camera."

"There must be some mistake." He stood. "Someone set this up. Why would any Jordan harm you?"

"I was hoping you'd tell me." Her anger bubbled just below the surface, but she kept it in check. "Maybe it would make it easier if I was out of the way—after all, you didn't even acknowledge your own son's death."

"Do you really think that little of me that you would even consider I would put your mother through that again?" His face crumpled, and he fell back onto the sofa. "You saw her. She was devastated when Dylan died. One visit from you and she is already talking more like herself. How do you think she would handle *your* death?"

Holy shit. Of course her father wouldn't be so cruel—at least not to her mother. "I'm sorry."

"And do you have any idea how hard it's been on me? Losing Dylan . . ." His voice cracked and he looked away.

Maybe his refusal to talk about it with Serena was more because he couldn't, rather than wouldn't. For the first time in her life her father seemed smaller, more ordinary, more touchable, not just the aloof Pride Alpha above reproach. He grieved just like any father who'd lost a child.

"Forgive me," she whispered, sitting on the coffee table opposite him. "I didn't know."

"And why would you?" He ran his hand across his face and glanced to the camera in the corner of the room, then turned slightly so he was facing away from it. "You think I don't know what happened to you? What Leon did?"

Kitt rocked back and sat straight up.

The Alpha's eyes softened. "Of course I did. That was why I had you exiled and why I sent Dylan with you. To keep you safe."

When Dylan had found her by the swimming hole, her skin bruised and clothes torn, he'd wanted to kill Leon himself, especially when the lion had the gall to petition the Council of Aeternus Elders for her hand.

"I knew why you married Emmett, but it only worked for a short time. Leon was determined to have you—this was the only way I knew how to protect you." Being the Alpha, Tyrone was bound by the laws of the Pride more than anyone else. He had to enforce them, not question them.

A thought struck her. "Mother's letters— It was you."

"Shhh!" He leaned forward, shaking his head.

All these years Kitt had thought he hated her. Tears filled her eyes and she dropped her head.

"Forgive what I'm about to say and do, but these walls have ears," he whispered and grabbed her by the arms, bringing her to her feet. "You have no right to come here and demand anything from me." His voice rose so anyone listening could hear. "I will look into this matter. If any Jordan Pride member has acted without permission, they will be severely dealt with."

He turned his back on her and walked to the mantel. She stood there, speechless, rubbing her arms. The closed doors burst open and Nathan stormed in with his bodyguard following close behind.

"What's she doing here?" he spat.

"She has brought something to my attention," Tyrone said, pointing to the print on the coffee table.

Nathan's eyes widened and he glanced at his bodyguard.

Tyrone's eyes dropped to the picture on the table and back up at her brother's companion, his eyes narrowing.

The male looked at Nathan with uncertainty.

"Show me your wrist," Tyrone demanded. "The one with that birthmark."

Her brother swallowed and straightened as his body-guard held out his arm. The purple birthmark on the wrist screamed guilt.

Nathan's bodyguard lunged at her. The air rushed from her lungs from the force of his big body slamming into hers. Tyrone exploded in a vortex of torn clothing as someone pulled her back out of the way. He blurred across the room and landed on the male's chest.

Tyrone was a growling fury of black fur and teeth, tear-ing out the male's throat while disemboweling him with his hind claws. Thick leather-clad arms held her out of harm's way and she looked up surprised to find Oberon's thunder-ous expression glaring at her brother.

Where had he come from?

Nathan stepped back as the large panther raised its bloody maw and focused on him. The angry rumble in the panther's throat echoed around the large room as more men rushed in, Leon included. A cold pain stabbed through her heart at the sight of him.

Her father changed back into human form and walked toward Nathan. His eyes glittered with bloodlust and wrath as he stood nose to nose with his son, the late bodyguard's blood covering his face, chest, and arms.

"Did you know about this?" Tyrone asked.

"No." Nathan didn't even bat an eyelash as he stared back at his father. "Of course I didn't. She's my sister."

The way he said *sister* sounded more like an insult, and Kitt knew he was lying. Nathan flicked his gaze to her and his chin rose in challenge.

"I have no proof to the contrary so for now we'll have to

take your word for it," Tyrone hissed. "But he was in your employ, and your responsibility."

Kitt's head was spinning. A female servant rushed in with a rich brocade robe and Tyrone shrugged it onto his shoulders.

Kitt pushed out of Oberon's arms. "I demand retribution, as is my right." She may as well make the most of this situation.

"The one who tried to assassinate you lies dead," Tyrone said to her and Oberon. "What more could you ask?"

Pride law was complicated. On one hand, she had no rights at all. But as a wronged party, Pride or not, retribution was hers to demand.

She crossed to stand in front of her brother. "I want my children with me," she said, watching Nathan's face closely.

His eyes widened and flashed dangerously. "Never," he hissed.

The shock must be getting to her. For a moment she thought his irises actually changed color. *It was probably just his anger—*

"Done!" Tyrone tied the belt on his robe.

"*No.* You can't," Nathan hissed at him.

"He was your man," Tyrone replied, then turned to look at Kitt. "While they attend the Academy and until they have their qualifications to work in the restort healers, they may reside at your apartment. But they remain members of the Jordan Pride and as such will be expected to behave accordingly."

"You can't have them." Nathan flew at Kitt.

Her father stepped into his path, wrapped a hand around Nathan's throat, and slammed him onto his back. Then bent low so only those very near could hear what he said. "Your man tried to kill her, and she's entitled to retribution. Be thankful she's not demanding your head." Tyrone's voice was soft, cold, and stiff. "Now, get out of my sight until I figure out what I'm going to do with you. And so help me, if I find out you had anything to do with this . . ."

Nathan climbed to his feet when Tyrone released him, and

straightened out his suit. He shot her a look of pure venom. "This is all your fault, bitch," he hissed.

"Enough," Tyrone roared.

"*No.*" Nathan sneered. "I've been loyal to the Pride for decades even though I know most talk behind my back. And now you choose this filthy whore over me, just as you always have. It was either her or Dylan. Never me."

Her father slapped Nathan, the guilt on Tyrone's face only confirming her brother's accusations. Her brother touched the cheek Tyrone had dared to strike and stalked from the room without even a backward glance.

Tyrone's shoulders slumped as he watched his son storm away in anger. "I'll have the girls delivered to your apartment within hours," he said without looking at her.

"Thank you," she whispered.

Tyrone bent over the dead felian and slid the gold ring from his finger. Cold anger burned his pale blue eyes as he twisted the piece of jewelry to catch the light, and then his face blanked as he tossed it to her. "You have your compensation. Now leave."

Her heart shattered into ten thousand pieces.

"Leon," he said as the male followed her with his treacherous, tawny eyes. "Ask Mr. O'Shea to come back in, please."

Her father wouldn't even look at her as she left with Oberon. This time she didn't think it was pretense. She'd taken away his last son and his granddaughters. That was a world of hurt for one day.

Kitt sat at the table, looking at the clock every five seconds. Night had already fallen and they still weren't here.

"Will you stop that?" Oberon said. "You're spilling your coffee."

"Stop what?" she asked, glancing at the clock again.

"That jiggle thing you're doing with your leg. You do it when you're nervous or impatient or even just plain mad."

She looked down at the untouched cup sitting on the table in front of her. The pale beverage had slopped over the side and a milky pool surrounded the cup.

He'd gone to a lot of trouble wrestling with her coffee machine to make her a latte just the way she liked, and she'd
just wasted it. She stilled her leg and gave him an apologetic
grimace.

A knock on the door sent her to her feet, and she almost
ran to open it. But before she did she stopped, patted down
her hair, and straightened her top.

"You look fine," he mouthed before she could phrase the
question. She painted a smile on her face and turned the
handle.

The twins stood in the hall outside the apartment, bags
slung over their shoulders and suitcases in their hands. Seph
wore her usual sullen look.

"Come in, please." Kitt stood back and waved them in
with her hand. Did her voice have a nervous, higher pitch to
it, or was she just paranoid? She glanced at Oberon, pleading for help.

He winked and climbed to his feet to take their suitcases.
"Follow me, girls. Your room is down the hall."

Kitt let out a sigh. They were here—now what? She looked
around and saw the puddle still on the tabletop.

Coffee, good idea.

She raced into the kitchen, put on a pot of coffee, and
grabbed up the dishcloth to clean the mess she'd left on the
table. Just as she finished wiping it up, Oberon came down
the hall.

"I'll leave you to it," Oberon said.

The panic started in the balls of her feet and rose with a
prickle up her legs to spike in her stomach. "You can't leave
me alone with them yet," she whispered.

What would she say?

What would they think of her?

What did they think of their new living arrangements?

Questions shot through her brain at lightning speed.

Oberon snagged the wrist of the hand she raised to tug on
her lip. "Don't worry so much; I'm sure they won't eat you."

"That depends on how much food you have in the house,"
Cal said, smiling. "Seph can chew her way through a live
cow when she's really hungry."

"Hey!" Seph slugged her sister in the shoulder. "You can talk, Miss Piggy."

For the first time, Kitt saw Seph smile, truly smile—with her eyes as well as her mouth. She sat down on the sofa and pulled one of the cushions into her lap.

"I'll have to do some shopping, but I thought we could order in some pizza or Chinese for now," she said.

"Can we get both?" Cal asked. "I'm starved."

Oberon grinned. "I can see you're a girl after my own heart."

"See. Told you"—Seph threw the cushion at her sister—"a major Miss Piggy."

Cal threw it straight back and laughed.

"Sure, why not." Kitt relaxed a little. "I think there's some takeout menus in the kitchen somewhere. Your uncle used to order from Mario's around the corner all the time."

"Well, on that note, I'll leave you girls to it." The ursian crossed to the door. "Take your time coming into work later."

Kitt found the tri-folded paper menus just where Dylan had left them, stuck on the side of the fridge with the Mario's Pizza number magnet. She took them into the living room and handed them to Cal.

"Besides a large pepperoni pizza, I want egg rolls, and noodles, and chicken wings," Cal said while looking at the Chinese takeout choices.

"I really miss a good feed of fish and chips," Seph said, looking wistful. "Battered prawns, calamari rings, and fresh barra."

"Barra?" Kitt asked.

"Barramundi—one of our favorite eating fish from Australia," Cal said. "Sometimes Raven would take us over to the territory and we'd go fishing for fresh barramundi, and cook it over a fire so the skin crisped up and the flesh would just melt in your mouth."

"Do you miss it?" she asked her daughters. "Australia, I mean?"

Cal tilted her head. "I guess so. It was a great place to grow up. I miss some things, and others I don't."

"I miss my friends." Seph looked down at the cushion

she'd retrieved and plucked at invisible lint. "Well, some of them."

"She found out a couple of weeks ago that her longtime boyfriend has been sleeping with Kylie, her best friend," Cal whispered. "They'd been seeing each other behind her back for nearly a year."

"Cal!" Seph said, looking a little annoyed that her sister was giving away all her private secrets.

"Well, it's true."

"Anyway, it's *former* boyfriend and *former* best friend." Seph puffed up. "And they deserve each other."

"So that's why you always seemed so unhappy to see me?" Kitt asked and sat on the sofa, pulling her left leg under her.

Seph shrugged. "Sorry about that; it was nothing personal. Raven always told us why you sent us away."

"Okay—I really want some of these dumplings too," Cal said, "and these spare ribs look good."

Seph looked at Kitt, a smile tugging at the corner of her lips, and then they both burst out laughing.

"What?" Cal said looking a little hurt.

"The phone's over there. Order what you like." Kitt sat back, feeling much more relaxed. They didn't hate her. In fact, they might even grow to like her.

30

Girl's' Night

"There's one more wing left," Kitt said, shaking the cardboard takeout box.

"I'll have it," Cal said, leaning forward and fishing out the chicken piece.

Seph groaned from where she lay on the sofa. "No more, please. I'm so full. I don't know how you can eat another bite."

"Serves you right for being mean to me." Cal sat on the floor across the coffee table from Kitt and ripped into the chicken flesh with her teeth, then smiled around a mouthful of macerated meat.

"Oh, gross," her sister said, whacking her lightly across the side of the head. "You're making me sick."

Cal grinned and took another bite.

"Do you really feel what each other experiences?" Kitt asked.

"Sometimes," Seph said. "Especially strong sensations."

"Though it doesn't quite work that way all the time." Cal chucked the bone on the plate with the rest of the leftovers. "Sometimes one will feel what the other is experiencing, even though the one it's happening to doesn't. Like now. I'm the one who's overeaten, but it's Seph getting the stomachache."

"Or like when one of us is with a guy, the other is . . . you know." Cal winked.

"Whoa!" Kitt held up her hands, laughing. "T.M.I."

"Yeah, Seph—look who's being gross now," Cal said. "You can't talk about sex in front of our mother."

Kitt's stomach flipped at being referred to as mother, but she didn't want to make a big deal of it.

"I love listening to your accents," Kitt said and sighed.

Cal screwed up her nose. "We don't have an accent."

"You do," Seph finished for her twin.

Kitt stood. "This has been fun, but I have to pick up some vegan blood for Tones on the way into work."

"We were sorry to hear he got hurt," Seph said, sitting up.

Cal looked back at her sister and nodded. "He's a nice guy."

Kitt picked up her coat and put it on, stuffing her gloves into her pocket. "Lock the door behind me and make sure you don't open it for anyone but me, Raven, or Oberon."

She swiped up her keys and handbag from the counter. "And make sure you stay in the apartment," she warned.

"Sure," Cal said, but Seph appeared a little cagey. It was hard to figure that girl out.

The blustery weather outside her apartment building sent a burger wrapper scuttling past as she hit the pavement. She pulled the collar up around her ears, then shoved her hands into her coat pockets and walked against the wind in the direction of her parking space.

The hair on the back of her neck prickled. She looked around. A few people were out and about. She lifted her hand and waved back to a human couple who lived down the hall. They were just ending their workday while she was starting hers.

People mostly kept their heads down and concentrated on getting where they were going. No one really seemed to pay her much nevermind. Yet the dark corners appeared a little darker, the shadows a little more sinister—as if something, or someone, was there, waiting for her to make a wrong move. She shook it off. Leon's attack still spooked her.

Kitt wrapped her hand around a can of paramace in her

pocket. Someone *was* following her. She couldn't hear anything, and dared not look over her shoulder either, yet sensed she was being watched. She quickened her pace a little but her urgency didn't lessen. It was time to get rid of Dylan's beloved T-Bird and start parking in the underground lot, she thought.

She jangled her keys in her pocket for comfort. The car was only a few feet away and she hit the central locking button on her car key.

Two steps away. She reached out to open the door when a hand landed heavily on her shoulder.

She turned, pulling the paramace canister out of her pocket, and let loose a full blast into the face of the large figure behind her.

Joshua fell to the ground, clutching his face as he screamed in pain. Jericho leapt out of the nearby car to rush to his brother's side.

Damn.

"I'm so sorry," she said, reaching into her car to pull out a bottle of water she always carried. She cracked the top as she dropped to her knees beside the writhing felian.

The other looked on as she peeled his brother's hands away from his face, then poured the entire contents over his red, blotchy flesh, which had begun to blister. He instantly began to quiet.

"What are you doing here?" she asked the unwounded brother.

"You dropped this," he said and picked up the black woolen glove from where Joshua had let it go.

She reached into her coat and pulled out its twin, then stuffed them both back into her pocket. Kitt spotted the black SUV on the other side of the street with the two bodyguards who followed the girls around the campus.

Jericho looked up. "Your brother disappeared this morning after your visit and your father wanted us to keep an eye on you in case he came after you again."

Probably scampered off somewhere to lick his wounds.

Kitt wasn't worried about having the extra protection around, especially in light of everything that had happened recently. She came to her feet as Joshua rose to his knees. "You should see a healer to make sure you don't have any residual aftereffects of the trace silver nitrate."

"Ah, don't worry about me, you missed my eyes," Joshua said, dusting off his clothes. "Besides, it's not the first time I've had a face full of paramace. I'll be all right in a half hour."

She picked up her keys from the ground as Jericho helped his brother walk back to the SUV. They would follow her, she knew, and it made her feel a little bit safer knowing they were the ones watching over her.

Raven heard her voice coming down the hall. It felt like weeks since he'd seen her. Yet it was less than twenty-four hours. He tried not to hurry, tried to keep his stride slow and measured, but his feet had other ideas.

"Are they sure?" Oberon growled.

"What's wrong?" Raven said as he came up behind them.

Kitt turned. She seemed happy to see him, yet something was obviously wrong. Something besides the fact her brother had tried to kill her. He'd found out the details from Oberon earlier.

"What's the matter?" he asked, reaching out to her.

"Nathan's gone missing," Oberon said. "At first they thought he was just off somewhere sulking, but they found his bodyguard and driver in his car, both with their throats cut and a lot of blood on the backseat, which is most likely Nathan's."

Raven put his arms around Kitt's shoulders and pulled her against him, and this time she didn't pull away. The scent of her skin and hair filled him with that familiar longing. Her warmth stirred the protecting instinct in him.

She snuggled against his chest for a moment, and let him comfort her. After a minute, she drew back, her eyes dropping to his neck, and turned to Oberon. "Why is he wearing an inhibitor?" she asked and turned to the ursian. "Take it off. *Now.*"

"No," Raven said. "He's right. When I heard you'd been hurt, poisoned, I wanted to rip the whole Pride apart. It keeps everyone safe, including me. I have great control, masterful control as an agent of the Draconus Nocti. But when it comes to you, all reason dissipates."

The ursian looked at him with a strange, unreadable expression. Then nodded with what looked like a new level of respect. "Besides, I've given him the combination, so he can take it off any time he wishes."

The ursian placed a large hand on Kitt's shoulder. "Come on. Let's get you home so you can tell the twins about Nathan."

Oberon climbed onto the big black customized Harley-Davidson with a beautiful scene of an American Indian woman and a large grizzly bear airbrushed onto the fuel tank. He turned the key and the machine rumbled into life with the distinctive potato-potato idle.

She climbed onto the noisy beast behind her surrogate brother as he revved the engine, and she gripped his waist as it leapt away, all power and growling menace.

The motorcycle rumbled between her thighs and her hair whipped every which way as she glanced behind to see the tiger brothers' SUV following close behind. Thank God that they'd stopped Raven from coming. As much as she wanted him with her, he would be in danger.

When they arrived back at her building, the other Jordan SUV sat where she had last seen it. Dark shapes were slumped against the windows. Her father would be furious to find his men sleeping on the job.

It was only as she got closer that she wondered at the odd angle of their heads. Oberon yanked the door open and the first bodyguard tumbled out onto the pavement, his head only attached to his neck by a thin strip of skin at the back. Kitt heard Oberon pull out his cell phone, but immediately ran into the apartment building. She didn't have time to wait for him or the elevator and took the stairs to her floor.

With trembling hands she managed to get the key into the lock just as Oberon caught up with her. The safety chain only allowed the door to open a couple of inches, and with frustration she pounded her fists against the wood.

"Cal, Seph," she called out. "It's me, Kitt. Open the door!"

But no answer came from within.

"Please, girls. You must let me in." Desperation cracked her voice a little.

Oberon's phone chirped in his pocket. He slid it open and answered with a terse, "DuPrie."

His eyes snapped wide and locked on her. "Right. Thanks. And Antoinette"—he held Kitt's gaze—"tell Raven."

He slid the phone shut and looked at his feet, frowning. "A young man has been found murdered only two blocks from here. The MO's the same as the campus killer."

"Just let me check on the girls and we can go," she said, turning to bang on the door again.

"They found something else beside the body," Oberon said, his voice low and heavy. "A girl's purse and cell phone—they belong to Seph."

Her legs lost all feeling and a pain stabbed through her sternum, tightening across her chest. Kitt braced herself against the wall for a moment, then turned and banged frantically on the door screaming, *"OPEN UP!"*

Oberon pushed her aside and hit the door with his massive shoulder. The wood around the doorframe exploded into splinters as the safety-chain housing gave way. Kitt raced inside her apartment and ran from room to room, looking for the twins.

She found Cal in the bathroom hugging her knees to her chest, rocking back and forth. She'd thrown up several times, and the haunted terrified eyes in her pale face stared off into nothing.

Kitt dropped to her knees, but the girl didn't seem to notice her at all. She reached out to touch Cal's arm lightly. She recoiled and began to shriek hysterically, trying to fight her off with flailing hands. Even Oberon seemed rattled by the terror in the chilling scream.

"You're safe," Kitt said, trapping Cal's arms against her body and drawing the girl into her chest.

"It's cold and dark," Cal croaked, horrified. "Uncle Nathan is here. I can't see him, but I can hear him begging and pleading with the other man."

Cal's throat worked hard as she swallowed several times. "That other man scares me. His voice is so . . . so dead."

The girl's pallid features twisted with revulsion. "He's touching Seph's face, calling her his angel."

Kitt rocked Cal back and forth, planting several kisses on her forehead. "You're safe—you're here with us."

The frightened girl returned to the room from wherever she'd been with her sister. Kitt could almost feel Cal's spirit reinhabiting her body as her eyes focused. Her tears welled and slid down her cheeks, and her lip trembled. "Persephone isn't."

Cal wrapped her arms around Kitt's neck and wept. "We have to save her, Mem. She's cold and frightened and helpless."

Kitt's heart not only broke, it splintered and shattered into shards of icy glass. It was the first time either of her daughters had called her that, but it was overshadowed by the fact she may be about to lose one of them.

Oberon grabbed a towel and handed it to Kitt. She wiped away the spilled sick on the girl's chin and fevered sweat from her face.

"Let's go into the living room. Oberon, make some hot sweet tea," Kitt said, helping the girl to her feet.

"We have to find her—save her from the evil man," Cal said, clutching at her with desperation. "She's in danger. I don't believe him when he says he'll never hurt her. He lies. He's insane."

Kitt bundled her up on the sofa with a thick blanket around her shoulders and took the mug of hot sweet tea Oberon held out. She helped Cal take a sip.

"She's awake again." Cal sat straight, speaking from far away. "I think I can connect with her."

Oberon took her hand. "Now tell her to be calm; we need her help to find out where she is."

Cal nodded, her brow furrowed in concentration. "She asks what you need to know."

"Tell her to concentrate. She may not be able to see, but she can use her other senses."

"She can't move. He's done something to her. She can't move."

Terror pierced Kitt's heart. An Animalian didn't regenerate like an Aeternus; if he'd disabled her the way he had the others, she might never be able to move again.

"No, wait," Cal said. "She can move, but her hands and feet are bound and she can't change either. Something's stopping her."

Kitt let out a sigh. *Thank God.* She wouldn't be permanently maimed—at least that's if they could get to her before— She really didn't want to think about what might happen if they didn't.

"Okay, Cal. Ask her what she can hear," Oberon prompted the girl.

Cal tilted her head, as if listening to something. "At the moment it's quiet. Wait, water, she can hear water dripping. It sounds . . . hollow?" Cal frowned. "No, it echoes."

"Good, what else is there? Or what else has she heard? Where is Nathan? Tell us about the man who holds them?" Oberon fired questions at her, causing her to grow a little agitated.

"Slow down." Kitt shot Oberon a warning frown. "First tell us about Nathan."

"She says he's a few feet away, slightly to her left. Sometimes he's silent, sometimes he moans, and sometimes he argues with the man." Cal frowned. "That's all she knows."

"What's he doing now?" Kitt asked. He may have tried to kill her, but he was still her brother.

"She can only hear him breathing." Cal opened her eyes and looked at Kitt. "She says she hears a rumbling periodically."

"Okay, what about the other man?" Oberon asked.

"He's insane and very angry. When he's not arguing with Nathan, he's talking to someone called Ealund. Maybe on the phone, though she can't hear any ringing or key presses. She thinks this Ealund might not really exist."

"Tell her she's doing very well." Oberon soothed. "Is there anything else? What can she smell?"

"Dirt? She thinks she's sitting on dirt, and she thinks she may be leaning against a rock—it feels too irregular to be concrete. And there's something else, something familiar that she can't put her finger on—like hot metal or something, usually around the time of the distant rumbling, screeching noise."

"The subway," Kitt and Oberon chorused.

"There are thousands of tunnels down there," Oberon said. "Both manmade and natural."

"Then we'd better get started," her father's voice said from the open door.

Tyrone came into the room with his hands behind his back, Jericho and Joshua flanking him. Then Leon walked through the door.

"Get out of my home," she hissed, and his arrogant smirk widened.

31

Danger Signs

So, Nathan's missing. Raven looked at the first images Tones sent through from the crime scene. The two bodies were in the front. The passenger's head leaned against the window, his white shirt soaked with blood from the neat line splitting his throat. The driver's head hung back, the cut yawning through to the bone. Arterial-pulse spray covered the victim's lap, the dash, and the windscreen.

Whether human or Animalian, it wouldn't have mattered—they both would've bled out in seconds.

"Raven!" Antoinette raced into the room. "One of your daughters is missing."

"What?" He stood up so fast he sent the computer chair flying back. "Which one?"

"Seph."

Oh, thank God for small miracles. "She can take care of herself better than Cal. How long has she been missing?"

"That's not it." Antoinette dragged her hand through her hair and placed the other on her hip. "They found her things at the site of a campus-killer murder."

Please God, let her be all right. Raven snatched his jacket off the coatrack and headed for the door.

"Wait," Antoinette called.

"NO!" He turned on her and stabbed a finger in her direc-

tion. "Jordan Pride be damned—I'm not going to stay here while my baby's in danger."

She held up a set of car keys. "I'll drive."

He nodded. "Right. Where're we going?"

"Kitt, Oberon, and Cal are making their way to the subway caverns. Cal's made a connection to her sister and that's where they're convinced Seph is."

Cal would be able to sense Seph. Raven had no doubt she was right.

Antoinette clicked the unlock button on her key and the taillights flashed on her car.

She climbed into the driver's seat and turned the key in the ignition—the V-8 engine roared to life.

She leaned over to the passenger side and opened the door. "So, are you coming or what?"

He jumped in and buckled up, suspecting Antoinette drove the way she did everything else. Full throttle.

And he wasn't wrong. She zoomed through the streets at breakneck speed, running lights where she could, effortlessly changing gears, heel-and-toeing the clutch and accelerator to get the maximum performance out of the machine.

Raven clung to the seat and dash. She changed lanes quickly and often, weaving in and out of the traffic, missing other vehicles by inches. But the whole time she worked the stick shift, brakes, and accelerator—especially the accelerator—she wasn't reckless. The female was in total control of both herself and the car.

She would've been an asset to the Draconus Nocti back in the day—the perfect operative. Smart, fearless, and more than a little crazy: the perfect point-and-shoot weapon.

He wasn't afraid to die. The only thing that scared him was not being there to save his daughter.

"Faster," he growled.

A cell phone rang. "Shit," she said as she clicked the hands-free receiver. "Talk."

"They've surfaced," the disembodied voice said. "And they're hunting."

"Fuck! Perfect timing," Antoinette spat and glanced over

at Raven looking torn. "I'll meet you at your place as soon as I can." She pressed the hang-up button. "I'm sorry, something's come up. I'll have to drop you."

She steered to the curb and brought the car to a screeching stop. "The subway entrance is a block that way. You should be able to catch them up."

"Thank you," he said as he reached for the door handle. "And good hunting."

She tilted her head and gave him a tight, deadly smile. "You too."

He'd barely closed the door when she took off in a cloud of smoke and squealing tires, narrowly missing a blue sedan as she changed lanes.

Raven willed the change, but nothing happened.

The inhibitor. He'd forgotten all about it.

He knew the combination, but couldn't see to remove it. *I can't change!* A great inconvenience, but his skills didn't rely on his canian abilities alone. Raven took off at a dead run along the pavement, moving as fast as he could, pumping his arms to match the stride of his legs.

"OUT OF THE WAY," he yelled.

Pedestrians hurriedly moved. He slammed his hip sideways to avoid a man bending over.

A woman pushing a baby buggy came out from behind a car. He dodged her, smashed into the side of a parked van and ricocheted off with barely a break in his stride.

He reached the staircase leading down into the subway and made it to the bottom with three well-measured leaps. There were so many people moving around, even at this time of night. But among the scents were two that stood out above all others: Kitt's and Cal's.

They led him to the edge of the station platform and down into the subway tunnel. No rattling or rumbling came from either direction and he dropped onto the tracks to follow their trail.

The light from the station grew dimmer behind him, but he was tracking by scent—following two of the three most important people in his life, and praying they would lead to the third.

The girls were not alone; there were four other felians. He recognized Leon and Tyrone Jordan.

That could make things interesting.

Along with the four felians, there was one big ursian scent. Thank God for Oberon. He'd protect them, especially from Leon.

A roaring rumble came from behind and he turned to see the subway train headlights speeding toward him.

A service nook veered off a short distance ahead.

The ground beneath his feet trembled.

Raven put on a burst to speed up and threw himself into the gap. The metal wheels clattered and screamed less than a foot from his head as the train hurtled past.

As he lay there panting, he picked up the scent trail going the same way. He was relying only on his sense of smell to guide him, it almost formed pictures in his mind.

The trail led him to an old, disused section of tunnel. At least he didn't have to worry about getting run over by trains. There were hundreds of miles of old and disused tunnels down here, and who knew what else.

He followed the scents to a fissure in the concrete wall of the tunnel, wide enough for a large man to squeeze through. It went downward, close to thirty feet, before it opened onto a natural cave system, which lacked the angles and lines of the manmade tunnels above.

They were close; the trail was only several minutes old. And what's more, an older scent, of Seph and Nathan, lingered here, both strongly tinged with fear. And traces of the killer's pheromone-charged odor faded in and out, something he'd never encountered before in all his years of training.

He ran carefully, his nose still leading the way. Voices came from up ahead, around a half mile. An eerie yellow glow flicked and disappeared as the voices moved around corners. Then it stopped and he moved in carefully until he came upon them. His heart leapt at the sight of his other daughter and her mother.

"We need to rest for a moment," Oberon said.

"No—we should push on," Kitt demanded.

"Look at Cal, she's exhausted," Oberon growled.

The cave had widened out into a sort of natural room. Cal was sitting on a rock, head hanging down, but as soon as he stepped into the subdued yellow light of several glow sticks, she seemed to sense him and raised her head to lock eyes with him.

"Raven?" she whispered, disbelief and ecstatic relief vying for dominance in her expression.

"You came!" she said louder, then she was on her feet, running to fling herself into his arms. She buried her face in his chest.

"Hey, baby-girl." He circled his arms around her and kissed the top of her head like when she *was* a little girl. Trembling, she hugged him closer.

He raised his gaze to meet several astonished faces. Including Kitt's.

Twenty minutes after dropping Raven off, Antoinette pulled up outside the warehouse where Tripper kept his van. Something wasn't right. Nothing seemed out of place, but a sixth sense warned her to be cautious. She slid open her cell and typed in the quick dial key with her thumb.

The phone went straight to voicemail. "Tones. I've just arrived at Tripper's and it's too quiet. It may be nothing, but just in case."

She slipped the phone back into her black cargo pants pocket and popped the trunk. Antoinette slipped the katanas out of their cases before closing the lid softly. She bent to check the laces on her combat boots and glanced at the door, hoping Tripper would appear.

He didn't.

Then she realized what was bugging her. No music.

It was far too quiet.

The scent of blood and death hung heavy inside the warehouse. Dog lay on his rug, stone still and she sighed. *Poor old thing.* But as she approached, he raised his head with a soft whimper and came awkwardly to his feet to meet her.

She didn't need her Aeternus abilities to sense the old dog

was scared. His tail was drawn up close between his legs, his body tensed, and his eyes had a long, nervous cast. She crouched beside him. He placed his jaw over her shoulder, hugging her in his own doggy way. As she patted his back, she projected a little calmness toward him to give him some comfort and examined the vast empty warehouse through narrowed eyes.

Tripper's system of perimeter cameras and alarms in the surrounding area would have warned him she was here. But where was he?

She followed the scent of blood. It was dead blood, carrion. The sticky pool was congealed under the stuffed leather chair facing the wrong way.

She stood, scratching the dog behind the ear, steeling herself to look at the body she could smell in the chair. A body that shouldn't be here—a body that didn't belong.

She walked around to the front and glanced down. Blood covered the chest from the wound in the throat and long hair was stuck in the tacky mess.

What is the body of a fang-whore doing here, and where is Tripper?

The scent of living blood came from close by. She reached behind and unsheathed one of the swords. The smell of stale dope smoke and the sound of his heart beating triple time came from up ahead and she followed it.

Tripper lay huddled near some old warehouse rubble. He shook with a fevered chill, tears marking clean tracks down his filthy face and crimson-caked mouth.

Her heart sank.

His face crumpled into a fresh flood of tears when he saw her, and she bent to help him stand.

"They made me do it," he babbled, coming up on shaky legs.

"I know," she said.

Tripper's fingers bit into her shoulders. "I didn't want to, but J.J. forced me."

"I know." She closed her eyes, not wanting to see his pain. Her heart grew heavy. She liked Tripper; really liked him.

More tears spilled from his eyes and down his cheeks. "He made me watch first, watch him feed on that poor girl, ripping at her throat like an animal."

Antoinette glanced at the body of the fang-whore in the chair.

"Please." He clutched the front of her T-shirt. "Don't let me be like that."

"You know what I have to do," she said.

He nodded jerkily and pulled her close so his mouth touched her ear. "Someone will be in contact to take my place. It's all been arranged."

He dropped to his knees in front of her, his shoulders shaking with his sobs as he fell onto his elbows and bent his forehead to the floor. Antoinette's eyes were dry as she moved behind him. She couldn't cry any more. But in her heart, the tears fell.

It had to be done. She knew it.

The katana grew heavy.

Tripper sat back on his calves and wiped his face on the cuff of his long-sleeve heavy metal shirt, then he nodded. "Do it," he said, the tremor gone from his voice.

"Tripper, I . . ." Antoinette was at a loss for words.

"It worked out for you, Antoinette, and I'm glad. But I don't want to end up like J.J. This is my only option." He turned and looked over his shoulder. "Make it quick and make it clean."

"Okay," she said firmly.

He looked straight ahead, puffing out his chest and straightening his shoulders.

With a heavy heart, Antoinette held the sword in front of her.

And sliced cleanly.

His head fell to the floor. Quick and painless—at least she hoped it was. Antoinette collapsed to her knees beside his prone decapitated body.

"Goodbye, Tripper," she whispered, watching the blood pooling on the filthy floor.

The dull thud sounded behind her, followed by a slow steady rhythmic applause.

32

The Belly of the Beast

He'd come.

For them.

For his daughters.

For *their* daughters.

The knowledge hit hard. Why hadn't she been on his side, the side that shared their children? She wouldn't send him away—and the decision would cut her off from the Pride forever.

Raven had every right to be here and she would stand by him. Both relief and fear washed over her, and a thick tension choked her. The closed-in space of the cave made it worse. Raven stroked Cal's hair and locked eyes with Kitt over their daughter's head. Leon and the Tiger Twins rushed forward. Kitt put herself between her family and the Pride.

"STOP!" her father roared.

Kitt expected to see surprise and shock, but there was none. Leon, however, was another matter. His hands balled into tight fists at his side, teeth bared, and shoulders hunched.

"Matokwe!" he hissed through gritted teeth. His hatred for them was well known. It was rumored the Matokwe Pack had started the fire that consumed the Pantella Pride. But it was never proven.

Tyrone held up his hand, silencing him. "We can use his tracking skills."

"We can't trust this dog," Leon spat.

Tyrone and Kitt stared at each other from across the floor, before his gaze flicked to Cal wrapped in Raven's comfort.

Tyrone knew—everything. Kitt could tell by the way he watched Cal and Raven.

"Dylan told you," she said.

He didn't answer. There was no need—his posture said it all.

Kitt glanced back over her shoulder at the movement. Oberon closed in behind Raven, lending his support and declaring his allegiance.

"I see you forgot this," the ursian whispered as he removed the inhibitor chain.

"Thanks," Raven said and pushed Cal gently into the bear's arms, then went to stand beside Kitt.

A warmth began to bloom in her chest at his nearness. She'd never felt more right standing beside him than at this moment. The three brothers advanced, crowding forward.

Tyrone waved off his men. "I said, leave him."

The Tiger Twins stepped back but Leon continued. Raven pushed her behind him as the lion came to a stop so close that Kitt could smell his breath.

Her stomach rolled, and she shot her father a pleading look. "We don't have time for this. We need to find Seph."

"Leon, stand down," Tyrone growled and jerked his head at the other two.

Jericho moved forward and clutched the lion's shoulder. Leon's eyes dropped to where Raven's other hand rested protectively against Kitt's hip.

"So," he hissed at her. "You would lie with this dog."

Cal pulled out of Oberon's hold and wrapped her arms around Raven's waist and Kitt joined her. Still her father didn't look surprised.

"You knew he fathered your grandchildren," she said flatly. "And you still put a price on his head."

"Of course I did," Tyrone said, looking from Raven to Kitt. "It was expected. The Pride council had convicted the Matokwe for murdering your husband. Dylan told me it was very unlikely anyone would ever collect." He shrugged. "But it didn't matter to me either way. It was just the dog who slept with my daughter."

Leon's face fell, then split into a nasty caricature of a smile. "You may have had her, but I had her first."

Oberon reached out and yanked Raven back, holding him firm so he couldn't reach the grinning lion. She stood in front of him, her hands on Raven's chest. He trembled under her palms, his face a mask of rage as he looked down at her. "So he's the one?"

She'd never revealed it was Leon who robbed her of her innocence because Raven would have killed him. "It's not important. Seph is the only thing that matters now."

Leon leapt and slammed his fist into the side of Raven's chin, rocking back his head and knocking Kitt on her ass. She looked up shocked as he closed in again. The twins moved quickly and hauled their brother back.

Oberon slowly removed his long leather jacket, then unbuckled his belt. Kitt flicked her gaze to him and the ursian winked, and she knew if Raven needed it, Oberon would come down on his side.

"Stop this," Cal cried, lifting trembling hands to her face. "Please, we have to help her."

Everyone stopped.

Cal ran to her father again and Raven stroked her hair, kissing the top of her head. "It's all right, baby."

"Can you find her, wolf?" Tyrone asked.

Raven glanced at Cal and peeled off his shirt. "I have to."

Tyrone looked at Cal. "Can you sense her yet?"

The girl tilted her head and closed her eyes. "She's still unconscious, but this is definitely the right way."

Raven said, "Some of the scents are confused, but they definitely came this way. The killer's is the strongest."

Oberon slapped him on the shoulder. "Then let's not waste any more time."

Kitt gripped her father's arm. "Thank you."

Then a piercing scream shattered the cave space, sending a spike of panic shooting down her backbone.

* * *

Antoinette turned to find J.J. pounding his hands together in mocking applause.

"Touching, very touching," the dreniac sneered.

Antoinette didn't even bother with any of the several curses that sprang to the tip of her tongue. She wanted to tear him limb from limb with her bare hands. But before she could reach him, someone stepped into her path and threw her backward into the faded green van.

She climbed from the caved-in metal side and fell forward onto her hands and knees in the glass sprayed across the floor from the blown out windows. A female Aeternus in heavy makeup, big hair, and spandex—like a rock queen gone mad—stood beside J.J. The same insane slant to the eyes Antoinette had only ever seen in one other—Dante Rubins.

Her hand came up to stroke J.J.'s shoulder. Antoinette shook some of the glass shards out of her hair and glared at them from under her lashes before climbing to her feet. Blood stained the ground from the cuts to her palms and knees. Her sword had landed not far from Marvella, who smiled as she brought her foot down heavily, snapping the blade.

"You're lucky that wasn't my favorite, bitch," Antoinette hissed.

Marvella turned to J.J. and ran her tongue up the side of his face, then looked at Antoinette. "Bring me her head, lover."

"My pleasure." J.J. grabbed the insane female around the waist and bent to kiss her throat. She threw back her head and let him, a throaty laugh echoing in the cavernous warehouse.

Antoinette feared the impact against the van had broken her other sword and she drew it with trepidation. But the blade slid out of the sheath with little resistance and she held it before her.

J.J. seemed more like a typical dreniac than last time she'd encountered him. Dark circles surrounded his bloodshot eyes, and his hands shook as he picked up a length of metal pipe. Marvella placed her hand on his shoulder and offered her wrist. He glanced at her before dropping the pipe again and taking it, biting deep.

She wasn't about to be polite, and she attacked while they were busy. The female saw her coming and leapt backward. J.J.'s fangs, still embedded in her wrist, ripped the flesh to the bone, covering him in her dark blood as he fell back. Antoinette's blade missed him by a fraction of a hair.

The bleeding dreniac snatched up the metal pipe on his way down and raised it to block Antoinette's next strike.

"Kill her slowly," Marvella spat from where she clung to the railing edge of the mezzanine overlooking the warehouse floor. "Make it really hurt."

"Come down here and do your own dirty work, bitch," Antoinette said.

The metal pipe J.J. wielded slammed onto her wrist, knocking away the katana. Antoinette had broken the first rule of self-preservation—never turn your back on the enemy. She'd let her emotions get the better of her.

Stupid, stupid rookie mistake.

She ducked as he swung at her head, then she propelled up and smashed her elbow into his nose. Marvella dropped from above and slammed her across the face with the back of her hand. Antoinette countered with a foot to the chest, sending the insane Aeternus into a jumbled pile of old cardboard cartons, tubes, and sacks.

She dived for her sword, but J.J. beat her to it and kicked it out of her reach before diving for it himself.

She grabbed his foot and yanked him back just as his fingers touched the blade. He turned and drove his boot into her face. Stars exploded behind her eyes, clearing in time to see him picking up her sword and turning around. Antoinette started to rise when Marvella grabbed her from behind, pinning her arms to her side.

"Cut the bitch," the female screeched at J.J. "And make her bleed."

J.J. approached slowly, savoring her predicament. Gone

was the twitchiness, gone were the red-ringed eyes. Now he stood steady and focused. It must have something to do with the blood Marvella had given him. Maybe that's how she kept control of her pets.

He grinned as he closed in. "I've been looking forward to this."

Marvella's grip was crushing. Antoinette threw her head back, but the smooching crunch of her skull connecting with Marvella's nose never happened. Instead, she only hit thin air.

The Aeternus female chuckled in her ear. "You're not the only one who knows a few tricks."

Then J.J. lunged forward with the sword.

33

sisterly love

Cal screamed again, turning Kitt's blood to ice. She dropped to gather her daughter in her arms as the others came over, forming a ghostly ring of yellow glow-stick light round them.

"Ssh-sh-shhh," Raven whispered, meeting Kitt's eyes. "I'm here, baby-girl."

Cal stopped immediately and looked up at her father. "It's dark. I can't see . . . we can't see—" Cal sucked in her breath. "We can't fight him, can't change. He's . . . he's . . . he's coming."

Without a word, Raven transformed and raced away down the tunnel to the left, his shredded clothing scattered in his wake.

Tyrone took Raven's place at her side. "And your uncle Nathan, where's he?"

"I don't know," Cal sobbed. "He was there, but now . . ."

Kitt watched her father's eyes turn almost black with rage and fear. He stripped down to his Abeolite, changed into his large black-panther form and set off after Raven with the tiger brothers and Leon following.

"It's okay, Cal," Oberon soothed as he squatted beside her and Kitt, placing a hand on the trembling girl's shoulder. "Tell her we're coming."

"Please hurry." Kitt instinctively knew it was Seph's voice, not Cal's. "He's too strong."

Oberon stood up. "Can you manage to change? You'll travel faster."

Cal sniffed back her tears and nodded.

"But how will we find them?" asked Kitt. "Raven's already gone."

Cal looked up at her. "I can use wolf form. My senses are better for tracking."

"Do it," Kitt said. She'd worry about her father finding out later, if she had to.

Cal transformed.

"Wait." Oberon crossed to the backpack he'd been carrying earlier and took out a fresh glow stick. He snapped and shook it into the yellow neon glow and tied it around Cal's neck. Enough light for her to see and lead them. Then he picked up the flashlight he'd dropped on the ground when things had gotten ugly.

"Does that feel okay?" he asked the wolf.

She moved her head and made a small noise. Like the rest, Kitt stripped down to her Abeolite and transformed.

Oberon tied another glow stick around her neck too. "I'll stay human and carry the pack. I'll keep up better this way."

They moved through the cave system and came to another cavern junction with three different exits.

Oberon shone the flashlight down each way and breathed in deep.

"Which way now?" he asked, looking between the two caves. "Both seem to have recent scent trails."

Cal sniffed around, going a short way into each tunnel, her long thick tail hovering just above the ground. Suddenly she raced toward the back wall and jumped up several small ledges to a ridge about fifteen feet above them. She looked down and yapped, then seemingly disappeared into the rock face. Kitt followed.

Raven had definitely come this way. As she crawled through on all fours, Kitt could smell the occasional hit of his lingering warm scent where he'd brushed the walls on his way through. It was a tight fit in some places. *Oberon may have trouble.*

Confirming her thoughts, she heard a male grunting and cursing as he tried to squeeze through what was little more than a fissure between rock.

Thankfully, it was short and opened out into another cavern after only a few feet. Kitt crawled out at floor level, which meant this cave was higher than the one they'd come from. She could pick up her father's scent and the others. *So they had found it too, after all.*

But how could the killer have gotten both Nathan and Seph through that small opening?

"With a rope I think." Cal sat with her back against the rock face, looking pale and sweaty in the glow of the stick.

The first thought that crossed Kitt's mind was why had Cal changed back?

Kitt only had to look at Cal to know the answer. The girl was exhausted. It took a lot of energy to change and maintain Animalian form, and hers was depleted. If only they had some fresh meat.

"So you can read my mind as well?" Kitt asked as she shook off the last tremors through her body from reverting back to human form.

"No!" The girl looked at her and half laughed. "It doesn't take much to know what you're thinking; it's a pretty obvious question."

Kitt glanced around the enormous cave. There seemed to be no ceiling and the floor dropped away only a few feet from where they sat. She walked to the drop-off and looked over the edge. Some of the side broke away under her foot, sending a shower of rocks and dirt clattering against the rock walls. She lay flat to creep closer to the edge and peer over. There was the sound of running water gushing down the wall opposite but nothing from below. The rocks continued to fall away into the netherworld. *How deep is the chasm?*

A light came shining from the fissure as Oberon hauled himself out of the opening and lay on his back panting. The cave lit up a little with the flashlight. All except the large black chasm and the ceiling above.

He climbed to his feet and moved to join Kitt.

"The edge is soft," Cal warned.

He stopped a few feet back, unclipped a glow stick from his belt and tossed it in. It fell and continued to fall until the yellow glow disappeared completely without hitting the bottom.

He turned to them. "Okay, which way now?"

All meaning of time seemed lost down here—Kitt didn't know whether it was night or day, or even how long they'd been in the cave. *Was it hours or days?* She couldn't tell.

Cal struggled to her feet and Kitt moved away from the edge to help her.

"Wait." Oberon dropped the pack to the ground and fished around. "This is not as good as fresh meat, but it will give you back some energy."

He handed her several sticks of jerky. Cal grabbed them and tore into the dried meat. An instant hit of protein, the fresher the better, was what she needed now. But this would work for now.

"Lead the way," he said to Cal when she looked a little brighter.

The pain seared through Antoinette's shoulder as J.J. twisted the sword. She bit down on her lip to stop the scream building in her throat from escaping.

"How does that feel?" Marvella whispered in her ear.

"I've had worse bikini waxes," Antoinette hissed through gritted teeth.

Marvella's throaty laugh echoed throughout the warehouse as J.J. pulled the sword out.

Antoinette panted through the pain as the wound started to knit, just before he drove the blade through her other shoulder.

Laughter bubbled up her throat and she couldn't hold it in any longer. Better that than scream. She may heal quickly, but it still hurt like a fucking bastard.

"What the hell are you laughing at?" J.J. asked, twisting the steel in her shoulder a little harder.

"This may hurt me now," she laughed, "but it's nothing compared to what I'm going to do to you."

J.J. pulled out the sword, then plunged it lower through her stomach, exactly where she wanted him to. It seared, twisted, and burned and she did the only thing she could. She pushed herself harder onto the blade. It went right through her and into Marvella, who let her go with surprise.

With her arms now free, Antoinette pushed herself further until she was able to drive her palm up into J.J.'s nose. He let go of the pommel, just as she knew he would. And she bolted up the nearby stairs.

Marvella recovered almost immediately and followed. J.J. did too, only instead of taking the stairs he leapt to the next floor to cut off Antoinette.

With J.J. in front and Marvella behind, Antoinette used both hands and gritted her teeth as she slid the sword out of her gut. With all the blood loss, her hunger rose. Even the smell of the corrupt, stale human blood floating up from the ground below started to smell good.

J.J. advanced from one side, Marvella from the other. There was only one way to go. Antoinette dived over the side, somersaulted in midair, and dropped to the floor below. J.J. vaulted the railing after her to land heavily a few feet away.

"GET HER—FUCK HER UP GOOD!" the insane female screamed as she leaned over the railing above.

He picked up another length of metal pipe and swiped at her. She blocked with her battered katana, the blade covered in nicks and indents. She would have to work on it long and hard to get back a smooth edge.

But it was sharp enough to kill these two. With a kick double-feint, she spun around and lopped off J.J.'s left arm at the elbow. He screamed. His right hand covered the wound and blood seeped through his fingers. Then she took his right leg at the knee.

Marvella was about to climb down when an arrow ricocheted off the metal just to the right and embedded in the wall behind her. They all turned to see Tones loading another bolt into a crossbow.

The eighties rocker chick seemed to lose her nerve. She looked at Tones and Antoinette, then finally at J.J. "Sorry, lover—it's been fun."

"MARVELLA . . ." J.J. screamed.

She ran along the metal walkway, her heels tapping loudly. Tones fired again, but she ducked and it sailed right past her head and into the wall again. She reached the end of the platform and made a swan dive through the large windows.

Tones took off after her while Antoinette stood over J.J. The dreniac was shaking and oozing dark blood all over the floor.

"Please, Antoinette, don't kill me," he croaked. "For old-time's sake,"

Antoinette lowered the sword and looked down at the pitiful shell of a once-great Venator. He had been her colleague, her friend, even her lover.

"J.J.," she said, pulling back the sword.

She sliced quickly. His head slid away in an almost graceful tumble.

A quick death. More than he deserved for Tripper.

She sighed. "For old-time's sake."

34

innocence lost

Kitt had no idea how far beneath the surface they were at this point. Cal had been following the scent trail, leading them deeper and deeper. Finally, they saw a glow up ahead. Cal ran straight for the light and headed for her sister as she entered another cave—yapping excitedly and licking her face before she changed back to human form.

Raven sat back watching the two girls almost collide in their desperation to make contact. They clutched each other tight, both seeming to regain color and strength as if healing each other with their touch. For the moment they needed each other more than they needed their parents.

Tyrone sat hunched over Nathan, who was propped against a large rock in the middle of the cavern. Kitt moved to examine her brother. Blood covered his temple; a matching splat of crimson and hair was stuck to the boulder he was leaning against. His wound was healing, though he still looked a little groggy.

Tyrone stood up, his mouth open, his expression strange as he watched his granddaughters' reunion. Kitt closed her eyes and sucked in her breath. The moment she'd been dreading.

"She came in as a wolf," Tyrone said. "What the hell are you trying to pull here?"

Raven came up and put his hands on her shoulders. She touched her fingertips to his. Her father looked at them. Oberon crossed to check on Nathan.

"My God," Tyrone said, shaking his head. "Could you and he have really created a . . . ? There must be some mistake."

She'd never seen him so rattled before, but it still wasn't the reaction she'd expected.

"Show him," Raven said in a quiet tone to their daughter.

Cal changed into wolf form again and sat on her haunches.

"So the other one is the felian," Tyrone said, his features taking on a skeptical cast.

The wolf rose up and transformed into a snow leopard. Even though she'd seen it before, the sight still gave her the chill.

"Dúbabeo," Tyrone whispered and stumbled back to sit heavily on a large rock. "And her sister?"

"The same," Kitt said.

Nathan groaned and Kitt dropped to his side. Their eyes met, and for the first time in years, he didn't look at her with hate.

"Kitt, I . . ." He lowered his eyes.

She glanced over to the twins. "Let's just get you all out of here first." Then Kitt placed a glow stick on the ground next to her brother.

"Will he be okay?" Tyrone asked.

"Yes, the wound's already healed."

Tyrone also squatted in front of Nathan. "Did you see the killer?"

Her brother shook his head. "He had me blindfolded in the car. I never got a real good look at him. The tunnels are dark and most of the way he made me walk ahead, carrying Seph."

This cavern also had different tunnels leading away.

"Do you know which way he went?" Tyrone asked as Kitt cleaned the blood off Nathan's temple.

He lowered his eyes again. "No. I was unconscious."

She placed her hand on his shoulder. "Do you know what he wanted?"

Nathan frowned. "He said something about a sacred pool

and sacrificing Seph to the Holy Dark Brethren or something."

Kitt stiffened and turned to Oberon. He gave her a tight shake of his head to keep quiet.

Tyrone stood and looked down at them. "I'm going after my men—I sent them ahead to track the killer. Nathan and Persephone may be okay but no one attacks my family."

"I'll go with you," Raven said, coming to stand beside him.

Oberon stood up near the twins. "I'll stay here and keep an eye out."

"There's no need," Nathan said. "I'll watch them; my head's just about healed. I'm sure you'd be of more use with them."

"You sure?" Oberon asked Kitt.

"Yeah," she answered. "We'll be fine."

Oberon clapped Raven on the shoulder. "Let's go, then?"

"Here, you might need this more than I will." Oberon handed her the heavy flashlight.

Oberon undressed and the three males transformed, then set off down the far tunnel.

"Go—see to your daughters," Nathan said, waving her off when they'd gone.

She could do little else at this point. "Okay, but call if you need me."

Kitt squatted beside Seph, smoothing her hand over her hair and down the side of her face. The dam Seph had been holding back broke and she choked as the tears came. "Are you all right?"

The girl looked at her sister and smiled. "I am now."

A leather-covered inhibitor chain lay on the ground, along with what looked like a cord made from the same material. Marks on Seph's wrists and ankles were made by being tied up with a silver cord.

No wonder she couldn't move.

Cal took her sister's face in her hands, leaned forward, and planted a quick kiss on Seph's forehead. "Don't you ever do that to me again."

Seph made a noise that could've been a laugh or a sob as

she buried her face against Cal's shoulder. Then she lifted her eyes to Kitt and glanced past her.

A frown creased her brow and she sat back. "Is Nathan okay?"

The glow stick sat next to his slumped form. He lay on his side away from her and her heartbeat skidded to a stop. The flashlight was on the ground next to her and she picked it up and went to her brother's aid.

"Nathan?" She crouched beside her brother's prone body.

"No, not *Nathan*." He sat up, grabbed her wrist with one hand, and held something sharp against her throat. Malevolent dark eyes stared back from under a mop of dark hair, his mouth twisting into an insane caricature of a smile. "I'm Gideon, my sweet angel."

35

Deal with the Devil

My angel.

The real one.

He could see it now. The others were just pale imitations, copies of the original . . .

"BRING HER TO THE SACRED POOL." Ealund's ghostly form crossed to stand behind the woman.

Gideon frowned. "Not this one. Take the offering I brought to you, but leave me this one."

"Listen to him, brother," Nathan said. *"She is not worthy of your admiration."*

"THIS ONE IS STRONG," Ealund admitted. *"MAYBE EVEN STRONG ENOUGH TO FREE ME FROM THIS HELL."*

Gideon shook his head. The constant babble was confusing him. His thoughts flitted around his head like fireflies. Impossible to catch—impossible to pin down.

There was only *her.* There was only his *sweet, sweet* angel.

His thoughts solidified. "You're trying trick me, brother. Take her for yourself. But she is mine."

"No, brother. She will deceive you," Nathan said.

For years, Gideon had been trapped in the body he shared with Nathan. Since a shaman had separated their thoughts as children, Nathan hadn't spoken to Gideon—but that changed tonight.

At first, Gideon had the power; then Nathan discovered Ealund was there and conspired with him against Gideon.

"YOU, GIDEON, MUST BRING HER TO ME AS A SAC-RIFICE." Ealund moved around Kitt, running his long pale fingertips down her left cheek. She raised her hand to touch the spot, as if she felt it. She looked around.

"SHE IS YOUR PENANCE FOR FAILING ME."

"Listen to him," Nathan whispered. *"Give him Kathryn, keep the others."*

"Shut up, shut up, SHUT UP!" Gideon shook his head and clutched his angel tighter as the knife shook in his grip. "Leave me alone."

"YOU CANNOT END YOUR INDENTURE TO ME." Ealund's dark voice echoed in his head. *"YOU WILL DO AS I ASK."*

36

Double the Terror

Kitt stilled as the prick of the silver blade burned the sensitive skin of her throat. Her brother's face twisted back and forth, changing, struggling for dominance. One minute Nathan was there as he'd always been, the next a darker version with black hair and blue eyes not unlike Dylan and Tyrone's.

The dark-haired one called himself Gideon and, besides Nathan, he seemed to be talking to someone else over her shoulder. He was clearly delusional and psychotic.

Gideon.

Nathan's lost twin? They're sharing the same body? And yet they were as different as night and day—at least in physical appearance.

One who is two—two who are one.

Kitt turned her head just enough to see the girls watching in helpless horror. Obviously, they had no more idea about this Gideon than she did.

"So, Gideon is it?" She signaled the girls with her hand to stay where they were and be quiet.

He stopped changing and solidified into the dark-haired visage. His eyes kept moving around the room as if watching someone; however, there was no one there. When he looked at the twins, his eyes narrowed suspiciously.

"Gideon!" She called his attention back to her and away from them.

He frowned, confused and unsure. Not the soulless windows into the mind of a psychopath she was expecting.

"Where's Nathan?" she asked.

"In here." He pointed to his head, his face lighting up in triumph. "Trapped in the same prison he's kept me in for years. Now it's my body."

"Do you think I can talk to him?"

"She wants him," Gideon said over her shoulder, pressing the blade harder against her throat and tilting his head to the side as though he was listening to something beyond her hearing.

She tried to turn her head, but the blade bit deeper and a warm trickle ran down to her shoulder.

"No," Gideon said. "Don't say that."

"Say what?" she asked.

His eyes centered on her again. "He says you are a soiled harlot, a temptress of men. You need to be sacrificed."

Fear skittered across her chest. "Who? Nathan?"

Gideon frowned. "No, Ealund."

Ealund? "Does he share your body like Nathan?"

He tilted his head and sneered, like she was an idiot. "He's right behind you." His grin widened as she looked past him.

This time he let her look, but the space was empty.

"There's no one there."

"It doesn't matter if you can't see him, because he sees you." Gideon's dark smile deepened.

There must be a third personality. What else could it be? Maybe with such a warped psychotic living in his head he's developed delusions. Then she felt the brush of a cold breeze on her arm. But there was no wind in the cave. A chill crept over her.

"Can you ask Ealund a question for me?" She thought she would try humoring him.

"Ask yourself, he can hear you."

An icy wisp kissed her cheek. She shrank away from the invisible touch and turned to search the air around her. *Nothing.* There was nothing there and yet . . .

"Who are you?" This time her voice did betray her nerves.

"I told you, Ealund," Gideon answered.

Okay, different tact. "What are you?"

The air shimmered and the impression of laughter filled the still cave, though she could hear nothing.

"He says you know what he is," Gideon said and pressed the knife against her throat again. The silver burned.

Kitt got a little closer to the male who was her brother and yet not.

"STOP!" he yelled, twisting her around, forcing her wrist high up behind her back, and the prick of the silver blade continued to burn her neck.

The girls, who'd been inching their way toward the tunnel Raven and Tyrone had disappeared down, stopped as Gideon commanded.

"Tether yourself with the inhibitor cord," he hissed into her ear.

"What?" she said, looking at the twins who were just as confused as she.

"Pick up the cord and tie your wrists together." His voice started to take on a panicky note.

Kitt tried to take a step but his grip tightened. "What are you doing?"

"What you said," she said, confused.

"No, not this you, that you." He flicked the knife toward the twins.

She suddenly realized that he saw the twins and her as one person. He was insane.

Kitt needed to buy them time. "Can I talk to Nathan?"

"No," the male snapped. "Now, do as I say."

"Please! I really need to speak to my brother."

As the air moved around her, a coolness swept past.

"No. I have control, not him," Gideon said. "Don't make me let him out. *Yes . . . yes . . . no.*"

It was like listening to a one side of a telephone conversation.

"I know I'm stronger now but . . . I understand."

Gideon shuffled her toward the twins. "Bind the wrists," he said to the girls.

They should have run when they had the chance. Kitt held her arms out and allowed Cal to wrap her wrists together in front. Now she couldn't transform.

Strength and fighting abilities weren't going to win this one, she was certain. It'd take more than brute force to solve the situation. She had to try to get Nathan back. Maybe he'd see sense.

"Please"—she tried to keep the panic wrapping around her throat from squeezing off her voice—"I need to talk to Nathan."

"No, I . . ." His voice trailed.

"Gideon is useless." Kitt recognized Nathan's tone immediately.

She could actually feel the difference in the way he held her too. Gideon pressed his entire body against hers, whereas Nathan tried to touch as little as possible. And she could feel the hate wrapping around them both. The cold certainty that Nathan would be no savior crept over her skin. In fact, she may have just leapt with both feet into a raging inferno.

"If you want to save the twins, you do as he says," he whispered into her ear.

"Who?" she asked.

"Ealund."

So, he shared Gideon's illusions.

Though she wasn't sure it was a delusion as a cold sensation swept past her again. "Okay." She tried to keep her voice even.

"Now tie the twins' hands together behind their backs with the other cord," he said, and then he lowered his voice. "And do it quickly."

She needed time for Raven and Oberon to realize their mistake and return, but she knew she couldn't be too obvious about it. God, she hoped they'd come soon.

He released her enough for her to bend, but kept the knife at her throat. She took the cord from Cal and purposely let it fall from her fingers so it looked accidental, which wasn't far from the truth. Her own bound hands made it much more difficult.

"Careful bitch," Nathan hissed and the blade bit deeper against her throat.

"I'm sorry," she said and picked up the cord again.

Cal looked up, her eyes conveying all the fear Kitt felt; Seph's just held angry hate. She was such the warrior.

"It'll be okay." Kitt schooled her features to show more confidence than she felt. The twins sat back to back so she could bind them together by their wrists. She kept the knots as loose as she dared, hoping they would be able to get free.

As soon as she was done, Nathan grabbed Kitt by the wrists and untied them, then wrenched her arms behind her back and roughly retied them together. He pushed her down on the ground and slammed the handle of the knife against her skull.

Stars burst behind her eyes, knocking her almost senseless. Dirt filled her mouth and nose. A distant cacophony of dispute erupted from the girls; she couldn't make sense of the words, but got the gist.

She could also make out the menace in Nathan's tone as he threatened them into silence. Her heart sank. While she struggled to rise on her hands and knees, she saw that Nathan was tightening the girls' bonds. Her hope for them to get out of those loosely tied knots was immediately dashed.

The other thing that struck her was Nathan appeared as he normally did, his hair color back to the same pale blond and his eyes the same angry amber. When he'd finished, he rose and stalked toward her.

"You didn't think I'd trust you?" He looked down at her with the burning hatred she'd seen many times before, but it was now tinged with insanity. "You wanted to take them from me, but I'm going to mold them to be everything our father wanted."

"You will save them from Ealund?" Kitt asked.

"Yes, by sacrificing *you* to Ealund." He smiled at her and she realized he was now more insane than Gideon. "The twins will be free to come with me. Ealund promised."

"Why do you hate me so much?" she asked.

The look he gave her was pure venom. "Don't pretend you don't know."

As he dragged her to her feet, Gideon returned. She'd learn no more of her crimes against her brother.

Gideon's blue eyes glittered with malevolent desire in the dim light of the glow stick and his lips twisted into a mirage of a smile. She shrank away from him as much as his grip on her upper arm would let her. At least he no longer held the burning poisonous blade to her throat.

He tilted his head, his brow creasing in confusion. "Why do you cower from me?"

"Because you're evil and sick and I don't understand what you're doing." The revulsion pitched her voice a little higher.

His features turned to stone. "No, I'm just doing my master's bidding. But I want to be free—for you."

Kitt knew she shouldn't be provoking him, but she couldn't help herself. "For me? Is that how your sick and twisted mind justifies the murder of innocent people?"

"THEY WERE NEVER INNOCENT!" he roared. "They were vile creatures full of lust for power."

"They were children," she said. "You didn't even know them."

"You lie. Ealund told me their crimes," he said, confused. "He promised me I'd be free and the body would be mine."

And then it dawned on her. Gideon *was* evil, but he just wanted to escape Nathan as much as she did.

"He'll destroy you," she whispered. "You will never be free of him."

"You lie," he shrieked and dragged her toward the cavern entrance, opposite to the one the others took.

"Where are you taking me?" she asked, terror constricting her throat again.

He didn't even look as he said something she barely caught. It took a moment to fill in the gaps and work out what he'd said. But she did and her blood froze in her veins.

"To the edge of the beyond."

37

silent and deadly

Raven transformed and held his arm out, bent at a right angle at the elbow, his fist clenched in the silent military-stop signal. He heard hushed sounds—whispering male voices. Tyrone stopped behind him and Oberon concealed the glow stick's light within his thick fur. The three of them crept toward the whispers.

Two dark shapes loomed ahead. Raven and Tyrone pounced and when they had them subdued, Oberon brought out the light.

Beneath them, hands held behind their backs, were two confused and pissed tigers. Leon stood a short ways back, dropped his hands to his knees and let out a bellow of laughter.

"What the hell?" Tyrone said through clenched teeth as he climbed off his captive. "Where did you come from?"

Raven stood and offered his hand to his hapless victim. The felian's lip curled into a snarl, then eased off to finally accept the offer. It took him a moment to work out it was Jericho, recalling Kitt's description of his tattoo.

The brothers were both solid, burly men. Perfect bodyguard material. He'd seen them before, but they'd never actually met face-to-face.

"So where did you come from?" Tyrone asked.

Leon pointed back to the way they'd come. "A few hundred yards back, the tunnel we were following came out into an apex—one way continued to go down and the other back this way. We followed the scent."

"He must have got past us," Oberon said.

"No." Tyrone went pale.

"The girls!" Raven said.

"Please . . . don't let me be right." Tyrone shook himself as they all set off at top speed. Raven changed to wolf midstep. The change in the footfalls behind him suggested the others did the same.

There'd been a gnawing feeling in his gut for some time, but he put it down to Seph being in danger. *I left them behind, unprotected except for a hurt Nathan! What had I been thinking?*

It took much less time to get back. They knew the way this time. He entered the cave and found the twins sitting back to back, struggling to free themselves.

They were safe, both of them. But his relief was short-lived. *Where is Kitt?*

He transformed back to human and rushed to help the girls. "What happened?"

"It's Nathan—"

"He changed—"

The girls were talking at the same time.

"We have to save them," Tyrone said, cutting the girls off.

Raven finished untying them. They rubbed their wrists and turned as one to look at their grandfather, both heads tilting left at an identical angle.

"Where's Nathan and Kitt?" Oberon asked, pulling on his earlier discarded leather pants.

Tyrone's eyes flicked to the twins and shook his head.

"He's taken Kitt," Seph said, looking at her grandfather. "She gave herself up to save us."

What did he know?

"He's taking her to the edge of the beyond, whatever that means," Cal said, also holding her grandfather's eyes—and then as one, the twins turned to Raven. "We think he's going to sacrifice her."

Raven didn't wait for more. He changed into wolf form and took off after the scent trail; he could hear the others following behind. The thought of Kitt's life in danger spurred him on—faster.

There was light ahead and he raced for it. Something bumped him and heavy jaws clamped down on his shoulder, tearing flesh and tossing him aside. He let out a howl of pain and caught a blur of red-gold as he fell over the edge of the yawning abyss.

Only his training saved him.

Raven transformed quickly back into human, starting with his hands. He reached out first with his good arm and caught a ledge as he dropped, then used his injured arm to slow down his descent. The black void fell away into dark nothingness under his dangling feet. His fingers gripped hard as his feet scrabbled to find a foothold and release the screaming pressure on his shoulder.

Leon.

He was going to kill that lion the next time he saw him.

The mangled shoulder popped as it healed and he was able to move again, and he reached up as one foot found support. His heart pounded in his chest as he cursed the lion's name.

Then the sides crumbled. As he moved to find another foothold, a chunk of rock hit him on the head and he glanced up. The worried faces of his twin daughters peered down at him over the edge.

Kitt struggled under Gideon's thighs, her arms trapped behind her back. He pushed down as he hacked off a part of his shirt.

"I'm sorry I left the disabling blade behind," he said. "I would have used it higher in the neck for you, so you wouldn't have to feel any of this." He moved to stuff the piece of shirt into her mouth.

"Wait," she said, trying to buy more time. "Why did you kill Emmett?"

"Who?" he said, his frown deepening then his face cleared. "Oh, the white tiger from years ago."

Gideon's face morphed into Nathan's pale features.

"Emmett was going to oppose me in the council. He laughed and called me a sad little male, then turned his back. I struck him with the knife so hard the blade broke. He was alive and looked at me with those surprised eyes. He wasn't laughing anymore, but I couldn't kill him. Then I blacked out and woke later covered in blood. I didn't mean to do it . . ." His voice trailed off.

Then Gideon returned. She was starting to feel dizzy, seeing Gideon and her brother swap back and forth was very disorientating.

"It was you," she said.

"Yes, that was my first." The strange dark version of her brother smiled sadly.

He looked at her again. "You know—that was the first time I escaped, and it was the first time I saw you. My sweet, beautiful angel.

He looked to the side. "Now I must finish," he said. "Ealund demands it. No more questions."

She almost choked on the piece of shirt he stuffed into her mouth and he brought the blade against her skin. As the pain seared, she fought her gag reflex at the scent of burning flesh. Her burning flesh. The silver in the knife blade exacerbated the pain tenfold. She tried to bite off the scream building deep in the pit of her stomach, but it ripped up her throat only to be muffled by the makeshift gag.

Gideon stopped and frowned. "There, there, my angel. It'll soon be over."

"STOP!" Kitt heard her father's voice ring out in the cavern.

Gideon climbed off and yanked her up before him, using her as a shield. "Hello, *Daddy.*"

There was absolutely no trace of surprise on her father's face as he answered: "Hello, Gideon."

The angel grew rigid in front of him. Gideon had wanted this for a long time . . . and for his father to see him again.

Father . . . huh. More like jailer.

"Have you missed me, *Daddy*? Have you missed me since

you had the shaman imprison me in my brother's head?" Gideon hissed.

The angel they called Kitt struggled against her bonds, her words muffled by the gag.

Tyrone's face fell. "I did it to protect my children. If the Pride discovered what you were, they would've killed you both."

"But why me?" Gideon pleaded. "Why not Nathan?" It was something he'd been dying to know for a very long time. "How did you choose?"

"The Pride had already seen your brother," Tyrone said.

The one called Kitt made a confused noise, still gagged.

"Tell her, Daddy. Tell her what you did to me," Gideon said.

"Two heart beats, all normal. But the birth was difficult. Things went wrong. In the end there was only Nathan." Tyrone hung his head for a moment. "We told the Elders that Nathan's littermate died in birth. It just seemed easier."

"You lied," Gideon whispered.

Tyrone held out his hands, pleading. "We didn't know. You didn't manifest, Gideon, until Nathan was two. We had to save our child."

"Wasn't I your child too?" Gideon asked in disbelief, his hatred increasing.

"HE WAS AFRAID OF YOU," Ealund intoned.

"Were you?" Gideon said, he tightened his arm around his angel. "Were you afraid of me?"

"What?" Tyrone's eyes flicked away. "No."

Gideon could taste the lie. This whole time Nathan had been strangely quiet in his head.

Tyrone stepped closer. "Like I said, if the Pride found out what you were, they would've demanded your death. So I had the shaman perform the ceremony in secret."

"They took you from me." Nathan spoke for the first time. "I was all alone."

"Your mother fought my decision. She demanded I tell the truth . . . She wanted us to leave the Pride and take you away."

Gideon's heart came into his throat. "She fought for me?"

"Yes. She loved you very much. But I was the new Pride Alpha." Tyrone paced sideways, his eyes taking on a far-away look. "She was devastated when she lost you."

"She loved me!" He had thought she hated him for so long—this was hard to believe.

"HE LIES! TO SAVE HIS OTHER PRECIOUS CHILD," Ealund whispered. *"TO SAVE NATHAN."*

Tyrone nodded. "She grieved so much for you, it sent her into estrus again. Dylan and Kathryn were conceived."

She did care. His mother was the real angel. Not this one.

"YES!" Ealund's ghostly form floated above the abyss. *"SHE'S UNWORTHY. SEND HER TO ME."*

"Yes, send her to Ealund," Nathan whispered in his mind.

Gideon nodded and he plunged the knife into the false angel's chest.

38
Time's up

Dirt and debris rained down on Raven from above as they reached for him, but his grip started to slip. He closed his eyes and spat out a mouthful of detritus.

"Hold on," the ursian's voice rumbled from above.

A second later Seph was lowered over the side by her ankles. She gave him an unsteady smile as she wrapped her fingers around his wrist.

"Okay," she called over her shoulder.

Raven brought his other hand to also grip her wrist, then Oberon hauled them slowly toward the top. Until the edge broke away.

"WAIT!" yelled Raven.

More small rocks and dirt rained down, and when the debris settled, Oberon continued pulling. Finally, they reached the top and he and Cal helped Seph up as Raven climbed over the ledge and to his feet.

He dusted off his hands and looked at Oberon. "Thanks."

"Don't mention it," he rumbled. "Just be a little more careful next time."

"Let's go," Raven said, slapping him on the back. "We must stop—"

A strangled cry reverberated off the rocky walls.

Raven didn't need anything else to spur him on. He ran

with his heart thumping in his throat, but he felt like he was running in treacle.

Finally he came out into a wide cavern with a great black abyss extending away in either direction. Two figures grappled at the edge while another lay on the ground a short ways off. Deathly still.

Kitt.

He raced to her, sliding on his knees to her side and lifting her head into his lap before brushing back the hair from her face and removing the scrap of material from her mouth. The silver knife was still lodged deep in her chest and he gripped the handle. She looked up at him through her pain, gave him an infinitesimal nod and closed her eyes, squeezing a tear from the corner.

He took a breath and held it, not wanting to pull the knife out but knowing that leaving it in was poisoning her. He flexed his fingers on the handle then yanked it out. She screamed, filling the cavern with echoes, then passed out. Blood spurted from the wound—*so much blood*. And because the knife was silver, the wound didn't heal as quickly as it should and would leave a scar.

He pressed his hands against the gash, blood flowing through his fingers. And it kept coming.

"Oberon, your shirt," Cal ordered as she kneeled beside Kitt.

In that moment Raven could see she was truly Kitt's daughter.

"What do you want me to do," Seph asked, a little more unsure than her sister.

"Take Oberon's shirt and press it against the wound," Cal said. "We must stop the bleeding long enough to give her a chance to heal."

Oberon removed his shirt and hung back, slinging his jacket over his shoulder.

Cal pointed at it. "Now ball that up and use it to elevate her feet. Raven, lay her head on the ground."

Everyone did as she said. Her tone commanded confidence and her actions were sure. She picked up the knife, careful not to touch the blade, and examined it. "The tip's broken off inside—that's why it's not healing. I need a knife. "

Oberon pulled a Swiss army knife out of his pocket. "Will this do?"

"Perfect," she said, taking it from him.

Raven's hands shook and he couldn't stop them. For all his training, for all his experience of war, it meant nothing when it came to seeing the woman he loved on the edge of death.

"Now what do you want me to do?" he asked.

"We need to keep her still. Oberon, take her feet. Seph, hold up that flashlight." His daughter didn't need him—she was definitely her mother's daughter, but then she looked at Raven. "Can you take her shoulders?"

He nodded.

Seph wore the same helpless expression he was sure he did. The flashlight shook in her hands.

A low snarling hiss broke through his single-minded focus on Kitt's condition. Two black panthers faced off in a furious ball of teeth and fur. The Tiger Twins stood nearby, frozen in indecisiveness.

Since Nathan was a snow leopard, the other panther had to be the killer. But where was Nathan?

The panthers broke apart, ears pinned as they hissed and growled at each other. They were identical in every way. There was no telling them apart.

"Which is Tyrone?" Raven asked Tyrone's men.

"We're still trying to work that out ourselves," one of them said. "We don't know who to help."

The big black cats continued to circle each other—hissing, snarling, and growling. The echoes of their aggressive vocal exchange reverberated off the rock cave walls, amplifying the volume. Raven flexed his hand against Kitt's cool skin. He wanted to tear something apart, to strike out, but he remained near, helpless and afraid as his woman lay dying.

"Okay," Cal said. "I'm going in."

His daughter closed her eyes and took a deep, shaky breath. The knife shook slightly as it was poised above the still bleeding wound. Then she steeled herself and cut. More blood flowed in rivulets over Kitt's skin and pooled on the cave floor. His stomach sank and his heart with it. Seph gave him an uneasy smile. He'd never felt so helpless, and couldn't bear to keep looking, to see her in pain a moment longer. He lifted his head to watch what was going on around him.

Oberon met his eyes with a long, slow blink. The bear's fear was also visible on his shaken features. Joshua and Jericho's worried expressions shifted back and forth from the ongoing battle between the large black cats and the drama surrounding Kitt.

Leon stood a short ways off also watching the battle. As if he could feel the force of Raven's stare, he turned. A slow smirk spread across the lion's face.

You are so dead.

As if he could read Raven's thoughts, he looked around at his brothers and cocked a bring-it-on eyebrow, confident his brothers would protect him from anything Raven had to dish out.

Raven's temper burned. As much as he wanted to fly over and rip out the cat's throat, he had to think about the safety of his Family. Jericho glanced at Leon, and then locked eyes with Raven for a moment. The tiger male's lips tightened. Maybe Leon wasn't as safe as he thought he was.

The two panthers continued to fight furiously while the others looked on. It wasn't wise to try to get between two fighting Animalians if you wanted to live. All they could do was hang back and wait for an opening to present itself. Raven shifted his grip on Kitt's shoulders as she moaned.

"Maybe if you tried to pull them apart, they may change back to human," Leon suggested.

The Tiger Twins turned to him with an identical are-you-insane tilt to the head.

The lion shrugged. "Just a suggestion."

Raven returned his attention to Kitt as Cal made another cut.

Kitt jolted and groaned, her unconscious features screwed up in pain. Cal's jaw set in a determined jut. He'd never been more proud as he watched her working, her brow knotted in concentration.

If a trace of silver entered Kitt's heart or brain, it could mean instant death. If left in the wound, the surrounding tissue would degrade into a major infection.

Cal felt around, her hands covered in her mother's blood up to her wrists.

She looked up. "It's dangerously close to her heart. I'll have to be careful not to push it into the muscle wall."

How could she look calm about it all when his heart thudded heavily in his mouth? She wasn't. He noticed the tightness around the mouth and the worried cast to her eyes.

"I have faith in you," Raven said to his daughter.

But it was Seph who sniffed and wiped away the tears. He took her by the hand and pulled her down beside him.

"Got it," Cal yelled, her face vibrant in triumph, and held up two bloody fingers with a bloody triangle of metal. She dropped it on the ground and wiped her fingers on the shirt used to stem the blood flow. He'd had never been so pleased to see such a tiny piece of poisonous metal. Seph held the flashlight up while Cal matched the broken tip against the knife on the ground.

"It's intact," Cal said with a light, relieved smile.

Kitt's breath exploded from her mouth, then her head rose from the ground and her eyes flew open.

"Shhh-sh-sh," Cal said. "You're going to be okay."

She's going to be okay. Raven carefully kissed Kitt's lips and smiled at his daughter, who began to shake, shock setting in now her work was done.

Kitt felt as if her chest had been wrenched open and all her insides scooped out. She tried to rise but Cal pushed her down.

"Stay there," her makeshift surgeon said. "You've lost a lot of blood."

"Cal got out the broken piece," Seph said as she took Kitt's head into her lap.

Raven looked at their daughters, pride burning in his eyes. "She was amazing."

Kitt shifted aside the crumpled blood-soaked cloth. The flesh beneath was knitting together nicely. Cal had done an excellent job.

A squealing roar set the hair on the back of her neck standing on end. She raised her head just enough to see two black panthers, torn and bloody. She realized Gideon was also a panther.

How astonishing he was, such a magnificent anomaly. But if an animal and a person could share the same body, why not two people? The Pride's backward mentality toward anything different had caused this tragedy. If not for them, maybe Nathan and Gideon could have been relatively normal and healthy. Maybe Gideon wouldn't have gone insane. And maybe Nathan wouldn't have ended up so bitter.

A roaring crash reverberated around the cavern and the two big cats vanished in a cloud of dust.

"TYRONE!" Kitt screamed, struggling to her feet.

She pushed Raven's hands away as he tried to hold her down. The pain in her stomach was nothing compared with the horrible sinking dread that her father might be dead.

Oberon and her father's men raced to the edge. Raven left Kitt in the hands of Seph and Cal and joined the men. The dust cleared, and neither her father nor her brother was anywhere to be seen.

"They're still there hanging on the edge—both of them," Oberon said. "Help me."

Kitt struggled to her feet, creeping as close as she dared to the edge and peered over the side. Her father hung by one arm on a large rock jutting out from the almost smooth wall of the abyss, about ten or twelve feet down. With the other hand, he gripped Gideon's wrist.

"We have no rope. How are we going to get them up?" one of the twins asked.

"Seph, take off your jeans," Oberon said, unbuttoning the fly on his leather pants.

Now he was completely naked and, as usual, wore no Abeolite underneath.

The rock shifted under the weight. Nathan's features replaced Gideon's and twisted in terror as he glanced over his shoulder at the blackness below. Then the rock shifted again.

"It's not going to hold much longer," Raven said. "We have to get them up now."

"SAVE ME," Nathan screamed, trying to scrabble over Tyrone. "HURRY, SAVE ME!"

"I don't think this material will support the weight of two." Oberon tugged at the knot he'd made by tying the pants and the jeans together. It gave way. The material was too thick to form a solid connection.

Again the rock moved. Nathan looked up at Kitt, hate filling his eyes. They stared at each other for those few microseconds. And then Gideon's darker features replaced Nathan's hate-filled ones. He didn't look afraid or insane and gave her a single, solid nod. She knew what he was going to do before he reached up and gripped their father's hand, prying loose his fingers one at a time.

"No!" Tyrone cried.

"I'm sorry, Father." It was the last thing Gideon and Nathan would ever say. With that, Tyrone's final grip was broken and they fell away, still looking at Kitt.

Just before the body disappeared from sight, Nathan reappeared. It was his arms and legs flailing, and his scream tearing from the open mouth.

With the weight gone, Tyrone gripped the rock with both hands and pulled himself onto the jutting ledge and closer to the top. Oberon and the tiger brothers formed a chain—feet to hands, lying flat on the ground as they lowered the leather pants which were now long enough to reach and hauled Tyrone up over the edge. When her father was once again safe on terra firma, Kitt collapsed into Raven's arms, stunned and numb. She couldn't feel anything at all. Nathan and Gideon were gone and she felt nothing.

Raven kissed the top of her head. She turned in his arms and looked up at him with a smile. Then the smile slid away, his expression hardening.

"I have something I need to do," he said. "Seph, help your mother."

Tyrone stood surrounded by his men, but looked over at Kitt. His usual stony mask melted into fatherly concern. He was her father again, her daddy. His features blurred as her eyes filled with tears.

As Raven closed in on the group, Leon stepped out to

meet him with a sneer. Without breaking his stride, Raven's hand shot out, struck him in the neck, then he continued toward her father.

The lion's face rounded in surprise as three jagged parallel wounds yawned across his throat. His hands ineffectually tried to stem the blood pumping onto the cave floor from the carotid artery. He dropped to his knees. The blood continued to spurt from the wound, flowing over his chest and down his torso, until he toppled sideways.

39

terror finales

Kitt's knees buckled, the prickling sensation of the blood draining from her face threatened her consciousness as she struggled to comprehend what she'd just seen. Only Seph and Cal's hold on her stopped her from collapsing altogether. It'd happened so fast. She could hardly believe it. Leon was dead and Raven did it. Elation, vengeance, and horror—each emotion flashed one after the other, but mostly she felt relief quickly followed by fear. Fear of what her father would now do to Raven for killing one of his men.

Jericho and Joshua moved forward as Raven got closer, but Tyrone held up his hand to stop them. Their usual stoic expressions didn't change as they turned to watch their brother's blood pool onto the ground, turning the dirt and rubble to reddish black mud.

Kitt was shocked at the quick violence of it all. Cal and Seph had stiffened beside her but continued to support her weight. Oberon's face dropped, the Tiger Twins tensed, but Tyrone never moved.

Raven dropped the misshapen clawed hand to his side and it returned to human form, still covered with blood. He stopped in front of Tyrone and glanced back at Kitt before turning again to her father. "I'm taking back what's mine."

He glanced at Kitt and his daughters over his shoulder. "All of them."

"You ask a lot for someone who just killed another of my men before my very eyes, Matokwe," Tyrone said quietly.

"You know he deserved it," Raven said. "And they're mine."

Her father sighed and dropped his head. "Maybe you're right, but how are you going to protect them?"

"I did before and I will again," Raven hissed, getting up in Tyrone's face.

The tiger brothers started moving forward again, but Tyrone stopped them for the second time, knowing Raven wouldn't hurt him; Kitt could see the certainty in her father's eyes.

Raven stepped back. "Do whatever you need to—double the price on my head if you want, but I am taking them."

"And why would I do that?" Tyrone crossed his arms and exchanged a glance with the Tiger Twins. "After all, you discovered the serial killer's identity, clearing your own name in the process, and helped to bring him down." His eyes flicked to Leon's body lying a few feet away.

Kitt's breath stilled. *What's he up to now?*

She wasn't the only one confused. Oberon's head shot around and nailed Tyrone with a piercing glare. "You mean Nathan or Gideon, or whatever he called himself."

"No . . . Nathan was unfortunately killed by the campus killer while trying to save his niece from a horrible death," Tyrone said, catching Kitt's gaze and holding it. "He died a hero."

Kitt suddenly understood. It would kill her mother if she found out what Nathan had done. Plus, this way Tyrone could give Nathan the honor in death he couldn't in life.

"I also think Calliope and Persephone may be unsuited for Pride life. They've been tainted too much by human ways. Maybe it would be best if they left," the Alpha said. "And I'm afraid I will have to deny your petition to rejoin the Pride, my daughter."

"Hang on a minute," Oberon said. "Won't people be able to alibi Leon at the time of the murders?" Oberon asked.

The Alpha smiled. "It's well known he's a violent male, and we will make sure there is enough evidence to pin it on him and no alibis exist."

Kitt turned to the tigers. "But he's your brother."

"We've known for years how unstable he had become and did everything we could to save him," Jericho said. "But after what he did to Rainbow . . ."

Joshua nodded in agreement.

"So, it's agreed, then?" Tyrone asked Oberon who stood stony-faced.

The Tiger Twins carried their brother's body by his arms and legs and tossed Leon into the abyss.

The ursian nodded.

"Train your daughters well, wolf," Tyrone said as the Tiger Twins joined him. "And take good care of my little girl."

After dropping the girls off at the apartment, Kitt made Raven bring her to the office. The silver may have been inside too long, the danger of sepsis increasing the longer it had stayed in her body. While both Oberon and Raven insisted they could get what she needed, it was easier to get it herself than try to explain what she needed.

Raven parked the SUV in front of NYAPS and Oberon pulled his motorcycle up a short way off. A crowd had gathered on the front steps, surrounding the smiling head of VCU.

"Looks like Agent Roberts is in fine form," she said as Raven helped her out of the passenger seat. She'd almost fully healed, but didn't really feel up to facing the gauntlet of the reporters pressing microphones at the smug agent.

Neil Roberts looked over the heads of the gathered reporters, his conceited smile growing even wider as Oberon climbed off the Harley. "This investigation has been handled with incompetence and I have successfully petitioned the Department for the VCU to resume charge of the case—and I'm confident my efforts will meet with favorable consideration."

"I've had enough of this crap," the ursian said and snapped the front of his leather jacket into place.

Cody Shields appeared from the side to intercept him.

"Don't worry," Oberon said with a grin and clapped a big hand on the Incubus's shoulder. "I'm about to wipe the smile off that asshole's face."

Cody stepped aside. Oberon stalked across the lawn, his leather coat flaring in the morning breeze as he pushed his way through the crowd.

"Excuse me," he said as he approached the top step. "There's been a recent development in this case that you should all know about."

Cody joined Kitt and Raven and leaned against the front of the SUV to watch the show. "I can't believe he's so calm."

"I can't believe he said *excuse me*," she said.

Both males laughed.

"You guys look like shit." It came out sounding more like *shet* with Cody's accent, but she was getting used to it now, which was just as well since the twins spoke the same way. "What have you been up to?"

Raven jabbed his chin in the direction of the cameras and microphones turned on Oberon. "I think you're about to be enlightened."

"Last night, while Agent Roberts was playing politics, we were looking into the death of yet another victim of the campus killer. The male NYAPS student was found dead in an alley. One difference in this case was the abduction of the young man's date, who we were able to track safely. We retrieved the girl. However, in the course of trying to apprehend the campus killer, he met with a fatal accident."

The reporters surged forward as one, all yelling questions and jockeying for key positions at the front of the pack.

Cody looked at them with surprise.

"Long story, mate," Raven said.

"*PLEASE*, please," Oberon shouted above the howling reporters. "One question at a time."

The Incubus leaned forward, absorbing the emotions flying around. Agent Roberts's face turned a fuming beet red as he melted into the background and away from the limelight he'd readily sought moments before.

Oberon held up both of his hands to call for silence. "The

killer was a felian who started with murdering a member of his own Pride twenty years ago."

"CAN YOU TELL US THIS KILLER'S NAME?" a reporter yelled out.

"The killer is . . . or rather was . . . Leon of the Jordan Pride." Oberon's gaze flicked to her and then back to the reporters.

"Okay, then," Cody said, moving quickly. "Let's get you around the back before they realize who you are."

"Sounds like a great idea," Raven said and swept Kitt up in his arms with a smile. "Lead the way, dude."

Kitt took another sip of wine and smiled. It was the first time she'd seen Antoinette and Bianca in over a week. They'd stopped by to check on her, see how she was recovering.

"And Tones ran after Marvella like a regular Venator," the Aeternus said with a touch of pride. "Unfortunately, the bitch gave him the slip. With J.J. dead, she'll have to find a new stooge to do her dirty work. Tones thinks she'll go to ground to lick her wounds for a while."

Seph was sitting on the floor, staring up at the Aeternus with the beginnings of hero worship. Kitt hid her smile behind another sip and glanced over the rim at Bianca, who winked. She was glad when the witch had come. It was a good opportunity to get to know her a little better now that Kitt officially agreed to be part of the team.

A knock at the apartment door interrupted the laughter.

"I'll get it," Cal said, starting to her feet.

"No, I'm closer," Kitt said, a little tired of feeling like an invalid.

Tyrone stood on the threshold, dressed in an expensive Italian suit and appearing every inch the Alpha of a prominent felian Pride. He looked her up and down, then smiled his usual tight polite smile. "We're returning to the Pridelands."

Kitt nodded and turned to look at the twins laughing with Antoinette. He dropped his voice so only she could hear him. "The council has agreed to release them from the Pride." He straightened to clasp his hands behind his back.

"And I would ask a favor." He moved to one side. "I have a lot to do, and would like to leave something here for you to look after until I get back."

Serena stepped into the doorway holding a tiny baby and Rainbow came up beside her. Tears blurred Kitt's eyes. Her mother smiled through her own tears as she stepped into her arms. It felt so good to hold her again.

"I'll be back in about an hour," Tyrone said, his eyes looking suspiciously misty. "But this business looks like it will turn into a regular event—at least once a month."

"Thank you," Kitt said, and she moved to peck Tyrone on the cheek. He looked away quickly.

Jericho stepped forward to hand the other tiny infant over to Rainbow. Kitt caught the soft look in his eyes as he looked at the female and saw the way his fingers lingered a little too long on the back of her hand as she took the babe. Then Rainbow smiled. It took Kitt back to the time they were children and Rainbow's crush on Dylan. It was that same smile.

Jericho nodded at Kitt and stepped away.

"I'll be back a little later." Tyrone's voice cracked a little as he turned quickly and left. Rainbow and Serena joined the others to much oohing and aahing. The tiny babies passed from one clucking female to the next with much delight. The twins smiled and laughed along with the rest and a lump in Kitt's chest shifted. She'd missed so much of their growing up, so much of watching them grow from children to the young women they'd become. She wished she could go back and change it all, but it was too late. The only thing now was to move forward.

Cal leapt to her feet. "Can I get you anything? Coffee, wine, soda?"

"Sure, soda would be great, thanks," Serena said.

Kitt patted the girl's shoulder as Cal headed for the kitchen. "Rainbow, did I detect a little something between you and Jericho?" she asked as she reached for her glass.

The felian female blushed. "They've both been really sweet since Leon died. Helping to take care of the babies and . . ."

"Both of them?" Seph asked.

"I don't think that's what she meant," Kitt said with a laugh.

"Well, actually . . ." Rainbow's blush deepened. "It's just . . . they're used to sharing things and I couldn't decide between them . . ."

"You go, girl," Antoinette said, impressed.

Serena patted the embarrassed female's knee. "Actually in centuries past, it wasn't unusual to take on more than one mate, especially when war thinned our numbers. But it's something that's fallen out of practice these days."

"Well, good luck to you," Antoinette said. "I have enough trouble keeping track of one man."

The laughter filled the room. Her apartment, once cold and gray, now sparkled with new life. A fresh batch of tears threatened to spill, but this time full of joy and happiness instead of grief and sadness. Kitt just wished Dylan could be here to share it with her.

Their time was over almost before it'd begun. Kitt stood at the window and watched as her father ushered her mother and Rainbow into the limousine on the street far below. Just before he got in after them, he stopped and glanced back over his shoulder. Could he see her standing at the window? Probably not, but she liked to think he could and waved.

She turned away from the window at the sound of someone rapping on the front door. This time Cal beat her to it.

"Looks like you lovely ladies had quite a party," Tones said as he surveyed the wineglasses, soda bottles, and snack plates covering the coffee table.

It had turned into a bit of an impromptu celebration.

"You're such the sweet-talker, Tones," Antoinette said. "But what are you doing here?"

"Oberon told me where to find you. I thought maybe we could all go for a drink at Buddy's. I'm in the mood for a little dancing."

"Hey, yeah," Cal said. "Great idea. I love that place. Come on, Seph, let's go."

"Not a bad idea," Antoinette agreed. "You want to check it out, Bianca?"

"I've heard lots about this place," Bianca said. "But are you sure you want to go back there after last time?"

"Hell, yes," Cal said with a grin. "Seph's been pissed she missed that bar fight."

"There'll be no brawling tonight, thank you very much." The words, sounding so much like her mother's, were out of Kitt's mouth before she could stop them. "Besides, I am a little tired. What I'd really love is a hot shower and bed."

Seph's face fell.

"That's probably a good idea," Tones said. "But we'll take good care of the girls."

"Maybe we should stay in too," Cal said, sounding disappointed.

Kitt shook her head. Actually it would be nice to have some alone time. "There's no reason for you girls to stay in. You've been babysitting me all week. Go—have some fun."

"But . . ." Cal started.

"But nothing," Kitt said. "I'm only going to bed anyway."

Tones choked and tried to cover it with a cough. *What's wrong with him?*

"Only if you're sure," Seph said, the concern on her face was genuine.

She smiled. "I'm sure—now go. And stay away from fruity, alcoholic drinks, especially ones with umbrellas."

Cal laughed and jumped up and kissed Kitt's cheek. "We will and sleep tight."

Antoinette hugged her as well. "We'll take good care of them."

After they'd gone, the apartment grew silent. But it was a comforting silence, a warm silence, not like before. Her cold apartment was now a home again.

Happy, Kitt walked into her room. Without turning on the light, she opened the closet door, unzipped her skirt, and let it fall to her feet before slipping out of her top. As she reached for the robe hanging on a hook behind the door, she stopped and smiled. "I really wish you'd use the front door. That's why I gave you a key."

A chuckle floated from the chair in the far corner of the

dark room. "Where would be the fun in that? I wouldn't get to see you take your clothes off like that."

She pulled on her robe and tied the sash before turning toward his voice. "You always did have voyeuristic tendencies."

"Only when it came to you." He leaned forward into the light streaming in from the window and grinned in the way that sped up her pulse and sent goose bumps skittering across her skin. He stood and moved closer, wearing nothing more than a pair of black jeans, not even any shoes.

He closed in, silent and deadly like a predator—and she was his prey. Her heart pounded in anticipation as he hooked his finger through her sash and pulled her closer.

"How long have you been in here?" she asked.

"A while." Raven bent and placed a kiss on the side of her throat. "I had to call for backup."

"What do you mean backup?"

"I thought they were never going to leave." He sat down on the edge of the bed, dragging her closer until she stood between his knees and he could snuggle his face against her chest. "So I called Tones for help."

"What if I'd gone with them?" she said, finding it a little difficult to concentrate with his hand massaging her thigh just beneath her right butt cheek.

"Then I would've had to think of something else." He pulled aside her robe and kissed between her breasts.

She closed her eyes. "We should probably get a bigger place, though I'd really hate to leave this apartment." The feel of his lips against her skin sent shivers to her toes. "But the girls will need their own space."

"That's why I've put in an offer on the apartment next door." He muttered between kisses.

"You what?" She lifted his face to look at her.

"I thought the girls could share that apartment. Maybe we could put in a connecting door through the living room."

She smoothed back his hair. "I see you've thought of everything."

He chuckled. "Not really. The girls overheard the woman

who owns the apartment talking about moving to Florida. They came up with the idea and talked me into it." He pulled the sash undone. "But let's concentrate on more pressing issues."

"And what would they be?" she said with a smile, pulling the robe closed again.

"Hmm, you look tired—maybe you should hop in bed," he suggested.

She pushed away. "Actually, I was thinking a shower would be nice."

He grinned. "Even better," he said, taking her hand and planting a kiss on her open palm, sending delicious tickles to her center.

She cupped his cheek. "Then later . . ." She bent to kiss him. "Much, much later . . ." She kissed him longer. "You tell me what you and Oberon are planning for the Draconis Nocti and our daughters."

He looked up surprised. "You are a clever little minx." Then he smiled and stood up tossing her over his shoulder.

"Hey," she protested, kicking her legs. "What are you doing?"

He slapped her ass playfully. "Taking you for a shower, as you requested. Then I am going to make love to you several times before the girls come home."

Kitt stopped kicking and smiled.

Home. Our home.

Glossary of Terms

Abeolite: Worn by Animalians and Facimorphs, especially in urban areas. The material has been scientifically formulated to expand and stretch to great extremes to accommodate the changing shape. There are mesh segments to allow fur to grow through and there is an overlapping split in the rear to cater to a growing tail. Abeolite is usually worn like underwear under clothes in case the need for transformation comes up.

Abomination: A child who is born to a woman embraced late in her pregnancy. Unlike a child born to Aeternus parents, who will awaken after twenty-five years, an Abomination will awaken after its first year, appearing to age only one year for every fifteen that pass. Most do not reach the age of one.

Aeternus: A race of vampiric people who must ingest human blood to live, although not the "living dead" of legend. The Aeternus have created a symbiotic existence with the humans that feed them. They are either born of Aeternus parents or created when a human is embraced (see *embrace* below). Those born to Aeternus parents live as humans until their twenty-fifth year, when they may or may not awaken to become an Aeternus. Those who do not awaken are known as Latents.

Alpha: The male leader of a Bestiabeo Family. He is responsible for taking care of the day-to-day running of the group and enforcing the laws, but he answers to the Council of Elders.

Animalians: Intrinsically, they are part man and part animal, but differ from shape-shifters. There are three main genera in the Animalians: ursians—man-bears; felians—man-cats; and canians—man-canines. Each genus is made up of several subgenera: that is, the felians have mixed families of tiger, panther, lion, cougar, etc. There is much infighting between the genera. Humans cannot be turned into an Animalian—they must be born. But it is possible for a human to mate with an Animalian, whereby the child has a fifty-fifty chance of awakening to their Animalian heritage. It is the same between the genera—the child of two different genera will not know its genus until it awakens.

Family: A clan or family group of ursians.

Pack: A clan or family group of canians.

Pride: A clan or family group of felians.

Atropa wine: Despite the name, Atropa wine is actually a distilled spirit, not a wine, made from the plant known as belladonna, a deadly nightshade. While toxic to humans, especially the illegally distilled version known as belladonna moonshine, Atropa wine is one of the few substances to act as an intoxicant to Animalians.

Awaken: A parahuman coming of age, which results in the activation of parahuman abilities. This occurs at different ages depending on the race.

Bestiabeo: The traditional name for what are more commonly referred to as Animalians.

Blood-sucker: A term usually used for a dreniac, but can be used as an insult to an Aeternus.

Blood-thrall: An extreme state of sexual arousal. In humans it's brought on by a small amount of Aeternus blood entering the bloodstream either by direct entry through a vein or cut, or a few drops into an eye. Latents are more susceptible to its influence. If a human is in the throes of blood-thrall, the Aeternus responsible may also succumb to the effects. Once a certain point in the Aeternus's arousal is reached, they must see it through to the conclusion.

Cubii: The collective term for the race of the male Incubus and the female equivalent Succubus. In centuries past, they'd been used as sex slaves, agents of espionage, and sometimes even as assassins. When the CHaPR Treaty came into existence over a century ago, the race was freed from the enforced slavery they had suffered at the hands of humans and parahumans alike. Fearing their freedom would not last, they went into hiding.

Dark Sleep: A long dreamless state that can last up to one hundred years. An Aeternus can slip into Dark Sleep if feeding and resting cease for a period of more than a week. Only time and copious amounts of blood can wake the Dark Sleeper.

Death-high: The state of intoxication Necrodreniacs enter when they have drained a human to the last drop.

Donor: A human who voluntarily donates blood through a donor agency to feed the Aeternus. A blood donation can be collected and bottled, or a live donation can be given with the Aeternus feeding directly from a donor vein. Donors are regarded highly, unlike fang-whores who are indiscriminate and little more than prostitutes.

Dreniac: See *Necrodrenia*.

Dúbabeo: Thought to be a myth, Dúbabeo are usually identical twins in the Bestiabeo world and have the ability to transform into both parents' animal forms instead of one or the other. In ancient legends, the Dúbabeo were there to serve the Bestiabeo and were little more than prisoners in a guilded cage.

Elder: The oldest and wisest of a race. The Council of Aeternus Elders makes decisions regarding the Aeternus within the edicts of CHaPR. Positions are honorary, as the council's authority was superseded with the formation of the CHaPR. The majority of the Council of Elders now serve CHaPR.

Embrace: To change a human into an Aeternus or Necrodreniac through the eternal-kiss. A dangerous process often resulting in the death of the recipient human, with only one in ten embraced humans achieving successful transition. A human embraced by a Necrodreniac will become a Necrodreniac, complete with an addiction to death-highs. It is rare for Necrodreniacs to exert the self-control necessary to embrace humans. Humans who've survived the eternal-kiss are known as the embraced.

Eternal-kiss: A mix of Aeternus or Necrodreniac blood and saliva transferred from the mouth of the embracer to the mouth of the embraced. For an Aeternus to administer the eternal-kiss, permission must be given by the recipient, unless it is a life-and-death situation. Necrodreniacs usually don't ask—they just take.

Faciabeo or Facimorph: Also known as shape-shifters or shifters, they have the ability to bend their form to mimic other shapes through the use of magic. Once changed, they retain their own consciousness and only take on limited physical characteristics of the form they are mimicking— for example, flight when shifting into the form of a bird. Shifters do not become the animal they mimic unlike Animalians who are part human and part animal.

Facimorphic test: A standard test in most government departments and private industry, especially high-profile ones, to guard against infiltration of a shape-shifter masquerading as an employee. The test checks for specific shifting markers in the DNA of the test recipient.

Fang-mistress: A human kept in luxury by an Aeternus in return for exclusive feeding and often a sexual relationship.

Fang-virgin: A human who has never allowed an Aeternus to feed from his or her vein.

Fang-whore: A derogatory term for those who sell themselves indiscriminately to any Aeternus for blood, and usually sex, in exchange for money and/or blood for spiking.

Glar-Achni or **Glarachni:** An ancient race made up of several clans that came to earth ten thousand years ago. They adapted to their new surrounds by transmuting their DNA and mingling it with elements from their new planet. Each clan transformed into a different parahuman race according to the areas they chose to live in.

Latent: One born to parahuman parents who does not awaken in the designated year for their genus, instead continuing to live as a human.

Littermate: A Bestiabeo term for the siblings that result from the same pregnancy. Two progeny are the usual result of a Bestiabeo birth, one male and one female. While other combinations can happen, they are more the exception than the norm.

Mem: An endearment word for "Mother."

Mer-people: A little-known race of parahumans who live beneath the sea. They have been known to mate with humans; however, this is rare and the hybrid offspring seldom survive.

Necrodrenia: A disease that develops when an Aeternus completely drains a human while feeding, resulting in a death-high. Addiction is certain and immediate. Death is the only cure.

Orb or orbing: A crystal orb used by a witch to capture images from a subject as they tell a story. Commonly used to reenact crime scenes, but because of the subjectivity of the witness or suspect, the evidence is not admissible in court. However, it can supply valuable insight into the crime, which can give investigators leads to pursue.

Parahumans: Alternate humans that include the Aeternus, Animalians, shape-shifters, magic-wielders and Merpeople. All begin life as human and change to parahuman in different ways, depending on their genus and race.

Primara: A midwife in the old sense of the word. The female who is the spiritual and cultural center of an Animalian group and uses a mix of modern medicine and old herbal remedies to treat members of the community.

Shadow-combat: NYAPS state-of-the-art arena in the newly upgraded Venator training wing doubling as a venue for the sport of Shadow-combat. Also the term for the game in which individuals or teams, made up of human, parahumans, or both, are pitted against each other in mock-combat scenarios. It was first introduced in the Paris Academy of Parahuman Studies in the 1980s to help students hone their skills, and quickly gained popularity as a mainstream sport.

Shape-shifter or shifter: see *Faciabeo*.

Spiking: A human practice of mixing a couple of drops of Aeternus blood with a diluted amphetamine mix, which is injected intravenously. This increases the effect of the narcotic and "spikes" an extreme sexual high. Highly addictive and illegal, users eventually destroy their body's ability to produce white blood cells, eventually resulting in death. A human that spikes is known as a spiker.

Tech or Venator tech: The technical support for a Venator. They monitor police channels and other avenues, looking for signs of dreniac activity, and support Venators with intel and environment monitoring when on a hunt. Many can also excel in weapons invention, computers, and communications support.

Thaumaturgist (magic-wielders): Races that practice thaumaturgy to bend and use life-and-death energy—for example, witches, druids, shamans, etc. Each race uses magic in a unique manner and for a specific aim. For example, light witches use life energy for the benefit of others; and dark witches use death energy for self-gain and chaos.

Thaumaturgists—Druids: Druids are Thaumaturgists who use the power of plants in their magic. Their strong religious beliefs center on nature in all forms. They are one of the most sensual of the magic-wielders, and sex features strongly in ceremonies.

Thaumaturgists—familial witches: Require a bond to an animal familiar to be able to channel magic energy through.

Thaumaturgy: The art of invoking supernatural powers, such as magic, which are created from life or death energy.

Troubles, The: Europe in the early nineties saw unrest among the Aeternus community, which almost caused a split in CHaPR. Assassinations were rife and Necrodrenia was on the rise through deliberate infection, causing major friction with humans. These events seemed to cease after the death of Dante Rubins, who was much later named as the supposed instigator, although there was never any proof. The reasons behind The Troubles were never identified and seemed to die with Dante.

Venator: A type of bounty hunter who collects bounties for the capture or destruction of parahuman outlaws, and is traditionally human; but in recent years, parahumans have joined the ranks. Venators must be trained, licensed, and registered with the Guild before they are permitted to hunt. A Venator gains a license by attending the Guild Academy in their final year of training and passing a set of rigorous exams. Venators may specialize in various fields, including Necrodreniac destruction, hunting of dark magic-wielders, or tracking down rogue Animalians. When an Aeternus is in the grip of Necrodrenia, they are known as a Necrodreniac or dreniac.

Wolfsbane—*Aconitum vulparia* or aconite: a toxic poison, especially to Animalians

government and organizations

Academy of Parahuman Studies, the: A tertiary institution of parahuman studies for both humans and parahumans alike. All potential Venators must spend three years at the Academy learning their craft and preparing for the final exams—a set of grueling mental and physical tests to determine a candidate's suitability to becoming a licensed Venator and what specialization they will undertake—be it Necrodreniacs, Rogue Animalians, or Dark Thaumaturgists. Other courses are offered such as parahuman law, corporate thaumaturgy, and parahuman forensics to name a few.

Academy, the—NYAPS: New York Campus of the Academy of Parahuman studies—one of the first parahuman academies. Originally constructed in the early 1800s as an Aeternus stronghold, the complex has several underground dormitories and lecture halls connected through a large network of tunnels; years later, rooms and halls were built on the surface as well. When first converted to a center for learning, it catered only to parahumans, but in the 1960s, a period of integration for renewed human and parahuman relations, the Academy was opened to include human students studying parahuman courses. In the early seventies, the Guild moved their Venator training and testing facilities to the Academy to bring all parahuman studies under the one umbrella. Day and night lectures are scheduled to suit different student lifestyles.

Council for Human and Parahuman Relations (CHaPR): A council similar to the United Nations consisting of parahuman and human ambassadorial representatives. The CHaPR passes the laws that govern human and parahuman coexistence. It is governed by the CHaPR Treaty that was established in 1887 after a bitter and bloody war between the Aeternus and an alliance of Animalians and humans. Since its inception, a majority of the other parahuman races have also signed the treaty and are bound by the laws.

Department of Parahuman Security (the Department): The umbrella department responsible for enforcing the laws handed down by CHaPR. The Department consists of many divisions and branches. The following four divisions are only some of those that make up the Department.

Necrodreniac Control Branch (NCB): Responsible for monitoring and setting Necrodreniac bounties.

Office of the Chief Parahuman Medical Examiner— OCPME: The office that performs the autopsies for the Department.

Parahuman Intelligence Division (Intel): The intelligence division of the Department. This division gathers information (*or* "intel") on gangs and rogue parahuman groups, usually through the use of undercover agents.

Personal Security Branch: Personal security provides bodyguard detail to officials and VIP.

Violent Crimes Unit (VCU): A team that investigates serious violent crimes usually committed by or against parahumans.

Guild, the: An organization founded by humans as a part of the CHaPR Treaty and a form of protection against the parahumans. The Guild is responsible for Venator licensing. Once licensed, a portion of all Venators' bounty earnings go to the Guild.

Petrescu School of Training: One of the many small institutions that take a young human and train mind, body, and soul through regular academic studies supplemented with strong martial arts regimes. This school has built a reputation for preparing its students to enter the Parahuman Academies. This is not a Venator training facility; but those wishing to take up that line of work compete for a place in the school.

characters

Kitt Jordan: felian—exiled from her Jordan Pride just under eighteen years ago. Kitt studied human and parahuman medicine, then specialized in forensic pathology to eventually become chief medical examiner for OCPME. She recently resigned from OCPME to take up a teaching position at the New York Academy of Parahuman Studies.

Raven Matokwe: canian—Kitt's ex-lover and father to her twins. He has been missing for many years and is thought to be the killer of her husband. He has recently returned to the U.S. after the twins were discovered in Australia and returned to the Pride.

oberon's team

Oberon DuPrie: ursian—Current head of security at NYAPS and former VCU agent. He has put together a covert team of specialist to look into the possible recurrence of The Troubles of several years ago.

Antoinette Petrescu: Aeternus—Ex-Venator and newly turned Aeternus. Oberon offered her a job when she was expelled from the Guild after threatening several members.

Bianca Sin: witch—An expert in forensic thaumaturgy and head of Department of Thaumaturgy at NYAPS. Bianca is a nonpracticing familial witch and often called on by the city's law enforcement agencies to consult on cases.

Cody Shields: Incubus—Head of Admin at NYAPS, he looks more like a surfer than an office worker. Oberon uses Cody to diffuse emotional situations and as a liaison to external agencies. Cody is an Australian and has a strong Australian accent.

Tones (Antonio) Geraldi: Aeternus—Former VCU agent. Oberon poached the computer expert to work on his team. Tones is a humegetarian and a card-carrying member of Parahumans Against Animal Abuse.

jordan pride

Tyrone: The Pride Alpha and father to Kitt, Dylan, and Nathan.

Serena: The Pride Primara and mother to Kitt, Dylan, and Nathan.

Dylan: The littermate of Kitt, recently killed in the line of duty by an insane killer who was after Antoinette.

Calliope: "Cal"—One of the special twin daughters of Kitt and Raven. She and her twin were separated at birth from their mother to be brought up by foster parents in the distant country of Australia. They were recently returned to the Jordan Pride after they were discovered following news reports of their foster parents' death in a car accident.

Persephone: "Seph"—The other twin daughter of Kitt and Raven, sister to Calliope.

Nathan: Older sibling of Kitt and Dylan. He's had to work hard to overcome perceived unluckiness since his littermate died during his birth.

Emmett: Late husband of Kitt. Was murdered just before she gave birth to her daughters.

Jericho: Was taken in by the Jordan Pride at a young age along with his twin, Joshua (collectively, the "Tiger Twins") and older half-brother, Leon—the only survivors of Pantella Pride, which was decimated by a forest fire.

Joshua: The other of the Tiger Twins, twin brother to Jericho and half brother to Leon.

Leon: The older, aggressive brother of Joshua and Jericho, well known for his mistreatment of women and bad temper.

Rainbow: Pregnant wife of Leon and childhood friend of Kitt.

Dreniac gang

Marvella Maria Molyneux: An Aeternus female who, in the eighties, was a famous rock-and-roll singer known as Marie Vella, until it was discovered she was creating dreniac slaves, then feeding groupies and followers to them.

J.J.: A former Venator turned Necrodreniac by Marvella.

other characters

Christian Laroque: Aeternus agent working for intelligence and Antoinette's lover.

Ealund: Dark Brethren—and incorporeal being that thrives on violence.

Gideon: A serial killer with a penchant for fresh heart, preferably still beating.

Mark Ambrosia: The new all-state Shadow-combat champion.

Murray: The security guard at OCPME.

Neil Roberts, Agent: The agent in charge of VCU and the man responsible for having Oberon kicked off the unit.

Rudolf: An old human expert on the Dark Brethren.

Tez O'Connor: Medical Examiner at OCPME and occasional lover of Oberon.

Tripper McKee: Ex-Venator tech whose brother was killed in a Guild setup. He now works freelance, gathering evidence against the institution that put him in prison for five years.

Trudi Crompton: Roving news reporter for local television station WTFN.